KILL YOUR DARLINGS

SHIVNATH PRODUCTIONS

FILM & PUBLISHING

KILL YOUR DARLINGS

Copyright © 2022 by L.E. Harper

Cover design by Shivnath Productions
allentria.com

Edited by M.J. Pankey
museandquill.com

Cover art by Jaka Prawira
ellinsworth.co

Interior art by Neiratina
instagram.com/saturneidae

ISBN: 978-1-7923-6662-8

This edition first printed 2023

Dedicated to the darlings I couldn't save:
Medusa, Skylo, and Oreo

TABLE OF
CONTENTS

FOREWORD

While there are many fantastical things in this book, I wrote from a place of truth. Herein, I offer my deepest truths—truths I am not proud of, truths that I believed would do more harm than good if I spoke them aloud.

For years, I've suffered from depression. On these pages you'll find—between all the dragons and magic—an account of how I spiraled to rock bottom. You'll be exposed to dark and sometimes visceral descriptions of mental illness, including self-loathing and self-harm. You'll hear an unkind narrative voice, for the voice of depression is one that twists the truth, turning you against yourself.

I understand these descriptions may be triggering for people who, like me, have hit the bottom, and have punched through to sink to new and unfathomable lows. These content warnings are provided to help you decide if this is a story you want to read.

Although my book descends into darkness and examines the internal narrative that can lead to suicidal ideation, it's ultimately a tale of hope. When I read the words I wrote, they remind me that I am more than my darkness, more than the sum of my mistakes, more than the traumas I've sustained. I began writing Kill Your Darlings as a love letter to myself, at a time when I felt no one else in the world loved me; but I honed it, revised it, and edited it, hoping it could serve as a love letter to the people out there who've suffered as I have suffered.

I wrote in the hopes that speaking about these topics would pave the way toward de-stigmatizing them. I recounted my emotional journey in the hopes that others would feel less alone. I described my internal battle in the hopes that one day these battles would be treated with kindness and understanding, rather than ignorance and dismissal.

As with all groups, people with depression aren't a monolith. My journey may not resemble yours. I've told my truths as best I can; that's all any of us can do. But if you're like me, and mental illness has lied to you, distorted your reality, and stolen your joy, then know I wrote this book for you.

I know the battles you fight—and I believe you can win.

All my love,

L.E. Harper

CONTENT WARNINGS

This book contains depictions of mental illness, including depression, anxiety, suicidal ideation, and self-harm.

Other warnings include adult themes and content such as language, fantasy violence, and character death.

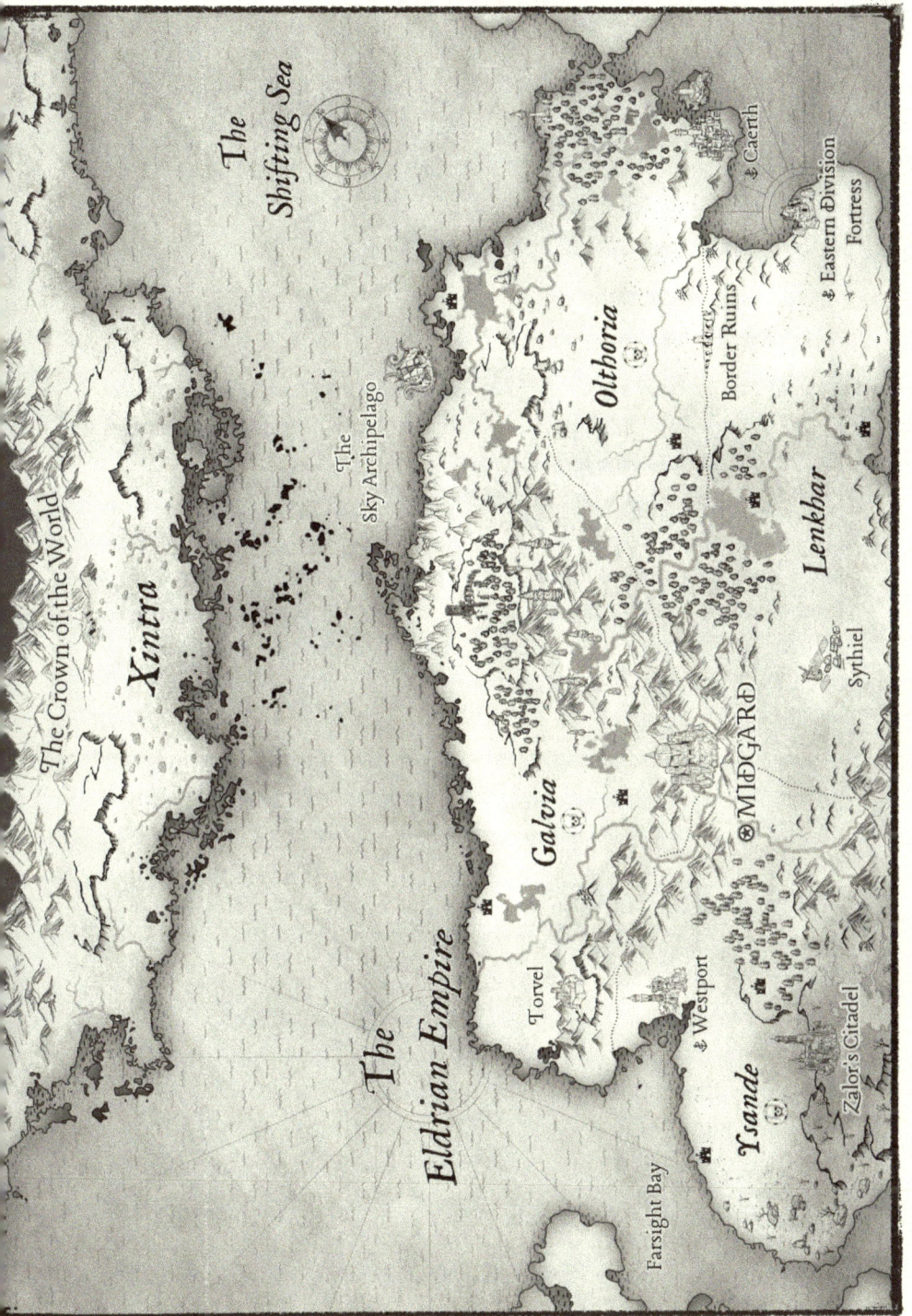

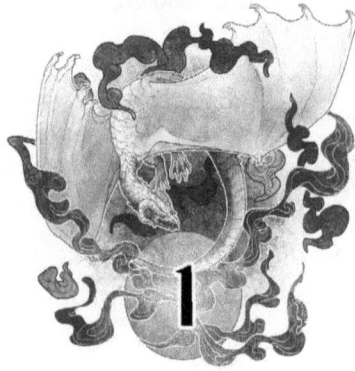

1

OBLIVION IS A FUNNY THING. It's human instinct to fear the proverbial abyss, but now that I'm here, it's not so bad. Calm emptiness consumes me. Cold darkness envelops me.

For a moment, an eternity, I'm lost.

Sensations trickle in from the edge of my semiconscious mind, and I become aware of a faint, coppery tang on my tongue. Scratchy linen sheets kiss my cheek. The heady scent of rain-dampened soil fills the air. When a faraway roar echoes like thunder rolling across distant plains, my brain sparks to life.

This is a dream, and I know it by heart.

Heat blazes through my veins as I realize what's happening. In my youth, I worked tirelessly—no pun intended—to achieve lucid dreaming. I kept journals, used mnemonics, performed routine reality checks. Now lucidity is second nature. My brain longs for this escape.

Starved of happiness in the waking world, it senses freedom and grasps for it.

The dream solidifies around me like a chrysalis. I drag myself away from the darkness, eager for tonight's adventure. Anxiety unhooks its dull, ever-present claws from my chest. Awareness of a new and wonderful realm billows outwards from me, and peace settles in my soul.

Peace. *Happiness.* I could chase those feelings to the end of eternity in the real world and never come close to catching them; here, they're always within my grasp.

My fingers roam beneath threadbare covers to find a warm hand.

I run my thumb over the callouses on the palm, smiling. If Valen is with me, that means it will be a good dream.

Obviously it will be good. I've returned to the place I love most. I know the pulse of every tree, the lore of every stone, the deepest desires of every creature. How could I not? I created them. This is my dream, my universe. And when I'm lucid, I can control it.

People in the real world, the mundane and tragic world, say authors have a God Complex. I wouldn't disagree.

Relishing the feel of my imaginary realm, I pick up the smoky scent of wood-burning watch fires. That means I'm dreaming about one of my war campaigns. A hint of pine in the smoke tells me I'm on the northwestern coast.

Weird. I can't remember a time when I've smelled anything in a dream. Then again, maybe I wouldn't. Maybe the sensations drain away when I wake, like sand through a sieve.

My main character, Kyla Starblade—whose body I inhabit whenever I dream about my fantasy novels—fights at the forefront of the largest and most dangerous battles of the Shadow War. Given the sensory clues, this must be the day after our army liberated the Shadow-occupied city of Westport.

I've arrived at the start of the fifth and final book in my series. Not surprising, since that unfinished manuscript dominates my waking life, haunting me. I'm not happy with it. Neither is my publisher.

Nope. Don't think about that. Focus on the dream. Enjoy the happiness while it lasts.

As if on cue, Valen's fingers twitch to life. They intertwine with my own, and I crack open an eye to look at him. Affection floods my chest, washing away every dark and distressing thought.

He's perfection.

Oh, I gave him flaws and pathos. He's his own person with his own goals. Uniting our forces into the Mortal Alliance? Valen's idea. The Westport victory? Valen's doing. Waiting three-and-a-half novels for Kyla to make the first move? Yes, that was Valen Stormcrest, pining idiot and Grade A cinnamon roll.

A thin glaze of sweat beads on his light-brown skin. His bare chest rises and falls with slow, steady breaths. Raven hair frames his sculpted face, falling in tousled waves across a noble brow.

They say you can't imagine a face you haven't seen. Every random face in your dreams is the real-life face of someone, somewhere, whose visage was engraved in your memory. Your brain rifles through its catalog and populates your nighttime visions with actual people.

Only I'm sure I've never seen anyone like Valen. The high cheek-bones, the long nose, the chiseled jawline—I would have *remembered* someone like that. The real world doesn't have anyone as extraordinary as that. When he turns to me and reveals sparkling gray eyes, as vibrant and ever-changing as a thunderstorm, my breath hitches.

"Kyla." He squeezes my hand. "You're here."

"Where else would I be?" My attempt at a flirtatious tone is cringeworthy.

"Usually you're gone before the sun rises."

Right. Kyla's a bit of a jerk. She's bad at communication and creates her own problems. While that makes for a compelling story, I'm not interested in drama now. I have more than enough of that in my real life, thank you very much.

"I wish I could stay here forever," I murmur.

Even the smallest, drowsiest smile is transformative on Valen. He pulls Kyla's hand—my hand—to his chest. "If only we lived in a world where we could. But the sun is up, and we have a war to win."

Yes, the Mortal Alliance is struggling to save civilians from slaughter at the hands of invading troops; but in dreams, I'm not obligated to focus on that. There's no need to stress my exhausted brain with problem-solving.

"The war can wait," I tell him.

He chuckles. "Who are you, and what have you done with Kyla Starblade?"

"I'm her evil twin." I close my eyes and snuggle closer, curling my body toward his. Even in the dream I feel sore, tired. Drained of energy, as if I, like my characters, have been fighting a war.

In a way, I have. I just lost the Battle of the Movie Rights, and Monday morning is D-Day, when I must deliver my final manuscript revisions to my editor.

I haven't finished those revisions yet. Haven't started them, actually.

"You could never convince me you're evil," says Valen, his deep voice tinged with playfulness. "Although it should be considered a crime for you to be so beautiful."

Under normal circumstances, such a mawkish sentiment would make me vomit. Unlike Kyla, I'm not in a relationship. Never have been, likely never will be. Truth be told, I don't want a relationship. At least, not with any real person.

Valen is different. I created him so I could love him (also because one of the unspoken rules of writing Young Adult fiction is that there must be a romantic subplot). Writing requirements aside, I made him everything I could ever want. I had no choice *but* to love him, in order to more convincingly write Kyla as she fell for him. And I'm able to love him because he's safe. Unattainable.

A perfect little figment of my imagination.

The lumpy pallet shifts. I open my eyes to find Valen propping himself up on his left elbow, leaning over me. At once, my rib cage feels thin and fragile, in danger of shattering around the heart that has begun to beat violently against it.

Lucid dreaming teaches you to recognize patterns: recurring symbols, events, and people. While I've dreamed of Valen plenty, this approach to intimacy has never happened before. Typically, I need at least three tequila shots before I can consider swapping spit. For this reason—or any number of deeper and darker reasons—it's hard to imagine kissing him. Maybe this is my subconscious's not-so-subtle way of sending me a message.

What the message is, I can't guess. Valen bends toward me, his lips about to close on mine. My brain and body are paralyzed. Should I allow this?

Do I *want* this?

Another far-off roar breaks the spell, fracturing the magic and the terrifying weight of the moment. A low, brassy note responds—the sentry's horn.

Valen raises his head and stares eastward, as if he can see through the canvas tent and into the sky where a dragon is approaching. I *can't* see through the tent, but I know that's happening because I wrote it. I know everything about this imaginary world, but it's clear I still don't know myself. While Valen is distracted, I shimmy Kyla's body out from under him.

"Cendrion has returned from patrol." He rolls to the far side of the cot and rises. The blanket falls away from a lean frame rippling with the muscles of a warrior. I don't avert my gaze as he dresses. I may not wish to act on desire, even in dreams, but that doesn't mean I can't enjoy the view.

He casts me a sidelong glance. "Are you planning to get up?"

No, I want to say, but the word sticks in my throat. Hyper-aware-ness notwithstanding, I'm not in the driver's seat of this dream. Events are progressing, despite my yearning for the contrary. If I let it play out, perhaps I'll find some inspiration to jolt me out of my writer's block.

I spy Kyla's pants and shirt on the bare earth floor and throw them on. When I try to follow Valen through the tent flaps, he stops me.

"We can't be seen leaving together this early," he whispers. "You'll have to teleport."

I suppress an exasperated groan. Like all the inhabitants of the world I created, Kyla can wield magic. However, I've never been able to harness her power, not even in my most lucid moments. Much as I've written about the magic system in the world of Solera, I don't have the first idea how to wield the energy that courses through every living thing here. I don't know what part of my brain to use, which muscle to flex.

Waving aside Valen's words, I start to push past him. "It doesn't matter."

He steps in my way, towering head and shoulders above me. "I'm the Commander-General of this army."

"And I'm the Lightbringer," I retort, using the honorific the military bestowed on Kyla.

"A position that's tenuous at best."

Shit. This dialogue isn't half bad. Maybe I *will* make some revisions. I'll add this to the beginning of Book Five. Never mind it's the ending my publishing team objects to.

"I promise no one will care if they see us together," I tell him.

"Even if they don't—which they will—and even if you've stopped worrying about your reputation overnight, it's my duty to protect you. Our relationship is a conflict of interest. The military adjudicators are looking for any excuse to punish you. Don't give it to them."

I huff a rueful laugh. Everything he's saying is true. This is so canon. Very on-brand for him. As the author of this story, I agree with what he's saying, even if it makes for an irritating dream.

"Fine." This will go easier if I stop fighting. "I'll meet you on the eastern ridge."

Valen scrutinizes me, his expression unreadable. "There's something different about you today."

"Good different, or bad different?"

The corners of his lips twitch—the infamous almost-smile, his signature move. "I'll let you know tonight."

"It's a date."

His face softens and he offers me a rare, full smile. Then he ducks through the flaps and emerges to greet the morning.

Squeezing my eyes shut, I try willing myself to the ridge, attempting a teleport spell. It's no use. The magic won't come. My real-world frustrations about feeling powerless in life, relationships, and career are determined to manifest in my dream.

Abandoning magic as a lost cause, I listen to the bustle outside. The troops will be queueing for breakfast at the far end of the encampment, exhausted from yesterday's battle and longing for a hot meal. I pace to the edge of the tent, crouch beside the cot, and lift a corner of the fabric wall. As soon as the path is clear, I wriggle out. The soil, damp from a storm and churned to mud by night patrols, is slimy and cold. The moisture seeping through my cotton blouse is as real as it gets. This dream is wild.

My spirits rise as I hike east, wiping my hands on Kyla's leather wyvernhide pants. I squeeze through a gap in the ring of earthen pikes around the tents, then ascend a ridge abutting the camp's border. Soothing birdsong floats on the breeze, and the clear rosy sky promises a gorgeous day. It's a far cry from the cramped and dirty tension of New York City.

I used to love the city. That love has faded, as many good things have faded from my life. Now the incessant urban hum grates on my nerves. Dour buildings loom like jailers, caging me in whenever I drift through the streets. I'm too tired for the flashing neon energy, too jaded to appreciate the metropolitan beauty I once saw.

But in dreams, my heart still thrums with the emotions life has wrung from my soul. This is Solera, the world whose fate I sculpt by whim, and I'm about to meet my favorite character.

As I crest the grassy hilltop in tandem with the sun, I can't help the tears that spring to my eyes. There, resplendent in the golden dawn, stands Cendrion: warrior, hero, and friend.

He also happens to be a dragon.

Dreaming of dragons is nothing new—hell, I made a career out of it—but something about Cendrion calls to me now as it never has before. Sunlight turns his white-scaled body into a faceted diamond. His amethyst eyes shine with unspoken reassurance. He understands me. He knows my soul as well as I know his.

What's left of it, at least. Cendrion is haunted by his past and future alike. I've entwined his fate with that of my world's greatest villain: Lord Zalor, the fiendish tyrant who started the Shadow War.

My thoughts darken as they turn to that villain, inner storms clouding my joy.

Kill your darlings. That's a saying we have in the publishing industry. In terms of writing, it means you must let go of attachments. For me, it holds a different meaning.

I've done terrible things to Cendrion. Unforgivable things. I'm overcome with the urge to apologize to him, to *all* my characters. Valen is already there, as are Kyla's best friends. Asher Brightstone, another human, and Rexa Faeloryn, a shapeshifter, stand side by side, looking at me.

"About time," says Rexa. Her natural form is humanoid but

chimerical. Dark-furred legs give way to a reptilian torso of mottled scales, like those of a python. The scales fade into the flesh of a human head, where her elegant features pinch in distaste. "What'd you do, crawl through the mud to get here?"

Words fail me. I'm transfixed by the majesty of Cendrion's ivory horns, extending upwards from each side of his skull in a graceful curve. The warmth of Asher's smile pulls at my heart.

"My darlings," I whisper, drinking in the sight of them. Silhouetted against the rolling emerald plains and pristine marble peaks of Westport, these four are the most beautiful creatures I've ever seen. The family I've always wanted. The friends I've never known.

I have friends in the real world—I *do*—but there are increasingly few of them. Such is life as a flawed, broken human who's bad at communication and creates her own problems.

Of course Kyla's based on me. She *is* me, and I am her. But I'm also all of my other characters. I'm every blade of grass on this hilltop. I'm the sun. The universe. I've never felt that as strongly as I do now, here, in this inexplicably heartbreaking dream.

I open my mouth to say something poignant and poetic: a creator speaking to her beautiful, perfect, doomed creations.

Before I can utter a word, Cendrion howls in pain. He rears up and flares his wings, revealing a shadowy shape behind him and the hilt of a dagger digging into his haunches.

Damn. *Damn* it all to hell. This is the first major plot point of Book Five. Lord Zalor sends an assassin to murder Kyla and her friends as retribution for the Battle of Westport. What an absolute asshole I am for having forgotten.

My characters launch into motion. As Cendrion twists to face his attacker, Rexa's catlike legs bend in a stance of aggression. She wields her changemagic, morphing into a fearsome tiger in the span of a heartbeat. Flesh and scale ripple into tawny striped fur, though her amber eyes remain human, sparkling with bloodlust.

Voltmagic crackles to life around Valen, and he hurls a blue-white bolt of lightning at the assassin. Asher, whose battle prowess lies with weapons, draws, nocks, and fires an arrow in one fluid motion. The assassin is too clever by half. He wields darkmagic and disappears into a wisp of shadow, rendering spells and arrows useless.

Cendrion glares around, nostrils flaring as if he hopes to track the shadowman's movement by scent. Blood trickles from his wound, scalloping across the scales of his left hind leg, but he pays it no mind.

"Fly to the healers," I tell the dragon, flapping my hands at him. "That dagger was dipped in poison."

His jeweled eyes flick to me. "How can you tell?"

Because I wrote it that way. Guilt turns my tongue leaden, and I can't bring myself to admit it aloud.

"This isn't over," says Valen. "Cendrion, return to camp and sound the alarm—check in with the healers while you're there. Starblade, defensive spells at the ready."

He doesn't even look at me when he addresses me, formal and distant. He's staring around, on the lookout for any trace of the assassin.

My jaw clenches. Suddenly I'm angry—not at Zalor, but at myself. What sort of idiot would waste a morning like this on attempted murder? I was so absorbed in my darkness that I couldn't see the simple splendor of this scene. Why didn't I write more about the fragrance of dew-kissed grass? The gleam of Cendrion's scales? The sensation of Valen's skin against my own?

The assassin materializes in front of me, rising from the shadows and coalescing into physical form. I take a swing at him, because that's the only thing I can do without Kyla's magic at my disposal. He sidesteps, produces another poisoned dagger, and plunges it into my chest.

"Lord Zalor sends his regards," the assassin hisses in my ear.

I've never been stabbed in the real world. I've written about brutal injuries, but without having known the injuries myself, I can't imagine what a stabbing would feel like. I can't dream about it.

Except I *am* dreaming it. The dagger's hilt protrudes from between my second and third ribs. Horrible pressure builds around its metal blade, which is burrowed in my left lung. I try and fail to draw breath. It's like the assassin has sucked the air out of me.

I'm in shock. Can one be in shock in a dream? I don't know. There should be an awful lot of pain, and I suppose there is, but my brain can't process it.

This doesn't happen in my book.

The foolish thought flashes through my mind. My dream wasn't following the flow of my novel, anyway—now it's gone completely off the rails. Fear crowds my senses, blurring my sight. Dormant survival instincts kick in. I want nothing more than to get off this vertiginous carnival ride-gone-wrong.

Blistering heat snaps me to attention. The scent of electricity burns my nostrils as Valen wields a searing fork of voltmagic and incinerates the shadowman.

The assassin's smoking corpse collapses at my feet, but his dagger remains lodged in my flesh. I sway on the spot and my knees buckle. My body crumples to the dirt, landing in such a way that I'm left staring into the shadowman's inert, empty face.

I'm cold. How much blood have I lost? None, because this is a dream. But I *have* lost blood before, and this reminds me of that: I'm lightheaded, I'm nauseous, I'm in shock. The pain's catching up to me, hovering at the edges of my spinning mind, but I can't process it because I'm in shock, I am in *shock* and I am *not* having a good time anymore and I want to wake up, even though I hate the real world, *I want to wake up*—

Kyla's friends surround me, calling for help. Someone yanks the dagger free, pulling the plug on a dam of sensation. Agony roars through me, ripping across my skin, digging claws into my nerves. With every breath I take, it feels like I've been stabbed again.

Valen hovers overhead. He presses his hand to my wound, staunching the flow of poisoned blood.

"I want to wake up." I force the words through breathless lungs, willing my subconscious to listen.

"Our lifemagic healers are on their way," he whispers. "Stay with me."

As the poison takes hold, I twitch and writhe. I wait for the telltale lurch that will jolt me back to my boring SoHo apartment, strewn with filthy clothes and week-old takeout containers. My muscles spasm, my spine arcs, yet I remain resolutely trapped in this nightmare.

I try to speak again, but I'm falling into darkness. Losing my grasp on my surroundings, on *everything*. Oblivion looms, ravenous and infinite, and it no longer feels calm. Now it's the jaws of a wicked monster closing around me, threatening to swallow me whole.

Screams die in my throat. Terror ignites in my soul. As I sink into the abyss, one final thought flickers through me:

Why am I not waking up?

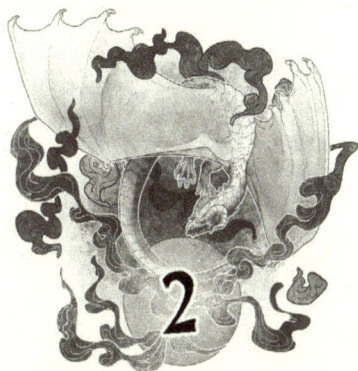

2

MY EYELIDS FLUTTER, and disappointment fills me. I'm awake, which means I must face reality in all its ugly glory. Not that I was particularly enjoying my nightmare by its violent end, but in truth, I'd prefer that to my monotonous routine.

Drag myself from bed. Burn a pot of coffee. Stare at my iPhone for ten hours to distract myself from manuscript revisions. Berate myself for being a miserable, lazy failure.

"She's coming 'round. We caught the poison early, thank Ohra. Treated the wound with mugwort before closing her up, so she's good as new. She should be on bed rest for a day or two, but she'll make a full recovery."

I feel my brows contract. Whose voice is that? I live alone.

"Thank you, Healer Farrow. We'll take it from here." There's another voice, familiar yet not—is that Eric? It can't be. I haven't seen Eric for months, since I lack the energy and desire to leave my apartment. I also suck at keeping in touch. Our correspondence these days consists of messaging each other depressing memes and talking shit about the G Train.

"Kyla?" That same gentle voice coaxes me from the nebulous place between sleep and wakefulness. My eyes crack open.

Impossible, I think, though my heart leaps. The poisoned blade didn't send me spiraling back to reality. I'm still dreaming.

"Asher," I whisper.

Asher's guileless chestnut eyes widen in relief. He bears an uncanny resemblance to my real-life best friend, Eric Samuel. Asher was based on Eric, so this makes sense. His suntanned skin, coiffed brown hair, and gold-rimmed glasses are all wonderfully familiar. Even the pitch of his low tenor is the same.

A large, white-scaled head crowds in, nudging Asher aside. It's more equine than crocodilian, complete with pointed horse-like ears on either side of his cranial horns—yet the visage is infinitely more elegant than that of any banal Earth creature.

"Why didn't you wield to defend yourself?" growls Cendrion.

He's not large by draconic standards—eight feet from talon to shoulder, with another four feet of neck—but he's formidable. His fangs, each as long as my thumb, glisten in a silent snarl. Anyone else would recoil from the reaction, but not me. I've loved dragons since I was a kid. When my debut novel hit the New York Times Bestsellers list, I became known as Earth's Foremost Dragon Authority.

"I can't wield," I reply without thinking.

"Pretty sure you can," drawls another voice. Rexa plunks herself down on the side of my cot, jostling my achy frame. The hem of her dark green cloak, which she wears to cover her natural form, trails across the trodden ground of the medical tent.

Wishing to steer the conversation away from myself, I look at Cendrion. "How's your wound?" I ask. Since the tent isn't tall enough to accommodate him, the hind half of his body sticks out through the canvas flaps across from me. "Shouldn't you be resting?"

He blows a dismissive snort through his nostrils. "It was barely a scratch."

"A *poisoned* scratch—"

"The healers patched me up, same as you," he interrupts. "Not even a scar to show for it."

My eyes widen, and I raise a hand to my chest. Smooth skin greets my fingers as they roam beneath my shirt collar.

"Wow," I murmur. "That's amazing." It's one thing to write about the healers' skill with lifemagic, manipulating body processes to aid and speed recovery; it's quite another to benefit from that skill. An injury that might have taken months to heal on Earth has taken mere hours on Solera.

Rexa leans in and knocks her scaly knuckles against my head. "What's with you today? Did that poison give you amnesia?"

I shrug. The acerbic stench of Healer Farrow's mugwort poultice is making my head spin. My brain's working at half-speed. No, that's not right—it's working at *triple* speed, but I have too many trains of thought, and they're all on a collision course.

Asher glances at Valen, who stands by the tent flap. "Should we bring the healer back?"

"No, I'm fine." The last thing I want is for some doctor to come poking around and ruin my dream.

Unless it's not a dream.

A tingling frisson suffuses me. That, of course, is my go-to fantasy: being transported into a world of magic. I've spent years, *decades*, wishing to stumble into the realm I love. I begged the universe to whisk me away from my wretched reality and bring me somewhere better. Somewhere I could be happy.

While I may be unhinged, I'm not quite insane. I know such things aren't possible. Still, my delusions have never been this deliciously, all-consumingly real.

Why not enjoy it while it lasts? Stabbing aside, this is what I've always wanted. Besides, it's not like I need to wake up to *do* anything, apart from revisions (and I'm mentally incapable of addressing those).

That knowledge churns my stomach with guilt, but I can't force ideas to come when my brain refuses to cooperate. The revisions will have to wait. Sleeping the day away and luxuriating in my favorite fantasies is a far more tantalizing prospect.

"If Lord Zalor sent an assassin, that means he's rattled," Valen's saying in the background. "We should build on the momentum of our victory. Once Kyla recovers, we can start the march to Torvel and—"

"Oh no." I sit bolt upright. "Going to Torvel is a bad idea."

Valen hooks one quizzical brow. "You were singing the praises of this plan yesterday. Why the change of heart?"

"I...have insider information. You have to scrap it."

"This *is* Kyla Starblade, right?" says Rexa. "Not some doppelgänger Zalor's planted to bring our army down from the inside?"

Her dry tone is at odds with the crease of tension on her brow. Her full lips are pressed in a thin line; her amber eyes are tight. A bubble of fondness swells within me. That familiar expression comes from my cousin Lindsay, who was the closest thing I had to a sister. She was the blueprint for Rexa's character.

The bubble wavers, threatening to pop. I'm not a doppelgänger, but neither am I the hero my characters trust and love. If they knew the real me—if they knew what I'm planning to do, what I've already done—they wouldn't be so accommodating.

My lips twist. "So, uh, there's some stuff I should tell you about the war. First off, I'm no longer able to wield."

"This isn't a laughing matter," Cendrion growls. "If we lose you, we lose everything."

Unease trickles through my bemused euphoria. If I'm stuck in Kyla's place, unable to wield her power, the world of Solera is doomed.

Roleplaying is fun, but it's time for a reality check. Lucid dreaming prepared me for this. I use several techniques to identify dreams, but the simplest is the Hand Test. Holding my left palm flat, I attempt to push my right pointer finger through it. In a dream, focusing on this desire allows my finger to pass through my hand.

My palm, however, remains unyielding. With a focused scowl, I poke my left hand aggressively, achieving nothing except making myself sore.

"Kyla?" Asher's voice pierces my concentration, and I twitch. In my peripheral vision, I'm dimly aware of my characters exchanging worried glances.

Tensing, I pinch myself like a cliché cartoon. Digging fingernails into flesh, I squeeze hard enough to draw a ruby droplet on my left wrist. Waves of adrenaline pulse through my gut in protest of the pain, yet I remain asleep.

Or rather, awake.

A chill creeps up my spine. Whether this is a dream or a tequila-addled hallucination, my actions have consequences. "It's not a joke," I whisper shakily. "I have no magic."

"Do you mind explaining yourself?" says Asher.

"It's going to sound crazy."

"This whole day has been crazy," says Rexa. "Try us."

I'm sitting on the thinnest of fences, unable to decide what I believe. If this isn't real, then nothing I do matters. I can linger guilt-free, playing this game as long as my subconscious allows. I'll wake from this beautiful nightmare eventually, safe and sad in my proper body.

But on the off chance this *is* real...

I fidget with my blanket, running the coarse fabric between my thumbs. Written words flow from me with the grace of petals on a river, but spoken words always cause problems. Either I say too much, or I say the wrong thing, or I get flustered and can't explain myself. As such, I've developed the cunning strategy of avoiding conversations whenever possible.

Unfortunately, I don't think I can avoid this one.

"Okay." I proceed with the air of someone shifting their weight onto thin ice, delicate and cautious. "In this world, everyone is born with the ability to wield magic. You—*we* call our magicsources by different names in different countries, but it's universally acknowledged to be one's soul."

To the Solerans, this is like explaining that two and two make four. But I'm not trying to explain it to them, I'm trying to reason it out for myself. If this is real—and I'm treating it like it is, for everyone's sake—how the hell did I get here?

And why did it happen?

There's always a *why* in fiction. That's the difference between fiction and reality: fiction has to make sense. Suffering serves a purpose in stories, advancing the character or the plot. On Earth, suffering is meaningless. There is no point, no greater goal. Life grinds you down until you're a paltry echo of who you used to be.

"Kyla?"

Another prompt snaps me out of my thought spiral. Everyone's staring at me.

"Imagine there was another world." My voice is slow, uncertain. "A parallel universe, if you will."

Asher scrunches his nose, the same way Eric does. "A what-now?"

"Some scholars believe that every time a choice is made, the universe splits," says Valen. "Infinite parallel universes exist in quantum-magical superposition, each one different because the people within them made different choices."

A predictable flutter ripples through my chest. I love it when he talks science. "I've heard that theory, but this is something else."

"You're referring to a universe outside our own?"

Thank the gods of Solera I made this man a genius. Deficient though I am in conversational skill, he's caught my meaning. "Yes. A universe where people aren't born with magic."

Valen's eyes narrow. "They're soulless?"

"No—well, I don't know." Souls are a much more nebulous concept on Earth. Here, they're scientific fact. A soul is the immaterial part of a Soleran that's pure energy. It's this energy that connects every living thing, enabling them to harness and wield subatomic elemental power.

"Let's say the people in that other universe do have souls, but those souls are different," I continue. "And let's also say they can interact with your universe."

Rexa's expression darkens. "I think you mean *our* universe."

I ignore her pointed correction. "So, in some weird, magical, quantum-sciencey way—action at distance, or whatever—someone in that parallel universe could make things happen here. Sometimes good things, but, uh...mostly bad things."

"Kyla," Cendrion rumbles. I wince at the name. "I can't help but wonder where you're going with this."

I suppress a chuckle. I've always been an over-writer. Nasty habit. My editor and I have spectacular fights about this problem.

"Imagine there's a human in that universe who's a parallel version of Kyla. She knows everything Kyla knows—in fact, she knows everything about your *world*, from the natural laws of science to what you're thinking right now."

Asher and Rexa exchange another dubious look. Cendrion's bat-like wings stir at his sides. Valen's face is a mask, but a storm rages in his cloud-gray eyes.

They're all ridiculously easy to read.

"You." I point to Rexa. "You think this is a load of mumbo-jumbo. We're trying to win the most important war in the history of Solera, and I'm wasting time acting like a lunatic while Zalor's out there murdering people."

She folds her lizard-like arms. "Doesn't take a telepath to figure that one out, Kyla."

That name again. It's a knife between my ribs. I feel like I'm lying to them, though I'm doing my utmost to give them a truth they'll be able to stomach.

"You," I say to Cendrion, "think I'm cracking under pressure. You worry the war's taken its toll on me, because you know what happens when you dwell too long in darkness."

Cendrion's pupils narrow to slivers. An unamused growl reverberates through his barrel chest.

Pursing my lips, I face Valen. "You're worried too, because you know science supports what I'm saying. If that other universe can interact with yours, *interfere* with yours, you know how dangerous that could be. And you know I'd never lie to you."

That's true for Kyla, but it's just as true for me. I wouldn't lie to my darlings. I wouldn't hurt them.

I ignore the voice whispering in the back of my mind, reminding me I've already hurt them irreparably.

"And you." Last but not least, I raise my hand to Asher: a peace offering and a plea. "You're the kindest person in this world. You give people chances, even when they don't deserve them. You'd hear what I have to say and you wouldn't be afraid, because no matter what kind of ridiculous trouble I get us into, I always get us out of it."

Asher takes my hand, and sorrow nips at me. I can't remember the last time I held the hand of my real best friend. On Earth, I'm not this open, honest, or gentle. I've isolated myself; my heart has become malnourished from lack of human touch.

"I could do with a little less trouble," he admits, "but you've never failed us yet."

A smile brushes my lips. Good old Asher.

"You trust me?" I ask.

"Of course."

"And you wouldn't hurt me?"

He squeezes my fingers in reassurance. "Never."

"None of you would," I press, looking around the tent.

"We'd never hurt Kyla Starblade." Valen's tone is blood-chilling. "But you're not Kyla Starblade, are you?"

Goosebumps undulate across my skin.

"No, I'm not," I admit through a mouth that's gone dry. "I'm her creator."

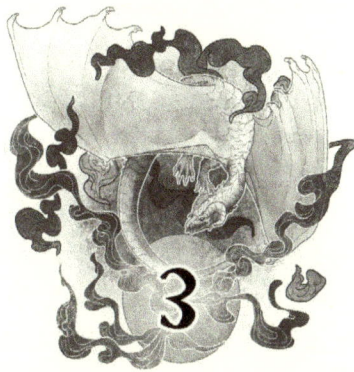

3

THREE HOURS INCH BY in the medical tent while my darlings tear into me like feral dogs, demanding impossible explanations. Though my knowledge of their world is encyclopedic, I stumble through my responses. I can't stand the snarl of distrust on Cendrion's face. Rexa's one wrong answer away from attacking me. The worried gleam in Asher's eyes makes my flesh crawl with shame.

See, this is why I avoid people. Interpersonal communication is too painful. By now, I'm ready to slither into a dark hole and hibernate for a decade, sleeping off the acidic adrenaline that courses through me.

"So, did I pass?" I ask, taking a stab at humor.

"I believe you mean no harm," says Asher, speaking before anyone else has the chance. The tension melts from my muscles, and I flop against my pillows.

"She couldn't harm us if she tried," says Cendrion. His voice, deep and smooth with a trace of the lilting draconic accent, isn't angry or suspicious. It's soft. Hopeless. "She can't wield."

"That's hardly a comfort. In fact, it puts us all in mortal danger," says Valen, fixing me with a glacial look. "Kyla Starblade is the only person in our army who could defeat Lord Zalor. Our strategy for reclaiming Shadow-occupied territory hinges on her lightmagic. If he finds out she's gone, there would be little to stop him from laying siege to the imperial city and claiming the Eldrian throne."

"I don't need the mansplaining, thanks. I literally wrote the book on this." My characters frown at the Earth reference. Valen's disapproving scowl suggests he wants to lecture me some more. Before he can, I scrape together my composure and add, "I've put you in a bad spot, but I'm going to fix it."

"How?" says Cendrion.

How, indeed? I can't win the Shadow War. My presence in Kyla's body has extinguished her magic.

I inhale, and strong scents ground me: the lingering stench of the mugwort poultice, the deep aroma of muddy earth, the subtle tang of magic. If this were a book, the answer would be straightforward, simple. I'd have my characters traipse off on an epic quest to save the world.

Slow warmth seeps from my heart, leaking through my body. Why *can't* it be that simple? I'll be the first to admit I suck at problem-solving on Earth, but here... here I have fantastical, otherworldly tools at my fingertips. Knowledge. Magic. Friends.

My lungs fill with anticipation and my stomach contracts with nervous excitement. With a stout nod, I sit up straight. "I'll bring Kyla back."

"Again," Cendrion presses, "how?"

A hurricane of half-baked ideas swirls through me. Planning isn't my strong suit, but that won't stop me here. Throwing aside my blankets, I jump to my feet. "I need to talk to the dragons. If anyone can offer answers, it's them."

For the first time since I revealed my identity, no one argues with me. I send a silent prayer of thanks to the mother-goddess Ohra.

My spirits rise once more as our ragtag troupe marches to the southern end of the camp. Solera lives and breathes around me. Solid, tangible, *real*.

The jury's still out on that last one, I'll admit. But if it looks real, sounds real, smells real, it may as well be real. What is reality but the sum of our perceptions? So long as this perception of reality lasts, I'll commit to it.

"Stand aside, please," I call to a group of guards, puffing out my chest as I strut toward the changemagic portal that shimmers behind them. "We must return to Midgard."

Kyla doesn't actually have commanding power in the army. She's classified as a special ops force and serves directly under the highest officer of the Mortal Alliance: Valen. Hello, conflict of interest.

The guards glance at Valen for confirmation. At his curt nod, they stand aside, allowing us access to the portable gateway that leads to Eldria's imperial city.

"Captain Ithryn," says Valen, addressing the lead guard. His voice is clipped and tense. "Send a message to General Praxus; he has command of the division while I'm on leave. Zalor's forces have withdrawn, but we must reinforce the airmagic shields around Westport and double the patrols on watch."

Ithryn bows and raises her left hand, where a silvery communication ring glints on her littlest finger. She murmurs to it as our group passes by, magically relaying Valen's orders.

I refrain from telling them that Zalor's busy with other things at this point in the tale, already plotting his next attack. Our division will be safe while we're away.

The Midgard Portal is a wispy aberration, a rip in the fabric of spacetime that has no width or mass. It stretches between two mobile, metallic boundary poles. Within the portal's foggy depths, a sparkling metropolis fades into view. I step from Westport to the imperial city, moving seven hundred miles in a single stride, reveling in the soft tingle of arcane magic as it warps around me.

There's a bounce in my step as I arrive in the Imperial Palace courtyard. I squint upwards, admiring the grandeur. White marble walls gleam in the afternoon sun. Cylindrical towers rise to spear fluffy, low-hanging clouds. Sculpted gargoyles crouch on high ramparts, spouting trails of water that thin to mist before ever touching the ground.

Magnificent though it is, I veer away from the palace, crossing the tiered flagstone square toward golden gates that lead to the city proper. The Midgardian Mountains rise in the far distance, blurred with summer haze.

I'm hyped. *So* hyped. Is it wrong to be this excited? Childlike delight bubbles within me. This rush of serotonin is better than any drug I've ever tried—and I've tried a lot of them.

I wasn't an addict, not really. I was just looking for something that could…well, something that could give me *this*. Happiness, pure and undiluted. Nothing worked (though tequila came close), so I never tried the same drug twice.

"How many dragons are in residence in the mountains?" I attempt to sound calm and professional, but my voice comes out high-pitched with eager anticipation.

"You mean your omniscient creator brain doesn't know?" Rexa sneers.

The true-to-character reaction warms me, and my lips quirk. "No, this isn't part of the story I wrote. This world started changing as soon as I possessed Kyla."

Ugh. That makes me sound like some gross poltergeist. This isn't a possession. I don't know what it *is*, but I know it's not as simple as that.

Rexa's eyes flash gold in the afternoon light. "So you admit you stole her body."

"I told you a million times, I didn't steal anything. This wasn't intentional."

Although if I had been able to do it intentionally—transport my soul from Earth to Solera, inhabit the body of my heroic protagonist—I'd have done so in a heartbeat.

"Enough arguing, Rexa," says Asher. As the army's ambassador, it's his duty to be a mediator within our forces. If a conflict arises, Asher's the one who sorts it out.

"I can't believe you're buying into her bullshit," Rexa says as the gates swing open on magical automated hinges, revealing the cityscape. "You're parading this parasite through our capital like it's nothing. What if she's an enemy shapeshifter trying to infiltrate our army?"

"How would an enemy know as much as she knows about us?"

"Wow, great question. I guess it would only make sense if Zalor had mind-controlled demons who could turn to shadow and spy on private conversations. Oh wait—"

"If I wanted to infiltrate your army," I interrupt, "confessing I'm from a different world has got to be the stupidest way to try it. Besides, you know why I can't be a shapeshifter."

As soon as the words are out, I realize I've crossed a line with Rexa. Her body fills with tension, a coiled spring ready to snap. We've left the palace proper, and I shudder to think how a brawl between two army officers would look to the city's civilians.

Rexa's a fighter in every sense of the word, just like Lindsay—but I haven't had a fight with Lindsay in years. She moved to Chile to reconnect with her birth family. After finding her birth mother and sister, she decided to stay abroad and pursue a career in teaching. With her so far away, she and I drifted apart.

Now Rexa leans close, and a surge of memories return to me. The way her eyes narrow, the way her cheeks color with emotion...it's like looking at my cousin. When was the last time I bothered to FaceTime with Lindsay? I can't remember.

"What do you know about the shapeshifters?" Rexa whispers in a venomous undertone.

I swallow, clenching fists that have become clammy. "I—I know you're the last one."

A snarl curls Rexa's lips. "I can't begin to guess why you're playing this twisted game, but you're going to slip up eventually, and when you do..." She draws a claw across her neck.

Asher steps between us. "I don't take chances when it comes to public safety."

From his wyvernhide utility belt—something he created himself, with enough hidden features to make Batman envious—he withdraws a tiny glass vial. Acid-green liquid glints within it. "You know what this is?"

"Soulbane," I say without missing a beat. "Not lethal, but toxic. It knocks you out when it enters your bloodstream *and* prevents you from wielding until it cycles out of your system."

He nods. "I won't hesitate to use this if I think you're a danger to yourself or anyone around you, but so far you haven't given me reason to distrust you."

Rexa scoffs, but thankfully, doesn't comment.

"I'm sure we all want things to go back to normal, including..." Asher hesitates, giving me an odd look. "We never got your real name."

"For sake of ease, it's best if you keep calling me Kyla."

He frowns. "That feels weird."

"She's right," says Cendrion, plodding along behind us. "This is a matter of national security. Zalor cannot discover that Kyla is compromised."

I glance over my shoulder and flash him a smile. He doesn't return it.

His reaction, coupled with Rexa's unrelenting death glare, sours my mood. I should have lied and pretended to be Kyla. It wouldn't have been hard. If only I'd come up with a better explanation, one that didn't turn my darlings against me.

We tromp west for a solid hour. The city has lost some of its vibrancy due to the ongoing war, but there are still plenty of people bustling about. Glittering skyscrapers, constructed through a combination of magic and mathematics, tower on either side of the packed thoroughfare as patrons browse street stands for food, clothes, and art.

Finally, we reach the city walls. Midgard perches on towering limestone cliffs surrounded by a moat. The ring of mountains beyond the river offers further natural protection.

Of course, without Kyla's teleporting abilities, I have no idea how we're going to reach the dragons' mountain enclave in a timely fashion. Midgard's fleet of enchanted airships is divided amongst the battlefronts, and it would take hours to cross the footbridge and climb the far slopes.

I stop once we're clear of the gates, but Valen strides ahead and does an about-face, pinning me with his icy gaze.

"So, I didn't think this one through," I admit. "I can't teleport us to the dragons."

"No, but you can summon them."

Ah. This is another test. He wants to see how much I know.

Cracking my neck and hiding a smirk, I sidestep Valen and continue toward the cliff. "It won't have the same effect without magic, but I can try."

I relish the sweet breeze that rises from the river, stirring my garments and lifting my loose hair in a cloud. The sun is sinking behind the western ridge of the mountains. Colorful, sparkling shapes traverse the skies: dragons high above, scouring the moat and slopes for an evening meal.

My worries melt away. Pure, unburdened joy renders me feather-light and giddy. This is all I've ever wanted—this beauty, this view, this feeling. I know the stakes, I *know* I'm insane, but for all that...I'm happy.

A lifetime has passed since I was last happy.

"*Drachryi, kemraté a'eos!*" Caught in the thrill of playing pretend, I thrust Kyla's hand in the air, pointing at a flying formation of six dragons. "*Vecerey rheenra aves te'oi!*"

The timbre of raw magical power that should be present when Kyla speaks Draconic is absent from my voice. Still, my inflection and pronunciation are spot-on. I roll my Rs and manage to capture the songlike flow of the language.

Asher's eyes go wide. While he's suitably impressed, Rexa is the perfect picture of haughty disdain: lizard arms crossed, fuzzy hip jutted, clawed foot tapping.

Luck's on my side. A twilight-scaled beauty swoops low, fixing me with a keen eye. Since I paid special attention to every dragon in my books, I recognize her as Temereth. Possessed of uncanny intelligence, even for the hyper-intelligent dragons, she's one of the few who's taken it upon herself to learn the Eldrian language.

A convenient happenstance to move this new subplot along. Suspiciously convenient, almost.

"*Temereth, tenerey qaersas arem evos arcanos,*" I yell.

Dragons don't deign to interact with mortals—who they view as crude and brutish—but they'll make an exception for Kyla Starblade. She wields their power, and they honor that magical connection.

Sure enough, Temereth banks and backwings, slowing her

approach. I retreat, giving her room to land. She alights before me, hooking pearly talons into crevices in the rocky ground. Her massive, membranous wings create miniature tornadoes of dust, and her dark scales glint sapphire when they catch the light of the sun. The scent of charcoal and minerals clings to her. It's accented with an indescribable aroma of magic, charged and vibrant.

I press my right fist to my heart and bow. I'm not sucking up—not consciously, at any rate. It's the appropriate reaction. Here's a creature four times my size who could rend me to pieces if she chose. If she doesn't deserve my respect, no one does.

"Lux'abria," she greets me, using the Draconic term for Lightbringer. "Quoras endrat inquios teos?"

"Do you mind if we speak Eldrian so my friends can join the conversation?" I gesture behind me, commending myself on my quick thinking. My Draconic is conversational at best. I invented a language for my books, but I had a handy-dandy cheat sheet I referenced whenever I was writing.

Temereth surveys my companions, passing judgment.

"Cendrion," she rumbles, staring down her snout at the smaller male. "It has been a month of moons since I saw you last."

His scaly lips curl in the faintest of snarls. "The dragons made it clear I was no longer welcome among them after the incident with Zalor."

I'm sure I'm the only one who catches the subtle hitch in his voice when he mentions that so-called incident. Incident doesn't capture the magnitude of the thing—it was downright cataclysmic when I wrote it.

The inner translucent membranes that protect Temereth's violet eyes rise and lower. A constellation of reflected light winks across her hide as she tilts her head toward me. "You claimed to have a question involving arcane magic."

"I do, and I ask that you keep an open mind when I tell you what happened." With that, I launch into my tale, explaining my identity and my relationship to the world of Solera. Temereth listens without a single interruption, standing at attention with the preternatural stillness of her kind.

"I had a bad week, and I wanted it to be over. So I went to sleep on Earth—I guess. I actually can't remember what I was doing, but I *must* have been sleeping, because next thing I knew, I woke up here, in Kyla's body, thinking it was just another dream."

I pause, reflecting on Earth. My memory's glitching. I recall languishing in my apartment for days on end, trying to force myself to do my damn rewrites. After that, it's a blank. The trail goes cold.

Some things remain crisp in my mind: Eric and Lindsay, my publishing team, my books. While the cornerstones of my identity are solid, the architectural details have blurred. I remember New York City, but not my favorite stores. I live near the 2 Train, but have no specific recollection of ever riding the subway.

I rub my temples, trying to massage away the beginnings of a stress headache. "Way I see it, there are two possibilities. The first is that I've suffered a massive psychotic break. This is a hallucination, and you're all projections of my subconscious."

Cendrion flattens his ears to his skull. "I'm not a figment of some human's imagination."

"Ah, but that's exactly what you'd say if you *were* a figment of my imagination."

I'm met with silence and unamused glares. No one appreciates my joke.

Clearing my throat, I hurry on. "The second possibility is that this is real. Everything in your universe, from the sun and the stars to the dirt beneath my feet, exists independently of me. But somehow I became connected to Kyla Starblade, and..."

I scowl, realizing the paradox as I stumble upon it. I'm connected to Kyla because she's the main character in my bestselling Young Adult novel series. I fabricated her life and personality from scraps of thought in my head. The connection only makes sense if this *isn't* real.

Temereth hums in thought. I can tell from the lowering of her rounded brow ridges that she, too, is analyzing the situation from every angle.

"There are many parallel universes that exist beyond our own," she says. "While these universes never physically coincide, it is possible through quantum-magical entanglement that they may interact. Since souls consist of molecules that adhere to the fundamental laws of energy, your Earthling soul and Kyla's Soleran soul could have become entangled."

"I'm sorry, are we taking this lunatic story seriously?" says Rexa. "You think it's more likely a transdimensional spirit possessed Kyla than that this is a disguised enemy?"

"Yes," says Temereth, in a voice that invites no room for argument.

Valen tries arguing anyway. "You also think it more likely than the possibility that this is still Kyla? The sustained traumas of war can lead to PTSD, psychotic breaks, and worse."

I hear the subtle edge of pleading in his voice. He's grasping at straws, hoping this is the answer. For a moment, I find myself hoping it is, too. What if I'm really her, the legendary, lightmagic-wielding hero? What if the twisted, fragmented memories rattling around in my skull are the dream, and *this* is my reality?

Surreptitiously, I glance down at my hands and poke my left palm again. My right pointer finger connects with solid flesh.

Real, my heart whispers, yearning for it to be so.

"Every soul has a unique energy signature, an infrared aura of magicthreads," Temereth continues in the background. "It is a mix of the elemental magic one wields, one's genetic composition, and electrical impulses in the brain and body. As a lightmagic wielder, I can see those auras, and I can definitively say that this is *not* Kyla Starblade. Her aura is alien, unlike that of any soul on the planet of Solera. Jagged, where yours are soft. Dull, where yours are bright."

The dragon's words are a punch in the gut. It's like she's insulted me, confirmed my inferiority. Worse still is the way Valen's face crumples as his last hope slips away. At least Temereth has solidified my story as truth.

Although we still don't have a *how* or a *why*.

As if she's read my thoughts, Temereth fixes her eyes on me. "I believe it's possible—not probable, but possible—that through your soul-connection to Kyla, you gained a window to our world.

Eventually, your connection grew strong enough that you phased out of your universe and into ours, which is how you came to inhabit the body of the Lightbringer."

She's right about one thing: it's not probable.

But it is possible.

Even in my old, boring universe, crazy shit happens on a quantum level all the time. Scientists can simulate magic in laboratories and particle accelerators. Is it so impossible to imagine I was touched by magic—perhaps selected, like the greatest Chosen Ones in Earthling lore—and pulled into a fantastical adventure?

I dismiss that notion. There's no magic in my reality. I was desperate for magic to come to me, like it does in the stories, but it never did. I used to sit in front of my parents' microwave as a child, hoping the radiation would turn me into a mutant, to no avail.

Huh. Come to think of it, that probably explains a lot of what's wrong with me.

I jolt from my musings when Rexa snaps her clawed fingers in my face. "Solera to Kyla. Are you in there?"

"No. That's why we're in this mess."

"Well, pay attention, whoever you are."

Temereth crouches, lowering herself to my level. "I asked if you can think of any reason this soul-phasing phenomenon would have occurred now."

I'm about to shake my head when I pause. I'm not on Earth anymore. I'm on Solera, a world where every action has a purpose, and every interaction drives the plot forward. It all serves the story.

And if there's one thing I do know, it's my story.

"If Temereth's theory is right," I say slowly, "then maybe I arrived at this precise moment in time to save you."

"Kyla is the one who's supposed to save us." This cutting remark comes from Valen. "Without her magic and skill, I fail to see how you can do the same."

I can admire his loyalty to Kyla while also feeling wounded. He's entitled to lash out. I would too, if I were in his shoes. He must hate me for what I've done to the woman he loves, stealing her body and shoving her soul into some theoretical limbo.

"No matter how powerful Kyla is, she's never seen the future," I retort. "She might have an advantage against Zalor's darkmagic, but she doesn't know what's coming next."

"And you do?" Rexa says skeptically.

Heat blazes through my veins. "Yes! That's my point. I connected to your world, and I know how your story ends."

As quickly as it came, the heat vanishes. My blood cools, turning to ice.

"Oh, gods," I whisper to myself. "This is it. The reason I'm here."

There's no easy way to put it. Best get it over with, like ripping off a band-aid.

"I believe I was sent to save you, because as it stands...you're all going to die."

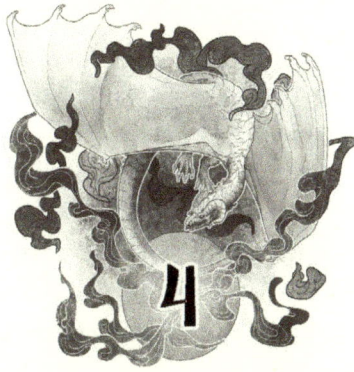

4

"BY THE END OF THE SERIES, Kyla learns enough to defeat Lord Zalor in the ultimate battle for the fate of the world. But it comes at a cost. Sacrifices must be made."

My characters stand spellbound before me, listening to their tale from a new and sinister angle. We've retreated to Temereth's private mountain cave for this conversation. There are spies everywhere—I should know—but none of Zalor's minions would dare trespass in the dragons' domain. Lightmagic is deadly to the servants of darkness.

"Asher and Rexa are slain in battle. Zalor murders Valen during the epic showdown. And when Kyla finally kills Zalor, Cendrion dies, too."

Those words hang in the silence. My companions' horrified faces shine in the cave's soft bioluminescence. Temereth has decorated her home with creeping starmoss. The plant sports tiny, white-blue blossoms that open and glow at night, bathing our surroundings with ethereal haze.

"My death, I foresaw," Cendrion growls, skirting the edge of a dark secret.

"What about the rest of us?" says Asher, looking at Rexa and Valen. Neither acknowledge him. Rexa's busy glaring at me, and Valen's busy brooding at the edge of the wide cave entrance.

I bite my lip. "Your deaths are, ah…surprise twists. To, you know, build tension."

Rexa lets out a derisive snort. "To *what*?"

"A story is nothing without conflict, and Kyla couldn't have everything," I say. "That would have made her a Mary Sue."

"Who the blood is Mary Sue?"

I groan and slap my hands to my forehead, dragging them across my face. "If Kyla had won a war, mastered her super-special magic without issue, and saved every single one of her friends, she would have been perfect. People in my world wouldn't have liked that."

That's what the writing experts would have you believe. Turns out readers *love* a good old-fashioned Mary Sue—because they, like me, long for escape. They project themselves into a hollow character, and suddenly they're everything they always wanted to be.

"Having Kyla lose everyone she loved made for a compelling end to the series."

"You're telling us you killed people for the sake of a good story," says Rexa.

"For the sake of a *great* story," I return blithely.

Too bad my publisher doesn't agree. The team on Earth was similarly horrified to hear of my characters' tragic demise. Hence the demanded rewrites.

"And there are people on your planet who would have read that story?" asks Asher.

"Yes."

"And they would have liked reading about our deaths?"

"No. The story was designed to make readers suffer."

"And you *wanted* to make them suffer?" Asher's mouth falls open. "Why?"

I shrug. "Because my reality is full of suffering. There are no perfect people or happy endings. Dreams don't come true. That's not how Earth works."

"Seeing as you're a self-professed murderer," Rexa cuts in, "how do we know you're not here to kill us ahead of schedule?"

"I don't want to kill you, I lov—" I can't get the word out, though it would be the purest truth I've ever spoken. I run my fingers through Kyla's messy hair. "I was just...going through a lot."

Yet the details of my misery elude me. Memories of Earth remain hazy—a fact that's increasingly troubling—and I can't summon the answer I need. "I was in a dark place," I say, wrapping my arms around myself. Temereth's cave is dry, and a little too cold for my liking. "Writing was an outlet for that darkness."

"You killed us because you were upset," Rexa concludes. "That's fucked up."

Her snide tone tells me she's not buying the soul-entanglement explanation.

"If you bothered to listen," I say, voice crackling with irritation, "you'd know it's not my fault. I just wrote what I saw happening. So, maybe the problem's here, hm?"

Rexa bares her fangs and takes a threatening step toward me.

"Easy," Asher murmurs, laying a hand on her arm.

She rounds on him. "You believe this crackpot story?"

"Frankly, I don't know what to believe. All I know is that this..."
He flounders for a suitable descriptor as he stares at me, eventually settling on a vague gesture in my direction. "She has enough information about our past and future to make me want to take her seriously."

Cendrion scowls. "Her knowledge of the past is understandable, but how could she know our future?"

"Hah!" says Rexa, pointing at me. "Explain your way out of *that*."

I can't. The paradoxes are piling up, each more frustrating than the last.

Temereth comes to my rescue. "Time is defined by space, and vice versa," she says, with the air of explaining that one and one make two. "The Earthling comes from a separate universe with a discrete space-time continuum, and that continuum will not necessarily run parallel relative to ours. Our future may be her present, which explains why she's seen our lives unfold."

I pinch the bridge of my nose, sighing. My brain hurts.

"This is all besides the point." Valen, who's been as silent and dour as a stone gargoyle, steps toward us. "We're focusing on the wrong problems. Right now, we need to figure out how to return Kyla Starblade's soul to her body."

A jolt of adrenaline shoots through me. "I can't leave. Your next battle turns into a massacre. Zalor's planning to ambush you in

Torvel. I know what happens—"

"And now you've told us. Consider us forewarned. We don't need you anymore."

His words drain me of warmth. I've written about his cold anger plenty of times. Only now that its full force is directed at me do I understand how cutting it is, how heartbreaking.

"If you'd rather have Kyla back, fine, but she can't save you in the end. The darkness that turned me into this sub-par person is in her, too."

Ah, yes. There's the real me, the queen of passive-aggression.

"I'll help Kyla guard against that darkness," says Cendrion, his voice quiet but firm.

"It's not that simple. You can tell someone a million times to be stronger, or happier, or *better*. It won't matter if they're not committed to changing."

"Do you believe Kyla wouldn't change to save the people she loves?" Valen demands.

I open my mouth, ready with a fiery comeback that dies on my lips.

Kyla is me, but she's also *more* than me. I had to make her likable so people would identify with her. I had to give her good qualities. Strength. Bravery. Selflessness. Qualities I lack—or, perhaps more accurately, qualities I lost somewhere along my long and tedious descent into darkness.

When I remain silent, Valen turns to Temereth. "Do you know any spells that might force Kyla's soul to phase back into her body?"

"Possibly," says Temereth. "We could perform an exorcism."

In Soleran terms, an exorcism is a complex arcane spell that separates the energy of a soul from a physical body. Only dragons have the power to wield it. I'm not sure it will have the intended effect if they perform it on me.

Yet I shudder when I consider that on Earth, an exorcism is meant to banish a malevolent spirit. In that regard, the spell would be ideal for whatever's going on between me and Kyla.

"An exorcism might force my soul out, but how would you get

Kyla's soul back?"

"A soul remains anchored to one's physical body as long as that body is alive," Temereth explains, "but two things cannot occupy the same space at the same time. You displaced Kyla's soul when you arrived; with you gone, her magical energy should find its way back to her body no matter where it is, in this universe or the next."

Something about that phrasing sends a thrill through me. "You think Kyla's soul ended up in my body?"

"Since the amount of energy cannot change within an isolated system, I think it quite likely that her soul left our universe when yours arrived."

The thought of Kyla Starblade wreaking havoc on Earth makes me laugh. It echoes in the cave, rebounding back upon me. "Oh, I hope she's there right now, wielding lightmagic. She'd turn my planet upside down. I'd be famous."

I'm already famous, so I'm not sure why I said that. My brain is no help, refusing point-blank to summon memories that I *know* should be there. I have a memory of my memories, but not the originals. Like I'm remembering the photograph of an event instead of the event itself.

"If this plan works, will the author's soul return to her Earth body?" Asher asks.

Warmth kindles in my chest. Despite everything, Asher's concerned for my welfare. More than I was, that's for sure.

"In theory," is Temereth's cavalier reply. "We'll find out when I wield the spell."

"Now you decide to be helpful," growls Cendrion. "Where was this helpful attitude when Kyla begged the dragons to join the Shadow War?"

Before, potential energy simmered in the cave; now the air feels brittle, like a single wrong move—or word—might shatter the trust we've built with Temereth.

"Surely you know why our kin cannot fight Zalor," she says, pinning Cendrion with a steely violet glare.

"Actually, I don't. You turned your back on Solera when it needed you most. I joined the Mortal Alliance because I believed my magic could make a difference—"

"And see where that belief has gotten you," she interjects. "You fought him and lost. He stole your lightmagic."

Cendrion bristles. A warning growl echoes along the length of his armored throat. My human characters scatter toward the mossy walls, removing themselves from between the dragons like any sane and rational-minded mortal would.

I, however, have proven myself neither sane nor rational. Instinct brings me toward Cendrion, and I place a quelling hand on his leg.

"It's not your fault," I murmur. "And it's not hers, either."

His eyes snap to me, narrowing. "What do you know that you aren't telling us?"

Oops.

"It's . . . complicated. I couldn't have the dragons join the Shadow War because then—well, then the story wouldn't have happened."

Rexa scoffs, and I wince. For someone who crafts words for a living, I sure do have a habit of choosing the wrong ones whenever I open my mouth.

"Kyla had an extraordinary gift," I say. "She shared the dragons' magic. There's a backstory—something to do with the Crown of the World—but that's not important. Point is, she was supposed to get them to join the battle against Zalor. The dragons *had* to refuse, because they're so powerful."

"Damn right they're powerful," says Rexa, now shooting a dirty look at Temereth. "Powerful enough to win the bloody war for us."

"Exactly! If they'd fought, they'd have won, and it would have been boring. There would have been no conflict, no journey for Kyla or anyone, you included."

"Given that my journey apparently ends in death, I'll take the boring version."

I fold my arms. "The problem with my rationale was that it made no sense, not even on Earth. Truth is, I don't know why the dragons won't join the war."

My editor says I need to reveal their reasoning in Book Five. I argued that I should leave the question open-ended, in case readers clamored for a prequel or a spin-off series. I thought that was a pretty slick excuse.

Wouldn't you know it, my publishing team saw through my bullshit.

I meet Temereth's appraising eye. "If this world is real, it means there are parts of it I haven't seen, secrets I never unearthed. So, would you finally like to explain *your* rationale, Temereth?"

"No."

I'm disappointed, but not surprised. If there'd been a reasonable explanation for their refusal, I'd have written it—or seen it, or divined it, or *whatevered* it—into my books.

"But know this: the dragons care about preserving Solera," Temereth continues, unprompted. "If we fight, we risk annihilation. Yet if we do nothing, Zalor will consume and destroy our world, taking it for his own. We cannot join you in battle, but I can perform the exorcism in the hopes of returning the Lightbringer's soul to us."

"Fine," I say. What can I do but agree? I'm surrounded by powerful wielders, none of whom view me in a favorable light.

Temereth nods, businesslike. "Tomorrow night is the summer solstice. The four moons will be in syzygy. The twelve magical energies of Solera will align, perhaps giving us the edge we need."

"We'll stay in Midgard until then," says Valen, glaring at me, "so we can keep this one under watch."

I bristle at the callous words. *This one.* That's what I've been reduced to in his eyes.

"Ambassador Brightstone," he says to Asher, now in full commander-general mode, "send word to the army, extending our leave. General Praxus will retain command of our division. General Faeloryn," he adds, turning to Rexa, "alert Fyr'thal. I want the Phoenix Division as reinforcements in Westport."

"On it," says Rexa, tapping the side of her head. One of her shapeshifter abilities is the power to speak telepathically with animals, so she's in charge of the army's creature factions. Fyr'thal is a phoenix friend of hers.

A sense of loss, shallow but bitter, worms through me. I'd have liked to meet Fyr'thal. I've been on Solera less than twenty-four hours, but all I can think of is how much I'll miss it when I'm gone.

There's nothing I miss about Earth. I can't remember much, but I know in the pit of my empty soul that I hated it there. I don't want to go back.

A rueful smile flits across my lips. I really have gone off the deep end, haven't I?

Ah, well. There are worse ways to go crazy. I could be strutting through Penn Station with a tinfoil hat on my head, ranting about how 5G airwaves are a plot to mind-control the population. This—waking up in the world I created—is the best outcome I could have hoped for.

It's a shame I'll have to leave soon, one way or another.

"Meet me atop Mount Oshir when the Bloodmoon clears the horizon and the aurora begins to shine," Temereth instructs us. "We will perform the exorcism and pray for a miracle."

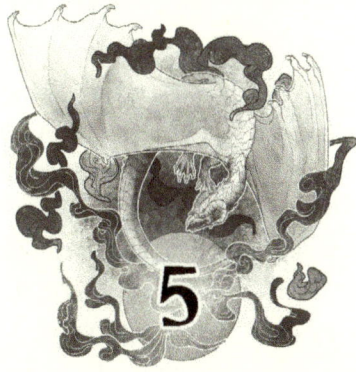

5

I'M DOOMED TO DEPORTATION from Solera, and everyone else needs to do damage control. With my fate decided, Temereth deigns to teleport us to the Imperial Palace.

Rexa goes to provide a vague update to the military personnel stationed in Midgard. Asher bustles off to inform the palace staff that, due to my injury on the battlefront, I'm confined to bed rest until tomorrow evening.

"She's to be monitored at all times," Valen instructs a liveried servant as we stride through the colonnaded entryway together. "For safety reasons."

"What do you think I'm going to do?"

His gaze flicks to me, and he gives me a nearly imperceptible shake of his head. He's warning me not to act suspicious—but Kyla Starblade would never go gentle into the night, and neither will I.

"I'm fine," I say, which is Kyla's favorite lie. "I don't need bed rest or a babysitter."

"You know why you must remain in Midgard." Valen's voice is deadly quiet.

"I'll stay, but first I'm having dinner."

With impeccable timing, my stomach chooses that moment to growl. I haven't eaten since I arrived in this world, and I have no idea when my last Earth meal was. I remember getting drunk mid-week after trying and failing to work on manuscript revisions, but tequila doesn't count as dinner.

I turn to the servant. "Thank you, but I'm not in need of your services."

He bows himself away, and I sashay toward the banquet hall before Valen can stop me. If I only have one day left in this world, I'm going to milk it for all it's worth.

I enter the grand chamber, basking in the finery. Built from the same creamy marble as the rest of the palace, the hall is bright with crystal chandeliers. Floor-to-ceiling bay windows create alcoves for private parties, offering breathtaking city views. Midgard is aglow with a million pinpricks of light. The mountains loom in the distance, black against the velvety night sky.

"What are you doing?" Valen hisses as he trails in my wake.

I flash him one of Kyla's most winning smiles. I know the effect that has on him—the sparkle in her eyes will melt his silly little heart. "Being myself."

"You can't be in a public space unsupervised—"

"Why?" I make a beeline for the buffet tables in the center of the room. The banquet hall remains open all day to accommodate war efforts, but by now it's almost midnight, and the crowd has dispersed. We're alone, apart from the servers. "I'm not stupid enough to give myself away. I know everything about Solera."

"You don't know why the dragons won't fight."

Oh. Yikes. That hurts. Like, *physically* hurts. A writer outwitted by her characters, forced into a corner by her own story.

"Well, I know everything Kyla would know." Irritation itches beneath my skin, but I plaster on a smile for the white-clad server behind the table, holding out my porcelain plate.

Everyone's had to tighten their belts during the war, but Midgard's earthmagic wielders have magically bolstered the city's food stores. There's less variety than there would be in better times, but the mingling sweet and spicy scents of Eldrian delicacies make my mouth water. The server heaps jasmine rice, candied Lenkhari purple yams, and cured wolfcat meat onto my plate.

"I'm not playing this game," Valen whispers, leaning so close that his lips brush my ear. I can't help but shiver agreeably. "Don't force me to discipline you."

"Don't threaten me with a good time," I retort from the corner of my mouth. I nod my thanks to the server before sweeping toward the bay windows. Valen follows.

"If you continue this insubordination," he says once we're out of earshot, "I'll have no choice but to place you under military arrest until the exorcism. Think of how that will look to the army. To the *world*. If Zalor suspects something's wrong with Kyla—"

"Relax." I slide onto a marble bench at a secluded table, grabbing the nearest set of utensils. "Nothing bad happens until the next battle you've planned at Torvel."

Valen sits across from me, straight-backed and rigid. "I can't issue orders based on your delusions. Give me tangible evidence that my troops are not currently at risk."

I'd be offended by his tone, except I've just lifted my fork and taken my first bite of Eldrian food. Something about the mix of tangy and spicy flavors makes it new and fresh, far more delicious than any meal back home. This is like ambrosia.

Perhaps, like ambrosia, I'll be able to stay here forever once I partake of the food. That's how it worked on Mount Olympus, right?

"You trounced Zalor's troops at the Battle of Westport," I say through a full mouth. "He's regrouping and planning his retaliation, and his army won't strike until Torvel."

A harsh laugh, devoid of mirth, breaks from Valen. "That's your idea of evidence?"

"Sorry, I forgot my three-page synopsis and battle diagrams in a parallel universe," I retort, chewing my dinner aggressively.

"You still talk as if this is a story, but it's not. It's bigger than whatever nonsense you've plastered on a page. You're gambling with millions of innocent lives."

I throw my fork down with a clatter and pinch the bridge of my nose. The gesture is mine, but thankfully, I also bestowed it on Kyla in the books.

"I know how serious this is. This is my world, too. I'm part of every character, and every character is part of me. I know this place and these people better than you know yourselves. I've cried and laughed and loved alongside all of you. I would never hurt you."

"Yet you claim to have crafted our deaths."

"You can't have it both ways, Valen," I say, holding his judgmental gaze. "Either you're a figment of my imagination and I'm a monster for murdering you in my manuscript, or you're real and I've seen your future. If it's the latter, then I'm not your enemy. I'm here to help."

The tension slips from his broad shoulders as my argument settles on him. Though my plate is half-full, I've lost my appetite. Brushing off my shirt, I stand and leave without another word.

I know my way through the white marble warren of palace halls. I drew maps of every important building in my books, so I find Kyla's room easily. All the military higher-ups have quarters here, including her. Up the bifurcated central stairwell, past the darkened ballroom, west down a corridor lined with plush, wine-red carpet runners.

Rounding a corner, I spy Asher and Rexa outside Kyla's gilded door. A traumatized servant huddles before them as they demand to know my whereabouts.

"*There* you are," Asher gasps when he spots me.

Rexa shoulders past him to point an accusatory finger at Valen. "Did you disconnect your brain? How could you allow her to go gallivanting around when—!" She bites off her words, glancing at the servant.

"Sorry for the inconvenience," I tell the poor man. "I don't need to be monitored, no matter what my friends say, so you're dismissed."

Seizing his chance to escape, the servant flees before anyone can countermand him.

"You're as troublesome as Kyla, I'll give you that," says Rexa. "Go in your room and stay there, or you'll answer to me."

"Cendrion's guarding the balcony," Asher adds. "I'll find a soldier to watch the door."

"No." Surprisingly, this comes from Valen. "That will raise suspicions."

"Not you, too," Rexa growls. "You can't be falling for her act."

"She made a valid point about our predicament. For now, I'm convinced she means to help. I'll remain in the city to monitor her. I'd like the two of you to return to camp and prep the division for our campaign in Torvel."

Asher goes pale. His glasses flash in the lamplight as he turns to me. "Isn't that the battle you mentioned? The one where we get ambushed?"

"The very same. Though now that you're *forewarned*, it's not really an ambush, is it?" I give Valen a falsely sweet smile, punching the word he threw in my face earlier.

To my shock, I catch the ghost of an answering smile on his lips. "It's not. So before you go home, *Kyla*," —he hits my name with the same pointed force I used, and my stomach lurches— "you and I will comb through every detail you remember about the rest of the war."

Rexa nods. "I'll come back tomorrow night."

"There's no need—" Valen begins, but she holds up a hand to silence him.

"You are the stupidest smart person I know," she says. "You might not realize it, but I see in your eyes that she's got you snared in her spell. It's clear I'm the only one who can be objective about her, and if something goes wrong, you'll need me."

With that, she stalks down the hall, waves of silky obsidian hair bouncing behind her. Her dark green cloak flutters in her wake.

Asher fishes out the vial of soulbane and hands it to Valen. "Just in case. Get some rest tonight. Both of you," he adds, looking at me.

"Thanks, Ash," I say without thinking.

He pauses before leaving, his face set in a lopsided scrunch. The expression is endearing, though not particularly reassuring. Eric makes that face whenever I do something dumb.

"I hope you know what you're getting into," he murmurs.

His words aren't angry or accusatory, and that makes it worse. Asher is worried.

He has every right to be.

With our unsatisfactory good-nights out of the way, I turn to Kyla's room. While my nerves are aflame with excitement, my body aches for rest. The door, enchanted to open only to its occupant's touch, swings wide for me when I clasp the golden handle.

The darkened chamber is small by palace standards, but I consider it luxurious beyond compare. A four-poster bed with downy comforters stands at the head of the room, draped with gauzy ornamental curtains. There's a small table and two chairs in the left corner. Across from me, a window bleeds silvery moonlight onto the bed, and double doors lead to a small balcony. Cendrion stands outside, a silent sentinel.

As I enter my quarters, movement registers from the corner of my eye. I wheel to face whoever's lurking in the shadows, anxiety-brain switching to overdrive. I open my mouth to scream for help, to summon Cendrion—

"Oh." My voice is a soft flutter, an exhalation of understanding. A mirror hangs on the wall to my right. "Just my reflection."

Only it's *not* my reflection. It's Kyla Starblade peering back at me, half illuminated by shafts of light streaming in from the hall. I put a hand to my leaping heart, and Mirror-Kyla emulates my action. I tilt my head. The reflection does the same.

It's surreal, this experience. There's something off about it, like hearing your own voice in feedback through a call. Your words register a millisecond after you utter them, and you slow your speech as you listen, as if you expect your disembodied echo to continue if you yourself were to stop talking.

Compounding my feeling of surreality is the fact that staring into the mirror and seeing Kyla's face feels surprisingly normal. My hand rises and brushes her cheek, and I realize I don't remember what I looked like on Earth. I do recall hating my body. Wanting to shed my skin, strip the meat off my bones—through surgical knife or baser weapons, I wasn't picky—and become someone, *any*one else.

A wan smile spreads across the reflected visage. That wish came true. I'm seeing a glimpse of who I could have been if I hadn't allowed life to beat the goodness and bravery out of me.

With a soft creak, the door opens wider to admit Valen. He strolls in like he owns the place, activating the enchanted light switch. The firelamp stand in the corner glows to life.

"What are you doing?" I ask. I thought we were done for the night, parting ways to reconvene tomorrow.

He shuts the door behind him. It locks with a *thunk*. "We have a war to discuss."

My stomach drops even as my heart soars, creating a maelstrom in my chest. "Can't stay away, huh?" I intended my voice to be dry as a desert. It comes out soft and shaky.

"Don't flatter yourself. Kyla is my responsibility."

"Oh, is that what you call it?"

"I intend to protect her body until the safe return of her soul," he says, drawing one of the chairs away from the table and folding his tall frame into it. "Since you are incapable of protecting yourself without magic, you'll have to suffer my presence."

Wait. Wait a gods-damned moment. Is this really happening? Did all the stars in my universe align to set me up in a There's Only One Bed trope? My *favorite*?

Mentally I'm not prepared. I want to spend every waking moment with my characters while I can—specifically, I want to be close to Valen. I want to hold his hand once more before I go. I want to wrap myself in the comfort of his safe embrace.

But I'm also a spectacular self-saboteur. Instead of inviting him to relax, my Earthling defense mechanisms kick in.

"Cendrion's outside. I think he's protection enough."

"Cendrion has his weaknesses, as you should know. Zalor stole his lightmagic, rendering him unable to wield."

"He's a *dragon*—"

"A dragon who was bested by a shadowman assassin this morning." Valen points to the seat opposite him. "Besides, you have work to do. I need a full, written report on the future of the Shadow War, starting with the Torvel ambush. So sit."

He's right, and that irritates me.

"Wow," I say, offering him an ironic bow before sinking into the second chair. "I wasn't aware you'd been promoted to Emperor of Eldria."

This time, the almost-smile glimmering at the edges of his mouth is evident. "Your Kyla impression is spot-on. A little too good to be an act, if you ask me."

If someone on Earth had attempted to dredge a droplet of emotional availability from me, I'd have clammed up and sent them packing. Valen is different. There's not a malicious bone in his body. He'd never think to mock another person, not even a person he dislikes.

And though I hate to admit it, I *am* a person he dislikes.

"Kyla was based on me," I say. "At least, I thought she was. I guess it's more like we're two versions of the same person in different universes. Star-crossed souls. A quantum-entangled, parallel-dimension duo."

"That would explain a lot," he murmurs, his eyes roving my face and body. "It's in keeping with certain theories of the multiverse, although I doubt you've lived parallel lives."

"You'd be surprised," I mutter.

"Oh? Tell me, how bad was the Shadow War on Earth?"

Ouch. Guess I underestimated how much he dislikes me.

"Kyla was thrust to the forefront of the Mortal Alliance, thanks to her lightmagic," he continues, crossing his arms. "When she begged the dragons for help, only Cendrion answered her cry. They strove to defeat Lord Zalor and failed with devastating results. Now the Eldrian Empire lies in ruin. Solera burns while our army struggles to fend off the forces of darkness. Did the same thing happen to you?"

In one paragraph, he's sucked the joy out of my chest. I feel like my old Earthling self: hollow. Bereft of hope, drowning in despair.

"There are no dragons in my world—one of the reasons it's so awful." My attempt at humor falls flat, even for me. "And though there's plenty of war, I wasn't involved in any of it."

Valen's gaze sharpens. I look down at my hands, picking at my nails and fidgeting with my sleeves. Absently, I tap my left palm. Still as solid as ever.

"But I had my fair share of trauma, and that . . . that ruined me. It was a slippery slope into self-loathing and self-destruction from there. I did terrible things to people I loved. To myself."

Funny how I can speak of my faults and crimes with such easy confidence, yet I can't remember any of the good things I've done.

Perhaps I never did any good things.

I hide a wince, refusing to entertain that thought. It's nonsense, of course—no one's pure evil, with the possible exception of Lord Zalor—yet it burrows into me, lodging deep within my chest, turning me cold.

Shit. My eyes are burning. If I blink, tears will fall. I can't let Valen see me cry. No one is allowed to see that. I tilt my head back and pretend to be fascinated by the ornate ceiling tiles, waiting for the brimming liquid to subside.

"I haven't fought deadly battles," I conclude, my voice thick with the strain of making it sound normal, "but I know what Kyla's suffered. And like her, my suffering has defined me."

She rose above it. I let it break me.

Valen is silent for a long time. Taking a risk, I lower my gaze. Water wobbles on the edges of my eyelids. His form distorts behind the liquid.

"Do you pity me?" The words are out of my mouth before I knew they were in my mind.

"If you're asking whether I feel sorry for you, the answer is no."

Ouch again. Well, I did ask—and at least he didn't say *yes*. Wallowing in self-pity may be one of my favorite activities, but I can't stand it coming from anyone else.

"I do, however, empathize," he adds, studying me like I'm one of his science books. "I know a fighter when I see one. You've been fighting a long time."

My heart lurches, caught off-guard by this unexpected olive branch.

"Yet I also notice a glaring difference between you and Kyla. If the roles were reversed—if she were displaced and wound up alone in a different world—she'd be desperate to go home."

"Home," I echo softly, turning the concept over in my mind. He doesn't understand why I yearn to stay here. I don't suppose most people would.

"The thing is, Earth didn't feel like home. This world does. I know I go on about magic and dragons, and those are wonderful things, but the true magic comes from the way I feel. The only time I felt alive was when I wrote about Solera. The only time I felt seen was when I was with you."

Valen is close. When did he get so close? We're inches apart. I can count his dark lashes. His eyes simmer with the energy and mystery of bottled lightning. Blinking, I pull myself to my senses. He hasn't gotten closer—I've leaned forward without being aware.

"All my main characters," I clarify, drawing away from him.

But especially you.

How can this be a dream if I have never, in all my wildest dreams, felt this way? This soft and loving ache is the realest, rawest emotion I've experienced. Maybe Earth was the Matrix, a pale and lackluster simulation of life. Or maybe *this* is the Matrix, and I'm trapped in some sort of hallucination stemming from . . . what? Expired milk? A bad batch of drugs? My own twisted mind?

"You know," says Valen, "Kyla is surrounded by people who love her, but sometimes she forgets that. Perhaps it's the same for you. Perhaps you're not as alone on Earth as you believe."

"It's not a matter of belief. I am who I am. I make myself alone, I build walls. And unlike Kyla, I don't have anyone in my life who cares enough to tear them down."

Is that true? It *feels* true, which is why I can say it with such confidence, but memories that were once crisp and absolute are now smeared like a child's finger-painting gone awry.

I stand, attempting to force my lips into a smile. They're uncooperative.

"You can take the bed," I tell him, too tired and broken to indulge in a fantasy that has no basis in reality. If I sink too far into the fantasy, reality will hurt that much more when I return to it. "I'll write my report on the balcony. I need some air."

Valen starts to say something, but I spin on my heel and stalk toward the balcony doors. I fling them open and slam them behind me. Cendrion's head shoots up at the noise.

"Sorry. I wanted to be alone. Do you mind if I stay out here?"

As he takes in my haggard appearance, the angry light in his purple gaze flickers out. "I have to keep watch," he says, "so you won't be alone."

"That's alright. We can be alone together." I press my back against the smooth wall and slide to a crouch. The blue-tinged Oldmoon shines high overhead. The smaller, red-tinged Bloodmoon lurks on the western horizon, peeking over the mountains. The other two moons, identical satellites called the Silver Twins, haven't yet climbed the eastern skies. "I like the darkness."

"Yes," whispers Cendrion. "The darkness is familiar."

6

IT'S THE NIGHT OF my scheduled departure. The Bloodmoon has crested the Midgardian Mountains. The Oldmoon hangs above, a perfect sphere in the star-studded heavens. The Silver Twins align beneath the two larger orbs. The ethereal colors of an aurora scintillate on the northern horizon, glowing greens melding with soft blues and magical purples.

Like on Earth, the aurora is caused by solar particles hitting the planet's magnetic field. The effect is augmented by the field of magic surrounding Solera, which stems from the north pole, the Crown of the World.

That place never made it into my books, but I know the lore. According to Soleran legend, that's where the dragons got their light-magic powers. Originally they were born with fire in their souls, in adherence with the Earthling cliché. But the dragons of prehistoric Solera discovered the Crown of the World, and there they were gifted new magic: the power of light.

Billions of years of magical history, a millennium's worth of mortal myths . . . it was all tucked in the back of my skull, a well to draw from if needed. Know the iceberg, write the tip.

I blink, remembering who I am and why I'm here. This isn't my world, as much as I'd like it to be.

And now it's time to leave.

Kyla's friends surround me on the mountain tableland. I face Temereth, whose hide is glazed with reflections of the four moons.

"Are you ready?" she asks, her voice soft and resonant with power.

I'm not. There was so much I wanted to do. Valen showed me a great kindness earlier, allowing me freedom to explore the palace grounds. I visited the vast library, smelled the jasmine and wisteria in the labyrinthine hedge garden, and stuffed myself with a hearty lunch of Galvian spiced seaweed and Lenkhari lentil soup.

I let the silence last too long. Temereth tilts her head and says, "There is no shame in being afraid."

"I'm not afraid." I look away from her luminous violet eyes. "Just sad."

Kyla's friends are my friends, too, though our interactions have been strained. These are the creatures who gave me comfort when I needed it, who saw me through the worst times of my life. Their steadfast presence helped me more than anyone on Earth ever did. I sank into this world with them when reality became too heavy a burden to bear.

Asher steps forward and offers his hand. "You're doing the right thing. And we're forever grateful for the information you gave us."

I didn't sleep last night. Instead, I spent my time writing out every detail of the upcoming ambush, the end of the war, and Zalor himself. His strengths, his weaknesses.

What sucks is that he doesn't have any weaknesses, apart from lightmagic. He's godlike in his power.

"I pray to Ohra that my information helps you," I tell Asher, grasping his proffered hand. "I hope you can change the ending of your story."

"I know we can."

A smile trembles on my lips. I wish I could believe the way he does. He makes hope seem effortless. "There's that unquenchable optimism."

Asher retreats, and I make a mental note to spend more time with Eric when I return to Earth. We've grown apart over the years, each absorbed in our increasingly separate lives. He has his career and his boyfriend and his photography hobby, and I...?

Well, I have my world. I have a surrogate character who fills the void Eric's absence has left in my soul. I never wish to trouble Eric with my problems, because I know how busy he is, but I think I'll give him a call when I get home. I can fill him in on the juicy drama with my publisher.

Ten years ago, I would have told him this tale, too: the tale of how I awoke in a different world. We used to love talking about magic. I know that much. The memories of my childhood remain intact, albeit indistinct. Blurred, as only time itself can blur them.

Eric and I dreamed of magic together. We'd frolic in midsummer thunderstorms, tempting fate, wishing for lightning to strike and give us superpowers. But the real world has a way of wringing the hope from you, squeezing out drops of joy with every heartbreak and failure and loss until you're empty. It's been ages since I treated magic as if it were an attainable thing. I'm not sure if that was a symptom of adulthood or major depression. Maybe both.

Drowning in nostalgia and caught between two worlds, I inhale a lungful of chilly air. The scent of fragrant featherpine trees fills my nose, a heady mixture of lavender fields and evergreen forests. I tilt my face skyward, letting the starlight kiss my cheeks.

"Do your worst, Temereth." My voice, at least, is steady and sure—unlike my heart, which stutters an arrhythmic beat in my throat.

The dragon's eyes glow as she embraces her magicsource and wields. Bereft of the power that flows through every living thing on Solera, I can't see the tangled tapestry of energy Temereth is twisting around my body.

But I can feel it.

My flesh tingles as an invisible net engulfs me. Magicthreads—strands of molecular energy that wielders manipulate to weave spells—leach warmth from me wherever they touch. I shiver and blink. Tears cloud my eyes again.

"For what it's worth," I say, "coming to your world is the best thing that's ever happened to me."

Asher dips his head in a sad, knowing way. Rexa, whose fists are clenched with nerves, does nothing. Valen's face is smooth, but the misty sparkle in his eyes betrays a hint of emotion.

A gasp slips between my teeth as the tingling sensation grows uncomfortable. It's less like a limb that's fallen asleep and more like acupuncture gone wrong. Needles are pricking me, steady and insistent.

Temereth's eyes flash, burning like miniature suns, and the needles become knives. A shuddering cry breaks from my lips, and my legs give way. As my knees crack against the mountaintop, my hands fly to my chest. Spectral claws close around my organs, trying to rip them from my body.

"Kyla!" Asher moves to help.

Cendrion throws out a wing, blocking his path. "Do not interfere," he warns. "The field of magic around her is too powerful. You might get tangled in the threads and snarl the spell, destroying her— or yourself."

The pain sinks into my body. No longer slicing against my skin, now it's in the core of my being. My lungs are on fire, filling with smoky fear. My heart thrashes, flinging itself against my rib cage. I regret overeating. The Eldrian food sloshes in my stomach as my abdomen convulses.

A ragged, grating wail tears my throat raw. The fire spreads from my lungs to my blood. Every vein, from my largest arteries to my smallest capillaries, is burning. I curl in on myself and slump to the side, twitching against the cold, rough rock.

"Has something gone wrong?" I hear Asher's shaky voice from a million miles away. "Should she be in this much pain?"

"An exorcism is one of the most complex spells to perform," Temereth replies. "And one of the most painful. We are divesting energy from mass, separating a soul from a body."

My vision's going dark at the edges. I suppose these are my last moments on Solera. I had hoped I'd end on a high note—or at least not an embarrassing one. Writhing in unendurable pain is not how I wish to be remembered.

Goodbye, my darlings.

The pain reaches critical mass. My brain short circuits, overloaded with agony. I scream. My body spasms. For one terrible, unending moment, I am nothing—

Nothing at all—

Unconsciousness, oblivion, no feeling, no thought, empty—

Then thunder cracks through my chest. Physical sensation comes shrieking back, but I'm still trapped in darkness.

CRACK!

Energy skitters along my nerves. My sternum is bruised, sore. It feels like someone punched me in the solar plexus.

"She's alive! Come on, breathe for me. Come on!"

CRACK!

Electricity surges into my body, defibrillating me. My back arches, and my heart—which has been stubbornly still—stammers to life.

I ache everywhere. I'm senseless, unable to comprehend what's happening, but I know I am not enjoying this experience. I've suffered enough. I don't want to suffer anymore.

"Kyla?"

Someone whispers in my ear, and clarity pierces my haze of confused anguish. I'm breathing again, but each breath is labored. With monumental effort, I open my eyes.

Against all odds, I remain on Solera.

My thoughts drift in pieces, shattered and scrambled by the torture I endured, yet this knowledge registers within me on a primal level. It fractures my foundational beliefs—or rather, fractures the limitations Earth imposed on them.

There's a difference between belief and hope. Before, despite all evidence to the contrary, I'd only *hoped* this was real—hoped it wasn't some elaborate maladaptive daydream or wild tequila trance. I *hoped* the rug wouldn't be yanked from under me when I awoke to the truth and found myself in my filthy New York City apartment.

Now, with the threads of my identity unraveled from the exorcism, I weave myself into a new tapestry. In a single heartbeat, everything's changed.

It's real.

Asher and Rexa hover by my side. Cendrion crouches behind them, and Temereth looms beyond. Valen's noble countenance, taut with fear, comes into focus. His hand is pressed against my chest. It was his voltmagic that saved me, shocking my heart into a regular rhythm.

"Valen," I croak.

He pulls me upright and wraps strong arms around me, burying his face in my shoulder. The touch awakens me like nothing else could, not even a thousand volts from an Earthling defibrillator. The fresh, clean scent of him illuminates the night. His warmth envelops me, making me whole.

"You're back." His voice is muffled against my neck. Though he holds me close, his touch is gentle, as if he's afraid I'll crumble if he squeezes too hard. "I thought I'd lost you."

He believes I'm her, the hero of Solera, the light of his life. For a moment, I dabble with the idea of pretending. I could do it easily.

But I'm an empty Earthling with no light to wield, and he would discover my deceit. If I deceive him, that will make everything worse by a hundredfold.

Just one more heartbeat, I think, savoring Valen's embrace. *Just let me live this lie for one more heartbeat.*

Never in all my years has someone held me this way. Like I matter. Like I am the universe. Every Earthling embrace I shared with a man came with insidious, tangled strings attached. My body has been starved for something this pure and gentle and safe.

Burning with regret, I raise my arms and place my hands on Valen's chest, pushing him away. "It's not her. It's me."

The way his face falls is more painful than the exorcism. One moment it's shining with relief; the next, it darkens in a rictus of disappointment. His brows contract, shadowing his eyes—and in those silver depths, I catch a glimmer of fear. Of uncertainty. Like me, I suspect his tangled beliefs and hopes have just been shattered.

"Why didn't the spell work?" growls Cendrion.

"There was no guarantee it would," says Temereth. "We were operating on theory."

"Where is Kyla?" Valen demands, standing and whirling to confront the dark-scaled dragon.

Temereth rotates her wing joints in a shrug. "That, I cannot say."

Valen rounds on me next, fixing me with a fever-bright gaze. "You must know something. There's something else you're not telling us."

"Stay your anger, Commander-General," says Temereth. "It will do no good to question her. There are some phenomena even the wisest minds cannot explain with magic or science."

I wrap my arms around myself, holding my throbbing body. The pain's dull but persistent. Guilt curdles in my gut, festering with the remains of my lunch.

Then I blink. Temereth's words tug at something in my mundane soul. This can't be explained by the magic in their universe or the science in mine, but what if there's an answer hidden in the place in-between?

Overhead, my characters start to argue. Asher and Valen trade heated words while Cendrion and Rexa attempt to bully answers out of a stoic Temereth. No one's paying attention to me, but that's alright. I'm having a Light Bulb moment, shaking with the aftershocks of Valen's voltmagic and the terrifying potential of my idea.

For two decades I've had a window to this world, a connection that allowed me to glimpse the past, present, and future of its inhabitants. The magic that brought me here is not native to Solera, but I know where I've seen it before.

In stories.

There are a thousand stories like this—it's almost a genre unto itself. The "Freaky Friday" trope, if you will. Two souls switch bodies. Only once they understand each other, learn a valuable lesson, or redeem themselves in some way do they return to their original selves.

Am I projecting my deepest fantasies onto the problem at hand? Yes. Am I sure this is the magical solution we've been searching for? Also yes. In the aftermath of the exorcism, considering the new possibilities unfolding before me, there's no question in my mind. The switch occurred, and to set things right, I must be the one to undo it. But how?

I don't have to gain an understanding of Kyla Starblade. Nor am I sure what lesson this place can teach me. I love this world, and I'm committed to doing anything in my power to save its people from the fate I've foreseen.

That leaves redemption.

A frisson of ominous certainty undulates through me. *That's the one.*

My brain can't dredge up any specific sins for which I must atone, but the truth screams from the depths of my heart. Even with the rest of my identity in tatters, this certainty remains: the knowledge that I'm a bad person. Worthless and undeserving.

I know I'm not a hero. I've known it for a long time, though it took me years to swallow the hard truth. Every misstep I took, every mistake I made—no matter how small or benign—drove the stake deeper into my heart. Not a hero; just a failure.

Like Cendrion, I'm haunted by the demons of my past and the fear of my future. I am, if I'm being honest with myself, a coward. Too scared of failing to keep trying. Too tired of pain to harness my power.

But I can change. Though I may have been a coward on Earth, this is Solera: a world spun from impossibilities, a world brimming with infinite potential. I can be like Kyla, embody her heroism, embrace her best traits. I can be noble and kind and brave. I can be selfless.

"I know what I have to do," I say, gaining strength with my conviction.

Everyone is arguing, and no one hears.

"Hey!" I shove myself to my feet. "I have an idea."

My outburst startles them into silence. They watch me, on guard, but the glowing truth in my soul is armor that makes me strong.

I've always doubted myself, second-guessing every choice and action. They will also doubt. They will question and fight me, but I know this is the way forward, and I'll do whatever I can to make them understand. I'll tell them every Earthling story and every gods-damned TV Trope in the book if I must.

"I know how to bring Kyla back and send myself home—but first, I must go on a journey."

"You're not going anywhere," says Rexa.

"Not on my own. I'll come with you and help you win the Shadow War. I'll keep you safe. I can prevent your deaths, and everyone will live happily ever after!"

Dubious looks pass between my darlings. I'm not explaining myself well; the exorcism fuddled my brain.

"How will you win the war without lightmagic?" asks Cendrion.

"Um, hello, I'm omniscient." I'm not really—there are plenty of things about this world I don't know, as I've already seen—but I'm the next best thing. "Plus, we have some of the most brilliant minds in Eldria gathered on this mountaintop. If we work together, we'll win."

Silence, ringing and brutal, yawns in the wake of my words.

"Please let me come." My gaze settles on Asher. "Your ending isn't a foregone conclusion. I can change it. I can save you."

Slowly, Asher approaches. He stares at me over his glasses, a furrow of consideration on his brow.

"You know," he says after a time, "I think you can."

Rexa tosses her hands up behind him, but Temereth nods. That strikes me as a good omen. Confidence blazes through me as my certainty in the plan solidifies.

"Kyla has to come with us anyway," says Cendrion. "We need to prevent Zalor from discovering the truth about her. She must be seen at the head of the army."

He glances at Valen, who has final say on military decisions. A muscle flickers in Valen's jaw as he studies me, weighing his options.

At long last, he gives his blessing: a single, curt nod.

"With any luck," he says, "we'll discover a more permanent solution to Kyla's soul-displacement on the road."

Not even his cold attitude can ruin my moment of triumph. I'm brimming with hope, ready to fight. My heart fills with love for these characters, this world.

I'm going on an *adventure*.

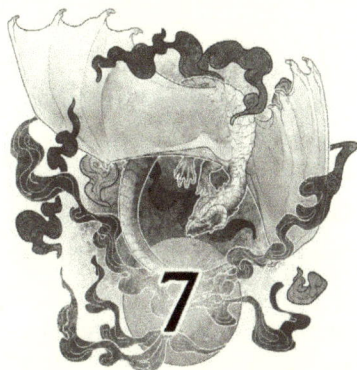

7

THE HERO'S JOURNEY is the oldest trope in the book of books. There's a beginning with high stakes. There's a middle with obstacles to overcome. Lastly, there's an ending—definitive and, if not happy, at least satisfying. The hero, having learned her lesson, is transformed.

I already feel transformed, though my epic journey to save Solera has just begun. I was suffocating on Earth. Like a frog being boiled in water, I couldn't feel the heat until all my positive emotions had evaporated.

"You're smiling too much," Valen mutters. "Take this seriously, or our cover is blown."

"I am taking this seriously," I retort from my perch on Cendrion's back as he leads the army column. We're marching to the northern kingdom of Galvia, zigzagging through verdant valleys and forests carpeting mountain foothills to avoid enemy eyes. "I can be dead-set on saving Solera and also be in a good mood."

How could I not be? Solera is *real*. If I didn't wake up from the excruciating pain of the exorcism, then I'm well and truly stuck here.

I stifle a laugh. *Stuck* isn't the right word. This is nothing short of a miracle. I've crossed between universes and landed in paradise. Although even here, in the Eldrian wilderness, traces of the Shadow War are evident. Suspicious splotches of withered plants dot the countryside—signs of Zalor's poison in this world, reminding me of what's at stake.

My plan for victory is simple: I'll use my knowledge to help the Mortal Alliance triumph against Zalor. Once he's defeated and I've atoned for my sins, the magical Powers That Be will allow me to return home.

This reasoning is "flimsy and asinine," according to Valen, and part of me knows that's true. But even if fulfilling my journey doesn't send me back to Earth, I'll still have saved the world I adore.

The mountain breeze tempers the heat of the summer sun. I close my eyes and soak in the golden warmth, for I've been cold since I woke from the exorcism. When a piercing call echoes toward us, I crack open a lid. A blaze of fiery phoenixes glitters between jagged peaks, adding a splash of ruby to the cerulean sky.

We halt at dusk to camp. Soldiers with earthmagic wield posts out of the ground, and airmagic wielders make quick work of settling canvas covers over the pillars.

I slide from Cendrion's back, surveying the bustling army. "Thank you."

He rolls his diamond shoulders. "It was nothing."

Emboldened by my newfound *joie de vivre*, I lay a hand against his scales. He glares at the uninvited touch, but I'm impervious to his ferocity.

"Dragons aren't work beasts. You're proud, intelligent creatures, superior to humans in most things. You did me a favor today, giving me that ride. I'm grateful."

Though his eyes remain narrowed, his slitted pupils widen to ovals, softening his gaze. "We must make them believe you're Kyla Starblade. I'd never carry a stranger."

"But you *did*. And I appreciate the gesture."

Cendrion's nostrils flare as he heaves a sigh. His warm breath rustles the wisps of hair around my face that have escaped Kyla's traditional battle braid.

"You are different from her." He starts plodding east, heading to higher ground. I get the feeling that the flick of his muscled tail is an invitation, so I hurry after him, taking four steps for every one of his.

"How so? I can be better at—"

"Oh, you've done a fine job masquerading," he interrupts. "The officers are fooled. I doubt anyone but your closest confidantes would see the difference."

"Valen said I was being too smiley," I mutter.

"On the contrary, your smile is where Kyla shines through most."

A guilty pang hits me. I gaze at the twilit peaks without seeing them as we hike through waist-high grass. I'm enjoying myself too much. The Eldrians are fighting a devastating war. It's wrong of me to feel so light.

It's wrong that I'm grateful the exorcism failed.

But come on—how many times do you get to save the world? Epic quests are few and far between on Earth.

"There are moments when something changes, and your eyes lose their light. That's when Kyla fades," Cendrion continues. "It makes me wonder what you're trying to atone for."

I chew my wind-chapped lower lip. It was pragmatism that convinced my darlings to bring me on this journey, nothing more. If word got out that the real Kyla Starblade was gone, there'd be hell to pay. I'm the only one who clings to the idea of redemption. But...

"I don't know," I admit to Cendrion. "Take your pick of the crop. I've done plenty of bad things."

Things, perhaps, that are neither deserving nor capable of atonement. Things I can't recall, which haunt me nonetheless. They hover at the edges of my mind, these half-remembered things—invisible but rancid, poisoning me with their sickly sweet stench.

A shudder whisks through me. In a bone-dry voice, I add, "Whatever set off this chain of events, it must have been really bad if it catapulted me into a parallel universe."

"A fellow tortured soul with a mysterious, haunted past." Cendrion tilts his head toward me as he ascends the foothills, an unmistakable twinkle in his amethyst eye. Thank Ohra *someone* enjoys my black humor.

"I thought I was supposed to be the all-knowing one."

"I don't need to be all-knowing. You are transparent. You don't bother hiding your emotions, whether they be happiness or pain."

The last glimmer of light fades behind the western ridge. Glowing starmoss and moon-blossoms shine in the dusk, setting the far slopes alight with soft, blue-white bioluminescence.

We've come to a rocky outcrop, a bald patch in the lush vegetation. Cendrion clambers onto it and stands in the deepening shadows. I take a place by his side, overlooking the organized chaos of the camping army.

"I wasn't like this on Earth," I admit. "I was real good at hiding emotions there."

"Not necessarily something to be proud of."

An itchy feeling irritates the lining of my chest, driving me to be contrary, to defend myself. But as I open my mouth, I discover I don't have the heart for it. "You have a point. Maybe that's something I'll change when I go home. Be more open with people. About feelings and shit."

The thought is as terrifying as it is alluring.

"To be fair, that's no easy feat," says Cendrion. Something in his voice makes goosebumps erupt on my arms. "Pain is transformative. It twists its way into every aspect of your life. It becomes an accent when you speak and a mask when you interact. If you're not careful, the mask becomes your reality."

I know these words. I wrote them. This is a scene from my fifth book. It's not supposed to appear until much later in the story, before the final battle with Zalor.

The words came from me—at least, I thought they had—but I didn't know how much I needed to hear them spoken aloud until this moment. I didn't know how heavy my soul had grown. Not from the pain itself, but from the loneliness of it. The isolation. Being trapped in my mind with nothing but darkness for company wasn't any way to live.

"Wise counsel," I say, taking special care to sound upbeat and unbothered. "I knew you were my favorite character for a reason."

Cendrion's ears twitch with interest. "I'm a favorite?"

"Of course. For starters, you're a dragon, and I'm Earth's number one dragon-fan. I will fight people about the physiological differences between dragons and wyverns. I've loved dragons since forever. But also, you're..."

My voice hitches. We're navigating into dangerous territory.

"Back when I thought this was just a story I'd invented, you were important to me. It might sound weird, but I felt like you represented part of my soul. Especially after the, ah...*incident* with Zalor."

A dam breaks in my heart, and the things I've been shoring away tumble forth in a rush: "While you struggled here, I struggled with my own demons on Earth. Maybe it was quantum entanglement, maybe it was coincidence, but we suffered the same emotional traumas. And that changes a person, you know? Something inside me got snuffed out. That's when you became an aspect of my darkness."

The starmoss on our rock has unfurled its tiny petals. The blossoms lift their glowing faces, straining for their namesake: the North Star, Akaerion. Their soft light turns Cendrion's pale profile luminous. His brow ridges draw together, and I'm suddenly afraid I've offended him.

"You're more than your darkness, of course," I add. "You have so much going for you. You're wise and determined and brave. I know it. I've *seen* it."

He remains immobile. Heat blooms in my cheeks.

"Too crazy? Too much?" A hint of mania creeps into my falsely cheery tone. "You're right, that was too much. Let's forget it ever happened."

"Forget what ever happened?"

"What I just—oh. Clever. I see what you did there. Yes, the new rule is: no more talking about Earth."

Or myself.

"Why focus on that world when I have to save this one? Speaking of, we've been gone a long time. We should return to camp for the war council."

"Indeed." Cendrion crouches. Instead of leaping skyward, he rolls his left shoulder. He angles the humerus of his wing behind me and stretches out his paw.

I recognize the gesture, but I don't dare hope. "What are you doing?"

"Offering you a ride."

Something balloons within me, pressing against my organs, making me feel like my feet have already left the ground. My hands fly to my face, where my mouth is widening in the dopiest grin of my life.

"Really?" I sound like my eight-year-old self again, squealing with joy on Halloween or shrieking in delight when the carnival came to town.

Cendrion jerks his head, inviting me to climb aboard. I can't help myself—I rush forward and hug the base of his neck, pressing my cheek to his smooth scales.

Something vibrates against my chest, a sound so deep it's felt rather than heard. Cendrion is rumbling, but it's not a growl. It's more like a purr, a deep, contented thrum. The sound dragons make when they're happy.

I scramble onto his back, hauling myself over the jut of his muscled wing joint. When I'm settled, every muscle in his body goes as taut as a bowstring.

"Hold tight," he says. With one mighty flap, we're airborne.

I let out a whoop of triumph as my stomach falls away, remaining on the ground while I catapult into the night. Wind whistles past me. Streaks of humid atmosphere condense over Cendrion's leathery wing membranes as he bears me toward the heavens.

My army uniform is thin for the summer, and the lingering effects of the exorcism have made me susceptible to the cold. A chill overtakes me, but I don't care.

I'm *flying*.

This is everyone's dream, though admittedly, most people don't dream of flying on a dragon. Nothing on Earth can emulate this, not airplanes, not wind tunnels, not skydiving. This is pure, unadulterated freedom.

The world unfolds beneath us. In the west, moonlight spills across rolling plains and farmlands. In the east, glittering lights march along the horizon: a series of cities on the serpentine Ysande River. The water in my eyes isn't all from the rush of air. This view could stop a heart—or start one. This is a view worth living for.

"May I ask something?" I call over the wind.

Cendrion tilts his head to fix me with one bright eye. The rising Oldmoon lends an ethereal light to his gaze and a silken sheen to his scaly hide.

"When Kyla asked the dragons for help, you were the only one who agreed. Why?"

I explained his reasoning in my books, of course. It's vital to the narrative, the cornerstone of Kyla and Cendrion's friendship. Yet now that I've met the real Cendrion, I feel like I never even scratched the surface of their connection. There are layers of depth I've been missing. Not just in my novels, but in my life. And I want *more*. I want to understand, to embrace those missing things.

We angle south in silence, floating on high altitude currents. From what I can see of the dragon's face, his expression is pensive. He gazes into the distance, eyes unfocused.

"I saw something in her I recognized," he says at last.

It's not much of an answer, but it's all the answer I need. We're kindred spirits, he and I, even if he doesn't know it.

I'm sorry, I think, too cowardly to say it aloud. It's hard to reconcile with the idea that Cendrion's downfall wasn't my fault. I merely transcribed his undoing at the hands of the Shadow Lord, yet guilt still pools within me.

Cendrion banks. I clutch at him to steady myself, grasping two of the pearly spinal protrusions that extend from his spine at even intervals. He angles toward the camp, descending in lazy spirals so I can have a few more moments of enjoyment. At the northern head of the valley, the large war tent is aglow. By this hour, the higher-ups will be gathered there to discuss tactics.

They're probably wondering where Kyla Starblade is.

For a moment, I wonder where the real Kyla is, too. Is she on Earth? If so, I hope she's having fun. With her magic, it should be easy.

And what of my real-life family, friends, co-workers, publishing team? How long have I been gone in Earth time? Have I missed the submission deadline for my manuscript revisions?

"I don't care," I whisper. Why waste energy worrying about the written world of Solera when I'm busy *living* in it? I'll worry when I return. If I return.

Would I be sad if I never found my way home?

I decide on the spot that the answer is *no*—a very definitive no. Eric is busy with his own life, my family has no need for me, and my publishing team will move on to the next hot author. On Earth I'm a phase, a trend, a mayfly.

Here, I'm a legend.

Cendrion backwings and stretches out his hind legs. I instinctively lean forward to balance my weight over his center of gravity. He touches down at the edge of the camp, flattening the grasses with each slow flap.

"That was the best," I say, breathless with exhilaration as I slide down his leg and land on unsteady feet.

"I have a reputation to uphold, as your favorite."

This time, the smile that blooms on my lips is one of genuine affection. It's not the idealistic love I have for a character I've created—it's the blossoming love for an autonomous, independent creature who understands me.

I've gained my first true Soleran friend.

Sometimes, dreams do come true.

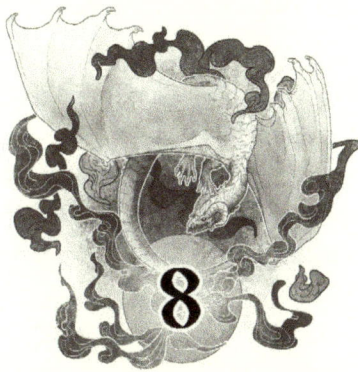

8

WE MAKE GOOD TIME on our march, reaching Galvia in under a week. Under cover of night, we wend our way through the rainforest, finding a hidden valley a little ways south of Shadow-occupied Torvel. Now our division camps amidst the mountains, prepping for battle.

"The Torvellan Pass is where the ambush will happen," I explain to my audience, gazing around the war tent. Today I'm addressing our cadre of generals, trying to warn them about the impending bloodbath without making it sound too suspicious.

"You mean where it's *likely* to happen," Valen corrects me.

"Right, yes. We've planned a surprise attack to liberate Torvel. Shadowtroops occupying the city will engage us, luring us up the cliffs." I trace paths on the maps spread across the central table. Weathered parchment rustles beneath my touch.

"We'll reach the city walls, but right when we think we've won, reserve shadowtroops will emerge from the escarpment cave systems and flank us. We'll be slaughtered."

Belatedly, I add, "That's the most plausible scenario."

"What makes you so certain this is Zalor's plan?" asks General Praxus, a tall and war-weary Olthoran. Though devoted to the Eldrian Empire, he isn't fond of Kyla. Like most of our officers, he believes if she'd gotten the dragons to fight, the war would have been over by now.

He's not wrong.

"I know Zalor," I say. "We dealt him a crushing blow at Westport. We've made it about more than controlling key territories; now it's about his pride. He has a pathological need to crush our resistance. He's angry, and he wants me dead."

"Torvel isn't a large city, nor does it have valuable resources," says General Novei, a native Galvian. Her ocean-blue eyes narrow in a scowl. "Why do you believe Zalor would expend such energy defending it?"

"For the same reason we decided to attack it. It's *not* an obvious pick." I survey the terrain visible through the open flaps of the war tent. The mountainous rainforest is peppered with karst formations. Pillars of quartz-sandstone rise through the mists, making for beautiful scenery—and difficult battlegrounds.

"We could have forged a path through major cities along the river," I continue. "We chose Torvel instead because we thought Zalor wouldn't expect that."

"But you're willing to bet he expects it," says Valen, playing into the ruse.

"What is your point in this thought experiment, Lightbringer?" Praxus demands. He's handsome for an older man, with a neatly trimmed beard and shiny scars peppering his copper skin. "Would you have us change direction on a whim?"

"No, I'd have us change strategy." I pause, considering how I'd rewrite this battle to ensure victory. "We proceed as planned with our attack, but anticipate a flanking ambush. We station the portal poles half a mile from the city cliffs. If an ambush comes, we activate the portal. We have the Midgard Reserves ready and waiting on the far side to come to our aid."

"That would leave Midgard without defenses," says Novei.

"Then we recall the Eastern Division to protect Midgard until Torvel is secure."

Praxus's russet eyes flash to Valen. "Commander-General, surely you won't entertain the notion of uprooting two branches of our army for this paltry attack."

"We'll send scouts to determine the number of shadowtroops in Torvel," says Valen. "If there's an unusually large concentration, I'll commit to the Lightbringer's strategy."

My hand shoots into the air. "I can go with Cendrion."

"Sending our two most valuable assets into enemy territory, unguarded?" Praxus scoffs. "Out of the question."

"We can take care of ourselves," says Cendrion, poking his head through the flaps to join the conversation. The tent's not big enough to house his bulk, so he's crouched outside.

"Can you?" says Praxus.

Valen shoots the other man a warning glance. "You're out of line, General."

"The last time Kyla Starblade took matters into her own hands," Praxus continues, unrelenting, "she confronted Zalor and cost Cendrion his lightmagic."

"I do not begrudge Kyla for what happened," the dragon growls, showing an excessive amount of fang. "Neither should you. The choice to fight was mine."

"Besides," I say, "we're not confronting Zalor, we're scouting for intel. I'll wield a lightmagic illusion to mask us from enemy eyes. No one will know we're there. It's the safest bet."

Not even Praxus can argue with that, though he does have some more generalized arguing to do before Valen dismisses the war council.

"That could have gone better," Valen says heavily, watching the higher-ups return to their respective battalions. Now it's just me and my core squad.

"It also could've gone way worse," I point out.

A tiny, mirthless smile tugs at his lips.

"So, did you just conveniently discover how to wield?" Rexa drawls as we leave the tent, veering north to avoid the main camp.

"I didn't need to. I know exactly how many shadowtroops are in the city *and* how many Zalor has stashed in the mountain caves."

I may not have magic, but being omniscient is a pretty good consolation prize.

"What will you do when it comes time to battle?" Asher asks me.

"Fight, obviously." He scrunches his nose, and I can't help but laugh. "Sorry. I have a friend back home who makes that exact same face whenever I do something dangerous and dumb."

"So, all the time," says Rexa.

"Pretty much. But I'm not gonna sit on the sidelines." There's nothing I hate worse than an inactive protagonist. Plus, if anyone would understand my desire to fight, it's Rexa.

Rexa, however, scoffs. She looks at Valen and says, "Are you going to allow this?"

"I don't see how we can avoid it," Cendrion says before Valen has a chance to respond. "We need her knowledge of the battle. It will be best if she stays with us as the skirmish plays out."

Rexa heaves a long-suffering sigh. "It's your funeral."

"It's no one's funeral," I snap. "I'll make sure of that."

"Kyla, we appreciate your offer to help," says Asher, "but people on both sides will ask questions if you don't wield."

"Not to worry. I'll fly with Cendrion during the battle—if that's alright," I add, glancing at the dragon. I feel solid with him, but I don't want to overstep my place by making assumptions about his willingness to cart my magicless ass around.

He meets my eyes and nods, pearly horns glinting.

"Now, if lots of fire were being tossed around me when I fly, I think the shadowtroops wouldn't notice my lack of light." Steeling myself, I turn to Rexa. "Could you call in some phoenixes for this battle? I'd like both you and them to fly with me."

I've said the magic words. The thrill of the hunt kindles in her gaze, as does the thirst for revenge.

"Fyr'thal and his blaze are in fighting shape," she says. "Nothing they like more than burning shadowtroops, and I owe Zalor a good whomping."

It's all I can do to contain my grin. Victory on two counts: Rexa's agreed to my plan, and I'll finally get to meet Fyr'thal.

"Excellent," I say, keeping my face neutral and my voice professional. I look to Asher next. "As for you, I need you to craft us something wild, something literally out of this world: a battery."

"A what-now?"

Solera is technologically advanced compared to many famous

fantasy lands in Earthling literature, but its technology is magic-reliant. There's little call for batteries when you have voltmagic wielders running around. There are enchanted firelamps, glowbulbs, and natural light-emitting crystals, but no wires and circuitry to accompany them.

"A battery is something that can store and release potential energy. Since I don't have a soul—or rather," I amend myself sourly, "since my Earthling soul is devoid of magic, our communication rings won't work on me."

The silver rings are enchanted to transmit one person's spoken words to another's ears, but they require energy to function. In the same way a car needs an initial spark of electricity to get the engine running, so do our comm devices. That spark is the soul itself: a person's magicsource.

"I'm happy to help," says Asher. He's great at crafting and inventing things. "But how would I go about making something like that? My earthmagic can only go so far."

"That's the beauty of it. A battery generates energy without magic. You'd create it through science and artistry alone. It, ah . . ." I pause, spirits sinking. I know everything about Solera, but—irony of ironies—very little about my home planet.

"Shit," I mutter. "Okay, so you have to find different metals that, like, create electricity through chemical reactions with each other. As an earthmagic wielder, you'll have a natural affinity with the raw elements needed, but without asking Google, I don't know *exactly* which materials to use."

"Who's Google?" Asher says guilelessly.

"Never mind. Bottom line, I'm an idiot and I never paid attention to the workings of Earth technology. We have three days for trial-and-error tests to see which metals can generate enough power for my comms device. Think you can manage that?"

He grins. "I'm up for the challenge. It'll be nice to get back to craft-wielding. It's been a long time since I had a chance to do anything unrelated to the war."

That's true, and it's a shame. Asher's magical talents are wasted in a military setting. Craft-wielding is an entirely different discipline than battle-wielding. It requires nuance, weaving threads just so, creating something greater than the sum of its parts. Battle-wielding requires its own skillset, to be sure, but the art of war is not the same as the art of... well, *art*.

"I'll need access to metals," Asher continues. "Not compound materials, but pure ones. That way I can test which of them work best."

"There are dwarven mines scattered throughout these mountains," says Cendrion. "I'm willing to fly you to the nearest one."

Asher bows to the dragon in gratitude. "That would be perfect. The dwarves wield earthmagic, too. They'll be happy to help experiment."

"You should go now. All of you," I say, including Rexa in my statement. "This battle isn't the end, it's the *beginning* of the end. Everything snowballs from here. We have to be prepared to win this war without Kyla's magic."

Their faces fall, and I mentally curse myself. We were working together for a brief moment, acting like a team. The reminder that I'm not their heroic friend is sobering.

"We'll be back before the battle," Asher promises. Cendrion crouches in invitation, and he vaults onto the dragon's back. With a mighty flap that kicks up whirlwinds of dust and leaves, they're airborne.

Rexa's body ripples, contorting as she shapeshifts. Her chimerical form shrinks. Brilliant red and gold plumage sprouts from dark fur and mottled scales. Her arms become sweeping wings. A blazing glory of rectrices fan behind her. A diamond-sharp beak elongates from her face, melding nose and lips into bone and keratin.

Suddenly she's a phoenix, half as tall as I am, gleaming and resplendent. She can't wield firemagic in this form—wielders are born with a single magical affinity, and Rexa's is changemagic—but she'll have the physical attributes of a phoenix, including speed and endurance.

Her amber eyes meet mine, and she dips her avian head in a small gesture of acknowledgement. With a shrill cry, she takes off, zooming south.

I watch her receding form for a while before I realize Valen and I are alone. A strange lightness twists my stomach into knots. My emotional response to him is automatic, but I don't want to betray any hint of attraction. I'm not Kyla, and I can't blur that crucial line.

"Good work today, soldier," he says in a neutral tone. "I'm glad you're thinking ahead."

"If I can change the ending of the story, I can save Kyla's friends. *And* Kyla."

"And the world," he adds.

Saving the world. Energy sparks in me, setting me alight.

Sluggish thoughts stir, surfacing from the darkness that shrouds my memories of Earth. I always dreamed about being a hero. As a child I was precocious, bursting with potential. I had big plans. I was going to help people.

Somewhere along the way, everything changed. I stumbled and fell, and never bothered to get up. It wasn't anything specific. I just started...*failing* at things. Career opportunities, keeping in touch with friends, taking care of my health. Even the simplest tasks, like leaving my apartment, became impossible obstacles.

I retreated to a different world for solace and sanctuary. *This* world. And when I signed my book deal, I thought everything would change.

It's a small power, writing things, but when millions of people read the things you write, that power grows. I wanted my story to be one of forgiveness and hope and redemption.

Then I killed my darlings in cold blood. Why?

It wasn't me. I didn't kill them, Zalor did. He still might, if I don't stop him.

I'm aware that I've drifted into a state of daydream stupefaction. Giving my head a little shake, I pull myself out of it. When I bring Solera into focus, I find Valen watching me.

"Sorry," I mumble.

"I didn't want to interrupt your thoughts. You had that familiar sparkle in your eye." His chest expands and deflates with an inaudible sigh. "I almost believed she'd returned."

My shoulders slump. Why does he have such power over me? How can he make me ache with longing and lacerate my heart in the same breath?

I turn to leave. "You should see to the troops. I'll make myself scarce."

Before I can take a step, a gentle hand closes on my arm. My pulse jumps as I glance at him.

"I delegated today's tasks to General Praxus," he says. "You and I have work to do."

"Work?" My voice is embarrassingly breathy.

"You said it yourself: we have to be prepared to win this war without Kyla or her magic. From your descriptions, it appears we'll be facing months of grueling bloodshed."

I nod, drowning in his gaze.

"Then you need to be able to protect yourself, and I need to make sure you can sell the illusion of being Kyla Starblade." He walks to a nearby patch of towering bamboo. With a spark of lightning, he slices through two thick stalks, catching them deftly. He pares these down with his belt knife, chopping off their fluffy tops and extraneous leafy protrusions, until he's left with a couple of sharpened sticks.

He tosses one to me. Instinct kicks in and I grab for it, catching it clumsily.

"Kyla is an expert swordsman," he says, squaring off in front of me.

"Swords*woman*," I correct him.

His lips quirk in the tiniest almost-smile. "I'm well aware," he murmurs, and his velvet tone sends a shiver right down to my toes.

I'm playing a dangerous game. Am I foolish enough to believe that Valen might fall in love with me, the person who upended his life and displaced the soul of his soulmate? Even if he did (which he *wouldn't*, because Valen is loyal to a fault), there can be no happy ending here. Like all my potential Earthling relationships, this one's doomed to fail.

"Mirror my ready stance," he instructs, all business once more.

"Arm out, elbow in. Knees bent, feet at perpendicular angles."

In my youth, I took fencing lessons. But that was years ago, in a different world. A different *life*. It's been a hot minute since I engaged in hobbies outside writing.

Still, as I shift my weight, my body settles into a long-forgotten, once-familiar stance. I'm struck for the first time by how very *different* Kyla's form is from my Earthling one. She spends her life wielding and fighting, while I spend mine hunched in front of a computer. She's also eleven years younger than me. I feel the easy give in her knees that my real, decrepit, thirty-one-year-old body would never have allowed.

I smile and roll my shoulders, embracing the simple power this body provides. *"En garde,"* I say glibly, and I lunge.

Valen parries my attack and whirls out of my way. He attempts a riposte at my unprotected left side, but I know all his tricks, and I'm already moving to dodge. Kyla's legs carry me to safety, though I wobble. My consciousness is unused to the motion her body has trained for.

He strikes again at my left flank. Since he's left-handed, and I—and Kyla—are right-handed, he thinks he can exploit that side. But I know this trick, too. He's feinting left in the hopes that I'll parry, then he'll disengage and cut at my right side. I ignore the feint and slash at his sword arm.

He evades with a bit of fancy footwork. Something burns in his eyes—the inner spark I've described in my writing so many times in such loving detail. Seeing it for myself is mesmerizing.

"You'll have to do better than that, *Adrai*," I quip, using the honorific for 'teacher' in his home kingdom of Olthoria. Kyla trained with him there for a year before she joined the Mortal Alliance, which is how they met and fell in love. Screw the Wise Old Mentor archetype, and not in the fun way. Give me a young, brilliant peer adviser any day of the week.

"You can't rely on your supernatural knowledge of my tactics to keep you safe," he chides, circling me. "What happens when you face an enemy you're not familiar with?"

"I'm familiar with every enemy."

I stab, adding a sneaky disengage. Valen doesn't need supernatural knowledge to block with ease. He was forced into the military at ten years old, and he's had a decade-and-a-half to master his swordsmanship.

"Besides," I continue, closing distance with him, "a great swordswoman knows her enemy intimately—"

Valen parries my blow and our bodies brush. My blood sings at the brief contact.

"—and employs that knowledge to her advantage." I know how his heart leaps when he stares into Kyla's eyes. He falters for a fraction of a moment, and I strike. My left hand leaves the bamboo sword and flies toward his neck.

Lightning fast, Valen's right hand intercepts mine and twists my wrist, forcing my arm down. A hiss escapes my clenched teeth and I buckle toward him, trying to avoid the pain of his subduing grip.

We're locked hilt to hilt, heart to heart. Indefinable energy flows between us. When my chest heaves, it touches his. I could soak in his warmth forever. It's doubly enticing now, since I can't shake the cold that's clung to me since Temereth's failed spell.

"So you *were* listening to my training lectures." His voice is halfway between a purr and a growl.

"Every word."

Despite my physical exertions and the dangerous lure of Valen's slightly parted lips, my heart slows. I shiver. It's only now that I've stopped moving that I sense something's amiss. I'm far too cold.

My mind rifles through a series of scenarios—a lingering scrap of poison from the assassin's blade? A new darkmagic spell wielded by an invisible enemy? A side effect of the botched exorcism?

My bamboo sword gives beneath Valen's applied pressure, and I collapse. In a flash, he drops his weapon and lunges to catch me. I hang in his arms, limp and pathetic.

"What's wrong?" His eyes scour my body. With a shuddering gasp, I struggle upright.

"Cold," I say, my voice trembling. "Don't know why."

He presses the back of his hand to my brow, then places two fingers against the corner of my jaw, taking my pulse. His face clouds.

"Brace yourself." His hand moves to my rib cage, hovering over my too-slow heart. At first I'm afraid he's going to shock me out of bradycardia. Instead, he begins unbuttoning my uniform.

"What are you—?" I can't get the sentence through my clenched jaw. My teeth begin to chatter. Even the terrifying intimacy of Valen's touch can't warm me or jolt my failing heart to life.

He slips his fingers beneath the collar of my shirt and presses his calloused palm against my bare flesh. My body begins to heat, energy spreading from his hand through my veins. As voltmagic-warmed blood flows to my extremities, I slowly return from the brink of disaster. My heart stutters, hitches, then catches in a familiar rhythm.

Valen retracts his hand. His eyes dart toward the encampment. No one can see us in such a compromising position. Not only would it fracture faith in Kyla's power at a moment when appearances are everything, the military higher-ups would use it against us if they knew we were in a relationship.

Which we're not. I must keep my identities straight. Valen loves Kyla, not me. He loves the sparkle in her eye, the jaunt in her step, the light in her soul.

"Can you stand?" His face is so close. He's still cradling my shoulders.

"I'm fine," I wheeze, shrugging out of his grasp.

In a perfect world, maybe someone like me could be with someone like Valen. Or rather, maybe someone like Valen would want to be with someone like me. But Solera is real, and is therefore inherently imperfect.

This other-world is dangerous. It always has been. Conflicts that once served simply to heighten tension in my writing are now far too real for my liking. What would have happened if my heart had stopped? Would I have died? Would my soul and consciousness have found a way back to my Earthling body, or would they have been forever lost in limbo?

He hesitates. "Are you still...?"

A new coldness surges through my body. Even here, no one cares about me. It's Kyla they want. Kyla they're worried about.

"Still me? Yeah, 'fraid so."

Valen's face falls. My spirits fall with it.

It's better this way. Even if I were trapped here forever and all the pieces magically fell into place and Valen decided he loved me—even *then* it wouldn't work. I can't give him what he wants. I could never make him happy.

I was better off on Earth, alone.

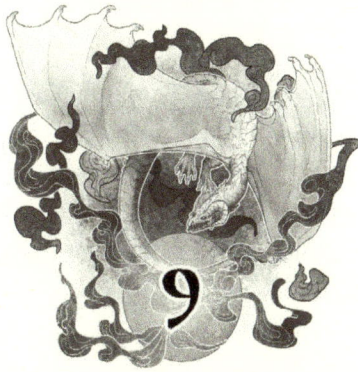

9

It's the morning of the attack. My body vibrates with compressed energy and jittery nerves.

Our troops are arrayed in diamond formation. Platoons of defensive specialists, high-powered offense, healer support, and reserve wielders are clumped throughout the slanted rank and file. Valen and the officers are at the core of the formation, keeping watch on all sides. I'm on a rocky hilltop with the double-reserves and the aerial unit, watching the ground troops move out.

"Moment of truth." Asher fiddles with his battery invention, a bulky metal bracelet. It doesn't look like much. Then again, I suppose a couple of nine-volts don't look like much to the naked eye, either.

He attaches the bracelet to my silver communication ring via wire. If it works, the ring's airmagic enchantment will carry my words to the ears of anyone else on comms. Its lifemagic inhibitor will limit audibility to whomever I think of while speaking.

"Is the metal coated?" I ask, inspecting the gadget in the sparse pre-dawn light. "I don't want to get electrocuted."

"Give me a bit of credit." Asher offers me the device, and I raise my arm. He clamps the bracelet around my wrist while slipping the ring onto my finger. "Go on, say something."

"Lightbringer reporting to Commander-General Stormcrest."

The bracelet warms against my skin. A moment later, I hear Valen's voice in my ear, as clear as if he were standing beside me: "Go for Stormcrest."

"Just letting you know the experiment was a success." I swallow a lump in my throat before adding, "Good luck and stay safe."

No reply. Surrounded by his troops, he couldn't offer any similar personal sentiments. That's the excuse I give myself to make the silence hurt a little less.

Asher watches me intently, peering over his glasses.

"Works like a charm," I say.

He breaks into a grin. "Let me tell you, this project was amazing. Learning about non-magic-based energy sources is huge. We could bring power to every corner of the empire, even the villages that can't afford voltmagic enchantments. I've got big plans for this technology once the war is over."

"Yeah. About that." I take him by the arm and pull him away from the crest of the hill, where Cendrion, Rexa, and her platoon of phoenix soldiers wait. Phoenixes wield firemagic (duh), and the natural glow of their plumage paints our surroundings with red.

"Quick spoiler alert," I murmur to Asher. "This is the battle where you...you know."

"Where I what?" His eyes go as round as the full Oldmoon. "Where I *die?*"

I nod, my lips thinning to a line.

"You didn't think that was worth mentioning before now?"

"I didn't want to upset you." I also didn't know how to say it. I still feel like I'm the Grim Reaper—the executioner swinging the blade, the demented puppet master pulling lethal strings. Even now, guilt shreds my innards. Asher's expression makes it exponentially worse.

"Consider me still very much upset."

I pinch the bridge of my nose and bow my head. So much for embodying Kyla's heroism. Here I am, being cagey, escalating conflict in my desperation to avoid it.

A soft touch on my shoulder makes me look up. Asher's face has softened. "I'm not upset at you. Zalor's the enemy. It's just a bit of a shock to hear I'm about to...you know."

Grief thickens in my throat. I don't deserve a friend such as this.

"You won't die, not if I can help it. You can stay by the portal for safety."

"Kyla, think about everything the Shadow Lord's done to us—"

"I am, and he's ruthless. Evil."

Asher draws himself to his full height. He's not tall, but he's got a couple inches on Kyla. "All evil needs to succeed is for good people to stand aside and let it spread."

"Excuse me, don't try to melodramatically dialogue your way out of this. This isn't the moment for your morals and heart of gold."

"There a problem here?"

I didn't realize how heated I'd become, how loudly I was speaking. I turn to find Rexa has joined the conversation.

"He can't fight," I say, pointing at Asher. "If he does, he'll die."

Rexa's sharp eyes dart between us. "Tell us how it happens so we can avoid it."

"Or—just hear me out—he could eliminate all possibility of death by *not fighting*."

Asher reaches out and takes my hand. In that moment, he looks indistinguishable from my best friend on Earth.

Whose name I suddenly can't remember.

My stomach swoops, but I can't waste time panicking about this precipitous drop in my mental capacity. I must focus on the war. Might be hard to do if my mind's turning to mush, but such are the ironic contradictions of life.

"You're here fighting for the people you love," Asher whispers. "Don't deny me that same privilege."

His words burrow through my chest to lodge between my heart and ribs. Goddammit.

"Thanks for making me look bad, Ash," Rexa drawls. "I'm just fighting because I hate Zalor."

"I arranged for most of our non-human factions to join the Mortal Alliance," says Asher, ignoring her quip. "The elves, the nereids, the ifriti—they're here because of me, and I'd be the worst sort of hypocrite if I didn't fight alongside them. I believe in Kyla's battle strategy. It'll be alright."

I clench my jaw, envying his quiet strength while cursing his hope-springs-eternal attitude. "You can stay with Valen at the formation core. Relay orders and translate as necessary for non-human troops, but do not engage the enemy."

When Asher opens his mouth to argue, I hold up a quelling hand. "This is already a compromise. And a stupid one. We need to win this battle, and you need to stay safe, or everything goes to hell."

He isn't pleased, but we're out of time. In the valley, the widest point of our army's formation is passing our rocky hill. Asher squares his shoulders and adjusts his quiver, preparing to join the march.

"Stay safe," I blurt.

He reaches out as if for a handshake, then pulls me into a hug. "You, too. When we win the day, it'll be your doing. It makes me wish I knew your real name."

A leaden ball drops into my stomach. I barely remember my Earth name, and there's no one in this world who knows the real me. No one who can remind me of the truth.

He nods at my silence and spins on his heel, hurrying downhill.

"Watch him," I implore Rexa, my voice breaking. "If anything goes wrong, pull him out of there."

Her arms are crossed, but her face is smooth as she scrutinizes me. "Huh," she murmurs. "You really care, don't you?"

"Of course I care. He's my best friend. No offense."

"None taken. I don't know you."

But I know her, no matter what she thinks. Her tone isn't sharp, it's dry. This is her idea of humor. I enjoy her ribbing when it's good-natured.

"Be careful," I tell her.

"*You* be careful. You're so busy fussing over us that you've forgotten you have no magic."

"Lucky I have the best fighter in Eldria watching my back."

Her eyes crinkle at the edges. "This doesn't mean I like you. It just means I really, *really* hate Zalor."

Rexa begins to wield, her body distorting. Today she's changing into a gryphon as large as a lion. She rears on her feline hind legs, avian forepaws slashing the air. Feathered wings sprout from her shoulders. She beats them once, twice, then she and her phoenix unit rise skyward together.

Now it's just Cendrion and me. He tilts his head to catch my eye.

"Ready for war?" he asks.

Perversely, a small part of me is excited. How many times have I been swept up in an action sequence while writing? How often have I found myself lost in the story, a puppet swaying on the strings of my imagination, a conduit for the words flowing through me as events unfold?

To see it, *experience* it firsthand, will be beyond anything I've imagined.

Cendrion crouches. I clamber onto his back and settle between his wing joints. A shiver passes through me in anticipation of the cold, thin air. I have no right to be cold; I stuffed myself into four layers this morning. I should be sweltering.

Eerie silence wraps around us. Our airmagic wielders stifled the sounds of five-thousand feet tromping through the hills, and the world has not yet woken. It feels as if Solera is holding its breath. I fidget, anxiety coating my lungs with ice.

Ahead, a ripple runs through the rainforest. Flocks of birds scatter skyward, dark against the gray dawn. Moments later, a low, brassy note reverberates.

"Lightbringer, we've engaged the shadowtroops." Valen's voice blooms in my ears once more. "You're cleared for take-off."

"That's the signal," I tell Cendrion. "Let's go."

The dragon trembles with a guttural growl. He kicks off and we're airborne. Wind whistles past my ears, and I squint against it. As we clear the tops of the rainforest trees, the first bands of sunlight brush the eastern horizon.

Cendrion stays low, skimming the treetops as we swoop toward the growing sound of battle. We clear a formation of rising stone peppered with stubborn jungle plants, and Torvel comes into view.

Saying it's a small city does it an injustice. It may be off the beaten path, but it sits atop a regal ridge with a sheer southern cliff face. Its burnished iron buildings—magically smoothed to a mirror-like shine—make for a striking silhouette against the lightening sky.

Enemy troops swarm out of the city walls, but the Mortal Alliance has gained a low foothold on the cliffs. A unit of earthmagic wielders helms the formation, creating a path for our soldiers. Pitch-black shadowbeasts—dead creatures who've been reanimated by Zalor's dark power—hound them from all angles, making the progress slow.

I wince at the carnage. Shadowbeasts are vicious foes. Zalor controls them, body and soul. Once resurrected, they become his demonic, mind-controlled slaves.

I draw a plain steel sword from the scabbard that hangs at my waist, gripping its hilt with a palm that has grown sweaty. "General Faeloryn, requesting backup on the front lines."

There's no audible response. Rexa can't speak in gryphon form, but as Cendrion banks over the valley skirmish, I see the telltale glow of phoenixes. Ten, eleven, twelve of the mythical birds rise, shrilling battle cries as they flank us.

Cendrion lets loose a roar of his own. It obliterates the ethereal echoes of phoenixsong and presses into my ears, reverberating in my skull.

The sound draws the shadowbeasts. The winged ones peel away from our ground troops and make a beeline for me. Of course, they think I'm Kyla Starblade, lightmagic wielder extraordinaire, she who has the power to kill the Shadow Lord.

They want her—*me*—dead.

Our phoenix friends dive. The foremost red-gold bird—whom I recognize as Fyr'thal—arrows toward the black cloud of shadowbeasts, his bronze beak a deadly point. Not to be outdone, Cendrion follows. He raises his wings, tucking me between his humeri, keeping me in place as he angles down. My sword sticks out over his right shoulder, my hand amazingly steady.

Then we're in the fray. Fyr'thal's body ignites with living flame as he clashes with the winged demons. His impressive seven-foot wingspan trails blazing sparks. A plume of errant fire clips me, but it doesn't hurt. Phoenix fire won't burn unless its wielder intends it to.

My brain stalls, overwhelmed. I've never, in all my life, had so much sensory input. Explosions of magic. Grating shrieks of demonic creatures. The searing scent of fire and blood. The seizure-inducing movement of a million bodies swirling around us.

Cendrion's neck recoils and darts out, a striking serpent aiming for a shadowbeast. The shadowbeast in question looks like it might have been a harpy when it was alive. Now it's something both more and less than a harpy: it died and bartered its soul to Zalor in exchange for a second chance at life.

The harpy no longer exists. It's an extension of Zalor. He's all there is.

Cendrion catches the hapless harpy in his jaws and crunches down. Black blood explodes from its wounds. Some of it flies back and hits my face, landing on my tongue in my open mouth. The acrid, burning taste and the foul smell of its body fluids—like human waste mixed with too-ripe fruit—jolt sense into me.

No matter how unprepared I am for the horrors of war, no matter how vulnerable I am without magic, I must fight. Who would I be if I didn't?

My old Earthling self, that's who. No more.

Cendrion snaps his wings out and levels off. Caught in the moment, I loose a battle cry of my own. My left hand closes around one of the pearly spinal protrusions on his neck. I throw my weight forward, leaning over his shoulder to stab at a winged demon.

The monster dodges my blow. I swing my blade wide and feel a nauseatingly satisfying *thunk* as I connect with my target. The shadowbeast howls and plummets toward the rocks, its corpse spouting black blood.

With that, something inside me changes. Darkness rises in my chest, taking the form of a familiar sensation: anger.

Wrath tumbles through my veins, burning me from the inside out. How dare these shadowtroops try to hurt my darlings. How dare Zalor try to ruin this beloved world of mine.

I make a private vow that I'll be the one to kill him before I leave Solera.

Cendrion banks to avoid a jet of deadly darkmagic. I hack at the shadowbeast wielding the accursed spell. This time, my aim is true. I slice through its neck, and it dies on impact.

My anger bubbles and mutates. A grin stretches my lips. I feel strong. The visceral horror of this moment will catch up with me later and I'll vomit, maybe cry. For now, I'm a puppet once more. As it has always been while writing a battle, I'm caught in a swift-moving current. I'm powerless to fight it. I don't *want* to fight it. I revel in it.

Passive-aggression may be my specialty, but I'm pretty good at aggressive-aggression, too.

The phoenixes provide an excellent defense as Cendrion carves through waves of shadowbeasts. With my left hand flat against the base of his neck, I feel his muscles bunch and sense what he's about to do. The first few times he banked, I was thrown off balance, but now I'm anticipating his movements. He dips right and I lean left, slashing with my sword as we circle a demon. It falls beneath my blade.

"You fly like a natural," Cendrion roars. Black blood coats his maw and streams down his throat. His eyes are wide and his pupils are the thinnest crescents of focus.

"It's all you," I call back, unable to contain my growing smile.

Am I a sociopath for enjoying this? I know the risks, but the feel of making a visible, quantifiable difference in the battle is exhilarating.

Another low, brassy note rumbles from the south, dousing my good mood.

"The ambush," I whisper, squinting over my shoulder.

I can't see through the storm of swooping phoenixes and motley demons—but I don't need to see what's happening. I know reserve shadowtroops are flanking our division at the base of the cliffs, the Torvellan Pass. I know, because that's how I wrote it. Everything's playing out exactly as it does in my manuscript.

My heart's in my throat. This is the moment my meddling must make a difference.

A shockwave blasts from the trees at the southern foot of the valley. Debris mushrooms in the air, creating a visible wave as the blast rockets toward us.

"Tuck your wings," I scream, huddling low and hooking my arm around Cendrion's neck. He does so not a moment too soon. The billow of air rams us, but we aren't caught in it—unlike the demon horde. I hear shrieks and the snap of delicate wing bones as our enemies tumble head over tail through the sky.

The shockwave of power came from the activation of the Midgard Portal. Our second division should be marching through to support the rear guard.

"Let's check the formation core," I call.

Cendrion dodges a dark spell and I swipe at an addled monster, making it shriek in agony and fall away. Cendrion falls too, angling into a controlled dive as we streak past the cliffs and approach the seething knot of battle.

The sun has risen, though hazy mist dilutes its light. It illuminates a scene of chaos. We're making headway on the cliffs. Our formation remains intact. The rear guard hasn't buckled beneath the ambush. It's holding against a snakelike band of shadowbeasts emerging from cliff caverns. Beyond, the reserve vanguard marches to assist.

My gaze floats over the army, coming to rest on the center. Valen is visible, distinguished by an occasional crack of lightning. He's technically not in a wielding position (he's technically not supposed to engage at all, being our highest officer), but he can't help himself. If he sees an opening, he takes it.

Asher stands beside him. I can't hear him over the cacophony, but I know he'll be relaying orders and shouting encouragement. Asher is an effortlessly good person. His bow is drawn. Like Valen, if he spots a weakness, he strikes.

"Nice shooting, Ambassador Brightstone," I call through the comms ring. His dwarf friends gifted him with combustible arrows, so whenever he hits a mark, his target explodes.

"So far, so good," he replies, his voice steady in my ears. "I'm still alive."

To the west, Rexa leads another band of phoenixes in an assault on Zalor's winged forces. She's a picture of perfect ferocity, flying as if she's never known fear—or, more accurately, as if she's already survived the worst fear and pain one can suffer. She is, without question, our greatest physical fighter. Beak and talons flash as she dodges enemy attacks and slices at her foes, striking with deadly accuracy.

"Shall we stay here or assist the rear guard?" Cendrion asks, pulling me away from my admiration of Rexa.

I glance south, but the Midgard Reserves have engaged the ambush. Zalor's minions are sandwiched between our divisions.

"Stay here. There are still plenty of demons to kill." To emphasize my point, I stand on Cendrion's back and swipe at a small creature who made the mistake of flying too close. It squeals in pain and droplets of midnight blood spatter my army uniform.

"How long does this battle last?" he inquires, banking to avoid an attack and nearly making me lose my balance. I drop to his back, lowering my center of gravity.

"Why?" I ask. "Are you feeling alright?"

"It's not me I'm worried about."

It takes me a moment to process what he's implying.

"I'm fine," I say, in exactly the sort of too-confident tone I'm sure Kyla always uses.

"I want to put a definitive end to this." He snags a demon and rips it in half. Soaring past the edge of the army formation, he drops the corpse into the midst of Zalor's forces.

"So do I, but . . ." I trail off. A dawning realization is creeping up on me.

"But?"

"I don't know what happens next."

This is no longer my story. I've changed the timeline just by being here, and now I've changed the course of the war.

The truth crashes on me like a tidal wave. My strength evaporates. I collapse against Cendrion's spine, shuddering. Cold—which I've been ignoring during the heat of battle—latches onto me and digs its talons into my flesh.

"Kyla? Kyla!"

"I'm fine," I repeat. Shaking my head to clear it, I heft my sword. "The enemy troops are thinning. Our army's nearly at the top of the cliff. Once we reach the city walls, maybe the shadowbeasts will concede."

"Concession isn't in Zalor's wheelhouse," Cendrion growls, banking to dodge a jet of darkmagic that comes too close for comfort.

I'm about to contact Valen for an update when the battlefield darkens. An eldritch hush muffles all noise. It feels like I'm trapped in my own little bubble of time.

Recognizing the signs for what they are, I choke on a gasp. The cold seeps through my skin and into the marrow of my bones, filling me with a despairing, all-consuming emptiness.

Unwilling to look behind me—for I know what I'll see—I turn my head.

There, borne on a billow of wispy black magic, is Lord Zalor.

10

When I said Cendrion was a mouthpiece for the darkness inside me, I meant the quiet darkness—the rueful shadow that floats behind you, reminding you of your dreams and how you failed to catch them.

Zalor, on the other hand, is a mouthpiece for the loud and violent darkness. The darkness that roars in your ear when you're alone at night. The darkness that keeps you awake with its screams, listing a litany of your greatest failures, turning you against yourself thought by poisoned thought.

Poisonous he may be, yet for all his evil deeds, Zalor's never been a mindless killer. He wants his subjects alive, wants to rule the world and make its creatures his subservient thralls. He would have allowed mortals to live under his thumb, but the mortals didn't think much of his plan.

That's why we're at war now. Obviously.

I hate to admit it, but Zalor's impressive. He looks the part of evil tyrant: he seems to suck the color from his surroundings, absorbing and devouring light like a black hole. His rotting, mummified skin is the color of death. It's too taut for his skull, and it rips when his flesh moves too drastically, revealing pitted bone beneath. Spiral horns protrude from either side of his head, making him seem as if he's wearing a war helmet. His eyes are solid sable orbs, scleras and irises swallowed by unbroken darkness.

Yet there's a charm that oozes past his barely human features. He's poised. Confident. He wears no armor, only dark plainclothes that reveal the muscled body of a warlord. His ghoulish visage is a manifestation of his godly power.

"By Ohra's bloody talons." Cendrion's voice is ragged. "He's here."

"This doesn't happen in the book," I say, knowing how stupid it sounds as the words leave my mouth. This isn't my book—it never was. It's a real universe with real people who, against all odds, I've learned to really love.

In my madness, I convinced myself of a foolish fantasy. I believed I could lead them to victory, and thereby gain redemption. I have to face the fact that this is reality. Reality is rarely sensical, and never kind.

"Kyla Starblade." Zalor's voice, a caress and a threat, is borne to my ears on a fell wind. His rich baritone makes my skin prickle. His smile leaches light from the world. The skies cloud and the wind shifts direction, turning cold and bitter. The Shadow Lord lifts his hands—

And a shockwave of darkness erupts from him. It breaks the sound barrier with an explosive *crack*, expanding from Zalor in a perfect sphere. Hapless shadowbeasts are caught in the blast, scattered asunder. In the blink of an eye, it hits Cendrion.

The shadow-wave slams into us, a wall of pure energy hurling us backward. For a moment, the world vanishes. I'm enshrouded in oblivion, every nerve screaming.

Then the wave is past. I blink, struggling to find my senses. Through some miracle, I've managed to cling to Cendrion. He twists in a weightless plummet and spreads his wings, righting himself.

"Oh, gods," I whisper, staring at the army below.

Our airmagic defenses were no match for Zalor's incorporeal dark energy, which penetrated the shields of condensed atmosphere. The Eldrian soldiers were flattened, thrown to the ground just as Cendrion was thrown through the sky.

"Retreat!" Valen's command reaches me through my comms device and as a faint echo. Someone's using an airmagic spell to amplify his voice, carrying it across the carnage to every soldier.

Asher's voice comes through the comms system a moment later, translating for the non-Eldrian-speaking species. As Cendrion gains altitude, I catch a glimpse of Rexa in gryphon form, regrouping her phoenixes. My darlings are okay.

But our army is not. I sense a shift in the tide of movement below. Soldiers flounder, struggling to reform the line.

"Kyla." Valen's voice sounds again. This time it's a whisper, and I know it's only for me. "You need to run."

He would have given this command even if I was the real Kyla Starblade, a true hero with the lightmagic necessary to combat Zalor. But Kyla Starblade would never have run from this fight, leaving her loved ones vulnerable and exposed.

Neither will I.

Leaning forward, I grasp the ridge of Cendrion's neck. "Let's get this son of a bitch."

Cendrion trumpets a challenge to the skies. With a mighty flap, he shoots toward Zalor.

The Shadow Lord is a mile away—his blast wave propelled us far from him. He sees us coming but allows our charge. At this point in the series, Kyla doesn't have the level of magical control needed to defeat him, and he knows it.

"Kyla!" Valen's voice is harsh this time, cracking like a whip. The name is a knife in my heart. "You can't win this fight. Retreat *now*. That's an order!"

The audible edge of fear in his tone nearly breaks me.

"I'm sorry, Valen." I pull the ring off my finger so I can't hear him, so I won't be tempted to give in to cowardice. It dangles from its battery line, and I tuck it into my sleeve.

A hurricane of darkness swirls around Zalor's hovering form. He's preparing spells, anticipating an epic death match. The heavens above him are a chaotic clash of sun and storm clouds.

His skeletal, clawed fingers twitch. With that simple gesture, he calls forth a new legion of shadowbeasts, materializing them from thin air. A thousand pitch-black airborne creatures—birds and bats and sylphs and a massive thraxwing—flock to their master, awaiting his next command.

I don't think the battered Mortal Alliance can stand against this fresh division of monsters.

Desperately I dig inside myself—one last, vain attempt to wield a power I'll never possess. I remain an empty husk, an Earthling to the bitter end. The only weapons I have are my blade and my brain.

I am so screwed.

"Zalor," I scream in my best impersonation of Kyla's bravado, "call off your troops!"

Zalor tilts his horned head. I sense, rather than see, his dead-black eyes flash. "It's far too late for leniency, Lightbringer." His words are clear, made magically audible to me. "I think the mortals must be taught a lesson for daring to defy me."

A bolt of darkmagic blasts from his outstretched palm. It streaks toward Cendrion faster than my human eye can process. Cendrion tucks his wings and rolls in midair, spiraling off-course to avoid Zalor's attack.

I clutch at the spinal protrusions on the dragon's neck, holding on for dear life. This close to annihilation, I find that life *is* dear. It would be a tragedy to have come this far only to lose the magic of Solera, and even the banalities of Earth.

As the world spins, a flash of fiery red flares in the corner of my vision. Cendrion rights himself and I twist my neck, owl-like. Fyr'thal the phoenix is flying toward me. Rexa's hot on his tail, talons and beak stained black with shadowbeast blood.

"No!" I scream, gesturing violently at her to flee. "Protect Asher— you promised!"

Rexa's wingbeats falter. Her amber eyes, eyes I'd recognize any-where, glint out of the gryphon's skull. I see defiance in her gaze, but even if she'd wanted to follow me into the jaws of death, Zalor's min-ions aren't giving her the option. A swarm of shadowbeasts ascends to intercept her.

With a feral call, Fyr'thal wields fire against the demonic undead. Rexa twists, rending her foes with her talons. Neither of them are as fast as they need to be. Magic isn't an infinite resource, it's an expen-diture of energy. After such a strenuous battle, they're at the end of their strength.

I turn to Zalor with murder in my heart, but Zalor's no longer paying attention to me. His head angles toward Rexa, watching her struggle. He wields, and another bolt of darkmagic streaks toward her.

The spell hits her wing and she shrieks, dropping. An echoing shriek of horror escapes me. Fyr'thal and his phoenixes close ranks around her, holding off the shadowbeasts while Rexa spirals down between two karsts, aiming for our ground troops.

Without communicating my desires to Cendrion, he dives after her. I lean past his neck, stretching a useless hand toward Rexa.

An irrational part of me believes this is my fault—like this is some twisted Final Destination scenario instead of reality. I spared Asher from his grisly fate on the battlefield; now destiny has turned its bloodthirsty gaze upon Rexa, who's next in line to perish in the books.

"This is your fault, Kyla." Zalor's voice pierces me, a sinister echo of the accusatory voice in my head. "You've led your friends to battle like lambs to the slaughter. Still, waste not, want not. When they die, they'll be mine."

I try to tune him out, but it's too late. He's loosed a flood of anxiety, sparked an inferno of self-loathing within me.

Rexa lands heavily near our front line soldiers. A lieutenant-general calls to her, inviting her into their ranks for safety, but even wounded, Rexa is relentless. She shreds at Zalor's ground troops, felling shadowmen left and right.

Hyper-focused on Rexa's plight, I don't notice the pitch-black wyvern hurtling toward me until it's too late. The demon slams into Cendrion, knocking him off-course.

Belatedly, I remember that I have a sword and I'm supposed to be a hero, not a pathetic wreck. I jam my blade into the wyvern's throat. It falls away, its corpse landing on several advancing shadowmen.

Unbalanced from the hit, Cendrion drops to the ground. Two hundred feet to our left, the rainforest looms, promising salvation through the portal. Ahead, our front line has bubbled outward, absorbing Rexa. I see lifemagic healers approaching, and I know they'll tend to her.

Yet Rexa still isn't safe. *None* of them will be safe until I end this.

"Incoming," screams the lieutenant-general. "Shields, now!"

If I were Kyla Starblade, I could have woven a spell of lightmagic to protect myself and my army. But I'm not her, and Zalor's dark spell hits us full-force.

It's like he dropped a bomb. A sphere of shadow strikes the spongy moss floor and explodes. Darts of black shrapnel fly everywhere, piercing air shields and armor. Soldiers collapse, dead on impact.

Cendrion's armored hide offers some protection, but I hear him grunt in pain and feel his body spasm. His legs give way and he stumbles. I pitch forward and topple past his shoulder, landing in the dirt.

Coughing, I shove myself up on my elbows and freeze.

I'm staring into the inert face of a dead Eldrian soldier. A human. His blue eyes are sightless, devoid of life. Crimson smears his brow.

The coppery stench of blood fills my nostrils and I retch—yet I can't tear myself away from the corpse. Lost in a stampede of chaos, he and I are connected in a timeless moment of death.

Then the corpse twitches.

I know this phenomenon. I've written about it countless times, but seeing it in action is beyond horrific. The blood oozing from the man's wound turns black. His pupils dilate, growing impossibly large. Darkmagic is spreading across his eyes.

He's turning into a shadowbeast.

Zalor tricks his prey, offering them a second chance at life in exchange for their souls. It might have seemed like a good deal to the dead man, but this is not a life. It's becoming an extension of the Shadow Lord, being beholden to his every whim.

The darkmagic spell consumes Zalor's newest victim, turning him to solidified shadow. The newborn demon sits up, holding my gaze. Through his eyes, I see his dark master staring back at me.

"There you are," the shadowman whispers in Zalor's voice.

Acting on instinct, I jam my sword into his neck. He goes still again, falling limp to the ground.

I shouldn't feel bad for destroying him, but I do. All shadowbeasts want is a second chance . . . but death does not offer second chances. Death is ultimate and absolute. Even on Solera, a world bursting at the seams with magic beyond imagining, that rule remains a constant. You can't bring a soul back once it's dissipated beyond the veil of mortality.

I shake myself and try to put the doubly dead soldier out of my head. The experience felt like it lasted an hour, but it's only been a few seconds. I push myself upright and stagger back to Cendrion. He extends a foreleg and I scramble up, resuming my perch between his wing joints.

"We need to cover the army's retreat," I breathe, leaning forward and resting my cheek against the side of his scaly neck. "Are you with me?"

I feel the growl inside him, though I can't hear it over the clash of weapons and spells. "To the end."

With that, he kicks off from the ground and launches toward Zalor.

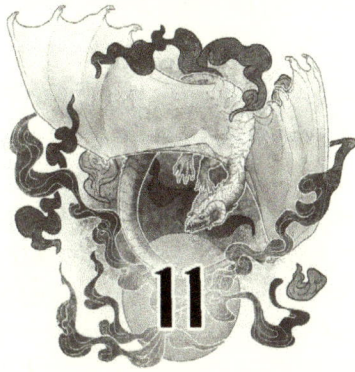

11

ZALOR'S SUPREMELY UNBOTHERED by the violence; his eyes are fixed on me. He lifts a clawed hand, and a deluge of shadow pours forth.

Cendrion dodges, but the phoenixes behind us aren't so lucky. As the dragon banks, I glimpse darkmagic soaking into the firebirds. It dulls their blazing plumage, enervates them, blunts their senses. One by one, they fall from the sky.

"He's enjoying this," I whisper, glaring at Zalor. His pleasure is evident in the cruel set of his mouth. He might not be a mindless killer, but that doesn't mean he's not a sadist. He revels in his supremacy.

Cendrion's muscles bunch as he gathers himself for a head-on assault. Breath rattles in his long throat. I can almost feel the blood-lust thrumming in his nerves.

"Wait," I tell him.

I know Zalor. Neither Cendrion nor I can defeat him without light-magic—but if I can make him pull his troops away from the army, my friends can retreat through the portal to the safety of Midgard.

"Zalor," I cry, "I have a deal to offer you."

"What are you doing?" Cendrion hisses.

I ignore the dragon and barrel on. "If you let my army go in peace, I'll give you what you desire most!"

The air around Zalor thickens with visible darkness. A miasma of shadow billows from him, making it seem as if a premature twilight's fallen on the northern skies.

"What do you know of my desires?" Zalor asks. His tone thrums with deep, primal hunger.

"I know you want unlimited control and power. If I give you my soul, there will be no one left to stand in your way."

"Kyla—!"

"Cendrion, trust me," I whisper from the corner of my mouth, not daring to move my lips. Zalor's eyes narrow, and I know it's no good. He's using his power to listen to every word I say. I add a dash of believable Kyla rashness for good measure: "I can take him. I'm ready."

That does the trick. Zalor raises a hand and his shadowbeast legion parts ways, leaving a clear path for Cendrion.

"You think yourself a match for me." Zalor's tone isn't angry or snide—it's soft. Calculating. I can almost see the cogs turning in his head. Omniscience *does* have its perks. Maybe I can weasel my way out of this with some good old-fashioned cleverness.

Despite my plot twists that keep readers on the edge of their seats, I've never been particularly clever. Knowing what I know now—that I didn't come up with *any* of those twists, I just witnessed them happening from another universe—I'd say I'm actually zero-percent clever.

Fear hooks its claws in my gut at that thought.

"What are you hiding, little Kyla?" Zalor asks, staring down his nose at me. "What trick do you have up your sleeve that makes you so bold today?"

"I'm asking myself the same question," Cendrion growls in an undertone.

"Don't worry," I tell the dragon. "I have a plan."

"That's what worries me."

I wince. I'm not a planner. I'm too much like Kyla in that regard. Why, I can't even plan book outlines. I've always been a spontaneous writer, following where the story takes me.

"You anticipated my ambush." Zalor indicates the battlefield with a sweep of his hand. "You put yourself front and center in a battle that you should have considered of little consequence. Now you offer the key to my victory in exchange for a moment of respite for your army."

He can smell blood in the water. With deliberate slowness, he drifts closer on his cloud of darkmagic. Cendrion tenses but remains where he is, hovering in place, refusing to give way before the Shadow Lord.

"Right, well." I clear my throat, stalling. "When I said to let my army go in peace, I meant forever. Make a binding pact with me. If you vow to call a truce, stop this war, and leave Eldria, then you can kill me. Right here, right now."

A sneer ripples across Zalor's face, cracking his dry, paper-thin flesh. "There's the catch. I have to admire your audacity. The mortals deserve *nothing*—no peace, no freedom, no hope. I will not stop this war until Solera is mine."

Fire and ice course through me, turning me feverish. His words ignite a burning fury in my heart, but the cold has returned to my body with a vengeance. I convulse at the drop in my internal temperature. Zalor notices my movement. His shriveled lips curl. He must think I'm frightened of him ... and I suppose I am. I know how powerful he is.

I also know his weak spots. He can't bear the thought of someone standing up to him. He wants everyone to think like him, assimilate to his dark ways—and if someone doesn't, he must first prove them irrefutably wrong before destroying them.

"Darkness begets darkness," I retort. "You believe you're trying to save the world, but it's not enough to simply save it. You must *change* it."

Thank Ohra I wrote a conversation very much like this one at the end of my manuscript. Maybe the story is salvageable. Maybe it's just reordering itself. I don't know. I can't devote energy to making assumptions, not when my plan hangs by the thinnest of threads.

Zalor flicks a wrist in disparagement of my argument. "I will change the world once it belongs to me. The mortals could have lived in peace if they had accepted my rightful rule, but they chose violence. So violence they shall have."

He's close. Shadowbeasts arc around us, hemming us in on all sides. There's no escape. Even if there was, I couldn't turn back. I must see my plan through.

Cendrion lashes out at Zalor, darting forward and swiping with his front paws. Zalor dissolves into shadow before the talons land. He reappears instantaneously behind Cendrion. I was expecting that move, and I'm ready for it. I lunge on Cendrion's back, stabbing at the Shadow Lord.

Zalor dodges my blow easily, lazily even.

"This is familiar, isn't it?" he says, leering. "A desperate hero trapped in an unwinnable war. Cendrion sacrificed himself for you the last time you challenged me, but he's outlived his usefulness. No one can save you now."

Cendrion bellows and charges Zalor again. Zalor phases out of reach, letting the dragon hurtle past.

"Why fight if you know you'll lose?" he taunts. "There is no hope for you, Lightbringer. Surrender and put yourself out of your misery."

I hack at him with my sword while Cendrion swipes with his claws. Zalor shrugs off our efforts. He knows he's stronger than us. Stronger than *me*.

That thought sends a fresh wave of rage tumbling through my body. Anger is Kyla's power emotion. She believes it's what makes her strong. I believe that about myself, too—and I don't care about the philosophical implications of using anger as a crutch, as a mask.

Anger is better than emptiness. Feeling something is better than feeling nothing.

With a ragged cry, I slice at Zalor again. He dodges, and a spectral black shockwave emanates from his body. The dark spell hits Cendrion and bowls him over in the air, sending me tumbling from his back.

I don't have time to scream. Moving like a glitch, like an atom popping in and out of existence in a quantum vacuum, Zalor appears beside me as I enter free fall. He nabs me by the neck, wrapping his fingers around my throat. My spine twists painfully. I'm thankful I'm not in my Earth body, where chronic back pain is my arch nemesis, not the Shadow Lord.

But now that I've been separated from Cendrion, I'm well and truly panicked. The dragon was my secret weapon. Without him, there's no hope for me.

If my stomach weren't empty, I'd be vomiting. Why did I think this was a good idea? Why didn't I heed Valen's command and flee when I had the chance? Not even Kyla Starblade with all her power could stand against Zalor at this point in the tale. What made me believe I was a match for him, magicless halfwit that I am?

Zalor holds me aloft, pulling me close. I kick and flail, trying to break his vise-like grip.

"There's something different about you today," he hisses, baring sable fangs. Cold, dry breath, scented like rotting leaves, wafts over my face. This close, I can see every tiny fissure in his flesh, every pockmark in the visible parts of his skull beneath.

"Good different... or bad different?" I choke out the words, half-delirious from the cold and lack of oxygen.

Zalor frowns. His grip tightens, claws puncturing my skin. I let out an airless scream as warm blood dribbles down my neck.

His claws dig deeper and I black out, reeling in endless horror. In my senseless state, I hallucinate. I imagine blood spilling from my body, pooling around me. I'm submerged in it, suffocating in it... and the blood is cold, so *very* cold—

For a moment, I am nothing—

Nothing at all—

Unconsciousness, oblivion, no feeling, no thought, not even a drop of blood—

Then humid air fills my lungs. With a shuddering gasp, I open my eyes. Zalor's ghastly visage swims before me. His face is slack, his obsidian orbs wide.

"Who are you?" he breathes.

The question is somehow the most terrifying thing he could have said.

A faraway roar meets my ears, shattering the moment of horrific intimacy. Darkness engulfs me. I become nothing again, but this time I remain conscious. It's different from the nothingness that gripped me moments ago. This is a warm nothing, a calm nothing, where I'm free of both physical and psychic pain.

I've been wielded into shadow, turned into an incorporeal wisp. I can't see the world rushing past as my savior whisks me away from Zalor's clutches, but instinct tells me I'm safe. When I'm reconstituted into physical form, thread by thread, tears of relief brim in my eyes.

"Cendrion," I rasp, my throat bruised and sore.

The white dragon crouches over me, hidden beneath a patch of giant ferns atop a karst. We're at the southern end of the valley. The army's retreat was successful; a flash of light followed by a thunderous shockwave of energy marks the closing of the portal. Our troops must have made it safely to Midgard.

"Quiet," he breathes. His sliver-fine pupils dance to the north, where Zalor is a speck in the sky amidst a tempest of shadowbeasts.

One of my shaking hands strains toward Cendrion. "You saved me."

"I can explain, but not now."

"No need." I bite back a hacking cough, wanting to stay silent in case any roving shadowbeasts are nearby. "I know what you are."

Cendrion's brow ridges arc up and his eyes turn liquid. He leans toward me and presses his snout against my hand, connecting us.

Kyla doesn't know what really happened during their first, ill-fated confrontation with Zalor. But I, the omniscient author, do.

"FIND KYLA STARBLADE!" Zalor's scream echoes throughout the mountains, causing a pressurized throb to surface behind my forehead. He must be furious that Cendrion snatched me out of his clutches. And that last question of his...as if he *knew*...

Did I hallucinate that?

The shadowbeasts scatter and Cendrion tenses. "We're not safe here. We need to leave."

I nod weakly.

"I want her brought to me," Zalor shrieks from the far end of the valley as Cendrion begins wielding, dissolving both of us into shadow. "And I want her *alive*."

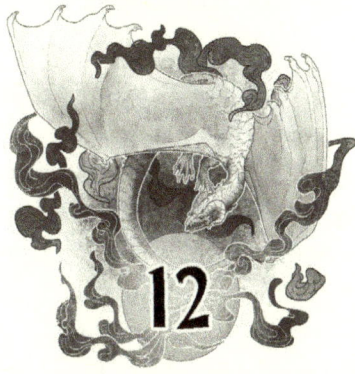

12

THIS IS A NIGHTMARE, and I know it by heart.

I awake in a small room, the dilapidated ceiling fan rattling above me. Coldness bleeds through a drafty window with dirty panes. The apartment shakes as the elevated N Train trundles past outside.

I live this nightmare every day. I can't summon the strength of will to rise from my aged mattress. Nothing's waiting for me beyond this dingy room, not even food in the fridge. All that's there is a half-eaten can of salsa and collard greens I bought when I was mentally healthy, thinking I'd one day make a meal out of them.

Ah, the folly of hope.

Kyla? Kyla!

My mind's buzzing, playing tricks again. I allow myself to drift into the hazy zone between sleep and wakefulness, focusing on ideas for my as-yet-unpublished book series. My brain seizes on its happy place and off it goes, whisking me into a dream, saving me from this dreary reality.

She's ice cold. Get her to the palace infirmary!

I *am* cold. The window is ill-fitting and doesn't close all the way, allowing winter air into my Astoria one-bedroom. I curl into a ball, hugging my comforter around me, and will myself to forget this world. When I immerse myself in Solera, I feel better. Some days, it's all that gets me out of bed.

I want guards posted by her bed around the clock. You can bet your last copper coin that Zalor will try to strike back.

Slowly, I float out of reality—or is this the dream? This dingy apartment, this empty existence ... I escaped this, didn't I? I wrote every day. I worked hard. I got out.

At least, I *think* I did. I can't tell what's real anymore, and I don't know where I belong. I don't even know my own name.

Kyla, please wake up.

Kyla ... is that me? It seems improbable, because the voice whispering in my ear is filled with tender affection that warms me from my core. Love so pure and perfect doesn't exist in nightmares, and I'm trapped in a never-ending nightmare. Stuck in place. Paralyzed.

There's nowhere I can go from here. I'll have to wake up eventually, so I can work a minimum-wage receptionist job, so I can struggle to pay rent and maybe have enough left over to feed myself next week, and I will repeat this grueling cycle until the day I die. Life is empty, and I am empty, and the emptiness frightens me.

When I feel nothing, I am nothing. And when I am nothing, then nothing matters.

Please, Kyla. We need you. I need you.

There's that voice again. Someone needs me.

The sense of being able to make a difference is what I've been missing all my life. Reality lacks structure. There's no definitive goal ... or ending. You achieve one thing and suddenly find you need to achieve something else. And it keeps going like that, and you're never happy.

But somewhere out there—in a parallel universe I know better than my own—my existence *does* matter.

The nightmare dims as I focus on that other, better world. My one-bedroom falls away in shreds, the vision receding into the darkest depths of my consciousness. The cold fades until it's less than a memory. With it gone, I can feel other things: a soft blanket against my skin, a luxurious warmth tingling in the air, a calloused hand gripping mine.

I crack my eyes open and blink, adjusting to the sudden brightness. I'm at the end of a long marble room, in a bed beside a window. Its pane is immaculate, and it's not at all drafty.

What an odd thing to think. No self-respecting window in the

Imperial Palace would ever dare to be drafty.

I shake my head, trying to shed the lingering remnants of the nightmare. The discomfort in my stomach, stemming from despair and a sprinkle of revulsion, dissipates. I pull a breath of Eldrian air into my lungs, dispelling the awful vision. The fresh scent of lemon and featherpine sparks life in my sleep-dulled brain.

"Kyla!"

Valen is beside me, holding my hand. He leans close, smoothing flyaway wisps of hair from my brow. The gesture feels oddly intimate, and my cheeks grow warm.

"Valen," I whisper, smiling drowsily.

His eyes dance with unspoken questions. A seed of darkness sprouts in my soul.

"It's not her. It's me."

Valen leans back. His left hand drops from my brow, but his right hand remains clasped around mine. "I figured as much. What the blood were you thinking, going after Zalor?"

"Not giving me a moment to gather my wits before you start with the lectures, are you?"

Hard creases appear on his face. He isn't interested in banter.

I swallow. My mouth is parched. "I couldn't let Zalor kill you. I had to distract him while the army retreated."

"Even if you *had* magic, confronting him would have been suicide!"

"Ah, you underestimate my willingness to die," I quip. "I'm a Millennial. It's in my nature."

"You're a what?"

"It's . . . never mind. It'll take too long to explain." I heave a sigh that turns into a cough.

Valen releases my hand, and my heart takes a tumble—but he's only done it to grab a pitcher on a marble nightstand next to my infirmary bed. I tilt my head to watch him pour a glass of water and notice that I'm hooked up to an intravenous drip. A silver needle is lodged in my arm, delivering vital fluids through a selkie-hide wire.

"Drink." Valen brings the cup to my lips. The water is deliciously cool, and, of course, I choke on it at once.

"Easy," he whispers. "You've been out for two days." His hand returns to my head, supporting the base of my neck. I sip more slowly this time, savoring the crystalline liquid.

Once I've had my fill, Valen sets the glass down and fixes me with a steely look. "What happened out there?"

I glance past him to check who else is in the infirmary. Most of the beds are filled, but the occupants are quiet, either sound asleep or in magically induced comas for deep healing.

"Zalor wasn't supposed to appear. I never wrote that in my manuscript—I never saw that happening. Your universe changed. Honestly, it changed as soon as I arrived. We're living in a different timeline now."

"We've lost our one advantage," says Valen, scrubbing a hand over his face. "We no longer know what will happen next."

"Maybe not, but I can guess. I know him. That's how I was able to stall him."

"And how is it you were able to *escape* him? General Praxus closed the portal to prevent shadowbeasts from following us to Midgard. He thought you'd be able to teleport to safety. I thought otherwise until the palace healers informed us they'd found you lying on the infirmary floor, out cold."

That's a good question. How did I get here? I wade through a morass of hazy visions filled with drafty windows and empty refrigerators, struggling to recall my last moments of consciousness.

"I spoke to Zalor. I offered him Kyla's life in exchange for ending the war."

Valen's eyes tighten.

"I'm sorry. It was the only bargaining chip I had, and it was a bluff. Zalor got a hold on me and I started feeling cold. I passed out. Then he did something—I think he wielded to bring me back—and he..."

My stomach sinks, twisting in a downward spiral.

"Valen, he knows."

"Knows what? Knows about *you*?"

"He must have seen something, or sensed something. We were—I don't know, *connected*. Maybe he caught a glimpse of my mind. Or my soul," I add in a hollow voice.

"How did you escape?" Valen asks again.

I falter, considering how best to respond..

"It's a secret," I say at last. His brows storm together. I reach for him and take his hand. "A secret that isn't mine to tell."

Valen takes a deep breath. It looks like he's gearing up for a lecture, but I squeeze his fingers, forestalling his arguments. "You'll know soon enough. Trust me."

I wince, because it's a stretch to ask for trust. I've done nothing to earn it. I led my friends into a battle that almost became a massacre, and I was flagrantly irresponsible with my custodianship of Kyla's body. That alone could have cost us the war.

It *would* have, if Zalor hadn't hesitated. If he hadn't seen something inside me. The truth, perhaps, of who I really am.

To my surprise, Valen nods. "There's work to be done. Are you well enough to stand?"

"I think so." With a pinching twinge, I pull the silver needle from my arm and toss the IV drip aside. I sit up, moving to swing my legs out of the bed, when I realize I'm not dressed. Gasping in horror, I snatch the covers to my chest, holding them tight.

"The work can wait until your clothes are brought." Is that a hint of amusement in Valen's tone? I narrow my eyes at him. He's staring determinedly at the ceiling, and his brown cheeks have darkened. "You were so cold, the healers had to weave air- and firemagic enchantments around you to maintain your core temperature. It was best performed against bare skin."

That explains the tingly matrix of heat enveloping me. Until now I was feeling good, despite everything: wonderfully warm, free of pain, happy to have survived my ordeal.

At Valen's signal, a lifemagic healer bustles over to examine me. She clears me for discharge and pulls a curtain in front of my bed so I can change. The smooth marble floor is cool against my toes, and a chill bleeds into me from the feet up as I dress, reminding me of . . . something. A nightmare I imagined when I was stuck between this world and the next.

A nightmare I never want to revisit.

"We need advice," Valen murmurs when I peel back the curtains to join him. "I'd like to speak to Temereth again."

"About solutions for the Shadow War?"

"Yes—but the more important war, I think, is being fought in your body. We need you healthy, because Solera is lost without you. Both of you."

That's the first time he's acknowledged me—the *real* me—as a useful individual. It sends renewed strength surging through my limbs. I straighten and nod, exiting the infirmary by his side.

"Would you like to eat before we go to the mountains?" Valen asks as we descend the elegant bifurcated central stairs of the palace. My eyebrows shoot up, and his rise in response, disappearing into his dark, tousled locks. "Why the look of surprise?"

"You're being suspiciously nice."

"I'm being pragmatic," he replies, cool as a cucumber. "You're unwell and you need to maintain your strength. I'm willing to bet you weren't eating properly on the march. I know how you feel about army rations."

"You know how *Kyla* feels about rations."

"And I've observed you picking over your pemmican and porridge like a princess."

We're trapped in a complicated dance. I shouldn't pretend to be Kyla, but I don't want to be myself. If I misstep, if I overplay my hand, I risk undoing all the progress I've made with Valen . . . but a parallel universe is as safe a place to flirt as there ever was. Why not enjoy myself while I can?

"Been watching me, Commander-General? Still afraid of what I might do?"

We've reached the second-story landing. Valen places his hand on the small of my back to guide me away from the stairs, into the corridor that leads to the banquet hall. The subtle touch sends lightning across my skin.

"Something like that." His tone is unreadable. It worries me. It's one thing for my lunatic, affection-starved brain to blur lines. It's quite another for Valen to do it.

But I'm weak. I can't reject a dream so freely offered, and I've never been one to turn down food. *Good* food, that is. He's right about those rations. Pemmican is disgusting. Google told me it was a mixture of tallow, dried meat, and berries. It did not prepare me for the texture or the aftertaste.

The banquet hall is busy when we reach it. Army personnel bustle to and fro. Midgard is on high alert post-battle.

"How's everyone else?" I ask.

"All safe. The city is too, for now."

I nod as I wait my turn on the long line. Neither Kyla nor I are renowned for our patience, but here, surrounded by the gleam of magic and a host of fantastical creatures, I could stare for years and never grow bored.

Solera is filled with species you'd find in every tropey tale, but they all have unique spins. Elves, for example, have fine scales like snakes, clawed fingers and toes, and golden, overlarge eyes with slitted pupils. When one elven officer approaches to consult with Valen, I admire the curve of her pointed ears and the otherworldly glint in her gaze.

There are also species here that you might not expect. I see nereids, water-dwelling creatures somewhere between humanoid and serpent; golems, earthmagic-using bipeds with leathery skin as tough as the stone they wield; ifriti, lizard-like fire wielders who bristle with glowing horns; and sylphs, which are basically big, fluffy manta rays that float around on airmagic.

Not long ago, I thought my overactive imagination created these wonderful beasts. I can't even be mad that it didn't. The fact that they're real is infinitely better.

The food today is hearty, featuring specialties from across the Eldrian Empire: Olthoran spiced meatloaf, Galvian pickled edamame salad, Lenkhari honeywheat bread. Valen and I find a secluded table in the farthest bay window and sit.

"I find myself at a disadvantage," he confesses after several minutes of silence while I stuff my face.

"Mmf?"

"You know all about me, but I know nothing about you."

I nearly choke on my too-large mouthful. "You know I hate army rations."

"Tell me something I *don't* know."

"Not much to tell."

Too late, I realize this is a Kyla quote. I'm deflecting, like she would. There's nothing safe I can tell Valen, because anything I say will reveal the depths of my twisted psyche. Any story I spin will end at a foregone conclusion of darkness.

I don't want to wallow in darkness tonight. I've suffered there too long. I want to forget Earth—and perhaps my reluctance to speak stems from the fact that I'm forgetting more of my Earthling life the longer I linger here.

I had family, didn't I? Friends? I must have . . . but if that's true, why were they so easy to forget?

Shaking off my disquiet, I fall back on my favorite topic of conversation—one that happens to be conveniently impersonal. "I love dragons."

"So I gathered. Did you always love them, or did it happen after you connected to our world?"

"I've been a dracophile since birth. I liked dinosaurs as a toddler, and I think my love of dragons stemmed from there."

"What are dinosaurs?" Valen asks, his head cocked at an adorably innocent angle.

"They're kinda like dragons without wings, magic, or the capacity for speech. Or so we gather. Their brains were comparatively small, but who's to say? The last dinosaurs died out on Earth sixty-five million years ago. Our scientists can only hypothesize what they were like."

Valen nods. "And do you have a favorite species of dinosaur?"

It's been decades since someone asked me this question, but my body is *ready*.

"Pachycephalosaurus." I grin as he raises a questioning brow.

"They were bipedal herbivores with really thick skull domes. We think they used to butt heads with each other." I form two fists and smack them together. This earns me a chuckle.

"Somehow, that makes perfect sense as your favorite."

I point my fork at him. "I'm taking the high road and not interpreting that as an insult."

"A wise choice." Valen's gaze locks on mine. Eye contact on Earth made my innards squirm with discomfort. I could never hold a gaze more than a few seconds, and even that was excruciating. But I could lose myself in his eyes, eyes that reflect the voltmagic in his soul.

"You like science," he says eventually.

"Of course. I based the magic in this world on the science in mine. At least, I thought I did."

"That explains how you know so much about magical mechanics." I catch the subtle edge of approval in his deep voice. He's impressed with the depth of my Soleran knowledge. Of course he is—he's a nerd in jock's clothing. He lives for this stuff.

"Oh yeah, I had lots of fun when I thought I was making it all up. Turns out our parallel universes have a lot in common. Or maybe it's one big universe, and our planets coexist within it."

"Ergo, the laws of subatomics would be consistent for both worlds—" Valen begins.

"—which would explain the similarities between them," I finish, brimming with youthful exuberance.

"Another difference between you and Kyla," he says. "She wasn't a scholar. Her eyes would glaze over whenever I spoke about science and math."

"I'll talk science with you all day, but please don't ever speak to me about math."

The shadows don't quite mask the curve of his lips. "Noted. You know, I studied science when I was young."

I do know, since I worked tirelessly on crafting Valen's past, but I don't interrupt. I want to hear the story from him. His voice is a song that calls to my soul. Plus, how many creators get the chance to talk to their creations? Or their not-creations? Potato-tomato.

"Before the war started, I dreamed of becoming a scholar. I wanted to unravel every mystery in our world and understand how everything worked. I even attended a specialized school where I grew up in Caerth, Olthoria's largest city."

"I grew up in a big city, too!" My voice is high-pitched, like a smitten teenager on a first date. "New York City."

"Was it nice?"

"That's a loaded question. It was obviously the best, but it was also very much the worst."

Valen laughs, *really* laughs, and it transforms him. "I know that feeling. Kyla loved city life, but it was never a good fit for me. If I'd had a choice, I'd have moved to a quiet village filled with dusty libraries and lived there happily for all my days." His face shines with wistful remembrance. Then his expression darkens, becoming overcast with regret.

"I joined the Olthoran armed forces when I was ten. Family business—my father and uncles were all in the military, so I didn't have a choice. Even while training to become an officer, I clung to the idea that I might one day be released from duty. Find a peaceful place to settle down." He shakes his head. "Of course, that was before Zalor came into the picture. As soon as he sacked Caerth, my division was deployed, and I had to give up my dreams."

I know this, too. I wrote it—yet hearing it spoken aloud tears at my heart.

"I want this war to be over," he whispers. "There's not a soul in the empire who doesn't want the war to end, but it's always felt personal to me. War destroyed who I used to be, as it does everyone; but it also destroyed who I *could* have been."

My throat tightens. I'm seized with the sudden urge to take him in my arms, comfort him, protect him.

"I'm going to kill Zalor," I vow. "I'm going to wreck him so hard that even his memory is erased from Solera. Then you can settle down in a nice village and read all the books in the world."

A sparkle returns to Valen's gaze. "I'd like that."

No doubt, no cynicism—what a wonderful breath of fresh air.

His quiet faith renews my resolve. My smile can't be contained, and I know how he feels about Kyla's smile. This isn't fair to either of us.

Valen is the responsible one. He clears his throat and stands, smoothing his uniform. "It's late. We still need to speak with Temereth."

And just like that, the spell is broken.

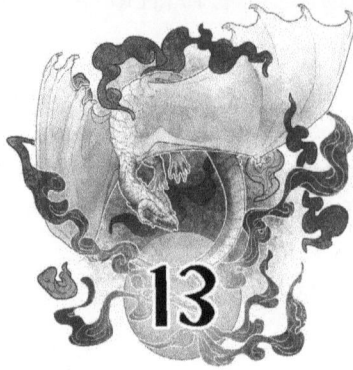

13

WE BUS OUR PLATES and take our leave. Fortunately, the recent battle is a perfect excuse to charter a carriage to the western wall. It takes three days for a magicsource to replenish to full capacity after expending all its energy. Well, 2.71828 days—the same as the base of natural logarithms, an important number in quantum-magical equations—but who's counting?

The Eldrians don't know I didn't wield a single thread of magic at Torvel. They think I'm unable to teleport because I'm still recharging, so our request doesn't raise suspicion.

The carriage that arrives is borne on an airmagic enchantment, hovering two feet off the ground for the gentlest of rides. It's also more economical than horses during wartime. Airmagic doesn't need to eat, nor does it take up valuable stable space.

Night's fallen by the time we exit Midgard's gates. City security has quadrupled. Valen explained that since the failed reclamation of Torvel, Lord Zalor has spread word across the continent, ensuring everyone from the simplest deep sea nereid to the oldest dragon knows he wants Kyla Starblade delivered to him. Alive.

He's even offered a reward, though in typical Zalor fashion, his reward is simply "ensured survival of the mortal races." Not much of an incentive, but it was enough to spike my blood pressure.

Guards patrol the wall ramparts. Fire crystals emit a harsh glow, suffusing the air with an orange haze. The near-invisible but unmistakable opalescent shimmer of a forcemagic field distorts the empty sky.

"We timed this poorly," I mutter. Dragons are diurnal, and most will be asleep at this hour. A few enterprising creatures still swoop through the thin clouds, but I don't recognize Temereth's silhouette. There's no guarantee she's out and about.

"*Felthys, vecerey aidos!*" I call to a young male dragon who dips low to scour the river for a late meal of fish. "*Tenrey corsiras aves Temereth. Te'as-endral naler eleros solendra?*"

My phrasing is inelegant, but the male tilts his head toward me in acknowledgment. Dragons can communicate with each other telepathically, so he's likely relaying my message to Temereth now.

The male swoops into the darkness, leaving us alone. Though the weather's temperate, I shiver. I resist the temptation to draw closer to Valen, who always runs warm.

A soundless, blinding flash cleaves the sky. Behind us, soldiers gasp. I screw up my eyes, but I hear the beat of long, leathery wings and catch the faint scent of charcoal and summer sand.

"*Lux'abria,*" Temereth hails me, having teleported to our location. I peek through my lashes and watch as the dark-scaled dragon alights at the cliff's edge. "What prompts this visit?"

Before I can open my mouth to explain, Temereth's brow ridges draw together. "Something is wrong with you."

Hearing her affirm it—so quickly, so easily—compounds the cold growing in my chest.

She wields again, teleporting all three of us. The sensation of a teleport is exhilarating but dizzying. It makes you feel like you're expanding to blanket the universe. You are, in a way, since matter expands as it increases velocity, and a teleport vibrates someone's molecules at light speed to move them between spaces. When the spell's over, you feel like you're being crammed into a too-small container: your mortal flesh prison.

We arrive in Temereth's personal cave. The dragon approaches me, lowering her head. I don't shy away from the massive snout or gleaming fangs. My instinct is to reach out, laying my palm against her nose. Her scales are pleasantly neutral—not too warm, not too cool.

Temereth tolerates the touch. Her membranous inner eyelids rise once and lower slowly.

"You are dying," she whispers at last.

That knocks the breath from my lungs. I sway against her as my knees weaken. "What?"

Valen is suddenly at my side. His arm slides around me and he hefts me upright, holding me close for support. I lean into him, grateful for his comforting presence. "How do you know, and what can we do to stop it?" he asks.

"I have sensed both Kyla's body and the Earthling's soul," Temereth replies. "There is nothing wrong with the former. The latter is causing the problem."

"My soul...?"

"Magic is the energy that powers our life functions. Yours is not a soul that provides wieldable energy, but it is a soul nonetheless. It was strong enough to sustain Kyla's body the last time we met; now it is fading."

"What did I do? Why is this happening?"

"I cannot be sure, but I can guess," says Temereth. "Despite the similarities between our universes, there remain fundamental differences that cannot be overcome. Like a saltwater fish in a freshwater pond, your soul is unequipped to survive here for an extended period."

"What happens to Kyla if the Earthling's soul dies?" Valen asks.

The question permeates my shock, sinks through my skin, and settles in my heart. My shivering redoubles. Valen's arm tightens around me but I push away, reeling backward.

"Kyla—"

"I'm not her!" The force of my cry echoes in Temereth's cavern and fades in the silence that has descended.

"If the Earthling's soul dies and vacates Kyla's body, it's possible Kyla's soul will return to its origin," says Temereth.

"Possible?" Valen repeats.

"I am operating on theory. This soul-phasing phenomenon has not been cataloged before." Temereth lifts her head and rearranges her wings in a haughty profile. The weight of her attention falls on me like a hammer on an anvil.

"You must find a way to win the Shadow War, and win it fast—else both you and Solera are doomed. The sooner you return to your natural body, the greater your chances of survival."

I swallow a lump in my throat. Grasping for a bit of levity, I say, "Don't suppose the dragons would like to join the war, huh? That'd solve... at least fifty percent of my problems."

Temereth's expression is blank and inscrutable, but I catch a flicker of darkness in the depths of her violet eyes. "The dragons cannot join this conflict."

"Figures," I mutter. "And I don't suppose you'd like to tell me *why?*"

She shakes her noble head, swinging it back and forth like a great pendulum. My brow knots with frustration, but I'm too tired, too cold to argue with her about plot holes and contrived conveniences.

"This is your journey," she reminds me.

"I know." But now that I no longer know the ending (or the middle, for that matter), I find myself far more reluctant to face it. My soul is dying, and with it, my hope. The light that flared in my heart now gutters like a candle at the end of its wick.

At Valen's request, Temereth returns us to the Imperial Palace. She sends us to the back entrance, which is less heavily trafficked. I slump into a quivering mass of defeat on the creamy marble steps.

Valen crouches before me.

"Ambassador Brightstone, General Faeloryn, I'm requesting your presence in the palace gardens," he murmurs, using his comms device to summon our friends.

He's close enough to touch, yet somehow universes away. I stare unseeingly across the grand gardens. The beauty of the hedge labyrinth, dotted with faerie lights, is lost on me. I'm oblivious to the radiant fireflies dancing in the dark. Unlike Earth fireflies, these ones wield actual firemagic. Could be a fun thing to enjoy, but I'm myopically fixated on the news of my impending doom.

Not surprising, I guess. Depression turned my Earthling mind to Swiss cheese. Trauma scarred my brain and changed it. It fixates on negatives and ignores positives. I've been stuck in an Ouroboros pattern of self-fulfilling failure for so long that I don't know how to escape.

Why fight if you know you'll lose?

Unbidden, Zalor's taunt floats to the front of my mind. It's almost as if he sensed my weakness from afar and sought to prey upon it. For the first time since coming to Solera, I'm inclined to agree with him.

Pounding footsteps reach my ears, heralding Asher and Rexa's arrival. I don't turn to greet them. I'm numb. Caught between one intolerable reality and another.

Valen explains the situation. Asher drops to sit beside me.

"Kyla?" The near-pitying tone causes waves of anger to crest in my sea of despair.

"I'm fine."

This draws a scoff from Rexa. "That's rich. You're moping."

"Rexa," Asher hisses in admonishment.

"What? She is. Moping when she should be fighting." Her cloak swirls around her dark-furred legs as she stomps around to stand on the step below mine, facing me. The suspicion that once lurked in her gaze has been replaced with something equally hard, yet infinitely warmer.

"We hit a minor setback. So what? Our goal hasn't changed. Win the war so we can get the real Kyla back and send you packing."

I want to wallow in my misery, but against my will, my lips twitch. Rexa spots it and smirks. She punches my shoulder in what she must think is a bracing manner.

"Ow!"

Rexa plunks herself down on my other side. "So, got any brilliant ideas?"

I can't cling to my bad mood when I'm sandwiched between my two best friends, but I have no clue where to go from here. I squeeze my eyes shut, pinching the bridge of my nose. "Come on, focus. Think."

Valen moves to stand in front of us. "You were convinced that defeating Zalor was the key to returning to Earth. We just need to come up with a winning war strategy."

The look he gives me takes my breath away. He's no longer hoping to see Kyla. It's me he's talking to. He thinks I'll pull some plot twist out of my bag of tricks.

I can't let him down. He's depending on me. *Everyone* is depending on me. I've been given a spectacular power, and I can't allow myself to sabotage it.

Determined to be the hero my friends need, I stand abruptly. "Okay. We attempted one solution to our problem and we failed, but that's to be expected. This is a natural progression of the story, facing challenges of increasing difficulty."

"Increasing difficulty," Rexa echoes. "Great."

I spin on my heel to stare at them. "To be honest, I sense something terrible on the horizon. But I also believe that if we stick together, if we all play our parts, we can triumph. Though the darkness may be infinite, it is weak—because even the smallest light has the power to shine through it."

I'm quoting myself, borrowing words I wrote in Book Five. A little melodramatic, but I don't care. We all need to hear it. Rexa nods. Asher grins. And Valen...

His expression is one I almost don't recognize, because I've never seen it directed at me before. The infamous almost-smile curving his lips, the strong set of his jaw, the energy in his eyes that makes him simultaneously ferocious and gentle.

My foolish heart strains toward him, reaching for something it can never have. All I've ever wanted is this feeling, this connection. On Earth, I was alone. Empty. How can I go down this road, knowing I'll be returning to misery if I succeed?

Damned if I do, damned if I don't.

My mind flutters away from my friends and seizes on something new. It's a plot line I dabbled with adding in my earlier books, but ultimately discarded.

Now it might just become my Deus Ex Magical salvation.

"There could be a way to kill Zalor *without* having to face him in battle," I say. "Have any of you heard legends about the Crown of the World?"

Only silence answers. If anyone's likely to be familiar with the lore, it's Valen, but even he looks lost.

"I have," says a voice behind us.

Instantly, everyone's on guard. Rexa balls her fists and hisses. Asher reaches for his bow and arrows, but pauses.

"Light of Ohra," he breathes. "So *that's* how you escaped Zalor."

I turn to find Cendrion materializing from the shadows of the palace's back foyer.

Rexa gawps at the dragon. "Since when do you wield darkmagic?"

"Since when do you wield anything?" asks Valen. He's schooled his face to smoothness, but his body is rigid with tension. "We thought you'd lost your powers. When you and Kyla first battled Lord Zalor—"

"I chose to stop wielding after the incident because Zalor infected me with a terrible curse," Cendrion interrupts. His neck and wings droop. "His spell snuffed out my lightmagic, replacing it thread by thread with darkness."

That's how their fate is entwined. Zalor's power lives in Cendrion, which means Cendrion will die alongside Zalor when he's finally defeated.

If he's defeated.

"You're more than your darkness," I remind Cendrion. "And since we're all on the same page now, we can start making use of it."

Rexa directs her glare at me. "You knew about this?"

Asher lays a calming hand on her shoulder. "It's okay. He's still the same Cendrion he's always been, no matter what magic lives within him."

Cendrion bares his fangs in a humorless grin. His talons clack against the immaculate flagstones as he approaches. "The darkness changed me and destroyed me in ways I could never have imagined. But it's been festering in my soul for as long as you've known me, so I suppose you're right."

My heart shrivels in my chest. I'm familiar with that feeling.

"I knew about Cendrion," I say, "but there are plenty of things about this world I *don't* know. The lore surrounding the Crown of the World could be one such example." I look at the dragon. "You probably know more than I do, if you'd like to tell it."

Cendrion inclines his head and begins.

"Long ago, Solera was barren, devoid of life and magic. As eons passed, twelve monoliths rose into being at the planet's magnetic north pole, each containing a different type of elemental energy. Eventually the monoliths cracked, setting their powers free.

"These magical energies mingled, creating the building blocks of life. Creatures evolved from each different strain of magic. Of these, none were more powerful or intelligent than the fire-wielding dragons." A touch of pride creeps into Cendrion's lilting tone.

"Our ancient draconic ancestors wanted to understand the universe, unravel its mysteries," he continues. "They followed traces of magical radiation to the north pole and found the Crown of the World. There they communed with the twelve monoliths, seeking answers. The Monolith of Lightmagic admired their quest for knowledge so much that it bestowed its power unto them, replacing the fire in their souls with light."

I know this portion of the legend. It's part of the untold explanation as to why Kyla wields lightmagic. I intended to give her a connection to the Crown of the World, but couldn't find a place to shoehorn that backstory into the books.

"Several thousand millennia later, Zalor comes into the picture." Here, Cendrion's voice grows ominous. "Zalor was once a mere mortal, a human who led a cursed and joyless life. He hated Solera, and longed for the power to reshape it in his warped vision of perfection. He sought and found the Crown of the World, and bound his soul to the Monolith of Darkmagic. Thus, he stole godly powers and became the Shadow Lord."

My nerves are electrified. None of these Zalor details had ever solidified in my mind, but as they settle in my dying soul now, certainty burns through me. This is more than legend. It's truth. My path has been illuminated.

"I have to find the Crown, too," I declare. Like the dragons before me, I sense that's where I'll find my answers.

The flat look Rexa gives me is so quintessentially her that I fight off a smile.

"You don't have to come." I wouldn't force this quest on anyone, let alone the people whose lives I'm trying to save.

She scoffs. "Yeah, I'll stay here twiddling my thumbs while you go gallivanting on an epic adventure. That sounds like me."

Asher, bless him, steps forward to pledge his support. "I'm following you, Kyla. If you believe this is the way, so do I."

"Sounds like a bunch of lunacy to me," says Rexa, "but no more loony than the other stuff you've come up with, I suppose."

I should tell them no, force them to stay here and remain safe. We'll be traversing lands unexplored, facing deadly arcane magics.

But I'm weak. Weak, and perhaps too rooted in my storybook fantasies. Is this not the ultimate dream? Going on a heroic quest with the creatures I love most in the world? Creatures who might be learning to love *me* for who I am?

As one, the three of us look at Valen. He's been unnaturally quiet.

"What do you think?" I ask him.

"I trust you," he says simply.

Those words are my undoing. I daren't speak, because my lips are trembling. Warmth pricks at the corners of my eyes.

"That's settled." Rexa claps her scaly hands and rubs them together. "When do we leave?"

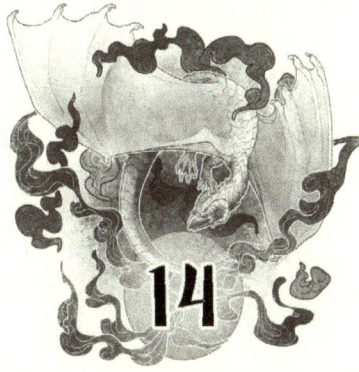

14

"I DON'T KNOW WHY," SAYS REXA, her voice dripping with sarcasm, "but I thought your master plan was going to involve something more exciting than research."

I hide a smile as I peruse the textbook in my hands. "Not every part of an adventure can be wild action and heart-stopping battles. A good story has calm parts."

"A boring story, maybe," she grumbles, slouching down the row and yanking random tomes from the marble shelves.

"There must be time for character development," I say, consulting the book's weathered pages. The Eldrians have different runes (which I've memorized), but our language is the same. The fact that Eldrian is actually American English doesn't make sense, but I don't want to consider the implications of that strange coincidence. "Part of the Hero's Journey is that the hero must change along the way. Otherwise, what's the point?"

"Have we changed genres, too?" Rexa's voice drifts toward me from the next row over. I can hear her irreverently rummaging through the stacks. "From action to snoozefest?"

Her predictable surliness is distracting. Not because I dislike it— she's making me laugh when I should be studying. It's hard enough as-is to read this alternate alphabet.

"Any luck?" The whisper is soft, but it makes me jump. I fumble the ancient book as I whirl to face Valen.

"Don't sneak up on me," I hiss. "My anxiety's through the roof. You're going to give me a heart attack."

"That wasn't my intention. I'm trying to keep your heart in working order."

I squint at him through the gloom. It's late, and the Imperial Library is deserted. The day lights have been turned off and the night lights—infrared orbs that hover in midair, bobbing gently like bubbles in a deep sea current—cast a ruby glow on our surroundings.

His face betrays nothing of his thoughts. I can't begin to guess what he was implying.

"It's slow-going," I say, skirting away from the sensitive subject of my heart. "Right now, all I have is a hunch. I'm finding whatever I can about the Crown of the World."

"So much for the claim that you know everything about Solera." It's unmistakable this time: there's a note of gentle teasing in his voice.

I give him a playful shove. "Shut up and help me search."

"As far as my officers know, I'm asleep in my room." He reaches for a stack of scrolls on a higher shelf and pulls them down. "I'll help however I can."

"Thank you," I say, returning to my study of the page.

It's only then that I realize how out of character those words are—not for Kyla, but for *me*. I always refused help on Earth. It's a trauma response, or so I gather. I never went to therapy, so I never had a psychiatrist tell me what the fuck was wrong with me. I had to get my information from internet memes.

In retrospect, refusal of therapy was probably one of the worst ways I hurt myself, but that's a different story—one Rexa would indubitably dismiss as "boring."

My acceptance of help makes a tiny bud of hope sprout from my desolate soul. Maybe these people are changing me for the better. Maybe I'm changing on my own, because I want to.

That's the single most important factor in changing. It doesn't come accidentally, it comes through intention. You have to work at it every minute of every day. I was too tired to try on Earth, but here— even though I'm dying—I feel powerful enough to do the things I couldn't do back home.

Valen and I emerge from the stacks into the library's central corridor, where stand long, narrow tables with cushioned seats. Asher's there, dozing with his head on a thick book.

I shake my own head fondly and take a seat a little ways away so as not to disturb his rest. He has enough on his plate with his ambassadorial duties. Zalor's decree sent every Eldrian species into a tizzy, and Asher's been putting out fires ever since.

Valen slides into a chair opposite me and arranges his scrolls on the table between us, unrolling one about arcane magic. Rexa emerges from another row of shelves and flings herself into a seat, still muttering about how she'd rather fight than study.

As I settle in for a long reading session, the aroma of the ancient pages wafts up to me, soothing my nerves and focusing my thoughts. Leaning down, I press my nose against the book and breathe in the familiar, wonderful scent. When I straighten, I notice Valen eyeing me.

"Can't help myself," I mutter. "It's one of my favorite smells."

He dips his head in understanding—and if I'm not mistaken, he's hiding the faintest trace of a smile.

After an hour of perusing books and scrolls, I open a tome of ancient history that contains lore forgotten and buried in the annals of Soleran time. Excitement growing, I find a section on the Crown of the World.

"This book confirms it," I whisper, scanning the page. "According to this, you can absorb the magical essence of one of the twelve monoliths—"

"We know. That's how Zalor got his power," says Rexa.

"—you can *return* a stolen essence to its monolith by connecting it with a power that is its equal and opposite. That's how we defeat him."

"We'd need lightmagic," says Valen.

"Which we don't have at our disposal," says Rexa. "The dragons refuse to fight."

"Dragons are the only creatures who *wield* lightmagic, but there are other things in this world that exude natural light," I say. "There are bioluminescent animals and plants, like starmoss."

"Yeah, let's throw some starmoss at Zalor. That'll show him."

"We'd have to throw it at the monolith," I tell Rexa, though I see her point. Starmoss does not strike me as an epic weapon, or even a useful one. "If we find something with enough inherent light, we can use it to sever Zalor's connection to darkmagic. He'll lose control over all his shadowbeasts and become mortal once more. We can kill him and end the war."

Across from me, Valen taps his chin. "What about a unicorn horn?"

"Ooh." My eyes widen. "That might be perfect."

"Unicorns were hunted to the brink of extinction for precisely this reason: dumb humans coveted their horns for selfish purposes," says Rexa. "There hasn't been a unicorn sighting in centuries. Good luck finding one before Zalor wipes us out."

"We need no luck," I say. "We have an almost-omniscient author and an animal telepath in our squad."

Her eyes widen, too, then narrow. "I won't use my power to kill an innocent creature."

"Good gods, we won't *kill* it. You'll ask for its cooperation. I'm not a monster," I add, though my gut twists in protest of those words, sensing a deep-rooted lie.

Rexa quirks a lopsided smile. "Fair enough."

"It's at least five-thousand miles from here to the Crown of the World," says Valen, "plus however far to find a unicorn. We'll need to leave immediately."

His words are a stark reminder of what I'm up against. My soul is dying, and we don't know what will happen if it perishes. My heart thuds. It feels like the ticking of a clock as I inch toward a deadline.

Deadline. Hah. I might not have come up with my book ideas, but at least I know I'm a wordsmith at heart.

"I'll call a war council at dawn and inform the officers of our plans." Valen reaches for his stack of scrolls at the same time as I grab one. Our fingers brush. Though it's hardly the first time we've touched, an inferno ignites within me.

"Sorry," I say, yanking my hand back.

No. Idiot. Why'd I have to open my mouth and make things awkward? At least the reddish hue of the night orbs will mask my blush.

I rise and gather a few scrolls into my arms, refusing to look at Valen. I do, however, make the mistake of catching Rexa's eye. She wiggles her brows suggestively. I'm torn between wanting to laugh and wanting to bury my head in sand. Turning on my heel, I hurry into the stacks to return the scrolls.

To my dismay, Rexa snakes around the table, following me. "You know, you're just like Kyla," she says in an undertone. "Not as subtle about Valen as you think."

I tense as I slide a scroll onto the shelf whence it came. I am utterly unprepared to deal with this level of drama. Flustered, I hurry off down the row of books. "There's nothing going on between Valen and me."

"For everyone's sake, you better keep it that way."

My scalp prickles. I'd think she was threatening me, except her voice is soft, and holds no trace of malice. It's odd enough to make me pause and glance over my shoulder, but Rexa's already gone. Vanished without a sound. Shaking myself, I turn the bookshelf corner.

And run straight into Valen.

"Need help?" he asks.

"I—I'm fine."

I'm not fine. Did he hear what we were whispering about? Has he noticed whatever Rexa saw that prompted her to confront me? I turn away from him, facing the stacks.

"Let me," he says softly, taking the scrolls as I stand on tiptoe, attempting to reach the shelf where they reside.

I'm short of breath, but it has nothing to do with my persistent symptoms of encroaching soul-death. I have no idea what I want to say, what I *should* say. This is a problem I'm intimately familiar with on Earth. I'll go nonverbal when faced with overwhelming negative stimuli. Though Valen's presence is in no way negative, my brain's sounding an alarm.

I hate talking. I hate stringing sentences together on the spot. That's why I'm a writer. I can formulate prose when given enough time to think about it, but a one-on-one conversation always spells disaster.

"Keep that," I blurt, pointing. "It had useful information and maps."

"Good thinking." Valen hands it to me and I clutch it against my chest, holding it over my thudding heart. Without another word, I slip out of the stacks in time to see Rexa give Asher a friendly punch on the shoulder, jolting him awake.

The four of us leave the library, moving in a tight-knit pack, speaking of schemes and strategies. I walk on the fringe of the group, staring determinedly at my feet. I feel exposed, like all eyes are on me.

Rexa is the first to peel off, entering her chambers with whispered assurances that she'll meet us at dawn. Asher follows soon after, since his palace guest room is a few doors down from hers.

That leaves Valen and me together. Alone. In the shadows.

His room is up ahead. Mine's around the corner. I force myself to remain calm as we approach his door. My sluggish heartbeat and constant coldness are banished to mere memories, for Valen walks past his room without hesitation. I pace at his side, my pulse thundering in my ears, my body a furnace.

This has never happened before—no, not even on Earth. I have no idea what to do. I'm reduced to a childlike state, caught in an adult situation I recognize but don't understand. Rexa's earlier warning is shunted to the back of my mind, forgotten. I can only focus on Valen, hyper-aware of the space shrinking between us with each step I take.

What should I say? For the time has come when I absolutely must say something. Yet again, I'm torn. Should I let this unfold in the name of science, or nip it in the bud?

"It's dark," is the brilliant witticism I land on.

"It's late," Valen says as we stop in front of my door. As in the library, the day lights in the halls of the Imperial Palace have dimmed. There are no infrared orbs here, but the shadows are enough (I hope) to conceal my flaming cheeks.

I can't bring myself to look at him. If I meet his eyes, everything will become impossibly difficult and devastatingly terrifying. I never expected I'd feel like this on Solera. The planets in this solar system have aligned to push me over the edge.

I don't know this story. I don't even know this genre. My brain stutters like a car engine that won't turn over, frantically trying to figure out what the dialogue should be. I'm paralyzed, torn between two worlds, two identities, two *realities*.

What I want…and what I am.

"Sleep well, Kyla. We'll need our strength."

I choke on a half-formed word and jerk my head up to find Valen retreating down the hall.

The heat flees, leaving me shivering. My heart's still racing, but now it aches too, throbbing with familiar emptiness. With longing.

A rush of Earth memories floods through me, unbidden. People together, happy and laughing, full of love and life. I don't remember their names—I barely remember their faces, and they appear as ghostly smudges in my vision—but I remember envying their love. Wanting what they had. Knowing I'd never have it.

Yet here it is, at the tips of my fingers. Within my grasp, but just out of my reach. If only I could *communicate* like a functional human being—

"Thanks." I force the single syllable out. It's all I can manage. The sound hangs in the air, and I wish I hadn't spoken at all.

"Until tomorrow," says Valen, inclining his head. With a whisper of his cloak, he vanishes around the corner.

I close my eyes and lean my brow against the cold, smooth door. My growing disappointment is eclipsed only by a massive sense of relief. I grasp at the memories that flashed through my mind, but the moment I touch them to reexamine them, they evaporate.

At least now I know why I'm losing my Earth memories. It's because my Earth soul is dying. As I weaken, so does my connection to the past.

Exhaustion slams into me, sudden and crushing. I open the door and trudge to my bed.

Nothing can happen, I remind myself. It wouldn't be fair to me, and it certainly wouldn't be fair to Valen—and I'm unequipped to consider how unfair it would be to the absent Kyla Starblade, whose life I've worn like a second skin these past two weeks.

The fundamental differences between her and me have never been so starkly illuminated. I can't remember much of Earth, but I know one thing for certain: I am not her.

If I allow myself to lose sight of that distinction, I'm afraid it will mean disaster for us all.

15

THE MORNING SUN PAINTS the eastern cliffs of the Midgardian Mountains with rosy light. I toe the line at the edge of a precipice, quivering with untapped potential, ready to take the plunge.

I feel lighter, younger, like a kid on Halloween. Halloween, of course, was far better than Christmas. Fantastical costumes, spooky décor, free candy. Even in my older years I loved it. When I grew up, Halloween was still Halloween, but Christmas became a barbed reminder of how alone I was.

"You have your assignments," says Valen, addressing the generals who've come to see us off. "Until we return, defending the imperial city and our reclaimed territories is top priority."

I won't say he's a natural leader, since he was forced into military life, but he *is* good. He's trained himself to be confident. He's worn his mask so long that it's become his truth.

"General Praxus has command," he continues, gesturing the older man forward.

Praxus threw a fit when we woke him at the crack of dawn to inform him of our journey, but he became considerably more amenable to the idea once Valen informed him of his temporary promotion.

Valen pins a band of color to the acting commander-general's sleeve: a distinction of his new rank. The other officers salute.

"Speed and safety to you," says Praxus, his russet eyes sweeping our party. "I wish you'd reconsider adding a protective unit."

"Bringing more people would attract unwanted attention as we move," I tell him. "We can't teleport, because no one knows where the

Crown of the World is."

Not even the dragons know its location. No creature on the mainland has stepped foot on Xintra, the northern ice continent, in centuries.

"You could teleport to the Galvian coast," he retorts. "You'd avoid crossing Shadow-occupied territory, and time is of the essence."

Well shit. Enthralled by the prospect of an epic quest, I neglected to prepare a better argument in the event of pushback. Of *course* Praxus has found a hole in my plot. No one knows we're hunting for a unicorn. They think Kyla's going to sever Zalor's connection to the Monolith of Darkmagic herself.

Thank the gods Valen's done his homework.

"Teleporting to any occupied region without a reconnaissance mission would be tantamount to suicide," he informs Praxus in his frostiest voice. "The Lightbringer will conceal us with illusions in enemy territory, and we'll determine strategic teleportation points along the way based on shadowtroop activity. These smaller hops will conserve her power for crossing the Shifting Sea."

Be still, my heart. A flawless excuse.

"It will add a few days to our journey," says Valen, "but I won't risk sloppy operations when we have a chance to end the war in one blow."

I exhale a slow, controlled breath of relief when Praxus concedes. He bows his head and steps back, giving us space.

"Good luck, Lightbringer," he says in clipped tones. "I hope the next time we meet, Zalor will be vanquished."

"Same," I mutter.

Brief farewells commence. Asher bids a tender goodbye to his long-time partner, Baelan. Baelan is a hulking, broad-shouldered elf, a lieutenant-general of the Southern Division. He's got a brutal reputation as a warrior, but he's gentle as a lamb with Asher.

A guilty pang of regret spears me as they embrace. The war has kept them apart more often than not. Plus, my problematic presence has dominated Asher's time, preventing him from enjoying the few moments he might otherwise have with Baelan.

Rexa, who's in gryphon form, telepathically confers with a congregation of animals both magical and mundane, from phoenixes and sylphs to mice and sparrows. She's surrounded by friends, but there's a heaviness to her movements, so subtle you'd miss it if you didn't know to look for it. No one in our group knows about her broken past, but at times like this, I can glimpse the loss lurking in her eyes.

When Zalor rose to power, he wiped out her colony, killing every shapeshifter in Eldria. Rexa's the only one who escaped the genocide. That's why she joined the Mortal Alliance, why she fights with such ferocity.

As for me, there are no farewells to dispense. While Kyla's not nearly as antisocial as I am, she's selected her inner circle with fastidious care. All her loved ones are here on this cliff.

Asher grips Baelan's scaly hands and whispers, "We'll be home and the war will be won before you know it."

The elf's golden eyes soften, and the two lean in to share one final kiss. Then Asher breaks away and comes to stand by my side.

"Maybe you shouldn't come," I murmur.

He shoots me a sidelong glare. "Why? Because I don't wield battle magic?"

"If that were the judging criteria, I'd be out," I say dryly. Growing serious, I nod toward Baelan. "You're the only one who has family here. You have something to lose if things go wrong."

"It's for precisely that reason I've decided to come. I won't let Zalor hurt the people I love. Plus," he adds, bumping my shoulder with his, "you're my family, too."

"*Kyla* is your family."

"Semantics," he says mildly.

I duck my head to hide my smile. Good old Asher.

Rexa ruffles her feathers and crouches, inviting him onto her back, and Cendrion does the same for me. I clamber up with as much grace as I can muster in my sleep-deprived, perma-cold state.

Valen approaches, joining me. My stomach and heart perform their predictable acrobatics. I should have realized this was coming. Even as a gryphon, Rexa is too small to carry two passengers. She can change her size, but larger shifts burn far more energy. On a quest such as this, we must conserve energy for when we need it.

I scoot forward on Cendrion's back, drawing my knees under me and hunching in the hollow between his wing joints. Valen now has plenty of room to sit behind me without touching, keeping up our appearances for the generals' sake.

He didn't have to come. By all rights, he *shouldn't* come. It would be better for him to remain at the helm of his army, especially after the recent clash with Zalor. But he insisted on joining us, and I didn't have the heart to say no.

Cendrion's muscles tense. His wings snap out, creating miniature dust tornadoes on the ground. He crouches, then springs forth, arcing over the cliff. I grasp one of his pearly neck spikes as we dive, reaching back with my free hand to steady Valen.

We level and shoot out over the emerald hills of Lenkha, the southeastern kingdom of the Eldrian Empire. Farmlands—diminished by the war but not destroyed—glimmer golden in the south, faint in the mid-morning haze. A shimmering band of blue snakes across the horizon like a giant serpent wending its way through valleys: the Sayrune River.

An ethereal cry echoes behind us. I look over my shoulder to see four brilliant, fiery-plumed forms rise to our level. Fyr'thal has come to grace our departure with a phoenix guard of honor.

I catch Valen's eye and realize I'm grinning like a fool. It's supposed to be a somber occasion. I know we may be flying to our doom, but I can't help it—I burst out laughing.

Valen smiles back, and it's not one of his almost-smiles. It's full and unreserved, and it changes everything. He's not old—twenty-six by this point in the books—but the grin lends a glowing youthfulness to his features.

"I should take this more seriously, huh?" I ask him.

"In a world darkened by shadow, it's refreshing to see such brightness."

His words were meant to be bracing, but they're sobering. I know this can't last forever. My days are numbered. One way or another, I'll be leaving soon. Returning home.

Unless my soul dies first.

The coldness reclaims me, and I look away from Valen. I lift a hand and let it hover, held aloft by the pressure of the air rushing past. Thoughts of home are bittersweet. Am I a terrible person for not thinking of the Earthlings more? How can I, when memories are slipping from my grasp like the thin trails of misty condensation flaring from my fingers?

I miss them.

That's a true thought, but it coexists with another that is equally true: I was lonely on Earth. I'll take credit where credit is due—I built walls around myself—but the people who claimed to care about me were not blameless in my suffering. None of them cared *enough* to tear those walls down.

Yeah, pretty sure these thoughts put me solidly in the "terrible person" camp. They make me a very unlikable female protagonist.

"Which way?" Cendrion calls.

"Due north," I reply. He banks left, heading into the kingdom of Galvia. The wind whispers promises of adventure. I shove aside my cranky musings, surrendering to its call.

No shadowtroop patrols spot us as we fly for hours. The altitude and mist provide good cover, but they also make me unbearably cold. Wind slices at me as Cendrion angles toward a jagged peak in the northeast. My shivering redoubles.

Then strong arms wrap around me. I'm too numb to react as Valen encases me in the folds of his cloak. He pulls me close, pressing me to his sturdy chest, and I melt against him. It might be voltmagic, it might be his natural body heat, but it's like oxygen and sunlight to me.

"Better?" he whispers in my ear.

"Mhmm." I wish I had more time to enjoy this, but we've almost reached our first stop.

It's a mountain lake in the wilderness. Towering shorea trees with sprawling, ridged roots create a tangled lattice near the water. These giants thrive at high altitudes where they soak up moonlight and turn it into magic.

Cendrion tilts and backwings, slowing his descent as he approaches the mossy shore. Rexa comes in for her landing next, skimming across the lake, tilting to let her primary feathers draw furrows through the water. She stretches out her hind legs and settles gracefully, allowing Asher to dismount.

Fyr'thal lands last. The other phoenixes returned to defend Midgard, but he remains. He's the only guard we can trust on this mission of many secrets.

Valen and I disentangle ourselves and dismount, surveying the untouched land. Ancient enchantments keep mortals away from this place, making it a perfect home for elusive creatures. You can only find it if you already know its location. Omniscience is one hell of a drug.

Rexa's gryphon form ripples. Feathers retract into her flesh, dwindling as she resumes her natural shape. I grab my travel pack and dig out her cloak, tossing it to her. She catches it and swings it around her shoulders.

"Were you able to sense anything on the flight?" I ask.

"Not a damn thing."

"That's okay, it was a long shot. The southern wilderness is too close to civilization. You can try again here, in the unicorn's forest." I gesture to the mighty shoreas.

There's no knowing where, precisely, the unicorn might be. Its territory stretches for miles in either direction from this isolated lake. If Rexa had sensed it at any point during our journey, we'd have landed then and there. Since she didn't, this is our best bet.

As night descends, Fyr'thal wields a hearty blaze—smokeless, thanks to his magic, so as not to give away our position. We dig into our rations and I huddle near the warmth.

The fragrances of burning wood and loamy, untouched forest remind me of Earth. Breathing deep, I close my eyes and allow the scents to unlock a torrent of memories I didn't know I still had. Visions tumble through my head: summers spent at day camp, nights roasting s'mores in an illegal firepit in a small Queens backyard, adventures in the forested parks of Long Island. Glimmers of innocence and fun.

There were good moments in my world. I loved all of that. I miss it.

But it wasn't anything quite like *this*.

Stars emerge overhead. The Oldmoon crests the ridge to the north, illuminating the glassy lake. When the Silver Twins rise to join it, their light awakens the magic in the shoreas. In the trees' highest branches, diamond-spun threads of bioluminescence flare along the veins of scabby bark, descending their trunks.

The glowing veins open small pods peppered throughout the leafy limbs. As the pods flower, they emit tiny, sparkling seeds that drift away, caught on gentle night currents. A constellation of natural magic glistens above us. Softly shining galaxies and nebulae coalesce and dissolve as the wind whisks the shorea seeds to new homes.

"Showtime." I tear my gaze from the mesmerizing dance of the starseeds. My friends turn their attention to me as I rise. "According to legend, there's only one surefire way to do this. A young virgin must venture alone into the unicorn's forest and sing to it."

I'd wanted to add the unicorn into my books, but researching specifics was too wild an adventure. For instance, googling "how to find a unicorn" will flood you with information on how to get a threesome going.

Suffice it to say, I abandoned the unicorn storyline—but the scattered tidbits of lore that I did find seeped into Solera's history along the way.

"Uh, problem." Rexa raises her hand. "I'm not a virgin. None of us are."

Yikes, super awkward. I know my friends' histories, but this is one aspect of the world I did not dwell on. The romance in my books was always fade-to-black, and whatever happened on the pages had a strictly PG rating.

"That's a garbage artifact from the stupid patriarchy," I say, waving aside her concerns and hoping my blush will be mistaken for reflected firelight. "If someone is good and pure of heart, the unicorn will come when they call."

She snorts. "You're putting a lot of misplaced trust in me, pal."

"*Goodness* does feel like an imprecise unit of measurement," Valen adds. "I thought we'd have something more concrete to go on."

"You want concrete, you've got it." I take Rexa's hand and pull her forward. It's the first gentle touch we've shared, but she tolerates it. "We have the only animal telepath in Eldria on our side. You have an amazing power, Rexa. You're strong and fierce, and you are good. I know that in my heart, because I know *your* heart."

Rexa's face—so often hard with resolve or anger—softens. "That was sweet enough to give me a gods-damned cavity. Careful, or I'll start to think you're flirting."

"I don't know how to flirt," I reply matter-of-factly.

"You sure?" she says in a suggestive undertone, wiggling her brows as she releases my fingers. Her catlike eyes glint yellow as they flick toward Valen and back to me.

"Very sure." I want to make that point clear. I haven't forgotten our little conversation in the library.

"That's what Kyla said, too." She grabs my arm and pulls me along as she trots toward the midnight gloom of the shoreas. "You want my advice?"

Advice is preferable to threats, so I nod.

"This situation is messy enough without romance complicating things."

"I happen to agree." It's Love Triangle meets Invasion of the Body Snatchers, and I am way out of my genre element.

"Someone's going to get hurt," she says. "Probably Kyla, maybe Valen, and *definitely* you. So watch your step."

"Gosh Rexa, I never knew you cared."

"This doesn't mean I like you," she says in an airy voice, leaving me at the edge of the low-hanging boughs. Before she vanishes into the forest, she glances over her shoulder and says, "But I owe you for saving Asher."

For a moment, the cold that's settled in my bones is replaced with tingling warmth. I smile after her, retreating to the fire to stand watch with my friends.

We wait between the shining forest and mirrored lake for two hours as Rexa works alone. Everyone else is tense, ready to surge into the trees at any sign of distress—but in my silent vigil, I've found a strange peace. I trust Rexa to do what needs to be done. And if I'm not mistaken, she might be learning to trust me. The closeness we shared, however brief, reminds me of something. Someone. Someone whose name and face I can't recall, but whose unseen presence in the shadows of my soul keeps me warm.

While admiring the moons above, the forgotten moon of my home planet rises in my memory. A distant echo of guilt—or is it sorrow?—reverberates in my heart. I'm not too proud to admit that Earth was beautiful in its own way.

No, I take that back. I'm way too proud. I'd never admit it aloud, but I can admit it to myself in the privacy of my mind.

When I return, maybe I should focus less on the drama of publishing and contracts and revisions. Maybe I should return to my roots, the real reason I started writing.

I bled my soul onto my pages—bled too much of it, which perhaps is part of the reason I became entangled with Kyla and ended up here. I spilled my innermost truths in black ink on perfect-bound cream paper, hoping to say something that *meant* something to someone, somewhere. Hoping to find connections through my words.

Before I sink too far into my muddy memories of Earth, eldritch light spills through the tangle of shorea branches. Rexa's returned from her sojourn. And behind her, emerging from the forest, a creature strolls out of legend and into reality.

The unicorn walks on long, willowy legs. Its cloud-spun mane floats on the air. Its pale, glossy hide is alight with shards of gold and silver, fire and stars. The shining horn on its brow is nearly three feet long, tapering to a diamond point. It floods our surroundings with soft brilliance.

The unicorn's effortless beauty steals my breath. It stops at the edge of the trees, but Rexa continues, returning to us. My friends clump together in silence, awestruck.

"Good news is, I found the unicorn," Rexa says unnecessarily.

"Bad news is, before it agrees to help, it wants to pass judgment. Too many humans have stolen unicorn horns for evil. I passed the test, but all of you must, too."

"No problem," I say, certain my darlings will pass with flying colors.

"The test is a little off-putting," Rexa warns us. "It seems dangerous, but no harm will come of it. Unless you're found unworthy, in which case you're out of luck."

Doubt trickles in, dampening my confidence. My darlings are worthy—of that there's no question. I, on the other hand, am a walking dumpster fire.

"I'll go first." I step forward. If something goes wrong in this phase of the plan, it'll go wrong because of me. As I pass her, Rexa slugs me on the shoulder. "Ow!"

"Just be yourself," she says, "and you'll be fine."

Being myself is what I'm afraid of. *Kyla* is the hero, not me. I can pretend to be good and brave all day long, and without magic in my soul, no telepaths can see the awful, incriminating truth. Pretending is one thing I'm good at. I did it for years on Earth. Hell, I've even fooled Rexa.

Somehow, I doubt my veil of lies will withstand the unicorn's test.

It plods forward on delicate cloven hooves, meeting me halfway between the trees and lake. My footsteps are leaden. I feel like this is my walk to the gallows. If I ruin this like I've ruined everything else in my life, what will become of the quest? Of Solera?

Of *me*?

The unicorn's iridescent eyes fix on mine. An aura of timelessness shimmers within those indigo orbs. It dips its narrow muzzle with excruciating slowness, a drawn-out drop of the headsman's ax.

I stay the course, because failure is not an option. The diamond point of the unicorn's horn comes to rest over my anxious, racing, unworthy heart.

We stand for a moment, an eternity, creatures of light and darkness facing off.

Then the horn pierces my chest.

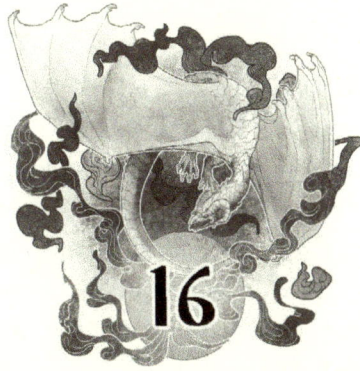

16

THERE'S NO PAIN WHEN the shining horn punctures me. My chest heaves as I draw labored, fearful breaths, but the horn continues its inexorable motion toward my core.

Let me see into your heart.

A shuddering gasp breaks from my lips. The unicorn's disembodied voice echoes inside me, rippling from my heart to my brain like waves on the surface of a still pond.

Do you want my magic for selfish reasons? the unicorn asks.

No, I think, because I can't summon the strength to speak. The horn connects us, transmitting my reply. Threads of light pulse in the spiral crevices of the bony protrusion, like neurons firing electrical impulses. *I want your magic so I can save my friends.*

Why do you want to save them?

My heart roars a staccato song in my ears, hammering as it tries in vain to flee the horn that thirsts for it. This strikes me as a stupid question with an obvious answer, but I suspect saying as much will not help my chances. *Because I love them.*

Solera fades around us, colors bleeding together and twisting in a cyclone of light and magic. I close my eyes against the visual stimuli, but the storm rages on behind my closed lids. It's a vision of Asher and Rexa. Wistful fondness throbs in my chest, creating pressure around the embedded horn.

If I save them, if I do this one good thing . . . maybe I can make up for all the not-good things I've done in my life.

So you seek to atone for your sins, the unicorn concludes. *What did you do that requires redemption?*

The vision of Asher and Rexa sharpens, distracting me from my defense. We're laughing and chatting, clustered around my computer, streaming a cheesy 80s animated flick.

Wait. That's not right. This isn't a vision. It's a memory, more distinct than anything I've experienced since coming to this world. That's Earth I'm seeing. My Earthling best friend, my cousin, and me. The unicorn has dredged my deepest desires from my soul, manifested them before my eyes.

The vision shifts, and my ghostly Earth-self is no longer laughing. She's withdrawn, guarded. When she smiles it pains me, because I see emptiness where there should be emotion. When she laughs it makes my flesh prickle, because I hear how fake it sounds.

She walks away from them, the only people in her life, and when they call after her, she doesn't look back. A heaping portion of happiness served to her on a silver platter, yet she can't taste it. An echo of long-lost contentment lingers on her tongue, turning to ash.

I don't know what I did, I confess to the unicorn. *All I know is I did everything wrong.*

I exorcised friends and family from my life, isolating myself and forgetting them. It was my fault. I failed them. Things fell apart.

I *allowed* things to fall apart.

Revulsion billows from my gut, swarming around the horn and burning my throat. I hate her, that girl. I hate the fact that she walked away from everything. And I know, I *know* she was tired—too tired to try—but seeing her like this, watching her ruin things when the solution seems so glaringly obvious, I want to throttle her.

She wasn't worthy of her Earthling friends then, and I remain unworthy to this day. I hope the horn lacerates my galloping heart. I hope my most foolish, most vital organ shreds itself to pieces on the unicorn's test.

I see conflict in you, says the unicorn. *Darkness and light at war.*

No shit. Though I try to keep this particular thought to myself, I get a sense the unicorn has heard. Oh well. RIP me.

The ripples of your fate will spread across the sea to touch far distant shores. The threads of your life are interwoven with those around you, in this universe and the next, in patterns you can never comprehend. The unicorn's voice is a mere whisper in my head. *Go then, and save your world.*

As quickly as the vision appeared, it vanishes. Gone is that empty ghost of a girl, snuffed out in a hurricane of shadow and light. The vision's colors whirl together, like water down a drain, and disappear from view.

I find myself trembling in Kyla's body before the unicorn. Our connection is broken—it's already moving on to its next victim, its indigo eyes fixed on Cendrion. My fingers fly to my chest, but there's no wound. Not even a tear in the fabric of my shirt.

"Kyla?"

I whirl and face my friends. They're watching me, tense and expectant.

"I guess I passed, right?" I ask, glancing at Rexa. She grins and gives me two scaly thumbs up.

"How was it?" Cendrion asks, bracing for impact as the unicorn advances on him. The subtle crinkling of his snout suggests he's afraid.

"Not bad." Though my voice is steady, my innards quake with the aftershocks of stressful conflict. The memory I glimpsed during my internal conversation dangles by threads too weak to support its weight. It falls away from me, like a dream that dissolves upon waking.

The unicorn's horn pierces Cendrion's armored chest with the ease of a warm knife sliding through butter. His eyes snap to mine, and a jolt of emotion ricochets between us.

How will the unicorn's light react to Cendrion's inherent darkness?

Yet no sooner has the horn pierced Cendrion than it retracts without leaving a mark. The dragon's taut muscles slacken with relief. He and I share a tiny nod. Regret sparkles in his moon-bright gaze. Though I long to ask what the disembodied voice whispered in his mind, I keep my mouth shut. It's bad enough we were forced to confront ourselves once; I won't make him relive his visions a second time.

Thrice more the unicorn repeats the process, on Valen, then Fyr'thal, then Asher. By the time the creature pierces his flesh, I'm sure we've won—until it tosses its maned head violently. Its horn snaps in two, half remaining on the creature's brow, half lodged in Asher's heart.

"NO!" I lunge toward my friend, terror exploding through every nerve and synapse.

But Asher calmly lifts his hands, grasps the broken horn, and pulls it from his chest. He, too, remains unblemished from his ordeal.

The unicorn dips its head, its half-horn glinting: a silent blessing for our quest. Then it canters toward the forest, dissolving into the night.

"We have our weapon," Asher whispers.

Shaking with nerves, I stare at the broken horn held flat on his palms. It shines less brightly now that it's no longer attached to its owner, but still it shines. Sparkling molecules of natural light dance across its translucent surface.

I reach out and run my thumb along the jagged edge, the place where the horn snapped. To my horror, its bioluminescence dims. The edge flakes beneath my fingers, tiny pieces crumbling into platinum dust.

I yank my hand back. The horn's glow returns once I'm gone, but it's fainter.

"What the blood just happened?" says Rexa. She looks at me for answers, but I'm as shocked as she is.

"The horn's fragile on its own," says Asher. "I can craft something to stabilize it, but I'd need the right materials to work with. The earth elements on this mountain aren't ideal."

"We're headed somewhere that might have useful supplies." My voice is low and tremulous. "The Sky Archipelago."

"Will it survive the journey?" asks Rexa, nodding at the horn.

"It will." Asher's voice is filled with quiet confidence. "It's resilient, it just needs some support and a gentle touch."

He raises his eyes from the horn and gazes at us, smiling. "We're halfway there."

Asher's optimism is bracing, but we are absolutely *not* halfway there. We're not even halfway to the Galvian coast.

We rest for a few short hours and set out at dawn, forging north. For three days we fly, zigzagging between Shadow-occupied cities to steer clear of our enemy. I don't need the map in the book I "borrowed" from the Imperial Library to tell me what places to avoid—I know the geography of Eldria inside and out.

The mountains fade into a tiered landscape of elevated steppes and sunken forests. It should be gorgeous, but the farther north we press, the more the land withers.

"It's the Shadow Lord's poison," Cendrion growls when we make camp on our fourth night.

We've stopped on the outskirts of a deserted town where the earth has sickened. Pitch-black splotches stain the ground. Withered plants dot the clearing where we've hidden. Desiccated corpses of small things, tucked into dusty corners where they crawled away to die before their time, fester in the shadows. A faint breeze stirs the morbid glade, wafting the scent of decay toward me. Once the putrid taste is in my mouth, I can't get rid of it.

Something about this doesn't feel right. Zalor's power is deadly, yes—but this destruction, mindless and random, isn't how darkmagic works. Whatever did this, it's darker than darkmagic. More sinister.

It almost feels like a *lack* of magic is making this place die.

I cast that notion aside. There are plenty of things about Solera that I don't know. I'm not the omniscient god I believed I was. Zalor is the Big Bad, the ultimate villain. It wouldn't make sense to introduce something worse than him so late in the game.

Our fifth day of travel dawns, blustery and cold. Valen's forced to hold me close on the flight to keep me warm, and I thaw at his touch.

In the late afternoon, he whispers, "Tell me about your world."

"*My* world?" I twist on Cendrion's back to give him a skeptical look. "Why would you want to hear about Earth?"

"I'd love to have a firsthand account of an alien planet. The fact that there's other intelligent life in some far corner of our multiverse has staggering scientific implications."

Of course. Ever the scholar.

"I d-don't remember much." A shiver runs through me. It's not because I'm freezing—it's because when I try to summon memories of Earth, nothing comes. It's one big, dark blank. "And there's not much to tell."

"A friendly tip: saying 'there's not much to tell' makes for a poor story. I'd think a professional author would be more inventive."

I shake my head at the gentle teasing and lean into his warmth. Closing my eyes, I try to summon something, anything, from the darkness. At first, nothing happens. I seek an anchor, a lifeline in the vast vacuum of my mind. With agonizing slowness, I unearth the forgotten foundations of my identity.

"I had friends," I murmur.

"Did you?"

I elbow him and he laughs. "Yes. When I thought Solera was something I'd made up, I based my characters on them. There was..."

I struggle to think of the name, willing the information to come to me. It's like a dream, a dream I once knew by heart. And if I'm lucid, I can control the dream.

Focus. Think. Remember.

"Eric." The word is a whisper, borne away on the biting wind. "He was my best friend. We grew up believing in magic together. I always felt safe with him because—"

I falter, and we fly in silence for a few moments. Valen doesn't push me.

"Earth wasn't as accepting as Solera," I finish at last, skirting the edge of memories I'm not willing to examine, truths I'm not ready to tell. "He and I were different. He knew it long before I did, but that's why I latched onto him. We were different in a similar sort of way. Other people didn't understand me, but he always did."

"He sounds a bit like Asher."

I embrace the recovered memory of my Earthling friend, welcoming it home. "He is. We lived in a cruel world, but Eric never let it break him."

"What of your family?"

"Oh, I was kinda the black sheep of my family. That's why I clung to—"

To who? My stomach drops. Who was the mysterious, warm presence Rexa reminds me of? Her name's on the tip of my tongue, but her memory hovers just beyond reach. I focus on the idea of her, trying to sharpen it.

"M-my cousin," I finish lamely, unable to grasp more than that. "She was Rexa's inspiration. We partied hard when we were young. Got into lots of trouble."

Though I can't remember my cousin's name, I remember our antics. She used to drag me into all sorts of unexpected adventures. She's the one who introduced me to nightclubs. It was there that I discovered tequila made the world—and most of its inhabitants—tolerable.

"She was the only family who understood me," I conclude, "but we drifted apart."

Valen's arms tighten around me. I absorb the silent offer of comfort.

"I loved my parents, but I couldn't tell them anything. Every time I tried to open a door, it was slammed in my face. But what can you expect from a couple of Boomers?"

"*Boomers.* Were they firemagic wielders?"

That's enough to elicit a belly laugh from me. The sound of such a peak-Earth word in his mouth is as ridiculous as it is strangely endearing.

"No firemagic on Earth, but there were fire*works*. Watching fireworks from the FDR Drive on July Fourth? That was something. And there were smartphones and airplanes and nanotech, stuff Solerans would consider magical. Pretty amazing, when you think about it."

"Is that a hint of homesickness I detect?"

"Not homesickness, but maybe . . . regret. I'm sorry I took certain things and people for granted. I wish I could tell them how sorry I am."

I miss my friends. I miss my family. I miss the mountains of upstate New York and the feel of a crisp spring breeze bearing the promise of a lush summer. I miss bumblebees and popcorn and roller coasters and driving on empty highways.

"Given your descriptions," Valen begins, "I'd say you and Kyla aren't the only linked souls. If Earth and Solera exist in parallel universes, it would mean Asher is linked to your Eric, and Rexa to your cousin."

I hadn't thought of it that way, but now that he's pointed it out, it makes sense. "That's how the multiverse works, right?"

"It's one theory," he says. "If only we had time to run experiments on the nature of your quantum-magical entanglement with this world. What if we discovered a method of controlling this soul-phasing phenomenon, allowing people to cross between universes at will?"

"That would be amazing," I whisper. "With the technology of Earth and the magic of Solera, I don't think there's anything we *couldn't* do."

We lapse into a comfortable silence, each of us absorbed in private fantasies. If only such a thing were possible. I'd have the best of both worlds—figuratively and literally.

"Who am I based on?" Valen asks after a while. His would-be casual tone delights me.

"No one. I imagined you, or so I thought. I made you unrealistic. Perfect. Someone I could trust and lo—"

Too late, I clamp my mouth shut. If I say that aloud, I shudder to think how it'll complicate things. Before Valen can reply, Cendrion angles down and we pitch forward on his back.

"What's wrong?" I call to the dragon. But as we descend from the cloud cover, I see what's wrong.

We've reached the Shifting Sea.

High above the turbulent water, floating islands dot the heavens, trailing wisps of vines as they drift lazily through the evening mist. My breath hitches at the dark beauty of the seascape, though my stomach twists at the thought of traversing the next thousand miles.

The waters beyond Eldria are notoriously dangerous. Wreckage dots the shoreline, poking through the waves: flotsam and jetsam of unfortunate watercraft and airships. No mortal has ever returned from the passage to Xintra.

Rexa, a wyvern today, banks close to Cendrion as we descend. Fyr'thal does the same. A swath of thick cloud obscures our group, masking us from prying eyes, and Cendrion wields us into shadow.

Darkmagic twines into the molecules of my body, turning me incorporeal. With sensation mercifully absent in my shadow-form, I'm no longer cold. I float in nothingness, content to drift.

We coalesce on a tempestuous coast. Ocean wind buffets us. Pewter-gray waves three meters tall crash against pillar-like rocks that jut from the water. We're halfway up a coastal cliff, but icy spray drifts up to us, landing on my exposed skin. The chilling contact chases away all vestiges of my lingering warmth from Valen.

Cendrion has brought us to the mouth of a cave in the sheer rock wall. Beside him, Rexa lands and Asher slides from her back. A bundle of fabric rests in his arms: our unicorn horn, swaddled in cushioning.

"This feels perfect," he says, crouching to place a hand against the damp ground. "I sense lots of pure earth elements in these rocks. Iron, nickel, cobalt... I can craft something powerful with those."

"G-good," I say, my teeth a-chatter once more. I was thinking we'd find materials on the Sky Archipelago, but working on the mainland is preferable. Those islands might *look* like floating Zen gardens, but deadly creatures inhabit them—creatures I'm hoping to avoid.

We enter the cave single-file, following tunnels deep into the cliffs. Here, too, I notice signs of decay: black fissures in the stone, small corpses in the shadows.

It has to be Zalor's doing. What other explanation is there?

The wind no longer reaches us after a few twists and turns, though its ghostly howling trails us as we walk. In a sheltered grotto, we make camp. Fyr'thal wields a fire, creating light for Asher to work.

Kneeling by the flames, Asher unwraps the horn with gentle reverence. Folds of cloth fall away from the crystalline weapon to reveal that its light has dimmed further. Despite that, it flickers with renewed life when he lifts it in one hand.

"How long will this take?" Rexa asks.

"You can't rush art," he says in lofty tones, closing his eyes and placing his free hand flat against the cave floor, fingers splayed.

Rexa huffs in impatience but refrains from pushing him.

Tiny flecks of stone begin to rise from the floor. They glitter in the gloom, drifting toward Asher, drawn by the gravity of his power. Soon a cloud of dancing motes forms around his left hand, the one that holds our fragile hope of victory.

There's nothing I can do until the crafting is complete, so I pull the library book from my travel pack. When I open it to the chapter on the Shifting Sea, the smell of weathered parchment wafts up to me, overpowering the stench of salt and seaweed.

Unable to stop myself, I bury my nose in the center fold, closing my eyes and breathing deep. The familiar bookish smell soothes my nerves.

When I open my eyes, Cendrion and Rexa give me quizzical looks. Valen, however, shoots me the shadow of a wink. My heart swells.

Yeah, he gets it.

"Once we leave the continent," I tell my friends in an undertone, "the main things we'll have to worry about are the moving islands, as they're designed to lure travelers off course; the unending sea storms; the violent water funnels; and the island dwellers looking for easy prey."

"Oh, is that it?" says Rexa.

"There might be more. I don't know everything. As I explore this world, I realize I know less and less."

"Between your knowledge and that book, we'll be fine," Asher says without opening his eyes. "Once the weapon is ready, we'll be unstoppable."

Safe and warm, surrounded by my darlings, I'm tempted to agree with his optimistic outlook. I lean against Cendrion, who's hunkered down behind me, and close my eyes.

In the place between sleep and consciousness, formless thoughts chase each other through my brain. Dreams rise and fall in my head like the crashing waves outside. Dreams of Solera, dreams of Earth. The two worlds blur in my mind until I can't tell what's real anymore, until I can't even tell I'm dreaming.

"Done!"

The shout yanks me from my slumber. Sitting up, I stare through the gloom, half expecting to see my SoHo loft . . . or maybe a dingy Astoria one-bedroom.

I must have been asleep longer than I thought, because the fire has died to flickering embers. Everyone else is lying in a restful state of repose—everyone except Asher.

"By Ohra's talons!" I scramble to my feet, aches and chills forgotten.

Asher has encased the shining horn within four slender metal spirals. It's suspended in a hollow space between twisting alloy rods that taper to a deadly point, like an oversized, ornamental dagger. There's even a hilt and a crossbar.

"You've outdone yourself," I tell Asher, approaching to admire his masterpiece. "What sort of magic keeps the horn suspended like that?"

"Not magic." Asher brandishes the encased horn. "Magnetism. I sensed a mine of magnetite in the back of the cave and crafted the cage with that."

"Brilliant. Pure genius. Zalor won't know what hit him. When we sever his connection to darkmagic . . ." I grin, picturing the epic conclusion to our journey. "Thank you, Ash. I owe you."

"It was my pleasure. Making the battery was a fun challenge, but this? This was *art*." A shadow of pain flits across his face, tempering our moment of triumph. "Maybe when the war's over, I'll go back to being a Crafter."

I bite my lip. Asher was once on track to become a professional artist. He won a scholarship that transplanted him from his tiny hometown of Sythiel, bringing him to the imperial city. Three days after he landed in Midgard to begin his apprenticeship, Lord Zalor struck the first blow of the Shadow War, dashing his dreams.

That's a common theme for my darlings, isn't it?

"I almost forgot what this feels like," Asher murmurs, running his finger along one of the twisting rods. "Doing something just for the love of it. It reminded me of peace."

Guilt oozes in my gut, though I know by now Asher's suffering isn't my fault. Stronger even than the urge to apologize is the urge to comfort him.

"I really thought this would be my life, once," he continues. "A quiet career in the arts."

"It still can be. You're twenty-one. You have your whole life ahead of you."

Asher hitches a smile into place. "That's true. I suppose it just means we have to hurry up and kill Zalor."

He turns the crafted blade, offering it to me hilt-first. I shy away, shaking my head. "I'll make the horn's light go out."

"Nonsense. It's stable now. If anyone should wield this weapon, it's you."

By my reckoning, I'm the least worthy character to be entrusted with it. And the one with the least claim to vengeance. The Shadow Lord ruined my darlings' lives, tore them from their loved ones, destroyed all hope in the world.

Not all of it, I think, staring at my best friend.

Hope may be fragile, but with the right combination of elements, it can become the strongest thing in the universe. I accept the gleaming weapon, and when my hand closes on the hilt, the floating horn flares brighter.

Asher's smile widens. I beam back and pull him into a hug. We stand together, bathed in the light of the coals and the light of the blade, ready for the next adventure.

I'll win this war for you, I promise him silently.

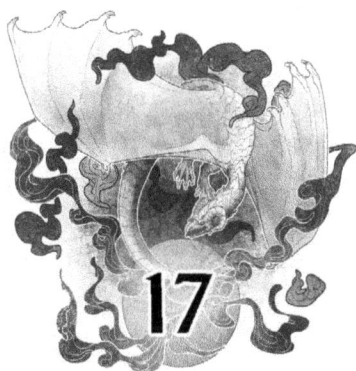

17

THE MORNING OF DEPARTURE is gray and bleak. Damp, desolate cliffs shine like black diamonds. Clouds have massed overhead and fog drifts in greasy strands. The Shifting Sea twists hungrily below, black water eddying around the coastal karsts. The wind is low but persistent, flecking my cheeks with sand and salt, whispering dark promises of what's to come.

A shiver snakes down my spine—not of fear, but of excitement. Crossing this expanse could spell disaster for any of my friends (not to mention magicless me), but this aesthetic of foreboding is just... *chef's kiss*. I couldn't have set the scene better if I'd tried.

"Beautiful morning, isn't it?"

This comes from Asher. I frown—sarcasm isn't his MO—but when I look his way, I see his tan face shining with admiration. He stands beside me inside the mouth of the cave, staring at the windswept horizon with something close to awe.

"You're serious," I say, half questioningly.

"Don't you think this view is stunning?"

"Well, yeah, but I'm kind of a lunatic." Most people would dread the thought of braving such unfavorable conditions. Valen certainly isn't thrilled. He paces the cliff's edge, raising his hand to gauge the direction of the swirling air currents.

Asher chuckles. "I wouldn't say I'm looking forward to the journey, but I appreciate the beauty of this place."

Before I can reply, Rexa returns from her patrol in the form of an arctic tern. As she comes to a fluttering halt, her bird's body ripples and distorts, legs elongating into their usual catlike, chimerical shape. She touches down before Asher and me, her expression grim.

"The coast is *not* clear," Rexa informs us. "A unit of Zalor's troops is approaching from the east."

Asher's face darkens. "What are your orders?"

I blink when I realize he's not looking at Valen, but at me.

"We don't have time to waste." Everyone leans in to hear my commands. I'm hit with a stray vision of Earth, reminded of a cartoonish football huddle-up when I was young, playing with the neighborhood kids at our local park. A smile, wildly inappropriate for the situation at hand, brushes my lips. "Cendrion will have to get us out of sight of the mainland."

"Shouldn't I reserve my magic?" the dragon inquires.

"We're reserving it for emergencies, and I'm pretty sure avoiding shadowtroops counts as an emergency," I say dryly. "If they spot us, we'll have to add Zalor's army to our master list of Things to Worry About."

Cendrion crouches. My nerveless fingers slip over his scales as I try and fail to clamber onto his back. My hands ache from the cold. I flex my digits, trying to force warmth into them. Bad idea. The ache spreads through my tendons into my wrists.

A strong arm snakes around my waist, brushing past the unicorn dagger that hangs at my hip. I look up to find Valen. He and Cendrion exchange a subtle nod, and the dragon flattens himself to the cave floor. Valen effortlessly hefts me into his arms and clambers up Cendrion's extended forepaw.

"I'm fine, I can do it," I insist, though Valen has already settled me in the space between Cendrion's wing joints.

"I know." I love him for the lie. "But we have to hurry."

Rexa transforms again, becoming a snow amphithere—a legless winged serpent. Her sleek design will serve her well for carving through storms, and her fuzzy white coat will keep her and Asher warm.

"R-rings on," I stutter through a jaw quivering with cold. I raise my right hand, where my battery-powered comms device glints.

Asher and Valen don their devices.

A nearly inaudible growl rumbles through Cendrion's body, and Solera fades. I'm looking forward to sinking into the weightlessness of darkmagic and losing all sensation. Unfortunately, when I turn to shadow this time, the cold and pain linger within me. They aren't as sharp as they were. They're more like memories—like they're floating just out of reach, and if I think about them too hard, they'll crash into me.

I do my utmost *not* to think about pain. But of course, thinking about not thinking about it only makes me think about it more. The imagined ache in my hands spreads to my forearms.

I hate my brain.

Then the pain becomes jarringly real. Cold knifes through my chest and my arms burn. With a jolt, I'm solid again. Cendrion wobbles in the air. An indignant squawk from Fyr'thal and a worried warble from Rexa tell me they've re-solidified, too.

"What's wrong?" Valen and Asher both ask. Despite the wailing wind, their voices are clear in my ears thanks to my comms ring. Cendrion tilts his head. Behind his translucent inner membrane, his dark pupil is a thin crescent of shock.

"I was wielding, and suddenly my threads . . . *bent*," he growls. "I don't know how to describe it. I've never felt that before. They twisted, and I lost control, so I dropped my spell."

I stare around. We've drawn level with the smallest outlying islands. They hover in the sky, vines whipping in the wind beneath their jagged, inverted peaks. Their tops bristle with vegetation.

"We're still within sight of the mainland," says Valen, squinting south at the receding shoreline, "but I think—"

Wham! A streak of darkness shoots from overhead and slams into Cendrion's wing. He roars and tumbles in the air. Valen and I are flung into the sky. I flail in free fall, arms screaming in protest as I wave them.

In my panic, my sight narrows. I'm focused on the fast-approaching whitecaps, but I vaguely register shapes materializing around us. Pitch-black shapes. Shadowbeasts.

The breath is knocked out of me as something collides with my rib cage. I writhe in the clutches of whatever foul creature has caught me.

"Relax," comes Cendrion's voice. "It's me."

His forepaws are clasped around my torso. He dives, heading toward the sea. Craning my neck, I can see past his tucked wings. A unit of shadowbeasts tails him—a couple wyverns, a hippogryph, and a few other monsters I can't distinguish, all the inky, hopeless color of death.

"Valen? Asher?" I ask shakily, focusing on reaching them through my comms ring.

"Here," Asher assures me through the ring. "Rexa has us."

I loose a breath of relief. Before I can draw a fresh lungful of air, Cendrion rolls to avoid an attacking shadowbeast. My head whips dangerously.

"Cendrion, turn us to shadow!"

"I can't." He levels out several meters above the ocean and shoots across the churning waves. The answer frightens me more than his death-drop.

"Valen!" I search the skies for him, my poor, bruised neck protesting the movement. "Can you—"

CRACK! A brilliant blue-white light flashes at the corner of my vision. Looks like Valen is two steps ahead of me.

Cendrion banks again, avoiding the grasping claws of a shadowbeast. As he tilts, I glimpse Rexa. High overhead, she has Asher and Valen on her back. Fyr'thal loops around her. Smaller and more agile, he darts back and forth between four shadowbeasts, keeping them away from her lashing tail and leathery wings.

With another thunderous crack, Valen wields voltmagic at his foes. But something's seriously wrong. Though Valen aims at his closest foe—a resurrected harpy, from the looks of it—the electricity curves in a wild, errant arc. It forks toward a tiny floating island and collides with the inverted peak. The rock slope explodes, sending rubble bursting outward.

"I'm losing control of my magic." Valen's low voice hums in my ears.

I can't reply. A gigantic wave crests and spin drift drenches my feet. I gasp with the shock of new cold in my extremities. Cendrion hisses and rises sharply, angling toward a much larger floating landmass.

To my left, Fyr'thal wields a jet of flame against the same harpy shadowbeast. Like the others, his spell goes awry. The fire curves and clips Rexa's wingtip instead of the demon. She jerks in midair and shrieks.

"Everyone stop wielding," I cry. "Look at the shadowbeasts. *They* aren't wielding. They must know something. We're wasting energy, doing more harm than good."

My mind races as I try to put the puzzle pieces together. I can't focus. I'm cold and my body hurts. Some sick, detached part of my writer brain loves the thrill of this chase, but the rational part of me readily admits that this is not fun. I'm not having a good time. I'm in so much pain. *I want to wake up.*

"It's not a dream," I growl through gritted teeth. "This is real. A real world. Real magic system that works in accordance with real laws of nature, and you know all those laws. So *think.*"

Then it hits me. Of course—how could I be so stupid?

"It's the islands! I always imagined they'd be floating on airmagic, but that can't be right. It's *forcemagic.* They're being held aloft by the magical warping of gravitational fields!"

"Are you sure?" says Cendrion.

"Well . . . no, but—"

"Give me a moment and I can confirm it," comes Valen's voice.

Cendrion banks and rises again. He's almost reached the massive floating rock ahead of us. I peer behind him and glimpse a small flash of voltmagic. It forks toward the nearest island.

"I see forcemagic threads," Valen informs us.

I grin. He must have sunk into the deepest part of his magic-source and connected to the core of his power. If a wielder focuses hard enough, they can see magicthreads when they're in that state. They can actually *see* the molecular, magical fabric of reality. What a wonder that must be.

"Forcemagic will reign supreme here," I tell my friends. It makes sense. It's so perfect. We're on a quest to reach the magnetic pole of Solera—of course we'd be entering a minefield of magic alongside it, magic that reflects its biome. That's how it is in every Eldrian territory: the magic of the region defines the region.

"If we want to shake the shadowbeasts," I add, "we'll need to rely on physical attacks."

"I'm on it," says Asher.

An explosion assaults my ears. A fiery plume flares behind us, engulfing one of the shadowbeasts.

I grin again. My cheeks ache, too—the wind and water have turned them to ice. Asher's combustible arrows won't be affected by the magnetic fields of the Sky Archipelago. They're enchanted to explode on impact, but they don't rely on magic to fly.

"Kyla." Valen's voice whispers in my ear. "Have Cendrion fly beneath Rexa and prepare to attack. I'll draw the shadowbeasts to me so we have clean targets."

I clench my frigid jaw against the thousand questions and protestations that bubble in my throat.

"Cendrion, can you double back? Valen's going to try something."

Cendrion whips his lithe form, turning on a dime. The shadowbeast behind him—a pitch-black thunderbird—wasn't expecting so bold a maneuver. Even without magic, Cendrion's a force to be reckoned with. He's a *dragon*, an apex predator, honed to perfection by millions of years of evolution. He lashes out, raking talons across the shadowbeast's neck to land a killing blow.

Of course, this forces Cendrion to drop me.

I hurtle toward the waves, and a midnight-plumed hippogryph darts in. Its black claws close around my legs. Even though I'm dropping toward the sea, I twist madly, trying to break free.

The hippogryph opens its beak, and horrifically, Zalor's voice emerges.

"You can't outrun me," he hisses, speaking through his mind-controlled servant. "You can't escape me. I know who you are, and you aren't strong enough for this."

Though my mind buzzes with panic, a pang of bitter sorrow ricochets through my dying soul. He's right. After everything I've seen and done, I'm still a useless Earthling. No magic, barely any fighting skills.

But I do have an epic weapon.

This might be a mistake, but I'm the reigning queen of mistakes. Rational thought is shoved aside in the face of impending doom. I grasp the unicorn dagger, yanking it from its secure loop on my belt. Bending upwards, I thrust the crafted blade into the hippogryph's avian leg.

My shadowbeast enemy explodes on impact, bursting into a cloud of pitch-black dust. I let out a startled whoop, and choke on a lungful of the ashy particles. I was *not* expecting that. If that's what the dagger does to a shadowbeast, the Monolith of Darkmagic won't stand a chance.

Cendrion races to catch me. He beats his wings, angling beneath me, and I settle on his back.

We level out of the dive and begin another laborious climb. Triumphant though I am after my shadowbeast encounter, I'm shivering uncontrollably, succumbing to the cruel cold. Darkness closes in at the edges of my vision.

No. I can't give up now. Three shadowbeasts remain between Cendrion and Rexa. Another four hound her above, some of whom have shadowmen riders.

I can help. I *must* help. I must do something, because stagnating in the swamp of failure, wallowing in the morass of nothingness, is a fate I can't accept.

I refuse to be the one who kills my darlings.

But my darlings (who are far better at heroism than I could ever hope to be) don't give me the chance to do anything. A fiery explosion erupts in front of Cendrion. Asher has felled a shadowbeast, and the dragon carves through a haze of black demon blood. Flecks impact my cheeks and tongue, smelling like waste, burning like acid. Coughing and spitting, I look up in time to see something that makes my heart stop.

Valen has jumped from Rexa's back. He's hurtling toward the water, and he's drawn the attention of the remaining demons. With a flash of silver, he whips his sword from its scabbard and slashes at the third shadowbeast who'd been pursuing Cendrion. It's a lucky stab. The monster goes limp and drops.

With a smoky explosion, Asher fells another foe. They're easy pickings now that they're in a straight dive toward the Shifting Sea, plunging after Valen. Cendrion angles beneath Valen, ready to catch him.

Then Valen's trajectory shifts. His eyes widen as he curves sideways, away from Cendrion and me.

Cendrion puts on a burst of speed. The push carries him way beyond Valen. He overshoots his mark, speeding toward a massive floating island.

Panting, Cendrion tries to wheel in the air. His muscles strain and bunch beneath me, but his efforts have little effect. We continue to career toward the island. Above us, so does Valen.

"What's happening?" Asher's voice reaches me through the comms ring.

"I don't..." The words die in my throat. Beyond the tufted top and inverted peak of the floating rock, I've glimpsed distortion in the air. Clouds oscillate unnaturally, and as Cendrion skirts the edge of the island, I spot a rising tower of seawater and detritus.

"Water funnel!" I shout. Given the fact that dust, leaves, and chunks of rock orbit the swirling liquid edifice, I'm guessing this isn't merely a weather phenomenon. Forcemagic must be involved—and it's reeling us in.

Cendrion stops fighting the funnel's pull, instead using it to increase his momentum. He reaches out and nabs Valen, who's also been drawn sideways.

Tucking the unicorn dagger in its holster, I lean over Cendrion's shoulder and offer my hand to Valen. He clasps my fingers and hauls himself onto the dragon's back beside me.

"Any ideas on how to get out of this one?" Valen whispers, holding me tight. We crouch together, hunkering against the whipping wind as Cendrion tries and fails to angle his trajectory away from the funnel. It's massive, more than half a mile in diameter. If forcemagic is involved, and we can't wield, I doubt there's anything we can do to escape.

A grating shriek rises above the howl of the seething hurricane. Valen and I look up. Rexa, Fyr'thal, and the rest of the shadowbeasts—two wyverns with shadowmen riders, a gryphon, and another harpy—have also been caught in the relentless magical pull.

Asher draws an arrow, sighting on one of the shadowwyverns, covering Rexa while she strains to break free of the funnel's gravity. He shoots, but the arrow arcs wide of its mark, like our wielding did earlier. It's pulled toward the funnel, faster and faster. I watch as it whips around the edge of the spinning water, lost in a swirl of chaos. Asher yanks out another arrow, and—

"NO!" The scream tears itself from my lips. A stray chunk of flying debris crashes into Rexa, bowling her over in midair. Asher is hurled away from her, careening past the shadowbeasts.

Cendrion launches after him, but we've reached the misty outermost edges of the funnel, and the forcemagic is too strong to resist here. The dragon's wing catches a watery gust, and he, too, spins in the sky. I scrabble against the scales of his neck, desperate for a handhold.

"Don't let go!" Valen cries.

I don't want to let go of him—not now, not ever—but with a nasty lurch, I'm wrenched from his arms.

I vaguely register voices shouting through the comms ring, but I can't discern words over the funnel's roar. Thunder shakes the sky. Stinging gobs of water pelt me like bullets. Head over heels I whirl through the air, caught in the hurricane's rocketing spin.

I'm going to die.

Centrifugal force shoves my blood into my extremities, making my vision go black. Nausea grips me. My body's weightless, light as a feather, yet my head feels like a leaden anchor pulling me down, down into darkness. I thought my withering soul would be the thing to do me in. Looks like nature's beating it to the punch.

I'm going to die.

"Valen . . ." I whisper, but I don't know if the word has reached him. I'm not focusing on transmitting my thoughts through my comms ring. I'm not focusing on *anything*. My brain rattles loosely in my skull, spinning like a top as the funnel absorbs me into its watery walls.

I underestimated the Shifting Sea and its storms. I thought we'd be strong enough to make it through. Now everyone will pay the price for my hubris.

I don't want to die.

That's my final thought before I surrender to oblivion.

18

I'M HAVING A NIGHTMARE AGAIN.

I awake in my drafty Astoria one-bedroom to the dinging of my iPhone. Rolling away from the grimy window, I check my notifications.

> ERIC: Brunch tomorrow at Dante??

I don't want to go to brunch. Apart from having no money, I have no energy to interact with other people. Swaddled in my blankets, I watch the N Train trundling by in the smoggy distance and contemplate how to best let him down.

> ME: Can't tomorrow. Maybe next weekend.

Another ding. I glare at the screen.

> ERIC: What's your excuse this time?

Dull anger flickers. I type a snide response:

> ME: Cause I'm exhausted and depressed, primarily.
> ERIC: That means it's time to leave your room and get some sun.

If one more person tells me I just need to go outside to cure myself, I will douse them with gasoline and light them on fire. The sun doesn't help. Fresh air doesn't make a difference. Nothing I do makes a difference, and I'm tired of *trying*.

But I can't say any of this aloud, not even to my best friend.

Most people are tired, yet they soldier on. They manage to come home from work every day and fight for their dreams. I see them. I envy them. The envy is corrosive, and it festers into impotent hatred.

I look at them and I wonder, *Why not me?*

Why can't I fix my life? It should be easy. This stagnation is my fault. If I tried a little harder—if I tried at *all*—I think I could do it. Hang out with my friends, get a better job, move to a better place, find Prince Charming, start working on my dreams.

The problem is, I can't move. I'm stuck. Detached from my body, unplugged from reality. I think to myself, over and over, *Get up. You must get up.*

But I can't. A void grows inside me, expanding through the depths of my soul. The emptiness is worse than the anxiety. Far worse. At least when anxiety comes upon me, I feel something. When the shadow consumes me, I feel nothing. The nothing is always worse. The nothing frightens me more than any panic attack I've ever succumbed to.

I stare into the emptiness, contemplating. It's an abyss.

What would happen if I fell?

My body jerks. It pulls back from the abyss in the dream, my underutilized self-preservation instincts kicking in at long last. With that twitch, the vision falls away.

I open my eyes. The nightmare was so mundane, yet the nausea of adrenaline lingers in my gut. I saw a place I don't want to revisit, a mindset I don't want to return to.

It takes a moment for Solera to come into focus. As reality sharpens, the nightmare fades. Memories of Earth recede, and my pain spikes.

I blink rapidly, clearing my fuzzy vision. I'm on one of the floating islands, out of the wind, sheltered in a copse of thick vegetation. Vine-draped tree limbs obscure the sky. Giant spotted toadstools, glowing with faint bioluminescence, crouch between mossy boulders and prickly brambles.

"Oh, gods," I moan, clasping my throbbing head. A low, muted howl persists in the background, ceaseless and maddening.

"Kyla?" A wide-eyed face pops into my line of sight. "You're alright!"

"Asher," I wheeze. Relief surges through me, followed fast by confusion. "Where are we? How'd we escape the water funnel?"

"We didn't. We were pulled into the eye of the storm, and we landed on this island in the center of the hurricane. It's a miracle we survived."

It is objectively a miracle, but right now, it sure doesn't feel like one. Everything hurts. I suppose that's to be expected, since I was wrenched through a hellstorm and cast onto this gods-forsaken rock.

Asher lays a hand on my brow. His face scrunches with worry. "You're ice cold."

"Yeah. Where's Fyr'thal?" Some phoenix warmth would do me a universe of good right about now.

Asher's face drains of color. He doesn't respond.

"Where's Fyr'thal?" I repeat, sitting up. A wave of lightheadedness makes the world spin. It's only then that I realize Asher and I are alone in the clearing.

"He and the others were captured," he whispers.

"What?!"

"Shh!" He raises his hands to quiet me, because I've tried to surge upright. In my enervated state, the best I can do is wiggle on the ground, like a turtle that's been flipped onto its shell. "Everyone's on the island. You and I were the first to enter the funnel, so the shadowbeasts didn't see where we landed. I pulled you to safety, but I couldn't...couldn't help our friends."

His voice hitches and his throat bobs. My heart skips several crucial beats.

"Are they alive?"

"Yes," he says. I go limp, sending a silent prayer of thanks to Ohra. "But honestly, I don't know why. Zalor's approach is usually kill first, ask questions later."

"Because of me, I expect. They want to draw Kyla Starblade out. The shadowbeasts know she'd try a rescue mission."

Asher nods, hefting his quiver and offering me his hand. "Then let's do it."

I have to save my friends, there's no question of that—but I'm tired. My body hurts, and my brain pulses with pressure. The idea of expending energy to fight a battle I can't possibly win is nauseating.

You aren't strong enough for this.

I flinch away from Zalor's disembodied voice ringing in my ears. During the fight with the shadowbeasts, he said he knew who I was. Can he look into my mind, as he does with his minions? Has he glimpsed every battle I've lost? Did he see every one of my failures?

Those failures—unsuccessful job interviews, manuscript rejections, damaged relationships—rise and roil in my brain, threatening to consume me. I couldn't even handle responding to text messages on Earth; what makes me think I can fight literal demons?

Don't listen to him, I think. *Get up. You must get up.*

I must find a way to save my friends. Besides, I'm not alone in this fight, and that makes all the difference. I have Asher. While we're free, while we're together, there's hope.

I accept his proffered hand, swaying as I rise. Asher pulls my arm over his shoulders, bracing me. I resist the urge to struggle, biting back a lie that I'm fine.

We hobble through a thicket of brambles. As the trees thin, the sky grows visible and the muted thunder of the hurricane grows louder. My stomach lurches when I observe the wall of spinning water stretching into the heavens. Given the muddy flavor of the ambient light, I can tell dusk is falling beyond the storm. We've been here for hours.

"Careful," Asher whispers. "Just beyond these rocks."

We stop behind a smattering of jagged boulders. I ease away from Asher, crouching to peek past the edge of a stone that glitters with a rusty tinge.

My stomach swoops. My darlings lie a hundred feet away on the rocky coast of the sky island, perilously close to the precipice and eddying tempest. Rexa, still in amphithere form, is sprawled on her side. Only the slow rise and fall of her ribs proves she is, in fact, alive.

One of the shadowwyverns hunches beside her head.

The other wyvern guards Cendrion. Fyr'thal lies beyond, his flames languid and weak, and the gryphon stands watch at his side. Valen's closest to the edge, and the harpy looms over his crumpled form. Two shadowmen patrol the perimeter of the small camp.

"That one's the leader of the pack," Asher breathes in my ear, nodding to the taller shadowman. "He did something to our friends, but I couldn't see what."

"Probably used soulbane," I murmur. Along with causing unconsciousness, soulbane prevents wielders from using magic for up to twelve hours. Zalor's shadowmen use the toxin to capture (and torture) prisoners.

"That's good news, if so," says Asher. I shoot him an incredulous look. How he's managed to find a ray of sunshine in this situation is beyond me. "It means our friends will wake up from the initial dose soon. Then it'll be an even fight."

"We can't wait around for that," I hiss. "Zalor knows everything his mind-controlled demons know. And if his mind-controlled demons know that Kyla Starblade and her friends are heading into the most dangerous territory in the world with an epic weapon of light..."

Asher winces. "He's probably on his way to us as we speak."

I rake my fingers through my hair and squeeze my eyes shut. "Escape plan. I need an escape plan."

But I can't focus. My brain isn't cooperating, and it's not just because I'm riddled with anxiety. I feel...slow. Like my thoughts are forcing their way through jelly to reach me. Like my nervous system's running out of battery.

With my eyes closed, my nightmare resurfaces, ruining all possibility of me coming up with solutions. I'm trapped again, stuck in that old one-bedroom. Unable to move. Unable to do anything.

"Kyla?" Asher whispers. I flinch away from the gentle tone, the hated name.

"How many combustible arrows do you have left?" I ask, trying to shed the dark memory of my old life. Asher unslings his quiver and shows me a single remaining arrow.

"I lost the others when I fell through the funnel. Still," he adds, "one might be enough."

It's official: his optimism has strayed into the realms of insanity.

"If I show myself to the shadowbeasts, they'll come after me," he reasons. "That would leave you free to rouse the others and escape."

"And what, abandon you on the island with a bunch of Zalor's minions?"

He nocks the arrow to his bowstring, offering me a brittle smile. "If I'm lucky, I can take a few of them with me when I go."

"You're not *supposed* to go!" Anger blisters my nerves. It fills the void inside me, the void that's been draining warmth and hope from my dying soul. "I am going to save you. That's why I'm here. That's why I'm here!"

My eyes fill with hot liquid. I'm *angry*, so why am I on the verge of weeping?

"I have to save you." I rock back and forth where I crouch on the ground. The world is caving in around me. My chest is about to burst. My thoughts are a shattered mirror, reflecting glints of a thousand shameful, half-forgotten truths. I'm bleeding. I'm dying.

A panic attack, here on Solera?

It's because of the nightmare. It has to be. Those dark memories made me fragile. Or maybe I've been a ticking time bomb. Maybe I just needed the tiniest provocation to relapse into my true self.

Asher lays down his weaponry and places both hands on my shoulders. His grip is firm and calming. He stills my mad rocking and looks me in the eye. Normally I'd shy away from eye contact, but something about his chestnut gaze is mesmerizing. Haunting.

He reminds me of Earth.

"I don't want to lose you," I whisper. "I can't."

"You won't. We'll figure something out."

"You don't know that. You don't even know me."

"I'm not sure that's right. You and Kyla are connected, and Kyla would never give up without a fight—"

"I'm not her!" I cover my face with trembling hands and swallow the sobs building in my chest. The last thing we need is for the nearby shadowtroops to hear me over the dull roar of the storm.

"This world was supposed to be better," I moan. "I was supposed to have a happy ending."

Asher's hands tighten on my shoulders. "Of course the story isn't happy right now, because this isn't the end. You haven't written that part yet."

"This isn't a book." I press the heels of my palms into my mouth, digging my teeth into my flesh. The pain brings clarity, pulling me away from psychic agony and making me focus on physical sensation.

"It's not, but stories exist for a reason. They teach us things about ourselves. This is your story now, Author. Your actions will dictate the ending."

I peek at Asher through my fingers. He's always been the wise one. Always knows just what to say.

Stories do exist for a reason. A good story has a magic of its own. A great story has the power to change the world.

"You didn't call me by her name," I whisper.

"That's because you're not her. If you wanted to give me your real name, I'd be honored to have it."

I open my mouth, then close it slowly.

I don't remember.

I'm pretty sure if I focused, I could siphon it from the morass of my mind—yet I don't want to. Though I'm not Kyla, no longer am I the Earthling who always tried to fly and always fell flat on her face.

On Earth I was bitter and jaded, but Asher has reminded me that hope isn't foolish. It's brave. And a hero must be brave, mustn't she? Otherwise she wouldn't be a hero.

As I contemplate the many inconvenient differences between Kyla and me, a thought pops into my head. A thought so crazy it might actually work. Zalor wants me alive. His troops use soulbane to subdue their targets. Soulbane is toxic to wielders—but I am not a wielder.

"My name isn't important." I've wasted enough time with my mini mental breakdown; I don't need to waste more on reintroductions. "And I think I have a plan."

19

WHEN I WAS TWELVE, my parents took me on a rafting tour down the Colorado River. Every so often, we'd stop and explore side gorges of the Grand Canyon. On one of these expeditions, I strayed from the group. Energetic, enthusiastic, and incredibly stupid, I wandered off alone to go rock climbing.

I found a perfect spot. I'd always been a good climber, and I was confident in my ability to scale the canyon wall. I scaled it alright—got right to the top of a sheer, craggy cliff.

Getting down, though . . . I hadn't considered that part of the equation.

This memory of Earth popped into my head, crystal-clear, and now I can't shake it. It plays in a maddening loop as I smooth my jacket, draw a breath, and leave Asher sheltered behind our smattering of boulders. Pushing through the bramble thicket, I emerge onto the flat stone coast.

"Hey assholes," I call to the shadowtroops patrolling the island's edge. "I'm the one you want. Let my friends go."

Their reaction is immediate, and so exaggerated it's almost comical. The pitch-black beasts hiss in shock, flaring their wings at the sight of me. The gryphon arches its spine like a startled cat. The two shadowmen recover from their initial surprise and bear down on me, drawing small syringes from their belts: darts filled with acid-green liquid.

Soulbane confirmed.

My stupid brain flashes back to my stupid Earth memory. There

I stood, stranded at the top of a gorge. No one knew where I was. For the first time in my life, I *feared* for my life.

But if I'd climbed up, I reasoned that I could climb down. I sank to my stomach and eased my legs over the red, dusty cliff. My body shook as my feet roamed blindly beneath me, seeking the toehold I knew had to be there. It was a drop that required me to let go of my handholds and fall several inches, trusting my instincts would land me safely.

What I'm doing now feels a bit like that first drop.

The shadowmen close in, flanking me on either side. I dodge a blow from the shorter one, ducking beneath his fist. I pivot and try to land a punch of my own, but he sideslips and backs up.

His companion is larger and faster. He bears down on me, and I jab at his face. He stops my fist with his free hand, squeezing my fingers so hard that pain lances through my arm all the way up to my shoulder. With his other hand, he aims the soulbane dart at my neck.

I brace for impact. I'm letting go of my handhold, praying my instincts are correct. My climbing talent saved me back then—once I made that first step, it was a smooth descent. Now, again, it's the moment of truth.

The soulbane dart punctures my flesh. I choke and gasp as pain pinches through my throat. Adrenaline spikes my pulse. I go limp and collapse.

"Finally," says one of the shadowmen. A booted toe collides with my shoulder, kicking me onto my back. "She barely put up a fight. Not so tough when you can't wield, are you?"

"Enough," says the other in a deeper, darker voice. "Lord Zalor wants her alive."

"I wasn't gonna kill her," grumbles the first demon. "Just rough her up a bit."

He grabs me under the arms and hoists me upright. My heart thuds so loudly, I'm sure they must hear it as they drag me across the sky coast and drop me unceremoniously. My cheekbone cracks against uneven rock. I've landed face-down.

Perfect.

As the shadowmen murmur to each other, their words inaudible over the buzzing swell of the storm, I dare to crack open an eyelid. In the faint light of Fyr'thal's plumage, I see they've dumped me beside Cendrion. The guard wyvern shifts its weight closer to me.

My brain stalls, snagging on the moment twenty years ago when I let go of my handholds and allowed myself to *trust* myself.

I gather a breath deep in my chest.

"NOW," I scream. I plunge my hand into my jacket and yank out the unicorn dagger. In one fluid movement, I roll sideways and jam the crafted blade into the wyvern's foot.

The wyvern explodes into pitch-black dust. It gives me a bit of cover, which I use to surge upright and wheel around. The shadowmen are in shock, and this time, they don't recover fast enough. I thrust the dagger at the smaller of the two, catching him on the shoulder. He bursts apart, his obsidian ashes swirling in a chaotic flurry.

The taller shadowman bares sable teeth and launches at me, pulling another soulbane dart from his belt. He can jab me with those things all he likes. I'm a plain old Earthling. Without magic, I'm immune to its worst effects.

The other shadowbeasts have flown into a frenzy. The gryphon is closest. It bunches its hindquarters and pounces, thirsting for my flesh.

Before the gryphon's talons find their mark, an arrow zooms through the periphery of my vision. A fireball erupts around the shadowbeast and it shrills an agonized cry. I stumble out of the way as its smoking body thuds to the ground in the place where I was just standing.

"Find whoever's out there and kill them," cries the shadowman.

The remaining wyvern and the harpy launch from the ground. The force of their wings stirs the ash of their deceased brethren into miniature tornadoes. I squint against the dust cloud, watching my opponent. He's smart enough to keep distance from the unicorn dagger.

"How are you awake?" he snarls.

"Soulbane won't work on me. I'm Kyla Starblade, bitch!"

Okay, I admit—in my moment of triumph, I've found power. Enjoyment, even. Fighting and *winning* is a balm on my broken soul, a soul that's grown too accustomed to failure.

The shadowman casts aside his dart and yanks a knife from his belt. Its razor edge glints in Fyr'thal's light as my enemy crouches, pointing the blade at me.

He lunges before I've gathered my wits. I stumble sideways and parry his thrust awkwardly. His knife slides down the metallic rods of the unicorn dagger, producing a noise like chalk grating on a blackboard. It sets my teeth on edge. When I try to riposte, the shadowman shoves me. I stumble back again, nearly losing my balance.

Kyla has the muscles of a trained warrior, but I've caused her body to waste away with my soul-death. I'm too weak for this fight.

Seeing my tawdry footwork, the shadowman advances. I hold my dagger between our bodies, realizing then how small a protection it truly is. As that dispiriting thought settles in my mind, the dagger's light flickers and dims.

"No," I gasp, horrified. Instinctively—and foolishly—I raise my right hand, bringing my weapon closer to inspect it for damage.

In my moment of distraction, the shadowman strikes. He slashes at me, and I don't have time to correct my mistake. I can't deflect his blade with the unicorn dagger. The best I can do is raise my arms to shield my chest and face.

I cry out as the shadowman's knife slices through my layers of jackets and shirts, biting into the skin of my left arm. I cringe aside, blunting the impact of his swipe. His blade also catches my right arm, but it's not as serious an injury.

Hissing through clenched teeth, I stagger backward. My left arm drops to my side, pulsing with pain. My right arm shakes as I lift the dagger again. I note with disquiet that the unicorn horn has dimmed another notch.

"You can't kill me," I say.

"My master wants you alive," the shadowman growls, "and I will deliver you as such. But he did not specify whether he wants you in one piece, or several."

He advances. My foot twists on a rock and I fall backward. I'm not having fun anymore. In my mind, dying is easier to face than torture. I don't like pain, and I don't want to suffer. I don't even want to fight anymore, because I'm suddenly certain I'll lose.

And I am so, *so* tired of losing.

Before the shadowman can reach me, a deep growl rumbles behind him. He twitches, falters, turns—

And comes face to face with Cendrion. My heart leaps. The dragon has awoken from his soulbane stupor. With a brutal roar, Cendrion clamps his jaws over the shadowman's head and twists. The demon's head pops clean off his neck with a sickening crack and squelch. Black blood erupts from his body.

Cendrion spits out the shadowman's skull and turns to me.

"Good timing," I say in a shaky voice.

"You know me. I like to make an entrance." Cendrion plods toward me. He lowers his bloodstained snout to my brow in a draconic gesture of respect. "You saved us."

"I haven't yet." Now that my opponent's dead, I turn and look for the other two shadowbeasts. I spy Asher instead, safe and sound, emerging from the bramble thicket.

"You good?" I ask.

He nods. "I found a branch to use as a makeshift arrow. Shot the harpy in the wing, finished her off with my crafting knife." He pats a sheathed blade hanging from his utility belt.

"Excellent. And the wyvern?"

"It tried to escape the eye of the storm, but the winds were too strong and kept blowing it back in. The last time it tried, it struck the island's edge and fell."

"We'll watch for it," I say, "but what matters now is getting off this island before anyone else finds us. Believe it or not, there are worse things to fear in the Sky Archipelago than Zalor's demons."

"The others may be sleeping off that soulbane for some time," said Cendrion. "I'm not large enough to carry more than two humans, and I'm not sure I'm in flying shape."

Damn. Here's another obstacle I didn't factor in: waking everyone

184

up and getting them airborne. Soulbane has adverse effects, including dizziness, nausea, and impairment of senses.

"Asher, you have the first aid kit, right?"

"Yes," he says, unslinging his travel pack. His face scrunches and he stares at me over the tops of his glasses. "Are you hurt?"

"I want to see if you have any mugwort in there," I say, ignoring the question and trying to ignore the throbbing in my arms. My inner sleeves are cold and moist with blood. I haven't assessed the damage, but I know it won't be pretty.

"Probably." He starts rummaging through the pack, seeking the kit. "But mugwort is an antiseptic. It won't wake them from a dose of soulbane."

"As a treatment, no. But it has an abusively pungent smell."

Asher smiles as he produces a rectangular metal box. "Homemade smelling salts. I like the way you think."

He finds the mugwort at once. I'm not surprised, seeing as most Soleran first aid kits come with it. Asher kneels beside Rexa and carefully uncaps the bottle beneath her nose.

I can smell the acerbic stench of the poultice from where I stand several feet away. Asher holds his breath, waving the bottle next to Rexa's nostrils. Her fuzzy snout wrinkles and her lips curl. With a snuffling snort, she opens her eyes.

"Praise be to Ohra," says Asher, quickly capping the bottle.

As Rexa shakes herself awake, Asher moves to Valen. He comes to with a coughing fit, sitting up and holding his head. I sidle closer to my friends, suddenly awkward. Even now, at this stage of our adventure, I'm not certain how my presence will be received.

There I go, second-guessing again. Guess I peaked when I was twelve. What I wouldn't give for some confidence in my social interactions.

"Thanks, Asher," says Valen, clambering to his feet. "I was worried for a moment there."

"It wasn't me." Asher stoppers the bottle and stows it away as Fyr'thal stirs beside him. "We owe it all to our author."

Valen turns to me. His eyes wander my face and a slow smile

blooms on his lips. Gone are the days when I could tell what my darlings are thinking. I have no idea what's running through his head.

Rexa extends her coiled neck. She blinks at me once, twice. I recognize the code: *Thank you.*

"Welcome," I murmur. Her approval means the world to me.

Her nostrils flare. She tilts her head and her gaze snaps to my injured limbs. A concerned, warbling growl echoes in her throat.

"What's wrong?" Asher, who's also familiar with her animal noises, hurries over to me.

"Nothing." I twist my left arm, suffering the twinge of pain to hide the dark stain seeping through my torn gray jacket sleeve. "I got a scratch from the fight. No big deal."

"We could put some mugwort on it so it doesn't get infected," says Asher, holding up the first aid kit.

"No," I say firmly. "I don't need it, and besides, we can't waste time on that. We're still in sight of the mainland. It's been...what, ten hours since the shadowbeasts drove us into the funnel? Zalor's forces could have reached the Galvian coast by now. We need to leave."

Faces darken, but no one argues. As one, we turn to the wall of spinning water.

The momentary high of my victory, of my friends' approval, fades in the face of the obstacles before me.

Now I have to figure out how to get us out of this gods-damned storm.

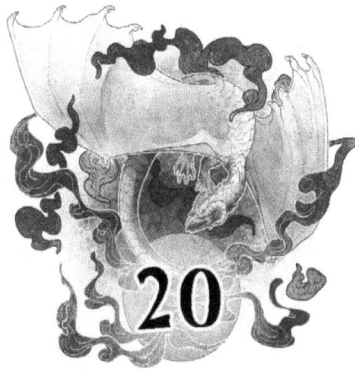

20

WE GATHER AT THE EDGE of the sky island—*The skyland*, I think with an inappropriate snort. I like that portmanteau, but I shiver as I contemplate the whorls of the tempest. If the shadowbeast wyvern couldn't escape the funnel's magical pull, I'm not sure we'll be able to. Especially not with our flyers reeling from a dose of soulbane.

Cendrion extends a tentative wingtip over the abyss. Though the skyland is somehow protected from the raging elements, his leathery membrane flaps in fierce gusts the moment it stretches beyond the coast. His wing whips sideways in the gale, nearly knocking him off his feet.

"Trapped," he growls. "We'll be sitting ducks for Zalor."

"Maybe we're starting in the wrong place," says Valen. He has a gleam in his eye that makes him look both unfocused and intense. It's the look he gets when he's connected to the core of his magicsource.

"There are forcemagic threads everywhere," he continues, sweeping a hand across the coast. "They're prevalent in the funnel, but they're also on the island itself. They're arcing over us, almost like a cage."

"Oh." Asher scrunches his nose, and a similar unfocused look enters his eyes. He's also sunk into his source to view the tangled web of threads. "If the Sky Archipelago floats on magnetism, and the islands are composed of magnetic earth elements, then it would follow that each of the islands has its own magnetic field of forcemagic."

"Like Solera itself," I add. *And Earth.*

"If we can find the island's magnetic pole," says Valen, turning away from the storm and gazing into the dark forest looming behind us, "we might be able to launch from there."

"And fly straight up, I imagine," Cendrion says heavily, tipping his snout to the sky. It's as lightless as a shadowbeast's hide by now. Night has descended beyond the funnel.

"I'm afraid so. Are you up to it?"

"I'll have to be."

Valen nods. "Let's search for the island's pole. The forcemagic seems to arc toward a central point, but as you can see, there's snarled pockets of threads everywhere."

I can't see. Without magic of my own, magicthreads are invisible to me. As my friends spread out, traipsing into the midnight vegetation, a frisson of foreboding slithers through me. I trail after Cendrion, who stomps a wide path toward the center of the skyland.

Fyr'thal's nearby presence provides illumination for our hunt. Red phoenix-light paints the underside of multi-pointed black leaves and makes ropey vines gleam. Beyond the lattice of the canopy, the sky is obsidian.

My scalp prickles as we delve deeper into the forest. It's not because of the creepy scenery (actually, this is my aesthetic), nor is it anxiety over the threat of Zalor's approach.

"Cendrion, is there a way to be less noisy?"

The dragon twists his neck to give me a flat look. He's trampling foliage and scraping past trees, snapping branches and flattening brush with abandon.

"Sorry, it's just . . . we really don't want to run into the creatures who inhabit these skylands."

"If they weren't attracted by the sounds of battle, I doubt this will draw their attention."

"Actually," I whisper, "now that the shadowbeasts are gone, this would be the perfect moment for them to hunt."

As if mentioning them has spoken the creatures into being, I glimpse a hint of movement in the shadows behind Cendrion. A figure flashes briefly in the light before vanishing.

"Shit." I try to point, and my forearm screams in agony. "I think they've found us."

"Weapons at the ready. Pick up the pace and stay together," Valen calls from somewhere to my left. I can't see him through the wall of trees. "Follow me. I found the island's pole."

Cendrion and the others crash onward. I stumble in the dragon's wake. Fyr'thal's light isn't enough for me to see the twisted roots and jutting rocks, and my clumsy feet find every one of them.

"Help!"

I freeze in my tracks, horror gripping my throat.

"Wait," I yell to the others, turning away from them and peering into the forest.

That was Rexa. I'd know her voice anywhere. Maybe, like me, she fell behind as the group forged ahead. She has no limbs apart from her feathery wings, so she has to snake across the ground. That can't be easy to do with her bulk.

If she's using her human voice, that means she had to transform back to humanoid shape. Given the skylands' effects on magic, that's a dangerous move. The surrounding forcemagic could have twisted her threads and turned her inside-out.

Perhaps she was *forced* to transform.

"Rexa," I scream, kicking past a leafy fern and hurling myself into the sable forest.

"Help! Over here," she calls.

I've only taken a few steps off Cendrion's path when the vegetation thins and I spot her. She's alone in a small clearing. Shelf mushrooms, glowing a ghoulish shade of yellow-green, lend a sickly light to our surroundings. Their eerie shine illuminates a tall, athletic woman with wavy dark hair and bright amber eyes.

But . . . this isn't Rexa. It can't be. There's something unnatural about her appearance. I can't put my finger on it at first, and then I realize: she's fully human. Her clothes are unmistakably Earthling in nature. Jeans, a stylish pleather jacket, Converse high tops.

My lips part. I stare at the woman, so familiar and so alien. A word surfaces on my tongue. It's a subconscious act, summoning that word, like muscle memory. Like instinct.

"Lindsay?"

The woman takes a step toward me, raising her hands for a hug. That's when I realize those hands are coated in dark liquid. It's dribbling out of her jacket, trickling down her fingers, puddling on the moss.

Blood.

"Lindsay, what happened?" I'm frozen, aghast. My Earthling cousin. Lindsay Monroe. We were once as close as sisters. I thought I'd lost all trace of her as my dying soul shriveled away...or perhaps I readily surrendered her as I sank into my new world and identity without reservation.

She takes another step. My body wages an inner battle. Half of me wants to run to her, to help her, and most importantly, to let her know that I'm sorry.

I *am* sorry. I'm sorry we drifted apart. I'm sorry I lost touch and never let her know how much I miss her and our youthful tequila-fueled adventures. I'm sorry I hurt her, because I'm gripped with the certainty that her wounds are my fault.

But the other half of me—the half that's lucid, or perhaps the half that's dreaming—screams a warning. Earth is real, but so is Solera. And I know what manner of creature lurks in the Sky Archipelago.

There's no way Lindsay could have been transported to this world. Even if she and Rexa were connected the way Kyla and I are, even if they're parallel souls, she couldn't have appeared in Earthling form wearing full-on Earthling regalia.

This is a wraith.

Wraiths are vampiric changemagic wielders, and they've clearly evolved to use their power despite the skylands' magnetic fields. They leach memories from their victims, changing form to become whatever will lure you in most effectively. Then they siphon energy from your soul until you're dead.

My soul, already half in the grave, won't last three minutes in the wraith's range.

With a shuddering gasp, I snap out of the wraith's hypnosis. I turn on a dime to flee back to the path, only to find Asher has followed me.

"Ash, it's not Rexa! It's..."

But I stop again. Asher also looks different. He's wearing sneakers, skinny jeans, Ray Ban glasses, and—my mind warps, dredging names and memories and pop culture icons from the darkness—his signature Sailor Moon graphic t-shirt.

"Eric," I breathe, my eyes blurring with water.

This is my best friend, not Asher. I abandoned him willingly, eagerly even. I wished to stay forever on Solera, but doing so would mean never seeing him again.

As with Lindsay, it takes me a moment to realize Eric is also dripping with blood. He reaches for me, and I reach back. I can't remember the last time I held the hand of my real best friend.

Pain swarms through my injured forearms, shocking me to my senses. This isn't Eric. This is a wraith. I'm hemmed in, caught between a hunting pair of vampiric monsters who'd love nothing more than to absorb my essence.

"You're not real," I scream, stumbling sideways.

But they *are* real. They're the two people I loved most on Earth. It's my fault we grew apart. In my depression, I couldn't reach out. It was easier to isolate. Better to hide. I didn't want to hurt them, as I knew I inevitably would if I allowed them to see my darkness... yet it seems that in alienating them, I hurt them regardless.

The shimmer of ruby liquid on their bodies rips my soul to shreds. Its scent is pungent, rusty, tinged with an edge of sickening honey sweetness. I close my eyes, rejecting the gruesome sight, but the blood's surrounding me, painting the backs of my closed lids, staining my hands, coating my arms. I'm drowning in it.

"No," I shriek to the night. "*No!*"

Thorny bushes tear at my clothes as I struggle to flee. Sticky vines rasp against my cheeks. Eric steps forward. He's less than five feet away. Lindsay approaches, her blood-drenched fingers straining for me.

Crash! A hailstorm of twigs and leaves assaults me. I hunch my shoulders, cringing toward a tree trunk for cover. With a flash of white scales, Cendrion explodes through the underbrush, rearing on his hind legs and landing on the Lindsay-shaped wraith.

I scream as she falls beneath his scythe-like talons. More blood bursts from her—but as soon as the wraith is dead, its changemagic spell fades. It shrivels and shrinks until it no longer looks like my cousin. It's revealed in its true form: a grotesque creature, like a millipede with slimy, wrinkled gray skin.

The Eric-wraith shifts its attention to Cendrion. It shrieks, baring hideous fangs that look out of place in the mouth of my Earthling best friend.

Ignoring the blistering pain in my arms, I yank the unicorn dagger from its resting place at my side. Lunging forward, I stab the wicked point into Eric's neck.

His face contorts and he issues a blood-muffled howl. When his chestnut eyes flicker to me, a riptide of guilt roars through my chest. I imagine I see sadness in Eric's dying visage. I've hurt him. I've done something unforgivable.

There can be no redemption for my crime.

This, however, is not the real Eric. It's a wraith. Its face shrivels and grays as it collapses, transforming into its sludgy, insectile form. The blood leaking from its wound turns black. It stinks like three-day-old rotten fish.

"Kyla, run!"

I wrench my gaze from not-Eric and look at Cendrion. Asher is perched on his back, his hand outstretched—an otherworldly reflection of the Earthling friend whose face is emblazoned in my mind, my dying soul.

Tucking the unicorn dagger safely away, I crash through thorny bushes, reaching for Asher with arms that scream for a respite. I grasp his hand and he hauls me onto Cendrion.

"Your timing's impeccable," I wheeze at the dragon.

Cendrion shoots me a twisted grin as he snakes his body around. "If you're not careful, I might start to think you're becoming a damsel in distress."

"The dragon isn't usually the one who saves the damsel." Branches shatter, showering me with debris as Cendrion gallops away from the scene of my terrible crime. "But I see your point."

I shouldn't have run off from the group. In hindsight, it was the stupidest thing I could have done. If this were a horror movie I'd be dead, and I'd deserve it. It's just that Rexa's—*Lindsay's* voice called to my soul. I couldn't have ignored it.

We burst from the trees and emerge on a bald, flat expanse of rock. The real Rexa is there, Valen on her back and Fyr'thal at her side. The amphithere coils her serpentine tail beneath her and spreads her feathery wings. With a mighty flap, she's airborne. She struggles to gain altitude for a moment before an invisible updraft catches her. She parachutes her wings and hurtles upwards on the force of the air current.

Cendrion leaps forward. He lands in the same spot Rexa launched from, bunches his muscles, and springs into the sky. Asher and I are jostled on his back as his body twists beneath us, fighting the effects of forcemagic and regular gravity.

I feel the moment we leave the invisible net of forcemagic. Vicious wind slams into Cendrion. He catches it with his leathery wings and we rocket toward the sky, leaving the awful island behind.

The rushing roar of the water funnel is deafening outside the sky-land's protective magnetic field. In the open with the wind lashing me, I'm freezing again. The encounter with the wraiths sapped me of strength. Even in that brief contact, I know they siphoned energy from my soul—and unlike the Solerans, my soul doesn't have the ability to regenerate energy.

My deadline has just been moved up.

After a few minutes of rising, the darkness thins. The roar of the funnel fades. Cendrion begins flapping, straining after Rexa's ghostly form.

With one last mighty wingbeat, we burst from the cloud cover. My breath catches in my throat. An ocean of stars glitters above us. The arm of the Soleran galaxy bends at the peak of the dark hemisphere, bisecting the heavens. Before us shines the Oldmoon, a brilliant and beautiful shade of pale blue. Behind us, a crescent sliver of the Blood-moon peeks over the blanket of clouds. The Silver Twins hang not far beyond.

Cendrion banks away from the Oldmoon and turns toward Akae-rion, the North Star. He levels, his claws strafing the fluffy tops of the clouds, gliding on high altitude currents. Rexa does the same, falling into line with him.

I sigh and let the tension drain from my body. I'm exhausted. I hurt everywhere, outside and in. My dying soul aches with guilt.

I'd written off Earth as a bad job. I was miserable for reasons beyond my control, and I was all too happy to leave. I've barely thought of the Earthlings I abandoned. I've been unconcerned about their welfare, about how my absence is affecting them. What if Lindsay misses me? What if Eric needs me? What will they do if I'm not there?

Did I not understand the assignment? I never considered the possibility, being so dismissive of my origin planet and past life, but what if my Hero's Journey is making me realize what I've had all along? What if the universe is placing insurmountable obstacles in my path in order to lead me home?

Or rather, given the nature of story structure, to *prevent* me from going home?

21

WE DESCEND WHEN OUR FLYERS can go no farther. We haven't gone as far as I'd like, but there's no choice. The soulbane drained them of energy.

Cendrion dips beneath the clouds. The comforting moonlight vanishes, and we're drenched in icy condensation. Below the heavy cover, it's drizzling.

"Because we d-didn't have enough obstacles to deal with," I mutter, wet and miserable.

Fyr'thal moves to lead the pack. It's too dark to see any skylands, even with the nimbus of phoenix-light hazing the air. The wind batters us away from our northern bearing.

Asher fishes out a compass from his belt. He squints at it and groans. "It's going haywire."

Of course a compass will be useless amidst the forcemagic of the archipelago. Without stars or moons to guide us, we could be flying off-course. We could be heading back to the mainland for all I know, straight toward Zalor and his army.

If this were a book I was writing, what would I do? They say writing is problem-solving, but how the hell am I going to solve our problems without magic?

"Wait," I gasp, my head snapping up. "That's it! Valen?"

"I'm here." His reply is immediate, his voice transmitted to my ears through the ring.

"I'd like you to wield."

"That's dangerous, especially in this weather," says Asher. "His spell will go astray."

"I'm counting on it."

"You're hoping my voltmagic will be pulled toward an island," Valen guesses.

"You comfortable trying that?"

There's a brief pause. Then a blue-white tongue of electricity flashes to the left. I squint against the brightness, blinking rain from my lashes. Valen crouches on Rexa's back. His hand stretches over her shoulder, pointing straight down. The lightning bolt curves unnaturally, skittering off in what I assume to be a westwards direction.

Rexa banks, shrilling a cry to Fyr'thal. He wheels and follows her, and Cendrion joins him. The rain intensifies as we fly. Stinging droplets assail my frozen cheeks.

After a minute, Valen wields again. This time, his lightning splits. A small fork shoots left, but the brunt of it takes a wayward turn to the right.

The party realigns. We continue like that until a massive shape, dark against the even darker background, becomes visible. Fyr'thal zooms ahead to find a safe landing spot. He spreads his wings, turning himself into a beacon.

Cendrion lands hard on the rocky coast. Rexa lashes her tail around the trunk of a tree and angles into the wind. The blustery air provides enough resistance for her to sink to the ground. Valen leaps from her back, allowing her to tuck her wings and settle.

Asher slides down Cendrion's right foreleg. I follow, but my movements are stiff. Though my arms are mostly numb, a dull ache throbs beneath the cold. My nerveless fingers slip on the dragon's smooth scales, and I fall in a heap at his claws.

At once, everyone jumps to my aid. Cendrion crouches beside me, Asher bends to offer me a hand, and Valen strides forward, eyes flashing.

"What happened?" he asks.

"Nothing—"

"It's not nothing." Valen's gaze narrows on my left arm, where the bloodstain on my sleeve has crusted. "You said it was only a scratch."

"And it is," I say. "Most of this is wraith blood."

It might be true. Between the battle, the rain, and my ordeal in the forest, I'm a filthy mess. I'm not sure why I'm arguing, why I don't want them to see the extent of my injuries. Maybe it's more that *I* don't want to see the extent of my injuries.

"Regardless, you're not well," says Valen. "We'll carry you inland."

"My *legs* aren't injured," I grumble.

He ignores my protest, gathering me into his arms. His touch is sure and gentle. A whisper of increased pain pulses through my wounds, but subsides once I'm nestled in his grasp.

Cendrion stomps into the vegetation, folding his wings tight to keep them from snagging on branches. Fyr'thal flutters to the dragon's shoulder, lighting the way. Valen and Asher follow, tamping down bits of broken bushes to make it easier for Rexa to slither after us.

"How bad is it, really?" Valen murmurs as we move.

"I'm fine."

He shoots me an unimpressed look. "I'm fully aware that when you say you're fine, you mean the opposite."

"It won't kill me," I say, electing not to remind him about the myriad things on this quest that still might.

Our progress slows as Cendrion encounters older, larger trees, ones even a dragon can't muscle aside. He stops and peers into the foliage on our left. "We can make that work."

A massive, leaning rock juts through the brambles, creating a small clearing. The space is defensible, and the boulder will provide some protection from the elements.

Cendrion stomps the area flat, leveling a campsite. Fyr'thal sets up shop under the rocky overhang, and Asher brings him broken branches to set ablaze. I hover uselessly, unable to help as my friends make safe our little alcove. Whenever I move my arms, they bark in agony.

"Anything to eat around here?" Asher asks me. "Those mushrooms, maybe?"

"Poisonous. But there might be some non-toxic variants. I'll look."

"Not alone, you won't," says Valen. "I'll help."

I hesitate, torn between the desire to keep him close and my

natural contrarianism. Extreme independence is a defense mecha-
nism—I don't need a psychiatrist to tell me that. I'm preventing heartbreak before it happens.

But I trust Valen. And by now, he trusts me. I nod, accepting his
help and feeling better for doing so.

"Do you think there's anything on this island that's actually fit for
mortal consumption?" he asks as we enter the forest.

"There's starmoss." I indicate the trunk of a knobbly tree. Tiny
blossoms, aglow with cold light, perch on tendril-like fronds stemming from a dark emerald carpet.

"Is it edible?"

"I mean, technically yes. It won't kill you, in any event."

"We'll circle back to that," Valen says dryly. He moves on, straying
farther from the light of Fyr'thal's fire.

I, however, remain staring at the starmoss.

"Are you alright?" Valen returns to my side, peering at me with
the air of a doctor at a deathbed. His closeness, the intensity of his
stare, steals my breath. My stomach performs a flip as I admire the
line of his jaw, the dark stubble growing in on his lean brown cheeks.

I can't believe myself. I'm in the middle of a deadly adventure, and
I choose now to act like a sixth-grader with a crush. You'd think I'd
know better.

You'd think that, but you'd be wrong. All of this is new to me,
but in many ways this—this *attention* from a man—is the most novel
experience. I wrote the burgeoning romance between Kyla and Valen,
sharing their thrills and heartbreaks, but I did it from afar. There was
a universe separating them and me. I was an objective observer, safe
on Earth.

Just when I'm about to lie and tell him I'm fine, Valen tilts his
head. "Your eyes."

"What's wrong with them?" I raise my hands in an automatic
self-conscious gesture, and regret it when my arms throb anew.

"Nothing." His expression shifts to the one he wears when connected to the innermost part of his magicsource, when he's so in tune
with the energy of the universe that he can see threads. "They're

different."

"What do you mean, *different?*" Another flip from my stomach. My innards are competing for the gold medal in gymnastics.

Valen doesn't answer at once. He's spellbound, his gaze both impersonal and intimate. It ignites me, putting every fiber of my being on high alert. It's like he's looking *through* me, not at me. Staring past whatever's wrong with my eyes to see what's wrong behind them.

"They're not Kyla's eyes." He brushes stray hairs from my face, seemingly oblivious to what he's doing and the effect it has on me. "I didn't notice until now. They're..."

"Darker?" I supply in a humorless tone.

"No—at least, not in the traditional sense of the word." He's too close. We're holding eye contact way too long, yet I can't bring myself to break it. "Maybe 'deeper' would be the more appropriate term. They're dark only because there's more to see, the way an ocean is darker than a puddle."

Holy fuck.

When's the last time I received a compliment like that? I think the answer is *never*. Being unequipped to handle compliments of any sort, much less ones that sear my soul and cauterize ancient wounds, my instinct is to direct attention away from myself.

Yet when I open my mouth to say something flippant and meaningless, what comes out is, "Your eyes are like galaxies. Every sparkle is a star."

Valen quirks a brow, and I realize I've made a grave mistake. Men aren't often complimented on their looks to begin with, and Kyla's no poet. I'm not sure she, with her poor communication skills, has ever paid him a proper compliment. Their on-page chemistry came from playful YA fluff banter.

This is stupid. Worse, it's dangerous. It's a slippery slope from compliments to feelings to confessions I don't want to make. I have to shut this down.

"Um, anyway." I clear my throat. "I was thinking we could use the starmoss."

Valen blinks at the shift in conversation but goes with it. "Not my first choice for dinner, but I've had worse. Who knows? Perhaps it will be better than pemmican."

"Not as food. As a navigation tool. The farther north we go, the stormier the weather will be. We won't be able to rely on the stars to navigate. But the fronds of starmoss always point north, see? They're magically drawn toward Akaerion, the North Star."

The star that burns as bright as your eyes, my brain whispers. I stuff that line away, figuring I can use it if I ever decide to write a schlocky romance novel.

His lips curve at the edges. "Let's bring it back to camp."

Though our expedition yielded no food, my friends are thrilled by my navigation suggestion. Score one for starmoss. It has its uses, after all.

Asher pulls out a glass bottle filled with nutrient-packed sylph-milk, and my friends pass it around. He pours some of the protein-rich drink into Rexa's fanged maw before offering the last sip to me.

I shake my head. "You split the rest. I'm not doing anything."

"Are you kidding?" says Asher. "You've led us through countless obstacles."

"I'm not the one flying, and I can't wield—"

"But you're brilliant." This comes not from Asher, but from Valen. "We need you well and functioning if we hope to reach the Crown of the World. So, my little author, I suggest you drink."

I note Valen is also no longer calling me *Kyla*, but I'm too exhausted to register the full implications of this. My whirlwind mind, usually eager to seize on the tiniest thing and overanalyze it til I make myself a nervous wreck, is mercifully quiet. Asher tips the drink into my mouth. It has a neutral, earthy taste, and though it's ice cold from the flight, I feel warmer for drinking it.

"We should tend to your arms," he says.

"They're alright for now. Seriously," I add, when a warning growl rumbles along Rexa's throat. "They can wait until after we've rested."

So we rest, ragged and sodden. Between Fyr'thal and the crackling fire, I'm no longer a human popsicle. Cendrion and Rexa act as windbreakers, and with the added protection of the leaning rock, our clearing is safe from the biting gale.

One by one, the others drift off. Fyr'thal nestles against my side, drying my garments while he dozes. Asher snores peacefully, tucked up against Rexa's wing. Valen is the only one who remains awake. He sits to my right, feeding branches to the blaze.

"You should sleep while you can," I tell him.

For a time, he doesn't reply. He stares into the unending night, and I'm content to let him be.

"You once said you were a part of every character, and every character was a part of you," he whispers, breaking the quiet. "That includes the wraiths and the shadowbeasts? And Lord Zalor?"

"Oh, him especially." Valen's brows disappear into windswept locks that have grown long on the road, and I sigh. "Well, yes and no. He represented an aspect of my darkness. That's why he was important to me."

Silence spirals between us. The fire crackles. With my foot, I nudge another branch into the flames.

"Can you describe it to me?" he says at last. "Your darkness."

I hesitate. Valen is mentally stable. Well-adjusted. I'm afraid he won't get it. Unlike the people of Earth, however, I don't fear that he'll mock or scorn me. I blow a breath through my cheeks, bracing myself. Honesty requires bravery, too.

And a hero *must* be brave.

"It's a combination of things, I suppose. And it's different for everyone who suffers from it," I say, proceeding with the caution of someone tiptoeing across a minefield. "The fact of the matter is that my brain doesn't quite work the way it should. And no matter what, I can't fix it. I tried ignoring it, and I tried prescriptions—potions, to you—and I tried drowning myself in alcohol, and I tried . . . I tried *so hard* to be a different person."

The irony is not lost on me that I finally got my wish. I woke up one morning in Kyla Starblade's body, yet I remain haunted by the shadow of who I was on Earth.

"Why would you want to be someone else?"

"Why *wouldn't* I is the better question," I quip. "That's a much shorter list."

Valen isn't laughing. His eyes wander my face in a deliberate path, as if searching for something. "But you have so much to offer."

My heart lurches against my ribs—yearning for him, or mourning for me?

"They say to always be yourself," I whisper.

"They who?"

"You know, the generic *them*. Everyone. Society. The world." I shake my head, dismissing that world and its toxic constructs. "They say that, but they never tell you that being unique is often akin to being lonely."

"Would you rather have been like everyone else?" Valen inquires.

"I don't know. I guess not. But if I had been, I think life would have been easier. To like all the things everyone else likes and listen to the same dumb pop songs everyone else listens to and behave the way every so-called normal person is expected to behave . . . I think there would be a comfort in that."

"It seems to me like that would be the more lonely thing."

"It would be boring, perhaps. But wouldn't it be nice to be able to find *happiness* in mundane things? In anything at all?"

My darkness drained the happiness from everything I did, promising misery, forcing me to isolate. And now, as I try to examine my memories of Earth, darkness is all I can see.

"I'd like to be happy," I murmur. "Like, *really* happy. Not faking. To genuinely want to be around others. To have things in common with people. To get their jokes, and laugh alongside them, and . . . well, you wouldn't get it."

I steal a glance at him. The set of his chin suggests he's gearing up to say something important, and I'm suddenly afraid.

"I never wanted to be in the military, and now I command the Mortal Alliance," he tells me. "Every death and lost battle feels like my fault. Sometimes I think it would be easier to surrender to Zalor, so I wouldn't have to feel this way anymore. I think too much has happened, and I've fallen too far, and I'll never be able to dig myself out of this pit. I worry I'll never feel happy again."

I gape at him, thunderstruck. "You never mentioned this."

"There hasn't been much time for us to—"

"I mean, not *ever*. You never once told Kyla this is how you feel."

And I, the almost-omniscient author, never caught a glimpse of it in his head. How did I miss this beautiful depth, this tragic truth? Am I a shitty writer, or do the Solerans have more secrets than I ever could have imagined?

His mouth twists in a mirthless smile. "Kyla bore the violence well, so I never wanted to burden her with my worries. She was the strong one."

"I'm not sure about that," I say before I can stop myself. "She hid her feelings."

He lifts one shoulder in a halfhearted shrug. "That's who she is. I wanted her to reach out, but she never did."

In his pain, I see my own. To touch him now would be dangerous, but I'm compelled to offer him the sort of comfort I never received on Earth.

No matter how innocent my intentions, an embrace is out of the question. Instead, I take his hand. He starts at my touch, looking away from the fire to stare at me.

Flickering shadows dance across his expectant face. There's a universe worth of things I want to say, but I have no idea where to start. The Shadow War left invisible, indelible scars on my darlings. What *can* I say to that? 171,000 words in the English-Eldrian language, and none of them are enough.

"You're not alone," I whisper. "I'm here."

His eyes glisten and his fingers tighten around mine. We sit like that for a time, connected, drenched in firelight and cloaked in shadow. Neither one of us speaks again. Neither one of us needs to.

Somehow, I've said the right thing.

22

RUMBLING THUNDER WAKES US at dawn. It's hard to tell it *is* dawn. The clouds overhead are heavy, dark, writhing with promises of horror.

Asher spent his watch transplanting the starmoss into the empty sylphmilk bottle. The glowing fronds now brush the left side of the curved glass. We have our navigation tool.

"It's time to tend to your arms," says Valen.

I'm not looking forward to peeling off my layers. Apart from being frozen, I don't want to look at my wounds. The ache is dull but persistent. If I keep my arms limp at my sides, sometimes I can't even feel it.

But Valen comes up behind me and runs his hands over my shoulders, helping me shrug off my overcoat. The touch sparks a tempest in my heart as I recall last night's conversation.

I try to remind myself this is wrong. Me feeling this way is bad enough, but for Valen to entertain the notion of romance is confusing. Simultaneously thrilling and disappointing. I'm disappointed because he's loyal to Kyla—Kyla, who I am definitively *not*.

Air rushes from my lungs as he eases my arms out of my next layer down. I'm ashamed of myself for encouraging this . . . and for knowing I'm leading him on. A dark shepherd driving my one-man flock toward the unhappiest of endings.

"Asher and I can do this on the road." I twitch away from Valen's hands, aware my friends are watching. The glint in Rexa's amber orbs is a little too shrewd for my liking.

We launch from the skyland, Valen and Rexa in the lead with the starmoss compass. Asher rides with me on Cendrion, working on my arms. It's awkward for countless reasons. I'm half-naked, wearing a breastband and a sleeveless cloak. Fyr'thal, whose body is the size of my torso, nestles on my lap. His warmth keeps the biting wind from destroying me, but there's no helping the sheeting rain that batters us.

Asher rubs pungent mugwort poultice on my knife wounds. As I suspected, seeing the lacerations made them real to me, and they immediately started feeling worse.

"Good thing we have a tailwind," he says, thankfully not addressing my injuries.

It is good, as it helps us clip along at a steady pace, but the south wind brings ill weather. All too soon, we find ourselves in a vicious lightning storm.

"Close ranks," Valen's voice sounds in my ears, overriding the incessant roll of thunder. "I'll try to divert the worst of it."

He's a force of nature, Valen. His command of voltmagic is enviable. Though the magical mechanics aren't visible to my soulless eye, I know he's repelling lightning that shoots our way. Once his magicthreads interact with the naturally occurring electricity, the magnetism of the skylands kicks in. Bolts that stray too close are diverted left and right.

I watch him, contemplating how everything has changed.

Maybe I'm not what I thought I was. Or maybe I can be *more* than what I thought I was. I never wanted any Earthling humans. They never stood a chance, not when I had a glimpse of this perfect, magical Soleran. I was fighting a losing battle on my home planet, trying to force myself into a conformity that I neither wanted nor understood.

Yet here, I do understand it. That yearning, that lightheartedness, that mythical sensation of pure and unadulterated *happiness* that someone's mere presence can induce.

I should push these thoughts away, but the alternative is focusing on the storm. That's too much for me, so I allow myself to sink into a fantasy.

After reaching the Crown of the World and severing Zalor's connection to Darkmagic, we return to Eldria as heroes. Through the magic of Plot Armor, the Shadow Lord's defeat saves my soul from death. I'm allowed to stay in this world. Kyla Starblade, who's inhabited my Earthling body, is content to remain where she is. She protects my real-life family and friends. She's good to them in a way I never could be.

And on Solera, my little found family lives happily ever after.

I have to stop thinking things into existence. The universe ignored my dream and seized on my nightmare. As I think about the Shadow Lord, a shadow falls upon us. Through my closed lids, I sense it: a colder coldness than the wind. A darker darkness than the storm.

My fantasy pops like a soap bubble. My head snaps up. I can't see my enemy, but I recognize the signs.

"We're in danger," I tell my friends through the comms ring. "Zalor's here."

I was complacent. I let my guard down. Though he's certainly helping to drive the plot, he hasn't made an appearance in quite some time; this confrontation was inevitable. Lord Zalor is Solera's greatest villain.

Did I really think I could outsmart him? Out*run* him?

Asher, who's wrapping my arms in gauze, fumbles his work. His eyes widen with terror. I know what I'll find when I look over my shoulder, and I try to brace myself for how bad it'll be.

It's actually a little less bad than I imagined. Being a writer has some perks. I thought the Shadow Lord would descend on us with legions of the worst winged creatures who hide in the deepest, rotten crevices of this world.

Turns out he's come alone. Alone, save for the behemoth he's riding.

His pitch-black shadowbeast mount is a thraxwing. It's shaped like a wyvern, but it's massive. Multi-ribbed wings extend from its shoulders to the base of its tail, leathery flesh stretching between the bony fingers to provide lift. It undulates through the sky as if swimming underwater. Its wedge-shaped head tilts on a stubby neck, and obsidian venom sacs quiver between the dark fangs of its gaping maw.

"Running is futile." Zalor's stentorian voice needs no magical augmentation to rise above the thunder. "This foolhardy endeavor will bring nothing but ruin—to you, to me, and to Solera."

He's dwarfed by the thraxwing, whose wingspan is greater than that of Cendrion and Rexa combined. At first I wonder why Cendrion isn't wheeling to face our nemesis, and then I see it: Zalor's clawed hands are outstretched. He's wielding. A thread of darkness connects him to the dragon straining silently beneath me.

"Land," Zalor commands, as if we have a choice in the matter. "We have much to discuss, you and I."

"How can he wield here?" Asher breathes. He's drawn his crafting knife, but weapons are useless against the Shadow Lord.

Valen tries to counter-wield. A whip of lightning arcs from his outstretched palm. It starts on a course for Zalor but is yanked away, diverted toward the nearby skylands.

I've made another miscalculation. In leading my friends to the Crown of the World, Zalor's legendary birthplace, I've led them into his territory. The wraiths evolved to be immune to the effects of the magnetic archipelago; the Shadow Lord must have similar immunity.

Too late, I see the futility of my actions. Too late, I see the dangerous precipice toward which my dreams, my desires, have pushed us.

"Little impostor." Zalor's sibilant hiss reaches me over the storm. "I suggest you make your friends cooperate. My thraxwing is hungry and itching for a fight."

The thraxwing emits a guttural ululation. Its belly ripples grotesquely. It uses flesh-eating venom to incapacitate its prey, and we're well within spitting range.

A hundred possibilities tumble through my brain. My thoughts center on the unicorn dagger at my hip, but if Zalor has full command of his magic, none of us will get close enough to land a blow. Direct confrontation with him is suicide.

"Do as he says," I tell the others.

"He called you *impostor*," Asher whispers.

"He knows."

As Cendrion descends, guided by Zalor's darkmagic, I can't help but feel that the two halves of my story are colliding. The disparate truths burning at the core of my being have been at war, and the war is coming to a head.

Anxiety boils my blood. Maybe this is my Dark Night of the Soul, the moment when hope seems lost. Or—the thought lances from my brain to my heart, spearing me with a dread more profound than I've ever felt—maybe this is the end.

Solera isn't a dream, it's real. In reality, we're never guaranteed a happy ending. We're not even guaranteed a satisfying one.

Cendrion's rough landing on a skyland jolts me out of my spiral. No, this can't be the end of my story. My Earthling self gave up at every major pinch point. I don't want to be that person anymore. I want to burn the memory of her and never look back.

Steeling myself, I twist around to face Zalor. He hovers on the thraxwing, anchored in the raging winds by some manner of magical enchantment. The beast's pitch-black tail lashes, tipped with a poisonous barb. More poisonous quills bristle on its back beneath Zalor's feet.

"How long I've waited for this conversation," he breathes.

His voice is filled with a yearning so intense, so intimate, it makes me squirm with revulsion. My terror mutates, sprouting new limbs as I consider all the ways he could hurt us. "What do you want with me?"

"You overplayed your hand, Impostor. You thought I wouldn't see through your facade at Torvel," he says. "You thought I wouldn't recognize the darkness in your soul."

Another ineffective tongue of voltmagic lances from Valen. It falls pitifully short of its mark, skittering into the sky. Zalor doesn't address it, thank Ohra. My friends are beneath his notice. He's fixated on me.

"I may not be Kyla Starblade," I say, slipping the unicorn dagger from its loop and passing it to Asher, using Fyr'thal's trembling body as cover, "but that's my strength now, not my weakness. I had a window to your world, a connection to *all* of you. I know the way you think and act."

"Of course," says Zalor, spreading his skeletal hands. "Your connection to Solera runs deep. Little did you know that while you were feeding off of us, some of us were feeding off of you."

I freeze in the act of standing on Cendrion's back. Stuck in an awkward half-crouch, I stare at the Shadow Lord.

"It was not so much that you were transcribing our story," he continues. "It was more that you were *directing* it. The moment you touched Solera, you changed it. That's one of the quantum-magical laws of the universe, you know—by the mere act of observation, you have altered our reality."

"No," I whisper. That can't be. Wouldn't I need some sort of magic to influence Solera the way Solera influenced me?

"I sensed the darkness in your soul from worlds away and used it to my advantage, drawing power from you. Every battle I won was the direct result of your inadvertent collaboration with me. You needed conflict on the pages of your pathetic books; through your meddling, you enabled my greatest victories."

My legs crumple and I slip on Cendrion's rain-drenched scales. I slide down his haunches, careening past his wing to land hard on the unforgiving skyland coast.

Words have deserted me. I'm empty. My brain fills with a high-pitched buzz. Only the primal urge to argue remains. "That's impossible."

"Is it?" Sinister amusement tinges his rich baritone. "If you give too much of yourself to the darkness, you shouldn't be surprised when the darkness grows strong."

"But—" Freezing rain flies into my mouth, stinging my tongue, yet my throat is dry. "I have no magic."

"You have no Soleran magic." Lightning roars, illuminating him in all his villainous glory. "The magic in your native world is more nuanced and understated. Can you think of no time you experienced a rush of power, an embrace of something *other*?"

That rings a painful bell. It echoes in the silence of my unfocused mind and bleeding soul. As before, so it is again: I sense the irrefutable truth of his words.

"Writing," I whisper.

He claps slowly. Even through my fog of horror, I feel a faint jab of annoyance at his patronization. "There is magic aplenty spread across the multiverse, but most souls fail to ever grasp it. You were one of the lucky ones on Earth. How eager you were to throw it away."

I can't tell if I'm weeping, but I think I must be. The storm douses my cheeks. Wind tears at my cloak, tempting me toward the abyss. Part of me wants to hurl myself off the skyland. I deserve to crash into the Shifting Sea and die on impact.

It *was* my fault. I was complicit in all the destruction and murder. I wielded neither magic nor sword, but the mighty pen. If Zalor gained power from my darkness, then I'm as much to blame for the death of my darlings as he is.

"You thought you were strong enough to rewrite the ending," Zalor continues, "and still you believe you might. Hope springs eternal—but hope is an emotion as dangerous and futile as any other. You should know that by now."

I do know. I'm quaking with nerves. My dying soul flickers. It naively believes there could be a way out of this mess.

But I can't think of an escape. I should feel *something* after learning this wretched truth, yet I feel nothing. The nothing frightens me more than it has any right to. It's a black hole, and I'm at the event horizon, letting it pull me away from reality and identity.

"Kill me if you must," I say, forcing the words past the cavernous darkness inside me. "Just let my friends go."

"Kill you?" Zalor laughs. "I don't want to kill you, I want you alive. You belong to me, as surely as I belong to you."

"I don't belong to you. I refuse to surrender to you!"

A chill emanates from Zalor. It's impossible to tell where he's looking, since his eyes are spheres of unbroken night, but I sense his gaze has shifted to my friends. "Not even if it ensured the survival of this world you love so desperately?"

Adrenaline pulses through me. "Leave them out of this."

"They are intrinsic to this," he counters. "They are the key—the beginning, and the end."

Riddles? He's never been one for riddles. He's about as subtle as a baseball bat to the back of the head.

"Poor, deluded soul that you are, you've convinced yourself they care for you." He clicks his tongue in a pitying fashion. "If you knew the truth, you'd see surrender is the kindest option. You are not worthy of them. You deserve nothing."

I clap my hands to my ears, trying to block out his toxic words, but they're inside me now. They've burrowed deep into my soul, poisoning me. "Shut up! You're wrong about everything. And so help me Ohra, I will never give you what you want."

Zalor's ghastly visage buckles with disdain. "You're cutting off your nose to spite your face."

"I'd cut off my *face* to spite my face, so joke's on you."

"Let's be reasonable, Impostor. Remember, I want to change your ending, too. We can live in peace, you and I. I'll help you return to your life, you help me conquer Solera. Once Solera's mine, who knows what I'll set my sights on next?"

At his portentous words, something erupts from my emptiness. A memory. A name.

Eric.

Lindsay. My parents. New York City. Bumblebees. Mountains. Music. The moon. The sun.

I will not let the Shadow Lord consume and mutilate them as he has mutilated Solera. He destroyed too many things I love; I won't let him do any more damage.

The wind whispers. The rain sings. The abyss calls my name, and I know what I have to do. Zalor wants me alive. He's been feeding off my power to ensure his victory in the Shadow War. Without me poisoning the story, Solera can win.

I stand shakily. Finally I feel something, but it's not the fear I expected. It's sorrow.

Zalor smiles at me. I smile back.

Then I dive off the cliff.

His screech fills the sky, slicing through the elements to reach me. I surrender to the fall, and once I've surrendered, I barely feel it. The drop in one's stomach isn't due to gravity, it's due to fear. Relinquish the fear of the abyss, and it's easy to take the plunge. All you have to do is give up everything.

I'll pull Zalor after me—he'll follow, I know it. Through my sacrifice, I'll allow my friends to continue to the Crown of the World and finish our quest. Without my meddling, Solera will stand a chance.

"Goodbye," I whisper through the comms ring as I plummet into the unending darkness. "I'm sorry."

Out of a swirl of wind and water, the Shifting Sea fades into visibility. I hurtle headlong toward the mountainous whitecaps, gaining speed with each of my final heartbeats. If Zalor hasn't caught me yet, he never will. I'm close, so close—

Then dragon talons clasp my waist. Before I shatter against the waves, warm darkness envelops me. Familiar darkness.

I surrender to the kind oblivion and float away.

23

THIS IS A NIGHTMARE.

"Your readers are expecting a happily-ever-after," says Jen Perez, my editor. I sit across from her, only half paying attention. "You can't build up a Young Adult Fantasy—with romance subplots, no less— and rip the rug out from under your audience's feet."

My gaze wanders to the window overlooking Sixth Avenue. "I'm subverting expectations."

"There's subverting expectations and then there's this." She plops my manuscript on her desk.

"I made it realistic."

"It's *fantasy*. No one wants to read this depressing drivel."

Yep, thanks for stating the obvious, I'm aware. No one wants the ugly truth of who I am. They prefer the mask I've constructed—the halcyon, paper-thin facade of magical optimism and happiness.

"Gabi called me. I'm not going to do a line edit until you've rewritten the last two-thirds."

I grimace. If Gabi, my agent, has gotten involved, it's only a matter of time before everyone is breathing down my neck, demanding I change the ending.

"I know it's a big ask, especially with such a short deadline," Jen adds. "But you can't kill ninety percent of your main cast, including your MC's love interest and best friends."

"That's what happens. That's the story."

If I have to suffer in life, so too must my characters suffer. If I can't be happy, no one can.

"Stories are one thing. The publishing industry is another." Jen folds her arms. "This is a business. I know you like what you've written, but you need to scrap it."

Scrap it, she says, like it's that easy. *Kill your darlings.*

I grimace. That phrase has always irked me. It's my least favorite writing advice. It demands you give up the things you love to make your story fit society's narrow expectations. Sacrifice passion for practicality, creativity for commercialization.

Yet her words spark a distant memory—this isn't real, is it? None of this is real. This is a dream. There's another reality, somewhere far away. A reality I've destroyed.

Jen prattles on in the background, but I can't be bothered to listen. I didn't become a writer to suffer through meetings like this, I became a writer because I wanted to experience magic. I wanted my words to make a difference.

I latch onto the idea of magic and trace threads of memory to their origin. Somewhere out there is a world filled with magic. A world that needs me.

I stand and turn my back on Jen.

"Where are you going? We haven't started on my notes—"

"This isn't real," I whisper, ignoring her.

Jen calls after me, but I squeeze my eyes shut and block out the bustle of the posh office and muted sounds of the city beyond. This is a dream, nothing more.

I want to wake up.

With a groan, I open my eyes. I'm lying on the floor of a small, enclosed rock cavern. Fyr'thal perches on my chest, dozing peacefully, his warm weight a blessing.

"Thanks, buddy," I murmur, reaching to stroke his crested head. I can't, because my arms are cocooned in fabric. I'm bundled in blankets and spare coats.

My movement is enough to startle the phoenix awake, and also enough to remind my arms that they're in pain. Fyr'thal shrills an ethereal cry that reverberates in the tiny space. Moments later, a fissure appears in the seamless rock wall, and I recognize the signs of

Asher's earthmagic. The stone rumbles and ripples and an opening widens, revealing four backlit figures in a much larger cave beyond.

Valen is the first to enter my cozy grotto. He drops to my side and lays a hand on my cheek.

"I thought I'd lost you," he whispers.

Earth grows hazier by the day (I can't even remember the dream I just had), but I know no one has ever looked at me like this, spoken to me in such a way.

Like my dying soul, Earth was filled with lots of emptiness. Empty words, empty promises. On the rare occasions when people noticed something was wrong with me, I recall that they'd make empty offers: *I'm always here for you. I believe in you. You'll achieve your dreams if you work hard. Remember, you are loved!*

"Where are we?" My voice is cracked and dry.

"Xintra, the ice continent."

"What?" I struggle again, trying to sit up. Fyr'thal hoots indignantly and flutters away. The cold latches onto me as soon as his fiery form is gone. "How?"

"Honestly?" Rexa enters the small cave with Asher in tow. "Sheer, dumb luck."

"Your stunt threw everyone for a loop," Cendrion adds. He remains in the larger cavern, since he can't fit in with us, but he snakes his head through the opening to talk. "Luckily, it surprised Zalor more than us. He dropped the spell he was using to control me, and I jumped after you. Rexa had the good sense to follow."

"That doesn't explain why we're not all sea monster food," I say, taking in the concerned faces, the affection shining in their eyes.

"As Rexa said, that's down to luck. You fell so far that we left the magnetic range of the Sky Archipelago. I was able to wield us into shadow right before impact."

"I transformed into a leviathan ray underwater," says Rexa. "We navigated north from there."

"And you survived?"

She snorts. "We're hardly helpless. Although you did miss a nail-biter battle I had with an elasmodon. I won," she adds, as if there was any question.

A thrill moves through me. We're defying the odds. We escaped Zalor.

At the thought of the Shadow Lord, I deflate.

"I'm sorry," I murmur.

"For what?" says Rexa. "Hurling yourself into oblivion and abandoning us on an impossible quest?"

"No—well, yes." Misery sloshes in my stomach. "It's my fault. Zalor confirmed it. I did this to your world."

A tense silence settles on us. Not even Rexa has a snarky remark to contribute.

The words are out of my mouth before I can stop them: "You should have let me die."

Asher shakes his head. "Don't say that. We need you."

I love him for his loyalty, even if it doesn't make sense. He'd be quantifiably better off without me. They all would.

Valen snakes an arm under my shoulders and helps me rise. "If anything, Zalor's admission proves your true power. You, my little author, are the only person in the world who can defeat him."

Heat scorches my cheeks. From the corner of my eye, I see Asher and Rexa exchange a look.

"We'll give you two some privacy," Asher says after a charged beat. "So you can plan our next move."

"Yeah. *Plan*." Rexa sketches quotation marks in the air.

I'm dead. I'm dying. After everything I've survived, embarrassment is going to be the thing that does me in.

The others retreat into the main cavern, where a bonfire burns. Rexa glances over her shoulder at Valen. "I called that day one," she says in a carrying whisper, rolling her eyes toward the craggy ceiling and shaking her head.

Without Fyr'thal, my smaller cave darkens. Valen's arm provides warmth in the phoenix's absence. Soothing shadows fall on my face, and I pray to Ohra they conceal the blush I know must be spreading there.

"I'm sorry," I say again. It's the only thing I can manage with him so close. I'm not sure what I'm apologizing for this time—the list is a mile long—but I sense I'm at the edge of another abyss.

"I am, too," he says. "I didn't understand the magic that connected you to this world. Because I didn't understand, I was angry. And afraid. I was unkind to you when you first arrived."

Wow. Not what I was expecting. I make the mistake of turning my head toward him, but he's not looking at me. His eyes are downcast and a frown creases his face.

"Maybe I still don't understand," he mutters.

I don't understand, either, but a distant alarm bell has begun to sound in my subconscious.

"All I know is that I feel..." He scrubs his free hand over his chin, and I realize he's flustered. Valen, always so cool and collected, is struggling to find words. "I feel different than I've ever felt before. Different than I felt with Kyla."

My brain screams at me, trying to warn me away from danger. It's like I'm the sober friend, the designated driver who's expected to prevent disasters before they happen. He's intoxicated, and it's my duty to shut this down before he says something damning.

"Of course you feel different," I tell him. "I'm not her."

"I know that." Valen's voice cracks. "You—you're more than her. It's the way you love this world and how you understand the darkness I've always had to hide. It's you talking about science and smelling books and coming up with brilliant ideas."

My mouth falls open. There's no breath in my lungs to argue, to steer him off this collision course. I hate him for saying such nauseatingly wonderful things.

"I wish I knew your real name." He brushes a strand of hair from my face. "Because I think it's been you all along."

With that, something snaps in my chest.

"You love *Kyla*," I tell him fiercely.

"I do." His throat bobs. "But being with you . . . it's like I'm home. I look in your eyes, and I recognize you. Your soul's been entwined with her body for as long as I've known her. And it's the soul, not the body, that I lo—"

"Stop." My word is loud and sharp, filled with misdirected violence. "You have it all wrong."

Uncertainty flickers in his gaze. "Do you not feel the same way Kyla felt?"

The burning in my throat—is it grief or shame? "It's complicated."

We sit in excruciating silence as I formulate my explanation, the thing I've never said aloud, not even on Earth.

"How I feel is one thing. And if I'm honest, I feel the same way." My chest heaves with pent-up emotion. "But I can't give you what you need. I'm ... not the same as Kyla."

My innards writhe in discomfort. I don't want to have this conversation. There's a reason I avoided it for years. Decades. "It has to do with orientation. No, that's not right. Um, it's—it's about sexuality."

Valen tilts his head. Despite the nature of what we're discussing, I feel I've wildly overstepped my place.

Write what you know, they always say. But I know nothing about this.

"You and Kyla had a ... physical, sexual relationship." Oh yes, it's definitely shame that's gripping my throat and chest. "You both wanted, *needed* that aspect of a relationship. I ..."

Don't overwrite. State the truth and be done with it.

"I don't."

His mask has slipped, and he's become transparent. The vulnerability is as much heartbreaking as it is disappointing. Valen can understand quantum-magical entanglement, but he can't fathom this.

"But you just said—"

"I know what I said. All of it's true. That's why this is so difficult. I'm romantically attracted to you, but not sexually attracted. The word on Earth is *asexual*. I can experience love as deeply and completely as anyone. But I don't express that love physically, the way you do."

It feels like I'm apologizing. It feels like all I've ever done is apologize for who I am. We're from different worlds, he and I. That's never been as clear as it is now.

"I see," he says after a time.

"Do you?" My voice is sharper than I intended. "I want to be clear about this. It's her you love, not me."

He hasn't moved. We're close, but a mountain of unspoken things now separates us. By the time he finally opens his mouth, I'm convinced I don't want to hear whatever he has to say.

Why are you like this?

Is it because of something that happened?

Couldn't you try it?

Maybe you just don't know what you're missing?

Such ignorant statements would ruin him for me.

"This is a stupid conversation. You know that, right?" I speak before he has a chance to, pulling my arms from their fabric confines and pushing away from him. "Even if there was some outlandish universe where we could make it work, it's not this one. If I stay on Solera, my soul will die. So just forget the whole damn thing."

Slowly, Valen retracts his arm. He rises, smoothing the front of his coat. His mask is back in place. Not even his eyes betray a hint of what he's feeling.

"If that's what you wish," he says in a neutral tone.

"Yeah, that's what I wish." The lie grates against my throat. I hate this. I hate *everything*. I hate Valen, which surprises me . . . until I peel back the layers of that sudden, intense rush to find the truth.

The truth I've always known.

I hate myself.

And this self-loathing aspect of me, this inability to accept myself or forgive myself or whatever it is I must do to come to terms with the fact that this is who I *am*, compounds the hatred by a thousandfold. I burn in silence, thinking a million poisoned thoughts, incapable of expressing a single one of them.

"We've lost time recovering," Valen says in a soft voice. "I'll have everyone pack up so we can keep moving."

As he retreats to the main cavern, the tension ebbs from my body. For all that I just faced the Shadow Lord, this has been the more draining, painful altercation.

Why do I hate myself so relentlessly? There's nothing wrong with being asexual. And frankly, because I *am* asexual and I don't want sex,

I wouldn't have it any other way.

But there is something upsetting about being *me,* this particular person. This miserable, mean-spirited wretch who pushes people away to punish them, to punish herself.

You are not worthy of them.

Zalor's voice haunts me. I clasp my head in my hands, hunching over, squeezing my eyes shut. A whimper escapes my lips as I rock back and forth, trying to purge his words from my brain.

You deserve nothing.

I open my mouth to scream—in fury, in grief—but before I can, someone else's scream echoes through the caves:

"We're under attack!"

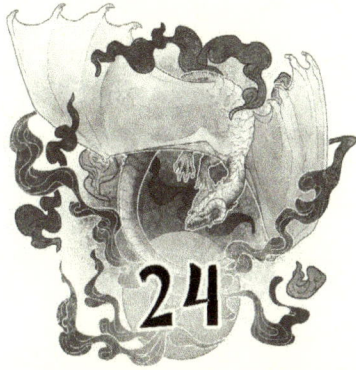

24

WRIGGLING FREE OF THE SPARE COATS, I stumble out of my grotto. In the larger cavern, Asher stuffs our belongings into travel packs. Fyr'thal flutters by the mouth of a winding passage, hooting with urgency.

"We need to leave," says Asher, hoisting the packs over his shoulder and motioning to me. "Now."

I swallow my questions and follow him into the tunnel, Fyr'thal lighting our way. Wind whistles toward us, flecking me with minuscule crystalline particles. Cold stings my nose and eyes.

Rounding a rocky bend, we emerge from our cave into a world of alien beauty. My breath catches in my throat. Vast ice canyons lie before us. Frozen formations rise and fall in whorls. Our cave nestles on a cliff facing north—I can tell because the sun is sinking behind massive mountains that stretch across the curve of the planet. In the low ambient light, the tendrils of Solera's aurora are visible.

For a moment I forget everything—Valen, my soul death, the fact that we can't go three seconds without some new disaster—and lose myself in the stunning sight of the aurora. Wisps of ethereal green and blue and purple oscillate in shimmering patterns, each hue bleeding into the next.

A deafening thunderbolt nearly sends me into cardiac arrest. I whip my head around and spot Valen, Cendrion, and Rexa a few feet away at the lip of a precipice. Loose snow sifts past me as I join them on the rocky ledge. Standing on tiptoe, I peer past Rexa.

My heart stutters. To the south, spiderwebbing through the heavens like fractures on a pane of glass, are threads of pitch-black. The

darkness seeps across sky and land alike. It's so profound it obliterates all trace of what it devours—glaciers and icewood forests and the
air itself vanish at the touch of the shadow.

Valen wields again, aiming at a lightless tendril snaking up the
southern slope of our little mountain. His voltmagic has no effect on
the inexorable, creeping darkness. The void swallows the blue-white
lightning, as it does everything else.

"I've seen a lot of horrors from Zalor," says Asher, "but I've never
seen anything like this."

"He might have changed tactics," says Cendrion. "Now that he
suspects what we're doing, he may be willing to use terrible powers,
the sort of magic he never wanted to resort to during the war."

Part of me knew this was coming. Another confrontation with the
Big Bad is the obvious climax, but now that I know I've been feeding Zalor power from worlds away, I fear he's unstoppable. Skilled
though our ragtag team is, hope, love, and fighting spirit are unrealistic weapons against the Shadow Lord.

Fyr'thal attacks next. Hovering beside Rexa, he opens his beak
and spits a brilliant jet of fire. The shadows refuse to flee the light—in
fact, his flames turn black the moment they cross the threshold of the
approaching void.

Rexa crouches, preparing to wield changemagic. I put a hand on
her arm and shake my head.

"If we can't fight it, we need to outrun it," I say.

You can't outrun me.

I steel myself against Zalor's voice and turn away from the void.

You can't escape me.

Cendrion lowers himself. I dig my fingers in behind his wing
joint and try to pull myself up his leg. My arms spasm as pain shoots
through them. Gasping, I collapse against his side.

Suddenly Valen is there. He scoops me up like it's nothing, like we
didn't just have a soul-fracturing fight, and hauls me onto the dragon's back. I'm too cold to protest.

Muscles bunching, Cendrion kicks off from the ledge. Valen holds
me tight as the dragon labors for a few wingbeats, climbing the skies.

"How the blood did Zalor do this?" Valen asks.

"His powers are unmatched." I make the mistake of looking back. From my angle on the rock ledge, I couldn't see the magnitude of the problem. Here in the air, I realize the void stretches across the entire horizon.

It looks like Zalor's taken the nuclear option. Where the void begins, the world ends. There's nothing in that pitch-blackness . . . and the nothing frightens me more than ever.

Why fight if you know you'll lose?

"Get out of my head," I whisper through gritted teeth.

Rexa, once more transformed into snow amphithere form, rises to Cendrion's level with Asher on her back. Fyr'thal glides on our other side. We fly in tandem, hastening north, until Fyr'thal shrills a warning call.

I look to the phoenix—he's gone into a death drop, heading straight down for a jagged ice chasm. I tilt my neck to see what he's fleeing, and find void tendrils descending. It's hard to gauge their position, since there's no light or shadow in their mass to denote perspective, but they seem to be curving, cresting like a great tsunami wave at its breaking point.

Its breaking point being *us*.

"Dive!" I scream.

Cendrion tucks his wings and plummets after Fyr'thal. Rexa follows fast on his tail. Valen and I cling to each other. I wish I could take comfort in his presence. I wish more than anything I could turn back the clock, undo our cave conversation—erase reality and return to the dream.

Ahead, Fyr'thal enters the narrow chasm. Cendrion zooms in next. Walls of rippled ice fly past us. Wind wails through the tapering gorge, screaming in my ears like a banshee portending my doom. We angle around a sharp curve. A quarter of a mile in front of us, our path terminates in a dead end of solid rock.

"It's too small to rise," Cendrion growls, his wing fingers scraping the chasm walls as he tries to ascend. "I'll have to wield."

Before he can weave a spell, disaster strikes.

The void drips in behind Rexa, black tendrils spilling over the walls. One moment, she's zooming in our wake; the next, she screams and dips. Her wings catch in the snowdrifts lining the gorge and she tumbles, face-planting in a poof of white powder. Asher is flung from her back.

Someone's screaming. A keening, piercing note shatters against my ear drums. It takes a moment to realize the scream is coming from me. I'm detached from my sense of self. I can't move, can't think. I can only watch, helpless.

A dark tendril touched Rexa's tail. Where the darkness connected with her flesh, she's begun to wither. A sable stain spreads across her white fur, infecting her with the void.

Rexa flounders in the snow, but her thrashing grows feeble as the void spreads up her tail. Asher stumbles to his feet and yanks his crafting knife from its sheath—a useless weapon against the oblivion collapsing from above.

"No!" I push against Valen, heedless of the agony in my arms. Sliding sideways off of Cendrion, I drop to the snow. The fall isn't far, maybe fifteen feet, and the powder cushions my impact. If there's more pain, I'm numb to it.

I dig myself out of my hole, yanking the unicorn dagger from my belt. Staggering upright, I strain toward Rexa and Asher. The wall of nothing looms behind them.

Rexa tries valiantly to slither onward, but the darkness has caught up to her. The tip of her tail, already blackened and shriveled, is lost in the void's relentless march. The stain creeps up her tail, spreads across her chest and neck.

Her gaze locks on mine. The pitch-black stain trickles into her lovely eyes, blotting out the amber that once shone so bright. She stills. Her head thuds to the snow.

And she's gone.

Gone.

I stand in an unending moment of anguish, unable to believe what I'm seeing. Clutched in my hand, the light of the unicorn dagger flickers—and goes out.

Something slams into me from behind. Cendrion has returned. He catches me in his jaws and lifts me up, twisting his neck to deposit me on his back. Valen reaches to receive me.

"I'm sorry, Kyla," he whispers.

That accursed name. If Kyla were here, this would never have happened. Instead I'm stuck in her place, trapped in this nightmare, and everything's gone wrong and I'm not having a good time anymore and I want to wake up, please god I want to wake up—

The world continues to move, though Rexa is no longer in it. Cendrion lunges for Asher next. The yawning maw of the void has consumed the corpse of the snow amphithere and is now only feet away.

Before it reaches us, everything dissolves. I recognize the feel of Cendrion's darkmagic whisking us to safety.

I try to cling to conscious thought, but my mind is weak. It seeks release from its misery, which the senseless state of insubstantiality can offer. I let go, allowing myself to drift in a thoughtless, dreamless fugue. Sensation and suffering are distant memories here.

My respite is not to last. All too soon, I'm corporeal again. Cold, pain, and grief slowly swarm back to me, one by one.

The first thing I see when I force open my eyes is a crackling fire and a sparkling blanket of snow beyond. Wherever we are, I suppose we've outrun the void.

Groaning, I sit up. We've made camp in an icewood forest clearing. The blue-barked trees, bristling with white needles and soft-glowing conical seeds, provide shelter. A dusky sky gleams through their branches, strewn with a smattering of faint stars.

Cendrion lies not too far from me, ribs rising and falling with deep, slow breaths. Firelight bleeds through the trees beyond, illuminating a broad-shouldered figure. Valen and Fyr'thal are on watch. Across from me in the clearing, Asher hunches on a stone. He clutches Rexa's dark green cloak.

My throat constricts. I roll to my stomach and crawl toward him.

"It happened so fast," he whispers. His voice is thick and stuffy. "I couldn't do anything. I—I didn't even get to say goodbye."

With a trembling hand, I touch the hem of the cloak. "It's my fault."

Asher shakes his head. "Don't say that."

"This is all my fault. I was supposed to save her. That's why I was brought here. That was my one purpose. And I failed."

Water sears my eyes. Sorrow claws its way through my chest, splitting my sternum. To have come so far, gotten so close, only to crash and burn within sight of the finish line . . .

Asher takes my hand, folding my fingers in his. "I wish we had time to grieve, but the void is still on the move. We were forced to stop because Cendrion ran out of energy. We'll have to keep going soon to stay ahead of it."

I shoot a backward glance at the slumbering dragon. Like any life function, wielding magic requires a wielder to burn energy stored in their body and soul. I imagine he's exhausted. How long can he survive on the run? How long can *any* of us survive?

"You should rest," Asher tells me.

I wrest myself from his grip and once more run my hands over Rexa's cloak. Asher doesn't stop me when I gather the fabric and press my face against it. I ache. I *burn*. I wish it had been me instead of her. It seems a cruel joke that I should live, while she—

A choked sob interrupts my introspection. I can't even think the word.

Slowly I rise. My feet crunch through an icy layer of snow as I put one foot in front of the other, trudging out of the clearing and into the night.

I'm on autopilot, not fully in control of my actions. Part of me doesn't know what I'm doing, but when the trees thin and I come to a ridge overlooking a midnight valley, I stop.

The once-distant mountains tower before me, dominating the sky. Their magnitude has created artificial night. Fanged peaks blot out the sunlight so completely that it's dark enough to see the aurora. I focus on the peaceful colors. This is a good place.

Kneeling, I set aside the cloak and begin to dig through the snow.

Every movement costs me. I'm hemorrhaging a disproportionate amount of energy, but I don't care. Losing myself in the simple mechanics of my repetitive motions, I dig and dig.

A crunch breaks the snow-softened silence. Someone's followed me.

"Do you want help?" asks Valen.

"I can do it." In contrast to his soft tone, my voice is harsh.

More crunching footsteps. I sense his presence next to me, but I refuse to look away from my work.

"I didn't ask if you *needed* help," he says, kneeling beside me. "I asked if you wanted it."

For the first time since coming to this world, a tear escapes my eye. Another follows, and another. They leak from me, and I'm powerless to stop them. Everything is wrong. Even the fact that Valen has managed to say the exact right thing is wrong—because it reminds me of what I can never have.

Sniffling, I nod. Rexa was his friend, too. Who am I to deny him this last act of honor? Besides, it's not weak to accept help when you need it. It might be the bravest thing I've done since we left Midgard.

Valen leans down and helps me dig. Asher joins me on my other side, chipping at the permafrost with his crafting knife. Fatigue weighs on me as I work. In addition to the constant ache in my arms, there's a disturbing sensation in my skull: pressure hovering on the edge of pain.

Between the three of us, we finish the makeshift grave.

I fold Rexa's cloak into the little hollow, smoothing its wrinkles. I want to say something poignant. Who better to deliver her eulogy than the writer who saw every facet of her life, knew every thought in her head?

When I open my mouth, nothing comes out. There are no adequate words to describe Rexa and how I felt about her. I can't immortalize her the way she deserves.

I think of my books, of the legendary adventures she and Kyla used to have. If this were a story, I could rewrite it so Rexa survives. Back home, it's as easy as pressing "delete."

But even if I do make it back to Earth, that won't change this reality. I've altered this world irrevocably. What happened here can't be undone by the stroke of a key or the scribbling of a pen.

"I'm sorry," is all I can manage in the end.

Slowly, Asher scrapes the misplaced snow into Rexa's grave. As the last scrap of green disappears, I break down and weep.

Distantly, I become aware of a weight around my shoulders: Valen's arm. Part of me wants to push him away, scream obscenities at him, tear things apart with my bare hands. I don't deserve his kindness... but I don't have the energy to resist.

I lean against his chest and release the howls I've been holding in. Valen enfolds me in his arms, smoothing my hair, rocking me gently. In the face of tragedy, our differences are forgotten. We mourn together as the Oldmoon rises.

It's freeing, in a way, allowing someone to see my pain. Allowing myself to show it. Lindsay saw me ugly-cry once, and I was mortified. I never lost it in front of Eric because I didn't want to burden him with my hardships.

Here, entwined with Valen, I feel no shame as I sob. Though his presence is a salve for my wounded heart, I can't find comfort in him, not truly. I fear I'll never know comfort again.

One of my darlings is dead.

How can I atone for that?

25

I FEEL LIKE MY OLD, WRETCHED SELF as we trudge north. Like the unicorn dagger, the world has grown dim. It has nothing to do with the ever-advancing void, which seems to suck color and vitality from its surroundings.

Rexa is gone, and a piece of my soul went with her. Grief comes in waves for the others; sometimes their brains allow them moments of peace. Not so with me. My misery is cruel, crushing, and constant. It compresses me into a singularity of nothingness.

Nothing offers relief, and nothing matters.

Objectively, I know that's a bad attitude. I still have a world to save and darlings to fight for. But when there isn't a single droplet of happiness to be dredged from my existence, fighting seems pointless.

Cendrion can't fly bearing three humans, so he blazes a trail north, stamping down the snow for us. He wields us into shadow whenever the void draws too close, but each time, his spell ends faster.

He's malnourished, exhausted, running on fumes. His magic-source must be nearly depleted.

"So," he pants after an hour of slogging along in silence, "what's the new plan?"

My shivering turns into a disconsolate shrug. "Same as the old plan. Find the Monolith of Darkmagic, sever Zalor's connection to its power, go home. Nothing's changed."

Except *everything's* changed. The mountains present an impasse. The dagger's light has dimmed.

And Rexa is dead.

Asher eyes the weapon bouncing at my hip. I look, too. The bloody starmoss would be more useful than the unicorn horn at this point, providing more naturally occurring lightmagic.

"Here." I pull the dagger from its sheath and thrust it at him. The moment he clasps the metal hilt, the horn blazes. "You do the honors. Have fun."

Asher furrows his brow at my tone and stares at me over the top of his glasses.

"I know it hurts," he says, "but Rexa wouldn't want you to give up. We can win. We *will* win, for her sake. Things seem dark, but you have so much to fight for."

The gentle encouragement makes me want to scream. I've sunk so far into my misery that I've become allergic to positivity.

"I'm still walking, aren't I? What more do you want from me?"

At once, I regret lashing out. I steal a sheepish glance at him, but he's no longer looking at me. He's staring over his shoulder at Valen, who trails our group as a rear guard.

"Is this about him?" Asher asks.

My body, already rigid with cold, tenses. He's guessed the nature of my cave conversation, but he doesn't know why Valen and I . . . is "broke up" the right term?

Asher sighs. "I know how hard relationships can be, but—"

"It's not a relationship." I really, *really* don't want to have this conversation. In light of everything that's happened, it's particularly idiotic. "Even if it were, it's different from what you've experienced. You're free to love Baelan, and everyone understands."

I wrote Solera as a world without homophobia because I didn't want such hatred and bigotry here. That might be the only good bit of meddling I did. Or maybe Solera is better than Earth, accepting of same-sex couples all on its own. Whatever the reason, Asher exists in a world where he isn't judged or hurt or discriminated against for his orientation.

I did *not* weave asexuality into the fabric of Solera—no one here will get it. It's not in any unexplored pocket of my lore. Truth be told, I didn't know the term existed when I started writing my books. That's why Kyla is a woman in a straight, allosexual relationship, while I am an asexual trash gremlin.

"It's absolutely a relationship," says Asher. "Granted, it's more complicated than most. There's a big moral dilemma here. Bigger than I can fathom."

No shit. But I don't want to deconstruct the philosophical and moral implications of unwittingly exerting control over Kyla Starblade.

"You could try talking to Valen," Cendrion suggests.

"I talked to him already. That's what ruined everything."

"And now you're avoiding him," says Asher. There's a subtle edge in his tone. He's frustrated. Growing tired of me. "Things are bad enough without you two fighting."

I bow my head and pinch the bridge of my nose. "I don't know what to say to him."

"You're a world-renowned author with an incredible gift. Surely you can—"

"You don't understand! You don't know how much energy it takes for me to talk to people, to be *normal*. It takes more energy than I can give to put on my mask and fake a smile and focus my brain."

I'm out of mana. The well's run dry. I cannot fathom the idea of torturing myself with another conversation.

My outburst silences Asher and Cendrion. Hating myself more than ever, yet unable to muster an apology, I rummage in my travel pack and pull out my book. I search the pages for a crumb of hope, anything to get us over the mountains. My stomach sinks as I peruse the text.

"You gotta be kidding me. The Frostspine Mountains are half again as tall as Mount Everest."

"I've suffered worse," Cendrion growls, glaring ahead at the peaks.

"Without an airmagic wielder on our team, we won't survive the atmosphere. Magically transporting us would drain you of more energy than you can spare. The effort would destroy you."

"Then I will consider it a worthy sacrifice on our journey."

He's alarmingly willing to hurl himself into the proverbial abyss.

He reminds me of myself. He *is* me—I understand that more intimately, now that Zalor's revealed the truth.

How much did I poison Cendrion? Did I pour too much self-destruction into him? Did I ruin him the way I ruined . . . well, everything?

"There has to be another way," I mutter, thumbing through the book. It's my fault Rexa died; I won't let Cendrion die, too.

My brain begins to fog as we plod on and on. It prevents me from focusing on the wounds in my heart, but neither can I focus on anything else. The Eldrian runes glaze before my eyes, blurring into black smears.

Thus, I'm unaware of our progress until Cendrion calls a halt to our trek. Blinking, I realize we've reached the mountain foothills. The hills abut sheer cliffs—the insurmountable edifice of the Frostspines.

Valen jogs up the slope to join us. "We should spread out and search for a trail. Unless you feel up to wielding," he adds, looking at Cendrion.

The dragon's head droops. His sides heave, and froth bubbles at his mouth. "Maybe a quick rest first," he wheezes.

Asher nods and turns west, kicking through thigh-high snow to inspect the mountains. Fyr'thal follows him. My vision's fading, along with my other senses. I can't discern much without the phoenix-light, but I get the sense that no trail will be found. The cliffs rise at a ninety-degree angle.

With nothing else for it, I head east. Boulders jut from the white expanse, giving me footholds as I approach the mountain face. I place a gloved hand against it, bracing myself as I totter along, searching in vain for a way forward.

"You shouldn't be alone out here."

I wince at the voice. Valen has followed me. He falls into step at my side and glances down. "We need to talk."

There they are, the four worst words in the English language. Shame and anxiety churn within me. I'm too tired for this shit. I'm ill-equipped to handle delicate interactions even at the best of times—and this is far from the best of times.

"No thanks, I'm good. Besides, I said everything I needed to say."

"You did," he agrees. "But I didn't."

"Okay, well, maybe this can wait. In case you haven't noticed, there are bigger problems at hand. So, why don't you look for a trail somewhere else?"

Yes, excellent. Push him away. My go-to method of conflict resolution.

Far from being deterred, Valen turns and plants himself in my path.

"This isn't the right time," I tell him.

His eyes flick south, toward the void, before returning to me. "It might be the only time we have. I don't like how we ended things—"

"Look, there's no point in talking anymore. You need sex in a relationship, I don't. We. Will. Never. Work."

I punctuate each word with obnoxious force. Murky memories writhe in the sludge of my mind. The more I scream at him, the more I understand the one I *want* to scream at is myself.

"There's more to life than sex," he tells me, his voice as cold as the unending winter around us. "I should think you, of all people, would understand that."

"Yeah? Tell that to the advertising industry, the movie industry, the cosmetics industry—"

"You know I don't understand your references," he interrupts, anger creeping into his tone. "And if you'd stop wallowing in self-pity and listen to me, things wouldn't be so bloody difficult. This is why you're alone on Earth. You're convinced it's impossible that anyone could care about you."

Oh, this bitch did *not*.

I long to rage and howl, but that won't help my cause. He'll think I'm emotional. Unhinged. Any response I make will turn me into a monster.

"I'm alone because I live in a society that isn't designed for people like me," I snarl. "If I were to hold someone, kiss someone, sleep beside someone back home, they'd think it was an overture to sex. That's the default for my world. That's the expectation."

Something flickers in his eyes, but in the perma-twilight, I can't discern what.

"It's not safe for me to hold anyone, or kiss anyone, or tell anyone how I feel about them, because then they'd expect something from me that I can't give. I'm alone because I can't force myself into society's stupid conception of normalcy. But you know what? Being alone is better than this." I gesture between the two of us.

For all that I don't like confrontation, I'm certainly good at escalating it. I intended to wound, and the way his shoulders slump tells me I've landed every blow. A brief pang of regret lances through me, but I smother it.

After several moments of excruciating silence, Valen visibly gathers his composure. He straightens, opens his mouth—

"I found something!"

Asher's faraway cry slices between us, breaking the tension. Valen's eyes widen. Without another word, he beckons to me, hurrying back the way we came. Stewing in misery, I follow. The running brings a delightful edge of nausea to my suffering. Just what I needed.

We pass a smattering of rocks and Fyr'thal's light becomes visible, casting Asher and Cendrion into silhouette several yards away. Asher excitedly waves us over. Screwing up my eyes, I spot what's gotten him so riled up.

"A tunnel," he says, pointing in triumph. Smooth and round, its interior is dark against the glacial midnight blue of the Frostspines.

"Probably the home of a flesh-eating ice wyrm," I say.

"I don't smell anything dangerous," says Cendrion, nostrils flaring as he snuffles at the opening. It's perfectly sized to accommodate his bulk. My suspicion sharpens.

"That doesn't mean it's a way through the mountains."

"Actually, I think it is. Beneath the scents of old ice and mineral rocks, there's a trace of magic: pure, charged, raw energy."

"Any sign of Zalor?" asks Valen, peering inside.

Cendrion shakes his head. "I know the scent of shadowbeasts— like compost and mold—and I know the scent of darkmagic. There's the barest hint of that, but that's the point, isn't it? We're heading toward the wellspring of all darkmagic on Solera."

He looks at me. So does everyone else.

"It feels too easy," I say at last.

"Why?" says Asher. "Because it wouldn't be this easy in your book?"

"Uh, yeah, that's precisely why. It's giving me big *Mines of Moria* vibes. If we go in there, it will turn into a deathtrap."

"Maybe this is less a trap and more a sign," Asher suggests. "What if this is a manifestation of your unique brand of magic? You want to save Solera, don't you?"

I nod, though my laggy brain can't discern where he's going with this.

"We know you've been influencing this world. What if you've done this without realizing it? What if it was your magic, your desire to make us succeed and bring us to the end of our journey, that created these tunnels?"

I frown, though not because it sounds unbelievable. It's not in keeping with the rules of the Soleran universe, nor the Earthling one—but cast beneath the blacklight of what Zalor revealed, it glows with a certain amount of eerie sense.

"Is there any other way through?" I ask, knowing that if anyone could answer that question, it would be me.

"I don't think we can spare the time to look," Cendrion murmurs.

He's right. The void in the southern skies, pushing us forward, pushing us *into* this tunnel, is close. Plus, considering my worsening symptoms, I'd say I'm on death's doorstep.

On Earth I'd pass this off with inappropriately morbid humor— "Yes please, hope this kills me, can't wait to die, hashtag-YOLO!" — but here, despite heartbreak and suffering, I do have things to live for.

After losing Rexa, I lost sight of that.

I want to save Solera. No matter what else changed, that never did. I crossed two continents and an ocean to reach this point. A true Hero's Journey.

I take a half step toward the tunnel. Then I pause.

The Hero's Journey is about *internal* change. In that regard, have

I changed at all? I've regressed to my self-destructive, self-isolating ways. I've been horrible to my friends.

I think of the wraiths, of the way they took shape to become my most beloved Earthlings. I know I love my friends and family; that was never in doubt. The question is whether I can show them I love them. That's the true character litmus test for me.

When I return, will I be different?

I don't trust that I've changed, but maybe that's the point. Change isn't gradual, it's intentional. I want to be better—not only to my Soleran darlings, but to the people of Earth. I want to be a good friend to Eric, a good cousin to Lindsay, a good daughter to my parents, a good human to the world.

"Let's do this." I take a step, and another, approaching the mouth of the tunnel. Bracing myself, I cross the threshold.

Nothing happens. No booby traps, no shadowbeasts, no darkness descending to consume me.

Asher joins me, Fyr'thal perched on his outstretched arm. The ridged sides of the ice tunnel cast a glittering pattern over us, a thousand mirrored pinpricks of phoenix-light. Asher gives me a bracing smile, and together, we walk on. Valen and Cendrion bring up the rear of our procession. The clack of the dragon's talons reverberates in the oppressive stillness.

Half a mile in, the hard-packed snow floor turns to gravelly rock. I stumble over the transition and sense Valen draw closer, a steadying presence.

We walk without incident for what feels like hours. Then a rumbling reaches my ears, so deep it's more felt than heard. The ground shoots up in front of us, walling off our progress. I spin shakily, but rough stone blocks us there, too.

"I knew it," I grate through clenched teeth.

Asher raises his hand toward the northern barrier, gesturing at the wall to wield it out of our way. His earthmagic has no effect. He tries again, gesturing more vigorously. Still nothing.

Fyr'thal shrills a cry that echoes in our enclosure, pressing on my ears. He wields a jet of flame against the ice siding. The fire splashes against an invisible barrier inches away from the glassy surface.

"Stop," I call. "No more wielding! There's forcemagic at play. Our threads might get twisted."

Everyone freezes. The only sound is the panicked beat of my heart.

Then Fyr'thal squawks. Cendrion growls. I look up to see what fresh horror has visited us.

It's not what I expect.

I was ready to find Lord Zalor himself, but the creature sitting in front of the northern rock wall seems to be solidified light rather than darkness incarnate. It's a beast both alien and immediately recognizable.

"Stop," I say again, flinging out an arm to prevent Cendrion from attacking. "It won't hurt us. It's a sphinx."

The sphinx trains slitted, moonlike eyes on me. Its luminous, silver-furred body is feline, but its face is disturbingly human.

I say *disturbingly* because there's something off about its too-symmetrical features. The flat, androgynous visage also looks out of place perched atop the figure of a ten-foot-tall cat. I can't help but admire it, though it's giving me an "uncanny valley" vibe.

"Why did it trap us?" the dragon demands.

"Ah. I guess I should say it won't hurt us *yet*."

The sphinx cocks its head. An inscrutable smile brushes its wide lips.

"Sphinxes wield timemagic," I continue. "It probably wasn't in the tunnel when we entered. It's possible it hasn't been in the tunnel for years, centuries even. When it sensed us, it wielded to intercept us at this precise temporal crossroads."

"What does it want?" Asher asks.

"I imagine it wants to ask us a riddle." I gather a breath and square off against the sphinx. "That's it, right? You're a guardian who's here to test our worthiness?"

The sphinx smiles again. A bald, ropey tail twitches behind it in a perfect rhythmic pattern, reminding me of a metronome.

"Worthiness for what?" Asher presses.

"Worthiness to pass."

"And what if we can't answer?"

"Then it will kill us," I return heavily.

"It can try," growls Cendrion. He steps forward to stand beside Valen and me, bristling.

"It's a master wielder. It can freeze us in time while it eviscerates us. Or it can accelerate time around us, desiccating us to corpses in the blink of an eye."

Although the sphinx remains unmoving (except for the ticking of its tail), its posture suddenly seems to suggest preening, as if it's proud of its ability to so thoroughly trounce us.

Cendrion blows a breath through his nostrils, like a noble warhorse protesting an activity that is beneath him. "If it wants to play games, then let's be done with it."

"Very well." I meet the sphinx's lustrous eyes and lift my chin. "Give us your riddle."

The sphinx doesn't open its mouth, but its voice fills the space around us. The sound is inhuman, echoing with chords of mysteries and magic. Its pattern of speech is lilting, hypnotic, almost like a song:

"Spun from silver linings and conceived from sparkling things—
Fly too close to seek our warmth and you will burn your wings.
Our golden aura lights a path for lords and paupers each—
Yet we can blind and maim our prey by staying out of reach.
One by one we fall away to chasms dark and lost—
Speak our name and tell us true if we were worth the cost."

The loudest silence I've ever heard stretches when the sphinx finishes its recitation. Asher's mouth hangs slightly ajar. Valen's giving the sphinx a run for its money in terms of being emotionless, but the tension in his shoulders betrays unease. A soundless snarl curls Cendrion's lips. None of them know the answer.

Yet something has clicked in my soul. The sphinx's riddle was meant for me, and me alone. Its voice still echoes in the hollow place inside me.

"Dreams."

There's a rustling as my friends turn to stare at me, but my gaze is locked on the sphinx. Its lips widen a fraction, but it does nothing else.

"Is that the right answer?" Asher ventures after a time.

"We're not dead, so...yeah."

"Then why are we still trapped?" asks Valen.

That's actually a great question. The sphinx should have granted us safe passage upon successful completion of the riddle. That's how all the legends go, both Earthling and Soleran.

It dawns on me, as I drown in the quicksilver depths of its cat eyes, that I haven't answered the riddle in full.

Speak our name and tell us true if we were worth the cost.

Dreams. What have they cost me?

My sanity, perhaps—not because I awoke one morning in a different universe, but because I drove myself to the edge of reason seeking things I could never attain. Things I didn't deserve, but coveted nonetheless. Love. Magic. *Happiness.*

What are dreams, if not the deepest expression of human nature? What drives human nature, if not the desire to be happy?

Yet in chasing my dreams, I destroyed my happiness. In trying so hard to attain something illusory, imaginary, I damaged my soul beyond repair.

Here, it cost me Rexa. On Earth, it cost me everything.

"No," I say before I can stop myself. "They weren't worth it."

My words are so soft that none of my friends catch them. But I see a flicker in the sphinx's eyes, and I know it heard.

"We appreciate your candor," the sphinx says without moving its lips. My friends don't react to the haunting voice. The echo was for my ears only.

As suddenly and inexplicably as it appeared, the sphinx vanishes. With another rumble, the earthen barriers retract into the ground. The ground itself begins to change: it smooths to a frictionless, sloping surface, and my feet give way. I thud down and slide forward, gathering speed. Around me, my friends have suffered similar fates.

"Is this a good sign or a bad sign?" Asher shouts over the rumble of the changing earth.

"Good, I imagine," says Valen. "We're moving faster than we could on foot."

This is true, but we're gathering speed at an alarming rate. The nausea returns to my swooping stomach. I'm dizzy, I'm miserable, I wasted my life on ridiculous fantasies, and here I am, in a world where my dreams are manifesting before my eyes, and somehow I've managed to *ruin* it—

Thump. The tunnel sends me bouncing as it gradually levels. My layers cushion the impacts, but the abuse sends shards of agony through me.

The five of us are forced together as our path narrows. I reach with both hands and latch onto whoever I can—a fistful of Asher's coat, a handful of Cendrion's tail—as we start to slow.

We crawl to a halt just before we reach the mouth of the shrinking tunnel. It opens into a bright, hazy mist. Nothing is visible through the stagnant fog.

"We made it," Asher whispers.

I nod, feeling the truth in the marrow of my bones. Through that exit lies the Crown of the World.

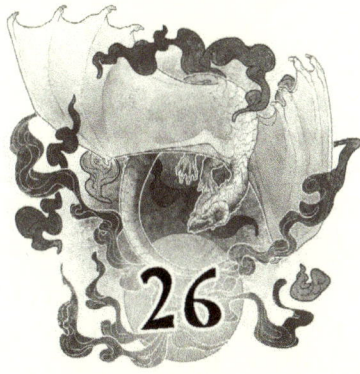

26

THE FOG IS INFINITE AND ABSOLUTE, and has a muffling quality. We're clumped together again, holding onto each other. Visibility is so poor that anyone could get lost if they stray from the party. Our voices sound faraway when we speak, like we're screaming to one another through bulletproof glass. It's enough to renew my shivers, though the extreme cold of the ice continent has abated.

After what seems an eternity, the fog thins. I hurry forward, encouraged. My arms—one linked with Asher, the other with Valen—throb. My head spins. But the end is in sight.

The world darkens as the fog dissipates. I become aware that the ground is gently sloping upward. It's composed of black granite sprinkled with iridescent flecks of minerals and magic.

"Should everything be darkening like this?" Asher tests his voice. It sounds normal once more, and there's a faint, collective sigh of relief from the others.

"I can't say," I admit. "We've reached the end of my knowledge. I don't know what happens next, or what lies beyond."

The sky grows visible through stringy strands of mist. Although it should be full daylight beyond the mountains, the heavens are also black. Multicolored shards of light hang suspended in the air, broken stars I could touch if I desired—but I dare not. I get the sense that any tiny part of this place could destroy me in a heartbeat if I put a toe out of line.

"By Ohra's bloody talons," Cendrion hisses. "Look."

The dragon's head is tilted to the south. Following his gaze, my stomach plummets.

The black tendrils have spread. They've crossed the Frostspine Mountains, just as we have, to permeate the Crown of the World. They stand out against the lightless sky, ink stains spreading across black parchment. Like shadows in the folds of a black velvet curtain, they put the surrounding night to shame with their absolute darkness.

A growl worms through Cendrion's throat. "Zalor is catching up."

Something stirs in the depths of my soul as I consider the void. I'm not sure this *is* Zalor's doing. This has a different quality from darkmagic. It's darker than dark, like death itself. It's indescribable and unknowable. It's stifling in its absoluteness, and I can't breathe.

For a moment I'm mesmerized, snared in the simplistic horror of the sight.

In that moment, disaster strikes. Bands of black mist burst into being, erupting from the ground. I gasp and lurch forward as they coil around me, like a serpent constricting its prey.

Cendrion roars and pitches sideways, wispy obsidian tendrils clawing at his wings. With a shout, Valen summons a bolt of lightning. The shadows withdraw from its brightness, releasing me. I gulp air into my lungs and try to still my quaking body.

Valen is powerful, but not even the brightest voltmagic can emit a pure enough light to banish darkmagic entirely. Nearby, writhing black shapes begin to take form.

"Shadowbeasts!" I scream.

Ambushed. Trapped by the villain who's always a step ahead. Have I changed enough to face him? To *defeat* him? I learned that I have strange magic of my own, yet I've done fuck-all with it. I don't know how to control it. I don't know how to win this fight.

Cendrion coils his lithe body and catapults forward, grabbing me in his front paws. I let out a winded *oof* as his clawed fingers tighten around my middle. Specks of brightness wink across my vision. My neck wobbles and the world spins.

Fierce and wild, Cendrion streaks into the sky, bowling past materializing shadowbeasts. His fangs tear at spectral winged bodies, lacerating enemies before they have a chance to fully form.

Squinting through the blur of battle, I spy something uphill. At the top of the wide northern slope stands a great monolith. In the haze beyond, I can make out another one. And another fainter one beyond that.

"There," I gasp, pointing. "The Crown of the World!"

We're within striking distance. If we can reach the Monolith of Darkmagic, we can sever Zalor's connection to his power. Reckless rage tumbles through me, and suddenly I hope the Shadow Lord *is* here. If he's here, we can end this in one mighty blow.

We—*I*—can kill him.

Cendrion tries to press north, but the shadowbeasts' numbers are too great. Stymied, he loops back toward Valen, Asher, and Fyr'thal.

Lightning fries the air as Valen does his utmost to hold the shadowbeasts off while Cendrion angles down. The dragon lands beside Asher, who's wielding two blades: his trusty crafting knife in one hand, the unicorn dagger in the other. Pitch-black dust swirls around him. The shadowbeasts hang back, cowering before the epic weapon.

"Take this," Asher cries, thrusting the dagger at me. In the whirlwind of battle, I don't hesitate to grasp it. It dims when it comes in contact with my skin, then flares as vengeful bloodlust rises in me. I'm ready to fight again. Too much is riding on the outcome of this battle for me to lose heart.

Before I can act, a puddle of ink spreads beneath my feet. Its frigid kiss slices into my soles. I scream as the dark maelstrom pulls me down. I jab with the dagger as I sink toward the rocky ground, but darkmagic is incorporeal. My attack has no effect on shadows; I might as well have tried to slice a sunbeam in twain.

Then the world dissolves, and darkness envelops me. Not the warm, familiar embrace of Cendrion's power, but the cold, unforgiving grasp of enemy darkmagic.

Sensation flees my body, and I'm blissfully free of physical feeling. My mind, however, clamors with terror. I've allowed myself to be kidnapped by Zalor's minions. I came this far only to fail.

If that's not a metaphor for my whole damn life, I don't know what is.

Without warning, reality comes rushing back in a crushing deluge. I've re-solidified on the slope leading to the monoliths. I find myself in the clutches of a massive shadowbeast that looks like it was once a manticore. Bright fire swirls around us—the flames forced my kidnapper to drop its darkmagic spell, returning to its physical form.

The manticore flashes a Cheshire Cat leer of malevolence, displaying sable fangs dripping with strands of black saliva. Before I can stab my aggressor, another eruption of flame burns painful spots into my retinas. The jet of fire incinerates the manticore, engulfing me in the process.

The fire doesn't burn. It's pleasantly tepid, sending tingles through me where it meets my flesh. Relief weakens my knees and I fall hard, my hip digging into the craggy slope.

Fyr'thal zooms past with a shrill cry and lands in front of me. The majestic beast is a comet, an inferno. Each of his feathers is limned with ruby-gold radiance. Sparks flare from his body, writhing in the superheated air around him.

"N-nice assist," I say through chattering teeth. The manticore's darkmagic leached what little warmth and strength I had, as it is wont to do. I crawl closer to Fyr'thal, awkward with the dagger, wincing as scree bites into my palms.

My guardian's molten warmth is a godsend. I huddle near his wings, hoping to steal some of that warmth for myself. Bands of phoenix fire arc around the two of us. Beyond the roaring flames, I see a wall of shadowbeasts seething, yearning to break through. I suspect the one who brings me to its master will receive a reward beyond measure.

In a fabulous display, Fyr'thal wields a spell that sends spears of fire lancing in all directions. Some shadowbeasts dodge, wielding themselves into immaterial scraps of shade. Others aren't so lucky. When Fyr'thal's fire collides with a solid body, it sears and rends and destroys. Dozens of onyx monsters die on impact.

With their numbers thinned, I grasp for boldness. I don't remember who I was, but I know it wasn't who I was *supposed* to be. I lived my Earthling life in fear of something—maybe everything—but I can't be that person anymore. Especially not now, at the climax of the tale, the Final Boss Fight.

I grasp the dagger's hilt with clammy hands, slick from my cowardice. Fyr'thal's fire won't hurt me, so I edge closer to the banded cage of flame. My movement tempts an enterprising shadowbeast near. It lashes out with lightless claws, hoping to hook me like a fish and pull me into its clutches, but I'm ready. I know how Zalor thinks, and I know how his servants act.

I dodge the predictable blow and stab. The shadowbeast bursts into ash, and I smile in grim triumph. The expression slips from my face when I notice Fyr'thal is losing steam.

"We have to reach the top of the hill. Think you have it in you?" I ask the phoenix.

He issues a soft hoot. The flames dancing across his feathers flicker. Not a good sign.

"We need backup," I shout.

But my friends are scattered. Cendrion glitches through the sky, popping in and out of corporeal form. A wall of darkness curves around him, making him unable to cross enemy lines. Now that the demons have seen our secret weapon, they've devised a way to counteract the dragon's strengths.

They're dividing us to conquer. On the ground, Asher and Valen are barely holding against such overwhelming odds. The sky rains black blood. Demon corpses litter the slope. I can't begin to guess how many shadowbeasts we've killed.

Asher's a few yards ahead of me, fighting to reach the monoliths, unable to break the barrier of enemies. We're overwhelmed, burnt out at the end of our journey, yet I'm so close.

And then—

A shadowbeast strikes. Ebony claws catch Asher's side, scraping his ribs. He cries out as crimson mists the air, blood spurting from his wound. He drops his crafting knife, crumpling in a heap on the ground.

Nauseating panic slams into me. No, no! He can't die. No one else can die. I can't lose anyone else—I won't survive that.

I cowered in the safety of phoenix flames instead of drawing the shadowbeasts to me, but no more. I don't want to be that person anymore. I want to be a hero. I want to change.

Gathering the last of my strength, I sprint uphill, spearing a hapless shadowbeast with the dagger as I burst through Fyr'thal's bars of fire.

"Come on," I call to the phoenix without looking back. "Asher needs help!"

The sight of mortal blood whips the shadowbeasts into a frenzy. They converge on Asher, scrabbling to finish him. Valen jumps in with his voltmagic, wielding a defensive storm, but the demons push forward, ravenous and relentless.

"No," I scream, swinging the dagger like a maniac. "*NO!*"

It's all I can think, all I can say. I have no plan. I can't fight the monsters, but I can't let them harm Asher.

Demons turn at the sound of my voice. They bare glistening black fangs, ready for battle. I charge to meet them, brandishing my glowing blade. In my racing, panicked mind, my enemies seem to be moving in slow motion.

Then I realize they *are* moving in slow motion. The nearest ones churn to a halt before they reach me. My vision—or perhaps reality itself—distorts. The farther shadowbeasts become elongated, stretching backwards, pulled into spaghetti strings to converge on a distant vanishing point.

I've reached the event horizon of a metaphysical black hole, crossed the threshold from one plane to the next. The laws of science and magic abandon me. Lying on the ground, clutching his wound, Asher moves at half speed. I strain for him, but he shakes his head.

"Keep going," he urges me.

"I can't leave you," I argue, though my body has been seized by a new source of gravity—one that tugs me inexorably toward the magical monoliths. I stumble past him on numb feet. "I have to save you!"

"That's how you do it." Asher nods to the crest of the hill. An eldritch ghost light silhouettes the visible dark pillars.

There's an awful logic to his words.

"We believe in you." His whisper somehow reaches me, slicing through the slow, deep buzz of frozen chaos.

To save him, I must win this battle. To win the battle, I must face the villain.

I pass a series of immobilized shadowbeasts. It feels like I'm slogging through a swamp of nothing, weightless yet painfully heavy. My head aches. My arms scream. My core temperature is dropping. I struggle on.

The monoliths are smaller than I imagined, and up close they look shiny. I place one foot on the crest of the hill. Then the other. Triumph sings in my sludgy blood. I've reached a flat plateau infused with a sourceless, fey light. I draw level with the nearest monolith, the first one I spotted. It's not colossal at all—it's my height.

I pass it, entering the ring of stones. Time resumes its regular speed and I sway from the sudden shift in magical dynamics. I'm at the magnetic, magical pole of Solera.

The Crown of the World.

Twelve monoliths—one for each of the twelve elemental magics— stand in a perfect circle, each equidistant from the others. They're shiny enough to be reflective.

I draw a long, shuddering breath, willing myself to be calm. I stagger to their center and turn on the spot. They look identical, each a tall, thin mirror of darkness. Which is the monolith I want, the one I must pierce with the dagger to sever Zalor from his power?

I catch my reflection in one of them and freeze. That isn't Kyla Starblade staring out from the burnished black plate of the monolith. That's... me. My Earth self.

My *real* self.

The dagger slips from my weakened grasp. It falls to the ground with a clatter, deafening in the stillness. Bewitched, I limp forward, gaping in horror.

What the hell is happening? Did I somehow win without realizing it? Is this a portal home? Was simply reaching the Crown a good enough way to end the story?

I shake my head, denying the abhorrent idea. That's unfulfilling.

This can't be the end.

Transfixed though I am by my Earthling visage, I spot something equally horrifying in the reflection behind me. My innards frost over and I whirl around.

"You," I growl.

Zalor spreads his hands in a convivial gesture. "Welcome, Impostor, to the place between worlds."

My fingers curl on empty air. I curse my unending stupidity. The unicorn dagger lies between us, closer to the Shadow Lord than to me. If I lunge for it—

"No more blades for you, I think. You've done enough damage."

With a twitch of his fingers, a shockwave of shadow erupts from him. It washes across the clearing, crashing into the monoliths. It does no harm when it hits me—but the moment it touches the dagger, the diamond spiral dissolves into darkness, magically whisked into voidspace.

"You may have the upper hand," I say in a shockingly steady voice, considering my epic weapon just poofed out of existence, "but you made a mistake telling me about my magic."

A bemused smirk cracks the thin, withered flesh of his mouth. I'm reminded of the sphinx, of its unknowable smile and its riddle of worthiness. "How do you figure that?"

"Because it gave me the edge I need." I plant my feet in a defensive crouch. The gesture is empty, but it lends me the illusion of strength. My arms cry for mercy as I raise them and ball my hands into fists. "It will allow me to fight you, and this time I'll win. I made a vow that I would kill you."

He lets out a mirthless chuckle. The sound lances into my soul.

"But my dear, you already have."

Without the adrenaline and physical exertion of battle, my brain fog is catching up to me. I can't wrap my head around his words. "That...that doesn't make sense."

"None of this makes sense, if you think about it." He twirls one clawed digit in an arc, indicating everything around us.

"Yes it does." My first instinct is to argue. Whatever he says is a trick, a lie. He's trying to throw me off my game.

Unfortunately, the tactic is working.

"It was a quest for redemption." Explaining my reasoning to the Shadow Lord makes it sound asinine. He's right. It *never* made any sense. Even with my disbelief willingly and fully suspended, there were glaring holes in the plot. "It followed all the story beats, and there was a Hero's Journey, and now I'm here at the climax to—"

"You have made a grave miscalculation." The subtle timbre of urgency in his baritone makes me snap my runaway mouth shut.

"This is not the end. It *cannot* be the end," he explains. "If it is, then you and I have both lost."

"I don't understand."

"You clung to this world," Zalor breathes. He's closer to me, though I haven't perceived him moving. Spacetime warps, sewing us together like the edges of a tear in fabric. "But it wasn't *this* world that needed saving. It wasn't this world that mattered."

"This is the only world that's ever mattered." My voice is ragged, desperate. "And I won't let you destroy it! You hurt Asher, you killed Rexa—"

"No, little Impostor. *You* killed Rexa. You destroyed everything."

"Shut up," I cry, though the voice in my head echoes Zalor's accusations.

"Is this the story you spun for yourself? It has a certain unsophisticated charm, I'll admit. You convinced yourself you could be a hero." He clicks his tongue, shaking his head. "Such a pity it was all a lie. Your delusions know no bounds."

I'm shivering head to toe, but not from the cold. Every nerve fires with panic, screaming at me to do something—maybe to run, maybe to fight, but I can't. I'm petrified, and though I don't want to hear what's coming next, I feel compelled to listen. Part of me is curious. What will his twisted version of events reveal?

"There was a Dark Night on Earth." He's closer again, less than five feet away from me. "And you fell."

"I didn't do my manuscript revisions because I didn't know how to change the story," I snarl, bristling in defense. "But I know now. I'm going to kill you."

He's right in front of me. Standing face to face, I realize for the first time that we're the same height. Looking at him is like looking into another mirror.

"Still you cling to your fairytale," he murmurs. "Would you like me to tell you the real story? Would you like to remember what happened, understand at last why you're here?"

My lips part, trembling. I'm suddenly certain, with every molecule of my being, that I don't want to know the real story.

"If I agree, will you let my friends go without harm?"

Zalor tilts his head. "That depends entirely on you."

I stare into his pitiless eyes. Then I nod.

He raises his clawed hand and lays it on my chest, over my stuttering heart.

The universe dissolves around me, and I sink into a dream.

27

ONCE UPON A TIME, *there lived a girl.*

She was young and full of promise, as all young people are. Her energy was boundless, her enthusiasm unfettered. Brimming with potential, bursting with dreams, she knew one day she'd change the world.

Her dreams were grand and sparkling. She was going to be famous. She was going to be wealthy. She'd find her Prince Charming and he would love her forever. She was smitten with the concept of being surrounded by her own people: people who cared about her.

The girl grew and changed, and for a time, it seemed everything she desired was within her grasp, at the tips of her fingers. She was close enough to brush her dreams, but try as she might, she was never able to gain purchase on the slope to the summit of victory. No matter how she strained, she never ended up where she wanted to be.

Angered by her failure, unable to comprehend why it was taking so long to do the things she'd set out to do, the girl pushed herself. She might have made it to the summit then, because she'd finally spread her wings, but invisible anchors weighed her down. She hadn't felt the snares around her ankles until she tried to fly.

The more she strained against them, the tighter they grew.

The girl's dreams diminished. She shrank them to accommodate for the harshness of reality.

Kill your darlings, the world whispered to her.

And with that first, fateful whisper, the girl began to die.

She saw it on her face. Fine lines around her mouth traced a history of hardship; translucent fractures around her eyes spoke of sorrow. She heard it in her voice. The girlish timbre of high-pitched excitement gave way to a slower, deeper monotone.

If she couldn't be famous, she could at least be successful. If she couldn't be wealthy, she could at least be comfortable. If she couldn't find Prince Charming, she could at least find a kindhearted human with whom to share her journey.

She tried to fit into the coffin-sized hole society had fashioned for her. Everyone else was content with their lot, so she reasoned she should be content, too. She worked and worked, praying for success, yearning for comfort.

None of her efforts paid off. Nothing she did was good enough.

Infuriated by her inability to perform, unable to comprehend how she—who had once been so young and full of promise—had fallen into the rut of self-fulfilling failure, she stubbornly forged ahead. But the harder she pushed, the slower she seemed to go. She'd lost her stamina. She was tired.

Kill your darlings, the world whispered.

Again the girl shrank her dreams, chiseling away at them, making them pocket-sized and realistic. If she couldn't be successful, she could at least be stable. If she couldn't be comfortable, she could at least be grateful for the things she had.

Yet gratitude seemed a distant memory. With the changing of the tide, her dreams ebbed. Bitterness and despair floated ashore. They festered on the damp sands of her consciousness, poisoning her one day at a time. The girl waited for high tide, for the return of her hopes and dreams.

It never came. Nothing mattered anymore. Nothing made her happy anymore.

She was trapped in an endless cycle. She had stumbled and fallen; she feared it was too late to get up. Why bother getting up at all? What destination was she forging toward? There was nothing in her future, no finish line to cross, no trophy to strive for.

Her dreams were dead, and so was she.

She was empty, she was nothing, and the nothing was exhausting. Without anything to counter the tedious pain of existence, existence itself was pointless.

The girl, whose youth and promise had been stolen by her own underachieving hand, who found herself drowning in despondency and bereft of happiness, considered her choices.

Life had stripped her of power. Caged by society, cornered in her own mind, there was little left to live for. Why should she torment herself when it would be easier to rest? To give up and stop fighting?

That was a tempting thought, yet morbid curiosity forced her to plod on and see where her path led. She would suffer in silence, endure for the people around her—parents and cousins and friends who would never understand her agony because she would never allow them to see it.

If she let them see her weakness, the illusion would shatter. The world would see a withered corpse in place of the girl, a corpse who wore her memory like a mask.

She suffered and endured. Every day she woke and donned her mask, hoping no one would see beyond her walls to who she really was, to what she had become. She faked her smiles and swallowed her pride and did as society expected.

The girl woke one morning and looked at her life. Instead of a castle, she lived in a drafty one-bedroom apartment. She was alone and miserable. She was suffering; she did not wish to suffer anymore.

She needed a reason to live, but when she looked for reasons, she found none.

So she decided to invent one.

She began to write—a "once upon a time" story, a fantasy, a fairy tale. A story about a girl who was very much like her . . . or rather, like who she had once been. The girl in the story stumbled, but always picked herself up. She was a hero.

The story took on a life of its own, and the author latched onto it. For the first time in years, she felt something. A shimmer. A spark. She relished in the sensation, marveling at the simple yet seismic changes happiness wrought upon her.

Her face shed some of its dullness. Her voice regained some of its shine. Her soul flickered, warmed by the magic of the world she crafted. Her heart began to beat for people who did not exist, except within the confines of her imagination—but nonetheless, it beat.

From the desolate ashes of her old, dead dreams, new dreams sprouted. She was going to be published. She was going to be a hero, just like the girl in her book. With her words, she would change the world. She believed the story she loved could make her better.

A fool's hope. She was broken, and no amount of storytelling or dreaming could heal the sickness hibernating deep in her core.

Slowly but surely, darkness crept back in. Her life began to fray at the seams, fracture along its fault lines. Taking care of herself was simultaneously too exhausting and too kind. She couldn't summon the energy to shower. She didn't deserve to eat. Dirty clothes piled up on her floor and bills piled up on her table. She lost touch with friends. She went into debt.

The magic of her story could only do so much. The heroes of the fantasy world she'd created were brave and strong, but they were no match for the fickleness of fate, the cruelty of life. She tried to share her story with the world, but the world told her there was no place for a voice such as hers.

Kill your darlings, said the world.

And the harder she fought for her final dream, the further it slipped away.

She was drowning, unable to get a proper lungful of air. There was never a day she woke when she didn't feel exhausted. It wasn't the exhaustion of too few hours of sleep, but the exhaustion of a ceaseless struggle beneath the deadweight of a crushing life. No rest would cure the fatigue that had seeped into her soul. That was the problem: her soul was tired.

A body can sleep. A brain can recharge. But a tired soul . . . there is no easy cure for that.

She had killed her darlings, shrunk her dreams, and in doing so, had shrunk herself.

One by one, the scant, slender threads that kept her attached to her mortal coil snapped. She dwelled on the certainty that there would never be another good day in her life. She was plodding down a path that had no happy ending. Her road led to a foregone conclusion of darkness, and she had no desire to continue such a journey.

She was trapped on a miserable ride, but she had one power left.

The girl woke one morning and realized she was free. She no longer cared about anything. The people around her had forgotten her, so she decided she didn't owe them any loyalty. Why should she suffer for them when they cared so little? Why should she force herself to live in pain when rest was within her grasp?

She debated how she'd let herself rest. Pills were too unreliable. Guns were too messy. Hanging took too long. She did not wish to suffer anymore. She had suffered enough.

There was something poetic, she decided, about bleeding out in a bathtub. A few drinks to numb the pain of the knife. A moment of courage to make the cuts, long and deep and in just the right places. Then she could lie back in the warm water, close her eyes, and drift away. She could be at peace.

There were no farewells to be dispensed, she discovered with a touch of regret. There was no one left who cared. They wouldn't miss her, so she wouldn't miss them. The only ones she would miss were the characters in her novels, her lighthouse in a sea of darkness. But they were no more than words on a page. Not even that—pixels on a screen. Her stories would never be printed, never see the light of day, never change the world.

They lived in her head.

They would die in her head, too.

This was the only part of the equation that turned her heart cold. This was the true tragedy. Her world would dissipate into the ether when she was gone.

Still, that knowledge was not enough to stop her. The idea had taken root. It lurked at the edge of her consciousness, darting in whenever she let her guard down. It dogged her footsteps. Hissed in her ear. Clawed at her soul—a soul already ragged and tired.

Kill your darlings, it whispered.

Finally she caved. She would do it, if only to silence the clamoring, howling, mad voice in her head. The voice that relentlessly assured her there was no happy ending. The voice that had devoured everything inside her until she was empty.

Once the voice was appeased, she could be at peace. No more failure. No more fighting. No more wearing masks and faking smiles and subsisting on stale crumbs of hope.

She could finally rest.

She left her job and returned to her apartment one moonless winter night. She considered her affairs, but found she had none to put in order. Her worldly possessions were few, and mostly useless. She had nothing to pass along but bills and the skeletons of long-dead dreams.

Her only possession of value was her laptop—not because it was expensive, but because it contained a summary of her soul. In zeroes and ones, it stored a universe. In spreadsheets and documents, it bore the recipe of her heart.

Perversely, she didn't want anyone to see the books she had written, the world she had created, if she was not there to share the experience. Poetic justice dictated that if the story began with her, so too should it end with her.

She dabbled with the idea of smashing the laptop.

She couldn't do it.

In the end, she shut it down and hid it in her desk drawer. She retrieved the scalpel she'd ordered online, grabbed a bottle of tequila, and went to her dingy bathroom. She ran the water until the room was steaming. She stripped naked, unashamed. Nothing mattered now. Nothing had ever mattered; she regretted that she'd been stupid enough to believe otherwise.

The water burned as she slid into the yellowing tub. Her flesh screamed in protest, but after four tequila shots she numbed to everything—the heat, the alcohol, the agony in her limbs as she split her skin with the blade.

Heat faded to cold as blood ribboned from her lacerations, staining the water, crusting the tub with crimson lines. Her arms pulsed with pain, chiming along to the beat of her racing heart. Her body froze. Her brain fogged.

She was faint.

She was falling.

And then...

And then...

I am awake. Awake, but dead.

For one terrible, unending moment, I am nothing—

Nothing at all—

Unconsciousness, oblivion, no feeling, no thought, empty—

"Not yet." Zalor's voice whispers in my ear. "I need you to see. I need you to understand."

I shudder and gasp. My breath flutters in the middle of my throat, sticking behind a lump. The nightmarish vision returns. The tub water swims before my eyes, dark with blood. I smell it, tangy and metallic with a touch of stomach-turning sweetness. I can't see it billowing from my submerged wrists, but I can feel it.

My head hangs at a sickly, hunched angle. A pearl of drool hovers at the edge of my parted lips. There is nothing poetic about this. My body, limp and lifeless as a crumpled tissue, holds no hint of martyrdom or power.

My vision blurs and darkness rushes in from the edges. I'm lost again, caught in the infinite, terrible nothingness—

"Not yet." Zalor's voice slices through the void of death.

His magic revives me and my heart lurches. He's forcing me to confront myself. There I am, exsanguinating in the stained tub of my Astoria one-bedroom.

Nausea rears its ugly head, but I'm too weak to heave, too far gone to expel the poison. The truth floats atop the blood water like an oil slick, gruesome and ignoble. It leers at me, taunting, torturing me.

I am not the hero of my story.

I am the villain.

28

"Now you understand." Zalor's voice splinters my shock.

I shake my head, unsure what I'm rejecting. Here, at the end of all things, perhaps I'm rejecting my decision.

I was struggling, but I didn't know how much. Not until now. Seeing the end of my journey made me realize what a long journey it was.

I listened to the voice that told me there would be no happy ending. I marinated in darkness, concocting schemes of self-harm. I bought a medical-grade scalpel on eBay. That could have, *should* have been the end of it. Any other person would have been repulsed by the frightening reality of my scheme. Not me. I committed to the violence, thinking it was the best ending I could hope for.

I ran the bath. I drank the tequila. I put the blade to my skin.

I killed myself.

"Not yet," the Shadow Lord hisses, responding to my thoughts.

I take a stumbling step back from him. "Leave me alone," I rasp, my voice throaty and cracked.

Let me die in peace.

He smiles softly. "I don't want you to die. I'm not ready to go gentle into that good night."

"Stop." I sway on unsteady limbs. "You won. What more do you want from me?"

"Have you learned nothing?" Zalor's voice rises and falls in a sneering fashion. "We are connected, you and I. Your death, Impostor, would destroy me alongside you."

A shuddering sob breaks from my lips. I'm cold, and my brain is . . . tired. So tired. Overloaded with a slurry of emotions, each more wretched than the last. I've see-sawed from fury to grief to disappointment. And finally, horribly, as I comprehend what he's implying, I land square in an abyss of self-pity.

This—*all* of this, my journey, my world, my darlings—was a dream. A hallucination. Nothing more than the collective, panicked misfiring of my expiring neurons. A final, frenzied attempt at self-preservation. None of it was real.

Scalding tears bloom in my eyes. An ocean of regret, a wellspring of shame. I valued my life so little—even now, teetering on the razor edge of death, I remember it with bitterness and scorn—yet my heart breaks for the world that never was. Solera will die with me.

I killed something beautiful. Something precious.

"Your power has bled into this universe," the Shadow Lord's hypnotic voice continues. "And I, of course, require your power for my own plans of domination. Therefore, I need you alive."

I take another cringing step backward. "You're too late."

"Am I? Your brain is still capable of conscious thought. Look."

Through a watery haze I blink at him. He gestures to one of the mirrored monoliths. I glance at the dark surface, where an awful vision of my limp Earthling body in the tub flickers. The mildewy sink is visible in the background. My phone rests on the jaundiced lip of the cracked porcelain.

My heart throbs, expanding against my lungs with wild, baseless hope. Could I reach it and call for help?

Should I?

I should be grasping for salvation. That's what a rational person would do. But there's a reason I'm in this mess, and it's not because I had a healthy outlook on my life.

"What happens here if I go back?"

"I expect, once your Earthling healers get you in working order, you and I can continue our joint venture." His gentlemanly smile is chilling, but his words give me pause.

Is there a chance this *is* real? Did my dying, displaced soul truly phase into a parallel universe? A universe I've been poisoning, but a real universe all the same?

"If that's true," I say, more to myself than to him, "Solera would still be in danger."

"From me, you mean? Yes, I suppose it would," he replies with sociopathic nonchalance. "You can't win this war, because you can't kill me. The death of one magic would mean the death of the other, and the only way to kill me is..."

He nods at the mirror-portal, where the grisly scene of my last and greatest crime leers at me.

Finally, I understand. I can't destroy the darkness without destroying myself. I truly *can't* win. My only two choices are to live and allow Zalor to seize control of Solera, or die and snuff it all out.

Life is draining from my soul like sand dribbling into a bottomless hourglass. I'm wasting time waffling. The choice should be simple. Easy.

Yet I hesitate.

As horrible thoughts burn between my struggling synapses, a familiar roar splits the air. The sound kick-starts my heart into regular rhythm. My legs give way from shock. I stumble and fall, reeling backward from the Shadow Lord and the monolith.

Before I hit the ground, everything vanishes.

Sight, sound, and sensation whisk away from me. I might have assumed I'd finally kicked the bucket, except I'm still capable of conscious thought. I don't know about the afterlife, but my outlook on that one's bleak, too. I don't think anything comes after.

That makes me want to hold on to *this* a little longer.

Now I recognize the telltale markers of darkmagic. Based on the roar, I gather Cendrion broke through the legions of shadowbeasts to save me. He's turned me to shadow and wielded me to safety.

I relish in the lack of feeling and sink into a dissociative state.

Here in the darkness, it's easy to divest myself from truth and reality and identity. Here, I can forget everything.

An eternity passes before I wake. Brightness filters through my lids. Crusted remnants of dried tears crumble as I open my eyes.

"Hello, little author." A diamond-scaled dragon crouches over me, keeping watch as I slumber. Pristine white marble gleams behind him, reflecting fiery light from outside.

"Hello, Cendrion."

"I'm sorry." His deep, rumbling voice quivers. "I saw you fall to Zalor and had to act. I couldn't let what happened to me happen to you."

I try to swallow, but my throat is bone dry. "How'd we get here? The void—"

"It dissipated when Zalor touched you. We fled back to Eldria, staying ahead of his forces—but only just." Cendrion bows his head. "It's my fault. I took you away before you could defeat him."

Stinging guilt bubbles in my eyes. "I wasn't going to defeat him."

Cendrion's amethyst gaze flickers to the window. We're in the infirmary of the Imperial Palace. Outside, the sky is a tapestry of eldritch horrors. The void has returned with a vengeance. Thick, black tendrils snake across blood-red heavens. It looks like the world is burning, and the darkness—more absolute than any darkmagic I've ever seen—is consuming it.

"We suspected something went wrong," he murmurs.

"Not something. Some*one*."

Cendrion's scaled brow ridges pull together in confusion.

"Me," I breathe. "I did a terrible thing."

Before I can elaborate, a bang echoes from the far end of the deserted infirmary. The thud of booted feet against the flagstone floor reaches me. Asher and Valen burst into view.

"Thank Ohra you're safe!" Asher launches at me, his arms spread wide. On instinct I lean toward him, yearning for the comfort of a kind embrace.

You destroyed everything.

Zalor's awful voice floods in, eclipsing all else. I raise a trembling hand, halting Asher in his tracks.

"What's the matter?" he asks.

"Apart from the obvious?" says Valen, nodding at the apocalyptic view. Is it my imagination, or are the city peaks of Midgard crumbling?

"Has the void advanced again?" says Cendrion.

Valen shakes his head. "It's stationary for now, but there's no telling how long that will last."

They don't know. They can't know, not if they're going about their lives, treating me as if I'm not a monster. I fade out of their conversation, but snap to attention when I hear them reference me.

". . . if the author wasn't able to defeat Zalor at the Crown of the World," Asher is saying, "then we have to find another way before it's too late."

"It's already too late," I blurt without thinking.

Everyone goes silent, staring at me.

"What happened back there?" Asher asks. "We saw you speaking to the Shadow Lord, but we couldn't hear anything."

I struggle to bring moisture to my dry throat. "It's going to sound crazy."

They wait, patient and concerned. I stifle a sob as I recall my first real (or not real, as the case may be) conversation with my darlings. How far we've come since then. How far I've fallen.

With a faltering voice, I tell my story.

"I tried to take my life on Earth," I conclude, staring at my hands, which are clenched around fistfuls of the hospital bedsheets. "That's why I'm here, living this dream, or nightmare, or hallucination. This is my life—the imagined life I always wanted—flashing before my eyes. It's over. The end."

I feel hollow admitting it.

"Of course it's not over," Asher says at once. I chance a peek at him. He's the only one of my friends who doesn't look horrified. "I never thought I'd say this, but Zalor is right. If you're capable of conscious thought, there's still hope! You can go back—"

"I don't want to go back."

Asher's eyes cloud behind his glasses. He sits on the edge of my bed and reaches for me.

"Why would you say that?" There's no pity in his expression, but there's plenty of worry. Right now, that's just as bad. "What about your Earthling friends? What about your book series? You have to finish your manuscript and give it to your publisher, don't you?"

I flinch away from his touch. "You're not getting it. That was fake. This is all fake. That life was a dream within *this* dream, nothing more. My friends don't care about me. My books weren't published."

Asher's face twists. I know he's struggling to wrap his mind around this. I can barely process the Inception-level bullshit my brain concocted, either. It was fake... but it offered a glimpse of what might have been. What could have been.

What now will never be.

"The fight with Zalor must have confused you," says Asher. "You know we've all lived full, independent lives here. Solera has millions of years of natural history, it's—"

"*Stop.*" The word is guttural and grating, harsh against my burning throat. "I don't want to hear it anymore."

I don't want to believe anymore.

"It was nice while it lasted, but I know the truth now. You can drop the act," I add, more to myself—encouraging my brain to close the curtain on this pathetic production.

Your delusions know no bounds.

Having supportive friends who enjoyed my company? That pushed the suspension of disbelief, but Valen showing romantic interest should have been the nail in the coffin. Of course this was a fantasy. There is no plausible universe in which someone like him could love someone like me.

"You can't give up," says Valen, and my stomach twists. His voice is as I've never heard it before: frightened. "You have to go back and fight."

"Why?" Again, I speak without thinking. I cringe, ashamed of my nihilism and my inability to repress it.

"So you can survive," Cendrion growls. "You owe it to yourself to—"

"To what?" I sit up so abruptly that they all draw back. "To suffer?"

"Everyone suffers." The dragon's voice is not unkind, but it sparks a burn within me.

"Yeah, I get it. I'm the asshole." Sluggish anger simmers in the pit of my chest. It's surreal, this conversation. I'm arguing with them like they're actual people, as opposed to projections of my desperate subconscious.

"Everyone has *those days*." I hook my fingers in the air. "The days where the voice in their head tells them they're ugly, and they're unlovable, and they're not good enough, and they're a failure, and they will never be happy, and in fact, they don't *deserve* to be happy."

Water spills past my lashes. My voice gains volume and strength. I'm not shouting, but every word packs a vicious punch.

"I should suck it up and suffer through those days, right? Everyone else does. But you know what? *Not* everyone's voice is so incessant that it drives them to the edge of madness, so loud that it drowns out happiness and reason, so unbearable that they want to rip off their skin, shed their body, become something else or nothing at all. Not everyone's voice distorts their reality, screaming at them nonstop, refusing to give them a single heartbeat of peace. Not everyone's voice makes their life a living hell, makes them *afraid* to live because living is so physically painful."

I'm spouting dark poetry. The irony isn't lost on me that only in death can I vocalize what I felt while I was alive.

"Not everyone's voice whispers to them at night, telling them that the only way they'll ever find the peace they want is to give up. I was never going to be happy, and if I go back, I never will be happy. I'll just keep suffering. So tell me, what is the point?"

Cendrion shakes his head, as if in denial of what he's hearing. "If that's what you believe, you're crazy."

"Fucking *obviously*!" The anger boils and bursts inside me. I throw my sheets aside and whip my legs off the far side of the infirmary bed, away from my darlings. Shoving myself upright, I stomp toward the window. "Healthy people don't do what I did. I had an illness."

The final symptom of which is death.

"You don't mean any of this." Asher probably intends his soft tone to be soothing. All it does is stoke the fire of my fury. "You don't want to die."

My nails bite into my skin as I clench my fists. *Stupid*, I want to scream at him—or possibly myself. *Stupid, useless, completely-missing-the-point argument.*

That's the one thing people don't seem to understand. No one *wants* to die. But no one wants to suffer, either.

I glare over my shoulder at Asher. His face, white with terror, brightens when he catches my gaze. He opens his mouth, but whatever he's going to say, I don't want to hear it.

"There is no hope for me," I snarl, pointing an accusing finger at him, "so don't start with your shit."

"Kyla," he says, staring at me aghast.

"I'M NOT HER! She's not real. *You're* not real. And suffering through your toxic positivity gets old real fast."

Word vomit. Spools of lava erupt within me, manifesting in fury. I can't stop. Don't want to stop. The angry things I've bottled up my whole life, the dangerous thoughts I was forced to hide on Earth . . . why waste the energy suppressing them here?

"And I don't want to hear about how I need to fight," I add, before anyone can say the infernal words. "I fought for thirty years, and what did it get me? A shitty one-bedroom, a dead-end minimum wage job, a bunch of fake Twitter friends who don't care and won't miss me when I'm gone. Don't tell me to fight when there's nothing to fight *for*."

No one dares reply. I've finally shut them up.

"The deed is done," I continue, convulsing with ill-subdued sobs. "Why would I go back and ruin the only thing I ever managed to do right?"

I turn away from them and lean my brow against the cold window pane. My broken breaths fog the glass as I stare at the burning world and the darkness devouring it, millimeter by millimeter.

From the corner of my eye, I catch a glimmer of movement in the reflection. Asher is retreating. Abandoning me to my fate. It shouldn't shock me after everything I've said, but it does. Cendrion, too, departs on silent paws.

"I know you're there," I growl. "I can feel your judgment burning a hole in the back of my skull."

Only silence answers. Some destructive desire to be awful, to prove beyond a shadow of doubt that I am irredeemable, makes me turn.

Looking at Valen still makes me ache with longing, though I now know what he is. In my Third Act clarity, I realize it isn't him I've been fighting with. It's been me all along.

My inability to accept my identity—as if this were a thing I could control—created a rift between my heart and my brain. These two essential pieces comprise my soul . . . but a soul at war with itself is doomed.

"Why did you do it?" he whispers at last.

I choke on a garbled laugh. "Were you not listening to my villain monologue?"

"I was. I just don't understand. You had so much to live for."

"I had *nothing* to live for."

Valen tilts his head. His eyes swim with reflections of the far-off fires and with . . . something else. Something nuanced and gentle. Something that breaks my heart.

"What about us?" He raises a hand, placing it on his chest before gesturing toward the infirmary exit, through which my imaginary friends have vanished.

The vulnerability, the raw hurt in his expression, is gut-wrenching. It's stupid to feel guilty, but old habits die hard.

"I'm sorry, Valen." The anger drains away, leaving me empty, tired, without armor to hide behind. "I never got published, it was all part of the dream. Your story never went anywhere. It never mattered."

"It mattered to you, didn't it?"

I open my mouth to argue, then close it slowly. I want to reject this wisdom, but something about it calls to me in a way nothing else has.

"That doesn't count," I say at last.

"On the contrary—you wanted to make a difference. What better way to be a hero than by writing a book that could save a life?"

The infirmary bed separates us, but I can trace every detail of his face.

"My life," I murmur.

"A life worth saving." He withdraws, leaving me alone with my dying thoughts. "That would be a story worth reading. But it can only be written if you go back."

THIS IS THE END OF SOLERA. The end of *me*.

Tunnel vision as everything crumbles. Unable to focus on anything but the creeping darkness in the sky. I'm suffocating. The weight of the world is too heavy. The tasks before me are too vast. Insurmountable in what little time I have left.

The shadows above are a reflection of the shadows in my soul. They consumed me until I was a shell, an empty husk devoid of love and hope and the desire to fight. The night I stopped fighting was the night I took my own life.

Tried to, anyway. I'm not quite dead yet.

Even if I wanted to go back, I don't know how. I can't see a path out of here. Try as I might to wake up, I'm trapped. Locked inside my dying brain, suffering through this prolonged fever dream, forced to watch as the darkness of death creeps ever onward.

I ghost through Midgard in my hospital shift on numb, bare feet. I'm losing my senses—touch first. It means I can no longer feel the ache of my bleeding arms or the nausea of blood loss or the pounding dizziness in my skull. But nor can I feel the fresh summer breeze, the sun-warmed stone against my soles, the whisper of the silk shift against my body.

"It doesn't matter," I murmur. "It's not real."

It reminds me of real things, though. Things I miss. Fragmented memories flash through my brain as I drift, zombie-like, along the city's eastern thoroughfare.

New York City sidewalks. Coney Island beach. Hot cocoa and fuzzy blankets and mindless movies on Friday nights. The Grand Canyon. Small moments of triumph when I let go of my handholds and did something brave.

A dull ache burns in the pit of my chest as pieces of my forgotten reality return. I huff a mirthless breath. All I'd dismissed as boring and banal calls to me like never before. The siren song of ordinary things wends its way through my heart.

Why do I yearn for those things now, when they're forever out of reach? They didn't matter. *Nothing* mattered. Earth didn't matter—and in the end, neither did Solera. There was nothing special about my world.

Except for what it meant to me.

Tears fog my vision. Here, at long last, I understand. The lesson is learned.

Too little, too late.

The citizens of Midgard wander in aimless patterns, bereft of direction or purpose. I pass sylphs and dwarves, nereids and ifriti, golems and elves. Their eyes have lost the sparkle of vitality. They know the end is coming, but they can't comprehend the magnitude of what that means. If they did, they'd be panicked. Fighting, the way all living things fight for life.

"I'm sorry," I whisper as I stumble past a cluster of humans. They don't acknowledge me. They stare at the shadows, chins tipped skyward. They'll have front row seats to watch their extinction in real time.

Like the citizens and the fiery sky, the infrastructure of Midgard is coming apart at the seams. Skyscrapers sport massive splinters in their once flawless surfaces. Cracks appear in the paved streets as I plod onward, abyssal fractures following in my footsteps.

Exotic plants lining the city thoroughfare wither as I watch. Verdant ferns turn black. Desiccated palm leaves skitter along sidewalks like tumbleweeds.

The wall grows as I trudge east. Finally I reach the gates. There are no guards, and a sliver of light shines between the massive doors. The heavy stone gives way when I push, grinding over the paved ground. Leaving the city behind, I approach the cliffs.

The Midgardian Mountains stand stark against the dark cross-hatching, a last bastion between me and death. Dragons, visible because their glittering hides wink like beacons beneath the red sky, perch on the faraway peaks. Sentinels guarding against the inevitable.

I get it now, the reason they wouldn't fight. Dragons wield a power equal and opposite to Zalor's darkmagic. That's why they never took action against him. If they destroyed him, they'd destroy themselves. That's the big reveal.

An apt metaphor for my situation—perhaps a little too on-the-nose for readers. Very obvious and lowbrow. No Nebula Award for me.

I expel a long-suffering sigh. It's all so meaningless.

And yet... they're beautiful, those faraway creatures.

There are no dragons on Earth, but I find myself missing the poor substitutes I had. Collectible figurines. Light-up Halloween decorations. A commissioned artwork of Cendrion. *My books.*

"You've come to face the end, too?"

A voice startles me out of my reverie. As if thinking of him has spun him into existence—which it very well might have—Cendrion arrives, padding toward me from the north, pacing the edge of the limestone cliffs.

My favorite character. Darkness incarnate. Not the cruel, violent darkness of Zalor, but the softer darkness. The shadow of what I might have been, had I not surrendered to the shadows inside me.

"I'm sorry," I say again. "For earlier. For everything."

My apology feels like a band-aid on a severed limb.

Cendrion joins me. As one, we turn east. Brilliant ruby light shafts between the bands of black, painting us with strange shadows. I inhale and exhale slowly. My sense of smell has succumbed to death. I can no longer enjoy the wild scent of the river, the hint of featherpine on the mountain wind, the subtle tang of magic in the air.

More memories flood forth to torment me. I can almost recall the way Earth smelled after a rainstorm. Hyacinths in full bloom in the spring. Fresh-cut lawns in the summer. The aroma of spicy cooking wafting through my apartment building—it wasn't meant for me, but I knew someone somewhere was guaranteed a warm, comforting meal, and there was a strange residual comfort in knowing that. There were things worth living for.

But is it worth returning to those things if it means I must also return to crushing failure, chronic pain, and unquenchable loneliness?

"And I'm sorry for what I did to you." I lean sideways, resting against Cendrion's sturdy frame. I'm numb to the sensation of his scales against my skin, the pressure of touch itself. This dream grows ever more dreamlike the further I slip from life.

"I made you suffer—in my books, I mean. I made Zalor infect you. You lost your soul because of me."

"It's not your fault."

"I think it is." If this is all in my head, my guilt is incontrovertible. On the off-chance Solera is real... that's worse. Zalor said it himself: I influenced the story. My darkness helped destroy this world.

"I do not begrudge what happened to me," says Cendrion.

"I begrudge it. You had so much potential. You had years of future ahead of you. I ruined it. I *stole* it."

I can't feel the heat in my eyes or the tears tracing tracks down my cheeks, but when I blink, water blurs my vision. I'm weeping for all the things that never were... and now, never will be.

"And for what?" I snarl. "Why?"

"Because reality is dark," Cendrion says easily. "Sometimes it gets the better of us, even the strongest of us. A soul is a fragile thing; a body, even more so. Reality forces you to make sacrifices. Food or medicine. Money or health. Dreams or peace. How can anyone be expected to find happiness when the world tells us every day to kill our darlings?"

"I don't know." Though I can't feel the sobs blocking my throat, my voice is thick with grief. "But I wish I hadn't done it."

When the world told me to kill my darlings, why did I listen?

What else could I have done?

Could I have waltzed through life, chasing errant dreams like butterflies in a field? The notion is preposterous. How would I have paid rent, bought collard greens doomed to spoil, gone to the therapy sessions I never had and so clearly needed?

Strange that humans were free to shape society however they imagined, and they chose to build their empire on a field of dead dreams. Dreams stolen from dregs like me—people who, by the accident of their birth, were unlucky enough to be caught in the cogs of a clockwork system of misery.

I bow my head in regret. "It's all my fault."

"It's not." The conviction, the *vehemence* in Cendrion's voice awakens something inside me—something I believed long since dead. My head jerks back up and I stare at him.

"It's Zalor's fault," he continues. "That is his greatest power: he lies to his victims. He distorts reality. He taints the truth with his darkness, turning you against yourself. Remember, as much as you were influencing him, he was influencing you."

I nod, watching through blurred eyes as a squadron of dragons flies south, fleeing the inescapable. Cendrion's wisdom smooths a broken piece of my soul that had turned sideways, pressing inwards and lacerating my heart.

"You once told me I am more than my darkness," Cendrion concludes. "That holds true for everyone."

"Even me?" I hate the quaver of uncertainty in my voice.

"Especially you. As long as you remember who you are, what you love, and what you're fighting for, the darkness cannot win."

Shivers dance down my spine. Valen's words from our first day together reverberate in my mind: *Infinite parallel universes exist in quantum-magical superposition, each one different because the people within them made different choices.*

During the course of this dream, I glimpsed possibilities of what my life could have been. I saw myself published, successful, an international sensation. In choosing death, I snuffed that universe out.

"I should have fought." For Eric and Lindsay. For my parents. For the agent and editor and publisher I might have gotten tomorrow, or the next day, or the day after that, if I'd only kept going.

"Then let us fight now," says Cendrion. His wings stir at his sides, fluttering with a whisper of anticipation.

I offer a trembling hand. He bends his neck in an elegant arc and rests his snout against my palm. I slip my arms around his muzzle, cradling his head to my chest.

I remember touch. Hugging my friends. Petting dogs. Rough bark digging into my fingers as I climbed a tree. Sitting in a quiet library with an age-softened book, absorbing the tranquility around me.

"Forgive me, old friend," I whisper, "but we won't win the Shadow War."

"No, I don't think we will."

I wince. Though Cendrion is a tortured soul, he's never been a defeatist. That role was reserved for me.

"You don't win this war, you simply fight it," he continues in a gentle tone. "There is no definitive end. Every day brings with it a new battle. Some days you lose—that is the nature of war. That is the nature of darkness."

I bite my lip to keep it from trembling and nod.

"But every day, you must resolve to win. And I promise you, little author, some days you *will* win."

An echo of sensation hums through my body. I remember field day in eighth grade, beating my classmates in a footrace. Receiving an award for a short film I made in college. Going to a mountain lakeshore with my high school best friends, splashing in the shallows, laughing as we danced beneath the halcyon summer sun. Days when life gave me gifts, free of charge.

"The war will rage on," says Cendrion, "but your ending is not a foregone conclusion."

"It's not," I agree, finding renewed strength in my voice. Lost in the darkness, I lost sight of that truth. While I'm still alive, I have the power to change things.

This is a dream, a dream I know by heart. And when I'm lucid, I can control the dream.

I break away from Cendrion to look him in the eye. "A piece of the Shadow Lord lives within you. You wield Zalor's power. In theory, you should be able to do anything he can do."

He raises a brow ridge. "In theory, yes. I've never explored the extent of those powers for fear of what they might do."

"What if…" I hesitate, unsure if my newest idea is genius or madness. Given my track record, probably the latter. "What if you tried resurrection?"

Cendrion flattens his ears and scowls. "Fight fire with fire? Create an army of shadowbeasts?"

"Just one," I whisper. "And maybe, if I help you, she won't be a shadowbeast at all."

The dragon's face softens as he catches on. He rotates his wing joints, squaring his shoulders. "I suppose there's nothing left to lose."

"And everything to gain," I add.

Unsure where to start but thrumming with the sort of energy I haven't experienced in ages, I stretch out my hands. Cendrion leans back on his haunches, raising his forepaws to mirror me. His eyes unfocus as he concentrates, contracting his fingers so his talons glint blood-red in the spectral light.

Please. I close my eyes and pray to whatever gods might be listening, focusing on what I want with all my soul. *Let this work.*

Brightness filters through my lids. Though I've lost all sense of touch, I hear the muted roar of wind and thunder. Something is happening, something massive.

Daring to peek, I let out a gasp.

Shining filaments stem from Cendrion's paws and my hands, pitch-black from him and glowing white from me. The threads collide and coalesce in the space between us, swirling and weaving together. They create a tapestry, a masterpiece.

Light scatters from our creation, as if we're feeding energy into an invisible prism. Our work refracts a rainbow, washing the cliffs and spearing the sky with glorious color. The muted roar of pure power rises, pressing into me with an almost physical weight. The brightness spikes, and I'm forced to close my eyes. Then it dims, and all is silent.

"Cendrion?" A shaky but wonderfully familiar voice speaks. My heart leaps and I look.

Rexa stands before me, hale and whole. She stares at her clawed hands, turning them over, patting her scaly torso as if to reassure herself that she's real.

Reality—such a nebulous concept. I beam as she turns on the spot, examining her chimerical form. Her amber eyes, sparkling with life, latch onto me.

"You," she breathes. "Did you do this?"

"It's all thanks to Cendrion." I nod at the dragon. He's panting from his exertions, but his fangs are showing in the widest draconic smile I've ever seen.

"The Shadow Lord can resurrect lost souls," he says. "It seems I share that ability."

"But..." Rexa spins again and runs her hands over her face, dragging her claws through her obsidian locks. "How come I'm not a shadowbeast? I mean, I'm not, right? I'm myself?"

"That depends," I say. "Do you have a deep-rooted desire to serve your lord and master, Zalor, and destroy everyone who stands in his way?"

Her face crinkles in a delighted grin.

"I do not," she declares.

"Then it worked. You're back."

By all rights, it *shouldn't* have worked—true resurrection goes against the magical laws of Solera and the scientific laws of Earth—but it seems we've found an answer in the space between universes. A fundamental truth unlocked at last.

"Rexa?!"

My heart leaps again and I turn. Asher and Fyr'thal are exiting the city gates, hurrying toward us. Whether they were attracted by the light of the resurrection spell or whether some subconscious part of me summoned them, it doesn't matter. All that matters is that they're here, and we're together.

Slack-jawed with shock, Asher races toward us. He hurls himself at Rexa and wraps her in a hug. "Gods above and below, I thought we'd lost you!"

"You did, I think," she wheezes, patting him on the back even as she tries to wriggle free from his rib-cracking grip. "I was gone for a while, there. Just... gone. Completely and utterly nothing."

She glances at me over Asher's shoulder.

"I'm sorry," I tell her. That's my hit single stuck on repeat, but it needs to be said. Again.

"Don't be." A silver sheen limns her eyes. "You brought me back."

Asher pulls away, giving Fyr'thal a chance to swoop in and greet her. She raises an arm and the phoenix alights on it, nuzzling his feathered head against her cheek. Then, as one, my darlings turn to me.

"You were right," I say. "All of you. There's still hope, and I want to fight."

"Better late than never," Asher and Rexa reply in unison. Asher's voice is kind; Rexa's is bone dry.

"I missed you," I whisper, holding my hands out, inviting them to join me once more.

Asher approaches. He came ready for war, bedecked in dwarf-made armor. Against all odds, he still believes.

"For what it's worth," he whispers, taking my proffered hand, "I never left. I was just keeping my distance. I wanted to give you space while you worked through . . . whatever you had to work through to get here."

"If I hadn't been such a colossal idiot, I'd have gotten here much sooner."

Asher squeezes my fingers, and I imagine I can feel something. Not his embrace, but something better: a dull, faint ache in my forearms. "I don't think so. This isn't a place you find easily. It only makes sense if there's a journey."

I can't help but smile. Good old Asher.

My journey has brought me from one universe to another, through shadow and hellfire and despair and triumph, to this moment. I know what comes next. The knowledge has been sewn into the fabric of my soul.

Every story I ever read, every tale I was ever told, made me believe that when the time came for me to be a hero, I could be one. That when at last I marched into battle, I would be ready and unafraid. That I would have gathered the tools I needed along the way to overcome the darkness.

I straighten my spine, ruining the effect with a sniffle. Glancing at Rexa, I ask, "Will you fight with me?"

She approaches, cracking her knuckles. For a moment she stares at me, her expression unreadable. Then she leans in and throws her arms around my neck.

"Let's fuck him up," she growls in my ear.

For the first time in what feels like a million years, I laugh. So on-brand. Her reaction fills me with warmth, only noticeable now because cold is creeping in at the edges of my consciousness.

Rexa breaks away. "This doesn't mean I like you," she assures me.

"Of course. I'd never dare to presume."

She snorts and slugs me on the shoulder. We're all in a loose circle now. I stare at my darlings, the things that have always been within my grasp. The things I wrote about and believed and *was*.

There's only one piece of the puzzle missing.

I turn, knowing I'll find what I seek if I will it to be there. Sure enough, standing on the southern cliffs, glowing with the light of sky-fire, is Valen. He's stopped outside the gates of Midgard, frozen as he takes in the impossible sight of Rexa.

Slowly, his gaze shifts to me.

"I love you," I tell him, and it occurs to me that this is the first time I've said that aloud. I never said it on Earth—I was one of those "You too" jerks. Someone else was always saying it; I, for whatever proud or broken reason, never bothered to say the words back.

I don't care how pathetic it is to love something that may or may not be real. It's real to me, and that's what matters.

Valen strides forward, but stops before we touch. He looks to Cendrion, then to Rexa, then back to me. I can almost see him putting the pieces together in his head.

"Nice of you to turn up," Rexa drawls. "We could use a commander-general."

He nods, though his gaze remains locked on mine.

"Anything within my power to give you," he whispers, "I will freely give it."

He's offering me the universe.

I offer him my hand.

"Just a hug," I whisper, more vulnerable than I've ever been.

He gently pulls me to him. I close my eyes and rest my head against his chest. A thrill runs through me, because I can *feel* it. The sleek, cool fabric of his Imperial military uniform. The rush of his heart against my cheek.

No kiss, no tearful professions of adoration. I don't need the former, and the latter would be disingenuous. I just want to know someone is on my side.

Even if that person is me, it counts.

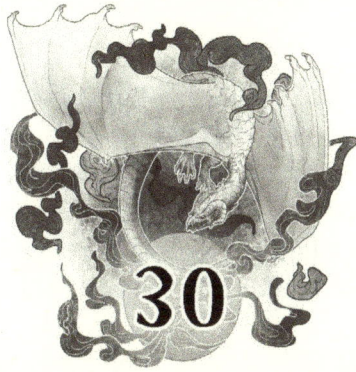

30

THE QUEST IS NEARING ITS END. I'm ready to return to the ordinary world, but it will come at a cost. To save myself, and by extension, Solera, I must forever leave the place I love.

It has to be done. And if I survive this battle, this night, changes will have to be made. I must act with intention to prevent myself from spiraling this far into the abyss again. If I am to live—*truly* live, rather than subsisting in a fog of self-hatred, which will inevitably lead back to self-destruction—then I must be committed to the idea of living.

I'll lose Solera, but I'll regain my future. My potential.

If we were to consult crusty old Joseph Campbell, he'd probably have a few things to say about my journey.

The returning hero, to complete her adventure, must survive the impact of the world.

I must reconnect with my Earthling body.

I don't know how.

"I'm at your service as Commander-General of the Mortal Alliance," Valen whispers, his lips brushing the top of my head, his breath rustling stray wisps of my hair.

"And you have my bow," Asher pipes up guilelessly from behind us.

I burst out laughing.

"Let's not turn this into a Lord of the Rings fanfic." I draw away from Valen to stare at my friends. Asher scrunches his nose in confusion, but I shake my head. "Stop me if you think this sounds crazy—"

"Might as well stop you preemptively," says Rexa.

"I think I have to reconnect with Zalor. The only time I touched my Earthling life was when I was with him. We'll make our last stand on the Midgardian Mountains, confront him on our own terms."

"We have no idea where Zalor is," says Cendrion.

"It doesn't matter. If I have the power to alter Solera's reality—and I think we've proved by now that I do—then he'll come when I call him."

"Let's get on with it," says Rexa. "We don't have much time."

We certainly don't. Judging by how dark my bathwater was, I'd say I've lost three or four pints of blood. Assuming I have less than ten pints in my body, I'm almost at the point of *no* return.

How much time has passed on Earth since I saw that vision in the Crown of the World?

"You can't march into your greatest battle wearing a hospital shift," says Asher. "We need to get you proper armor."

"We'll also need to amass a proper army," Valen adds.

My lips twitch. They don't understand the extent of my powers—how could they?—but I know what I'm capable of. I close my eyes and narrow my focus, concentrating on what I want. This is my dream, my universe. I *will* take control.

It's harder than I'd hoped, but easier than I feared. Though I'm lucid, I can't change the fact that worlds away, my physical brain is confused and weak from blood loss. I clench my fists, grit my teeth, and throw my heart and soul into shaping Solera.

For a few excruciating moments, it's like I'm struggling to unlock a door with the wrong key. Then, with an almighty heave of my subconscious, something slides into place with a satisfying *thunk*. Reality bends to my will.

I open my eyes to survey my rewrites.

Not half bad.

Instead of standing on the cliffs of Midgard, we're on the outer rim of the mountains, facing east. The crosshatched sky blazes red, as if an invisible afternoon sun burns beyond the lattice of shadow. Arrayed on the peaks, spread in rank-and-file formation, are all four divisions of the Mortal Alliance. Platemail gleams. Weapons glint.

The hum of potential energy swells as twelve-thousand wielders gear up for a battle of epic proportion.

I've also edited my outfit. Gone is my flimsy nightgown. In its place glitters the signature dragonscale armor Kyla Starblade dons in the fifth and final book of my unpublished, unknown fantasy series.

I raise my arms, admiring the overlapping white scales on my bracers. Each scale came from Cendrion as he shed them, and my characters painstakingly pieced this outfit together for Kyla to wear. My left hand drops to my hip, landing on the hilt of a magnificent sword: the unicorn dagger reimagined, a shining spiral three feet long, extending from a golden haft.

"Nice upgrade," says Rexa.

"Something's missing." I step forward, leaving the front line to march to the edge of the plateau upon which our regiment stands. I draw my blade and thrust it skyward, brandishing it with a theatrical flourish. The crystalline surface flashes crimson.

Just because I'm dying, that doesn't mean I can't enjoy my final moments on Solera. Gathering my breath deep in my chest, I open my mouth and call to the fiery heavens, *"Drachryi, kemraté a'eos!"*

It's like I've detonated a minefield in midair. Flashes of sound-less light erupt overhead, painting the mountains with blinding brilliance. Unlike the previous times I spoke Draconic (what now seems a lifetime ago), power lives in my words. The essence of magic sings in each syllable I utter.

I've become the Lightbringer, tapped into my potential, connected at last to Kyla's missing power. She and I are one and the same: just a couple of jerks who are bad at communication and create their own problems.

When I go home, I'll be kinder.

To others, yes—but most importantly, to myself.

Before I tackle that insuperable battle, I need to survive this one.

I blink to clear my vision and squint into the sky. Two hundred fully grown dragons hover overhead, held aloft by their lightmagic. I spot Temereth at the head of the pack.

"Lux'abria," she greets me.

"Temereth. I know why you couldn't fight." I hear myself speaking fluent Draconic. In accessing my power, I've unlocked the little pocket of neurons in my brain that fastidiously stored every word and grammatical construct of the dragons' language.

"Then you know we die if Zalor dies," Temereth replies in her native tongue.

"Actually, I don't think you will." I smile, noticing the subtle expressions of confusion spreading across scaly faces. *"On my journey, I learned that your ancestors gained their powers from the Monolith of Lightmagic."*

"So the legend goes," says Temereth.

"I also learned that you can return a magical essence to its monolith by connecting it to its equal and opposite power."

"A well-reasoned hypothesis, based on the givens presented."

"It so happens that Zalor wielded darkmagic while we were in the Crown," I tell her. *"And his spell hit every monolith there."*

Violet eyes flash as the dragons glance at each other. I imagine they're having a desperate telepathic symposium, exchanging thoughts at the speed of light.

"I follow the path of your logic," Temereth says at length, *"but your theory is flawed. As you see, my kin and I still have the ability to wield our lightmagic."*

"Yes, you still have the ability to wield it. Zalor bound his soul to the Monolith of Darkmagic and stole its power—but your ancestors didn't bind their souls to the Monolith of Lightmagic, did they?"

Temereth shakes her magnificent head. *"Lightmagic was gifted to them."*

"When Zalor's spell hit, it didn't sever your connection to magic," I conclude. *"All it did was sever your connection to the Monoliths—and, by extension, to him. Do you agree with this theory?"*

There's a moment of silence as the dragons ruminate. Then Temereth's scaly lips curl.

"All good hypotheses must be put to the test."

Beaming, I turn back to my friends, who are gazing upon me with something akin to awe. "We worked it out. The dragons are joining the Mortal Alliance."

Every mortal within earshot cheers. Rexa pumps her fists in the air. Cendrion, who understood every word of my conversation, dips his snout, offering me a bow.

"*I am not so lucky as my kin, I'm afraid,*" he whispers in Draconic so only I can hear. "*My fate remains entwined with Zalor's.*"

"*I'm here to save you,*" I remind him. "*And one way or another, I will.*"

Valen strides forward to join me on the cliff's edge, preventing Cendrion from arguing. He does an about-face, spinning to address the army. "Eldrians," he bellows, his voice echoing in the mountain peaks and canyons. Twelve thousand pairs of feet stomp in unison as the mortal races stand at attention.

"We are gathered today, all species of our world united, to challenge the Shadow Lord and defeat him," Valen booms. "The Lightbringer has secured our final faction, our most powerful allies. Generals, prepare offensive spells!"

Voices relay Valen's command down the line. The higher-ups are organizing their wielding units. From the corner of my eye, I spot General Praxus prepping his division to the north.

Asher, Rexa, Cendrion, and Fyr'thal come to my side. Rexa has taken the opportunity to change. She's become a mottle-scaled dragon. A fitting choice.

Fyr'thal shrieks an ethereal command, and a host of burning phoenixes rises from the army ranks. They soar upward to disperse themselves amidst their massive draconic brethren. The air shimmers, as it would with a heat mirage, and I know the magical birds are wielding superheated fire shields.

Fyr'thal tilts his head toward me. I reach for him, stroking his chest with the back of my hand. I'm not sure what he represents in my subconscious. He was a convenient thing to have on my journey, but he didn't necessarily stand for something the way my other darlings did.

Or did he?

"Your fire kept me alive," I tell him. He hoots and dips his head in acknowledgment. Then he flaps his wings in a burst of sparks and takes off, zooming skyward to join his people.

"I'm with Rexa," says Asher, shouldering his quiver and prepping his bow.

"Goodbye," I say automatically, stupidly. He pauses before he clambers onto Rexa's back.

"Is this the end?" he whispers.

I shake my head. "We'll win this one. Promise."

"I don't doubt that for a second." A small, sad smile wobbles on his mouth. "You'll see me again, but I don't think I'll ever see you again, will I?"

A sorrowful thrill shoots through me. Asher correctly interprets my silence as assent. He takes two long steps toward me and wraps me in a hug.

"Thank you," he whispers.

"Don't jinx it. We haven't won yet."

"Not for that. For everything you've done. If I have it right, I think we're all connected to you—and therefore, also connected to Earth."

I swallow a lump in my throat, snaking my arms around him. "Something like that."

"Well, I want you to know that Earth is beautiful."

"You've never been to Earth."

"No, but I've lived on Solera for twenty years. And Solera is beautiful beyond imagining."

I tighten my hold on him. "It is, isn't it?"

"Then by definition, that means Earth is beautiful." He draws back, holding me at arm's length. "You can only believe in the beauty of Solera if you had something beautiful to draw from."

How does he always know exactly what I need to hear?

"If I'd known I would get to meet you," I tell him, "I'd have killed myself way sooner."

Asher scowls and squeezes my shoulders. "That's not funny."

"It's kinda funny."

He's unimpressed, but behind him, Cendrion has a twinkle in his eye. Glad someone appreciates my humor. If you're not laughing, you're crying—and I'm done crying.

"Stay safe," Asher whispers. He retreats to Rexa and vaults onto her back. She spreads her draconic wings, allowing bloody sunlight to filter through their membranes. A wave of grief tightens around my chest, forcing heat up my throat. Finally, the right words come:

"Thank *you*." I thought this story was about me saving him, but in the end, he saved me. All my darlings did.

Not yet.

Another chill floods my veins. I'm not dead yet, but I'm hardly safe. The war on Earth is much less epic than the one I've sculpted here, but it will be far more deadly. The battlefield: my bathroom. The objective: reach my phone. Call for help.

Hell, I'll even accept the gods-damned thousand-dollar ambulance bill if I make it. It'll be a price worth paying if I survive the night.

I stretch out a hand, and Cendrion comes to me.

"I'm with you to the end," he says.

"As am I," says Valen.

Though my heart protests, I shake my head at Valen. "You'll be needed on the ground to lead the troops. This is not a done deal."

He frowns. "You can't control them with your abilities?"

"My brain is . . . fuzzy." I neatly avoid the term *dying*. "The narrower my field of focus, the better we'll fare. You command the army. I'll take care of Zalor."

Connect to the Shadow Lord. Connect to my body. Return to the land of the living.

Valen doesn't argue. He's a military strategist. He gets it.

"I want you to know that this is the realest thing I've ever felt," I tell him, gesturing between the two of us. "And it was nice to feel it, just once. I'll cherish the memory always."

There it is—the infamous almost-smile, visible only if you know to look for it. "You may well feel it again. If we win the day, you'll have your whole life ahead of you."

"I'm an obnoxious misanthropic jackass, incapable of normal human interaction, who wants a perfect Prince Charming to dote on me but doesn't want sex." My lips twist wryly. "I don't think you appreciate how difficult it'll be to find someone compatible on Earth. Asexuality is the *least* of my worries in that equation."

"You know none of that is true," he says.

My instinct is to argue, but I make the conscious decision not to. Valen is the smartest person I know. Maybe he's on to something.

I've been listening to my dark voice for so long that it distorted how I view myself. It told me I was a monster, and I believed that without question. Now that the veil has been lifted from my eyes, I see the truth: I am a complex, multifaceted, beautifully flawed human. I've lost some battles, yes—but by all the gods of Solera, I vow those losses won't be fatal.

"You are worthy of love, little author," Valen adds. Something in the timbre of his voice breaks my heart. "Never forget that."

"No promises," I quip.

Hugging him again would shatter what little focus I have left, so instead I hold out my hand for a shake. Awkward and self-sabotaging to the end. But hey—it's in-character.

His fingers, warm and calloused and comforting, grasp mine. He brings my hand to his lips and brushes a soft kiss on my knuckles.

Then he's gone, striding away to return to the army, barking commands to the thousands of shifting bodies. They're eager for a fight.

I'm dreading it. I've been delaying the inevitable, concocting a good and proper climax for our journey, but I can put it off no longer.

Cendrion crouches. My armor is bulky but lightweight, comprised as it is of hollow-honeycomb dragonscales, and I clamber onto his back with ease. A low growl gathers in his chest, building until it becomes a roar. He trumpets a challenge to the sky and launches from the cliff. The cacophonous cheers of the army follow on his wings, pushing us forward.

It's now or never. I summon my strength, gather my focus.

"Zalor," I scream, "I want a rematch!"

We wait for a response. The army's shouting fades, leaving the air empty. Eerie silence fills the vacuum. I'm afraid I've done something wrong, missed my chance, waited too long—but I *had* to say goodbye.

Without warning, dark thunderheads erupt before me, blotting out the light. Just as the dragons teleported to the front lines with blinding speed, so too do the shadowtroops amass.

A pitch-black legion of winged demons materializes. Our enemies coalesce into a writhing hurricane of death.

Helming their army is the Shadow Lord himself. He rides no epic mount—he's hovering on a cloud of darkness, alone and more terrifying than his horde of mind-controlled monsters.

"You know I don't want to fight you." His voice carries on the wind, making shivers crawl like ants beneath my armor. "I need you. I want you to live."

"Then it seems we're in agreement."

I can feel confusion radiating from his powerful form. "If you wish to return to Earth, foolish wretch, just say the word. I'll send you back, no questions asked, and we'll continue our arrangement as if nothing has changed."

"That's the problem. *Everything* has changed." I draw my sword and level it at him. "I'm officially rewriting the ending. You will no longer control me or feed off of me, you will no longer terrorize my friends, and I will *not* leave this realm until I know they're safe from you."

Zalor's desiccated, parchment-thin flesh splits in a smile. "You're in no position to bargain. Tarry too long and your time will run out. You can't waste precious heartbeats on this battle-for-show, not when the hour is so late."

He twirls a hand, indicating the lengthening shadows in the sky.

"I owe it to this world to give it the ending it deserves." I draw a breath through my nostrils and channel my focus into a blade, an arrow, a deadly ray. "I owe it to myself."

Brightness erupts behind the dark legion. Beams of lightmagic arc through the sky, encasing us in a glowing orb. I hear the terrified shrieks of shadowtroops and smile. The dragons made the first move. They've sealed off Zalor's escape. He'll be forced to confront me now. Or rather, I'll be forced to confront him.

"You dare challenge me?" Zalor thunders, his voice shattering against my ears. "I am omnipotent. My word is law. You can't defeat me—the only way to kill me is to kill yourself! You'll *never* be rid of me."

"That may be so. I can't win the war, not really."

He leers in triumph, reveling in my perceived weakness.

"But I can win this day. And I can win again tomorrow, if I try. I'll wake up every morning for the rest of my existence and I'll *fight* you, just to prove I can."

The flesh over his black-fanged mouth curls in derision. "You're fighting a losing battle."

"It's a battle worth fighting."

My focus has sharpened to a molten point. I unleash my power on the world. A beam of lightmagic erupts from my sword, hurtling toward the Shadow Lord.

And with that, the battle begins.

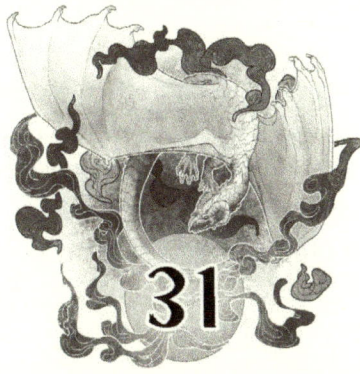

31

CONNECTED TO MY MAGIC, my world, I feel invincible. I'm dying, and everything is dying around me—but the thrill of an epic battle is, as it always has been, intoxicating.

The crush and swell of pitch-black demonic bodies is dizzying, but Cendrion navigates through them with expert precision. No longer does he hide his darkness—it's out in the open for everyone to see. He uses it to deadly effect, glitching across the sky, phasing us in and out of existence to avoid enemies and attack hapless victims.

He banks sharply. I lean left as he tilts right, instinctively counter-balancing. I swipe at an enterprising shadowbeast that dares to dart overhead, opening its belly with my blade. It emits a horrible squeal and falls away. Cendrion straightens and I adjust. I'm like an extension of his draconic body. We're a team, working seamlessly to forge a path toward Zalor.

My actions may have provided the Second Act Twist, but in my mind, Zalor is still the Big Bad. Perhaps foolishly, I've conflated connecting with him to *defeating* him.

A shadowbeast thraxwing, smaller than the one we faced in the Sky Archipelago, approaches us head-on, shrilling a dissonant cry. Its ribbed wings undulate. Its barbed tail thrashes. It opens its jaws and spits venom, emitting twin jets of pitch-black acid.

Cendrion pulls his wings in tight, keeping his humeri elevated. I'm sandwiched between them, kept snugly in place as he performs a flawless barrel roll.

The maneuver allows him to dodge the caustic liquid. He shoots past the thraxwing, twists, and attacks the creature from the rear. It shrieks in agony as his jaws close on its tail. He whips his neck, yanking the beast toward him. I lurch from the violent movement, squinting against the brightness of the blood red sky.

Cendrion releases the thraxwing's mangled tail and retracts his neck like a cobra, aiming to strike at the creature's head. I beat him to it. Hurling myself forward, I grab his spinal ridge for support and bury my sword deep in the thraxwing's skull. It dies without a chance to emit another cry, going limp and slipping from my blade to fall into the lightless chaos below.

"Nicely done!" I tell Cendrion. I recognize this battle—this is a play-by-play recreation of the final fight in Book Five. Although that fight was a bloodbath for my army, I can't help but feel bolstered. We're in familiar territory. I know this story.

Now I'm going to change it.

Cendrion tucks his wings up again, bracing me as he rolls sharply toward a shadowgryphon.

"To the north," I scream. Though my brain has identified this battle, it's still laggy, like an old computer struggling to run a powerful program. I don't have enough RAM to handle it—which is unfortunate, since this is *the* battle.

The battle where my darlings die one by one, until none remain.

My cry to Cendrion comes too late. The obsidian gryphon snaps its avian beak and catches him on the wing, as I knew it would.

"Don't disengage," I yell. "Push forward, trust me!"

Cendrion hisses and, thankfully, heeds my advice. He uses the gryphon's movement against it and bowls it over in the sky. It wasn't expecting that—it was expecting him to pull away. If he'd done so, it would have used its powerful beak to break the bones of Cendrion's wing.

With the gryphon unbalanced, Cendrion and I strike. He kicks at its side and I stab with my sword. I don't have the bandwidth to summon lightmagic again. My powers of concentration have shifted. Remember the battle. Change the ending.

Save your darlings.

The shadowgryphon convulses in pain and releases Cendrion. He wields darkmagic, bringing us to a lightless, senseless place before reappearing above the crush of war.

Cendrion's wing hasn't sustained too much damage, but he's not in good shape. I hear his labored breath. He's spent from wielding and fighting.

"I hate to say this," he pants, tilting his head toward me as he flies on, "but there are too many demons."

"We can take them," I say, reminding myself of both Asher and Rexa. Unquenchable optimism in the face of despair. The spirit to fight against overwhelming odds.

As I sharpen my concentration, bringing the battle into crisp focus, my stomach plummets. It's not just because Cendrion has dived to avoid another attack. Even with the dragons and their lightmagic on our side, we've barely made a dent in the shadowtroops.

To the west, an aerial battalion from the Mortal Alliance has risen. Sylphs, manticores, and water-maji have joined our airborne phoenix troops. The animal wielders of the four base elements work in tandem to repel Zalor's winged forces, but their combined efforts are not enough.

I note, with a painful thud in my chest, that the darkness consuming the heavens has spread to the land. Shadows seep across the gleaming cliffs of the Midgardian Mountains, blanketing the ground beneath the warring factions. The sky has also dimmed substantially. Beyond the dragons' magical shield, the pockets of visible red light have shrunk.

"We're losing," Cendrion growls.

"We are," I breathe. *But not to Zalor.*

It's me. I'm dying. And because I'm connected to Solera, my death will be the death of this world.

I was so sure that following this story structure would bring me where I needed to be. There *has* to be an answer. What if I concentrate on myself? Focus on sensing, *feeling* my Earthling body?

Though my brain screams at me not to disengage from the battle where my friends are fighting for their lives, my gut tells me it must be done. If ever there were a time to let go of my handholds and trust my instincts, it would be now.

As Cendrion dodges a crackling tongue of black lightning, I close my eyes. I cling to his scales. The clash of war grates on my nerves. Too much stimuli—I must blot it all out. This is a dream, and I can control it.

Except I can't. I'm torn. My focus rips like a piece of flimsy fabric, fraying between my two worlds. I'm caught in limbo, wanting to stay present with Cendrion and ensure none of my darlings die, yet *needing* to return to my body so I can end this nightmare. So I can save myself.

I do want to save myself. I was unable to see the things I had, unable to divine a path toward a happy ending. I was afraid.

And...I'm *still* afraid.

It dawns on me that I'm terrified. Trapped in a pocket of darkness, eyes closed, the sound and sensation of the Shadow War lessens and allows me to feel what I'm feeling.

I don't want to die, but I don't want to suffer through a miserable life.

I can't retreat, but I'm reluctant to advance.

The only way to change the ending is to survive.

It's this moment, the moment I'm torn between my two realities—because it would be a disservice to say that this world and these characters aren't real to me—when I feel a spark of something...Other.

I become aware, peripherally, of unpleasant sensations. I'm lightheaded, I'm nauseous. Pain from somewhere else is registering, hovering at the edges of my fuzzy, unfocused mind. I can't process it because I'm afraid.

Rooted in my fear. Drowning in it. I don't want to die. I'm not ready to die. I refuse that other reality, the one where I destroyed my own life. I want to take it all back because I'm afraid of dying and I am *not* having a good time anymore and I want to wake up, even though I'm terrified of the real world, *I want to wake up—*

"WAKE UP!"

The shout yanks me out of the in-between. My heavy eyelids peel open and a blur of red and black and gold burns my retinas. I shake my head, rattling my swollen brain around my skull. Echoes of pain and pressure shoot through my nerves.

I gasp for air. I focus.

Cendrion has broken through the shadowtroops and zooms toward the edge of the magical enclosure. My gaze snaps to the north. Zalor lurks there, hovering on his inky cloud. He's not making any special effort to escape the dragons' lightmagic enchantment—but neither does he engage.

Several shadowbeasts swarm in from the periphery of my vision, guarding their master. A pitch-black wyvern darts close, but a wyvern is no match for a dragon. Cendrion dodges, executing a perfect aerial loop around his foe and raking his talons down the other's spine. The wyvern shrieks and drops.

Gritting my teeth against the pain of movement, I swipe at a shadowgryphon. It falls away from the bite of my shining sword, spiraling down to its doom. Cendrion works like a well-oiled machine, rending three more demons to pieces.

Now our path to Zalor is clear. Though we're still a good mile away from him, I feel his gaze on me. A thrill shoots through me. He's waiting.

This is destiny dovetailing. The battles have converged.

Connect to Zalor. Connect to Earth.

Save Solera. Save *myself.*

There's a rushing, a roaring in my ears that has nothing to do with the battle. The roar bends, convulses, and becomes a rhythmic beat.

The beat of a war drum.

The beat of my blood.

I'd expected my heart to be pumping slowly, given my blood loss, but it's *galloping.* My gut clenches and adrenaline, more corrosive than thraxwing venom, sears my veins. Why would my body do this? Why would it speed up my heart, vomiting more blood into my bathwater? It's pushing me toward my death. How will I survive?

"You think you can change your ending?" Zalor's voice reaches me, each word an arrow fired from an invisible crossbow, puncturing me. His voice is no longer his. It's *mine.*

Just as I know him, he knows me. We're connected, and he knows my weaknesses. Knows how to exploit them for his victory.

"Don't forget, Impostor: I've had a window to your life, too. I've seen your soul. You're a failure. You're nothing. Thirty years of suffering, thirty years of blood and sweat and tears. Where has it gotten you? Do you think another thirty years will make a difference? Do you think you'll magically become the person you wish to be?"

I'm frozen on Cendrion's back, paralyzed by Zalor's—*my* voice. The voice that screamed at me. The voice that drove me to violence.

He's right.

"He's wrong."

My gaze shifts, flickering from the Shadow Lord to Cendrion. Though he valiantly wings onward, propelling us toward our fate, one of his amethyst eyes catches and holds mine.

I'm wrong. I've been wrong all this time. And I *know* that—I feel like I've had this revelation a hundred-thousand times in the last four chapters of this mad adventure—yet with each rapid fire heartbeat, I forget. My brain's unable to focus, to remember the things I've learned along the way: that I am not alone. That there is hope for me. That I'm a fighter, always have been.

A sob breaks from my lips. If I know all of this, why is it so easy to forget? I *hate* myself for forgetting. That's how I got here. I did this to myself because I'm stupid, and—

And there's that shadow-voice again. It's Zalor's voice, it's my voice. It screams awful things and makes me believe them. I mustn't listen to its lies.

Another sob as we zoom through the air, but this one doesn't stem from panic or self-loathing. It's at once an expression of relief and exhaustion. *This*, right here, is the nature of the Shadow War. It doesn't matter how many times I learn a lesson or win a battle—the fight will rage within me forever.

But I suddenly realize that's okay. As long as the fight rages, that means I'm alive. It means I haven't lost hope, and I haven't stopped fighting, and I've found ways to remind myself every day, every heartbeat, that I am worthy of living.

I *must* focus. I must remember these things. More importantly, I must forgive myself for the dark moments when I lose sight of them.

"You're wrong," I shout at Zalor, pulling strength from Cendrion's assertion. The light-shield pulses with energy, but the sky beyond its shimmering edge is almost completely black. I'm aware of darkness creeping in from the edges of my vision, too.

Is that a good thing, or a bad thing? Will I lose consciousness, leave Solera, and wake up on Earth? Or will I slip into a senseless state, slide down in my bloody bathwater, and die?

"I know you." Zalor's half a mile away, and the air is clear of shadowbeasts. Almost as if he's inviting this confrontation. "I'm a part of you."

"So is every character I've written," I retort. "And I won't let you kill them!"

My sword has been raised in challenge, but the weapon has grown too heavy. My forearms *hurt*, trembling as they struggle to hold the blade aloft. My head throbs. I sway on Cendrion's back as he careens toward the Shadow Lord.

Zalor sneers, revealing pitch-black fangs. His cloud of darkmagic bubbles, bearing him forward. He's come to settle the score. A one-on-one battle to decide the fate of the world, as it was always meant to be.

I know this ending. I wrote it. This is the moment of truth. Zalor's five-hundred feet away. As of now, I am *still* alive.

While I'm alive, I have the power to change things.

I gather the last vestiges of my focus, my strength, my determination, and I launch from Cendrion's shoulder, springing forward. The force of my jump sends the dragon askew. He hisses in shock as he spins off-course.

I, however, remain *on* course. Straight and true, I hurtle toward Zalor.

With a defiant war cry, I plunge my sword into his chest.

His lightless eyes go wide. His mouth contorts in a rictus of agony and hatred. He grips both my arms, digging razor-sharp claws through my armor and into my skin. The cloud of magic beneath him disintegrates. Locked together, irrevocably intertwined, we begin to fall.

Tumbling head over heels, everything blurs around us. The darkness of the sky eclipses the colors and motion of the battle until there's nothing. It's so dark I can't even see Zalor anymore—but I feel his claws in my flesh.

Then . . . the claws retract. Somehow, it doesn't help with the pain. If anything, my discomfort intensifies. Agony roars into me, ripping across my skin. I hate this. I'm dizzy and nauseous and in pain and my heart is racing and my head is pounding and I'm terrified and *I want to wake up.*

"I want to wake up," a slurred, weak voice mumbles. My voice.

And that's when it hits me.

I'm not dreaming.

This is real.

32

I OPEN MY EYES to find an ocean of blood entombing my body. Abstractly, I understand the bathwater's still warm. In Earth time, outside of my dream, only minutes have passed since I split my skin with the scalpel—yet my flesh is ice. I'm *so* cold.

But I have a mission, and I will not fail.

This is the most important battle I'll ever fight. The moment where the fate of the world is decided.

I raise my left arm. It's leaden, numb. The laceration throbs. As blood-water sluices from my flesh, I see darker, thicker rivers of crimson forking from the cut I inflicted upon myself.

My stomach roils, rejecting the sight. The tequila from earlier sloshes unpleasantly. Muscles tense as I heave, but nothing comes up.

Reality moves around me, making it impossible to focus. The room spins as if I've just stumbled off a merry-go-round. Splotches bloom and fade and bloom again across my scope of vision, simultaneously dark and bright. Like slow-burning fire creeping across parchment.

I blink hard. I must fight as I've never fought before.

I grip the edge of the tub and pull myself over the lip. Aching. Freezing. Every movement makes my nerves buzz with agony. My right arm's also bleeding. I cut both, like the masochist I am. How long do I have?

My fingers stumble on something. The discarded scalpel. I push it away as I twist, getting to my knees in the water, draped over the tub's edge. My head is too heavy to waste energy lifting it. I raise left arm, seeking blindly for the towel I know is hanging from a hook in the wall.

My heart rate spikes. The motion ignites a response within my body. My pulse flutters in my neck, in my stomach, stabbing through my wounds . . . yet the heartbeats feel shallow, as if they're not doing what they're supposed to. I expect they're not. My body doesn't have much blood left to work with. I have no oxygen.

In my detached state, a calm pocket of my brain can process this information and observe it with objective interest. The rest of my consciousness operates on auto-pilot. My fingers close on the towel and clamp down.

It comes free when I pull. The drywall crumbles around the hook I installed half-assedly. Thanking my past-self for her laziness, I proceed to wrap the towel around my left arm. Buy myself some time before help arrives. The left cut hurts more, feels deeper. Being right-handed, I made that incision first. That's the dangerous one, the one whence my life is draining, drop by vermillion drop.

I'm weak. Both arms shriek in protest as I twist the ratty fabric around myself from wrist to elbow. I don't know if I've made it tight enough. Every time I pull, my muscles collapse against the strain.

I finish my work. Not good, but maybe it will help.

Now the battle truly begins. I slide from the tub onto the tiled floor, a formless creature emerging from the primordial soup, grasping at a chance for life.

Dark liquid splashes around me, staining the yellowed grout. The coldness of the ceramic tiles burns my skin. Everything hurts.

But I am a hero, and I can work through the pain.

The bathroom is mercifully tiny. Thank you, shitty Astoria one-bedroom with 500-square-feet of living space. I bring my knees beneath me, huddling in a fetal position that gives me some extra height from the ground. I stretch my right arm as far as it can go, ignoring the ripping sensation that radiates from the wound I carved.

My nerveless fingers fumble. I clutch my phone.

It slips from my wet grasp, clattering into the sink. Against my ringing ears, the sound is louder than cannon fire.

Despair crashes on me. I try to draw breath and can't. It's like my lungs are deflating. My breathing is so shallow. I can't focus. No oxygen.

But I am a hero, and I can't give up.

I shuffle forward, scraping my knees across the icy, drenched tiles. The towel's turning red. The sickly sweet stench of my blood is nauseating.

I raise myself into a kneeling crouch. My head is about to burst, feeling at once like it's going to float away and like it's an anchor that wants to crash to the floor. I sway, and my cheek bumps harshly against the porcelain. I slump against the plywood side of the cabinet, but I have the height I need. My right hand snakes into the sink and closes on my phone.

Phone in hand, I collapse back into a fetal huddle. Less energy expended in this position. Flesh pressed together around my core, preserving what little warmth I have.

I tap the screen. The phone is unresponsive. Too wet. Fingers slick with blood. Liquid smeared across the shiny black expanse.

A horrible sound leaves my throat, something between a breathless scream and a hopeless sob. How much time wasted since my awakening? One minute? One hour? It feels like eternity has passed; every racing heartbeat marks a century of suffering.

But I am a hero, and salvation is within my grasp. I finished the quest. Found the magical MacGuffin. At last, the legendary artifact that can save the world is at my fingertips.

Focus. Think.

"Siri," I croak. My eyelids flutter and my pulse spikes again—not an altogether unpleasant feeling, because my screen has lit up in response. "Call 9-1-1."

Bleeding out, curled on the floor, I wait. Terror sets in.

Then, at long last, so faintly I think I've imagined it: "9-1-1, what's your emergency?"

"Bleeding," I mumble. It's all I can manage. There isn't much volume behind my voice, but my lips are close to the phone, lying in the puddle where I dropped it.

"What's your location?" the voice whispers from afar.

"Astoria."

Some unintelligible crackling. Either I'm fading, or the operator is. I suspect it's me.

"Broadway and 23rd," I clarify, pulling as much breath into my deflated chest as I can.

The person on the other end of my lifeline says something. I can't hear it. They're asking for instructions, perhaps—information they can use to save me. An address. Anything.

"Apartment 6H," I add in a stroke of genius. Then, more vulnerable than I've ever been, "Don't hang up. Stay with me."

I hear something that sounds like assent. Maybe they'll trace my exact location through my phone. I want to say more, but my energy's spent.

The shadows are closing in.

I curl my left arm, putting pressure on the wound. My right hand grips above my sticky left elbow—a poor excuse for a tourniquet. The towel is drenched. From blood loss, or the water on the floor? I can't tell.

Darkness spreads from the edges of my eyes, narrowing my blurred vision. My head is pounding, pressurized, cartwheeling.

I fight to hold on, but my body's shutting down. Fading in and out, I cling to the scrap of hope that help is on its way. That I managed to change my ending.

From that hope, a realization blooms, soft and beautiful as a rose-gold dawn.

My desire to make changes, to survive, was always centered around others: family, friends, darlings. Those were noble reasons to stay alive, to be sure, but I never once thought about doing it for myself.

A huge part of me believed life wasn't worth living. That's a hard battle to fight. Trapped alone beneath the suffocating weight of that belief, it's a battle I was doomed to lose. I could only hold on so long before my pain, and the need to escape it, won out.

But now, my chances of survival dwindling with every lost drop of blood, desire swells within me. It glows in my chest, pressing against my heart.

I want to stay alive. Not for anyone else, but for *me*. Because I want more from life. Because I deserve better.

This simple desire might be strong enough to change everything.

That's my final thought before the darkness claims me.

33

ALL THINGS CONSIDERED, I'm handling my death well.

No kicking, crying, or screaming. No *anything*, really. There's simply a vast expanse of nothing, as I always suspected.

My untimely demise is easier to accept than I imagined it would be. In the great hereafter, the place beyond, there is no sensation. My pain is gone. There's no emotional sensation either, so I can't feel any specific way about the absence of pain. I can't be relieved that my suffering has ended; I can't mourn the death of my future, my potential, my dreams—all the life I could have lived, had I not done what I did.

This isn't *really* nothing, though, is it? I am still, inexplicably, capable of conscious thought. It barely feels conscious, yet here they are: words and ideas that register within me on a primal level.

I'm thinking. Does that mean I'm alive? Or does it simply mean I've entered some special form of hell where I'm doomed to hang suspended in infinite nothingness, trapped with my own thoughts for eternity?

I shudder at the thought and realize—I can shudder. I can feel. And I feel... bad. I don't like that idea.

As I become more self-aware, the nothingness fades, falling away from me in spiraling whorls. I'm standing on solid but invisible ground. A phantom shine hangs around my naked body, not unlike an aurora. The shine flickers. Spectral wisps arc outward every so often, tiny solar flares. They're drawn, like iron filings to a magnet, toward a pinprick of light ahead.

The light grows steadily brighter.

Ah, fuck. I *am* dead.

Well, if I must choose between an eternity of semiconsciousness in the dark or an eternity of semiconsciousness in the light, I'll take the latter. I go toward the light, knowing I failed my last and greatest mission, but oddly calm. What's done is done. There's no going back. My life is over, but maybe I can make something of my afterlife. There *does* seem to be an afterlife, after all. Who'd have thunk?

The light grows, eclipsing the shadows. It's soft, and warmly comforting. I'm almost tempted to smile.

Then the light takes on a reddish hue, and a frisson of horror spears my gut. No Pearly Gates for me. That's the light of hellfire, I know it. I left a life of possibility only to damn myself to the eternity of the suffering I sought to escape—

Wait. Wait a gods-damned minute! There are shapes. Discernible shapes between the red. Black stripes. A blur of gold. A flash of sparkling white.

"Cendrion?" I murmur.

I blink once, and everything screams into focus.

I'm on Solera. Locked sword-to-claw with Zalor, whose furious face is millimeters from mine. The glow of the dragons' light-shield and the red of the sky bombards me from all angles as I spin, plunging with the Shadow Lord. Tumbling through the air, I spy the white flash again. And again, as I make another rotation in free fall.

Cendrion rockets after us, wings tucked and claws outstretched. He flares his leathery membranes and snaps them shut, giving himself an extra burst of speed. He's gaining on me.

I don't know how, I don't know why, but I'm back in my beloved world. It's heaven for me, though Solera is war-torn and dying. Or maybe—just *maybe*—Solera is real, and when I died on Earth, my displaced soul returned to its parallel resting place.

After a lifetime of waiting, chasing, yearning, is it so impossible to believe I've finally found magic?

This is a gift I don't deserve, but one I'll gladly accept. I'll never take anything for granted again. I learned that lesson too late, but I will not squander my inexplicable second chance.

With a thunderous roar, Cendrion's front talons close on my waist. Zalor hisses, coughing up black blood. It spatters on my cheeks and I grimace.

I let go of my sword—leaving its blade buried in his chest—and scrunch my legs, tucking them up beneath me as I did before I died. I kick at him savagely, breaking his hold on me. His claws unhook from my forearms. He spins away, hurtling toward the ground, while Cendrion spreads his wings and pulls out of his death-defying dive.

"I'm back," I call to the dragon. The whistling wind snatches my voice and flings it away as we soar skyward.

"Yes, because I caught you." He's oblivious to the fact that I lived and died in the time it took for him to zoom after me.

He banks and rises on a warm, dusty updraft. The raging Shadow War comes into view in the west. The air over the Midgardian Mountains is thick with a cloud of demons. The cliffs themselves are stained black and red, like the sky. Black from shadow. Red from blood.

"How's the army faring?" I ask, scanning the chaos and carnage.

"Not good. What did you do to Zalor?"

"Uh . . ." I hesitate, then figure it's best to be honest. I'll be *honest* in this new life. I want to be an open, honest, emotionally available person. I wasted too many moments on Earth hiding my thoughts and feelings. The truth of who I was, the burden I was carrying.

"I didn't defeat him." Not even a mortal wound from the unicorn blade managed to kill him. He's a godlike monster.

"I'm aware," says Cendrion. "Otherwise all his reanimated shadowtroops would have died. And so would I."

"Maybe not. I didn't defeat him, but I weakened him. The unicorn blade pierced his heart. I don't know what that means—I don't know if that's the sort of thing that would disentangle your fate from his."

"I can do nothing but hope and fight," he growls, putting on a burst of speed and dodging a shadowbeast phoenix.

That's all any of us can do. I can't guarantee Cendrion's fate, but I believe we have a chance. Though Zalor's weakened, my favorite character remains strong. And here in this other world, this other body, I'm strong, too.

As I squint at the fight, a vicious, frightening desire roars through me. "I can win this battle. Hoist me up. Let's end this."

"Do you have a plan?" he asks, and I catch the glimpse of a smile on his lips as he lifts me toward his chest. My fingers hook behind his wing joint. He stops flapping and glides, allowing me to scramble from his paws to his back.

"I've never been a planner." A bittersweet twinge echoes in my heart as I think of the writing I left behind. All the thrills, the fly-by-the-seat-of-your-pants battles, the near-death escapes.

I threw my work away when I took my own life, but I remember the story I wrote.

And dead or not, I still believe in the power of a good story.

"We have to do something to completely obliterate Zalor," I tell Cendrion as he nears the edge of battle. "Only then will we break his power."

Kyla Starblade did it in the finale of Book Five. I must find a way to do the same now. I focus, willing reality to warp, begging the universe to cave to my whims.

It doesn't work this time. My death changed something about my connection to Solera. Not surprising, perhaps, but very unfortunate given our circumstances.

That's life for you—or death, as the case may be. You can't control what obstacles are thrown your way. All you can do is overcome them as best you can with the tools you have available.

As Cendrion snags an unsuspecting shadowbeast in his claws, ripping it in two and creating a cloud of midnight blood, I force myself to recalibrate. I know this world, I know the rules.

I clench my fists and open them again. Reaching deep within myself, I focus and draw on the magical energy that courses through every living thing on Solera. Thinking of what I want, concentrating on a spell with all my might, I sculpt my will. Forcing it to manifest, I summon a beam of light.

It works. I lost my ability to change reality, but I can still wield Kyla's magic. Light sears the sky, shooting into the midst of the shadowbeasts and felling a dozen in one go.

I grin and let out a triumphant whoop, though the attack was ill-planned. I've drawn attention to us. A swarm of demons turns east, abandoning the Mortal Alliance and focusing on Cendrion and me.

"Author," Cendrion growls, dodging a spell of darkmagic and lashing out at the enemies closing in on all sides, encapsulating us in an orb of shadow, "I hope you have another trick up your sleeve."

My smile becomes wistful, sorrowful. I run my right hand over my left arm. "As it happens, I have several."

Cendrion snags a small winged shadowbeast, shredding it with his talons. Before he can turn his attention to anything else, an ear-splitting sound reaches us. A shockwave ripples through the demonic ranks.

I squint through their darkness to see that flaming stones have been launched from the artillery units of the Mortal Alliance. A second volley of projectiles flies from the rear line of my army. They arc through the shadowy bodies and explode. Burning shrapnel peppers the shadowbeasts from each airborne bomb. Massive fireballs engulf their numbers. The army has decimated Zalor's vanguard.

Cendrion rumbles a sound of approval. He takes advantage of the demons' confusion, speeding west. I lift a hand and summon another light beam, drawing my internal energy to my palm and focusing it into a laser. My magic melts more shadowbeasts.

It's a good start, but not enough. There are still thousands of enemies to worry about.

"*Drachryi, kemraté a'eos,*" I cry, again summoning the dragons to me. "*E'es colstraté!*"

Bright flashes erupt around us, sending shafts of brilliance through the mass of pitch-black creatures. I count four—four nearby dragons who heeded my call.

Additional light spells, far more powerful than mine, blast through Zalor's ranks. I spot Temereth gliding alongside us, clearing a path for Cendrion. Not only does her magic destroy an entire flock of demons, but the survivors peel away from us and focus on her, perceiving a new threat.

I wave and salute her. She twitches her head toward the cliffs as if to say, *Get on with it.*

"Faster," I urge Cendrion. "We have to find our friends."

Fyr'thal is the first one found. We don't actually find him—he comes to us. A jet of fire eliminates a shadowbeast sneaking up on Cendrion's left flank. I twist, squinting against the wave of heat and acrid ash, and find the phoenix gliding near.

"Follow me," I tell him. I'm forming the vague semblance of a plan. I'll gather my darlings in one place. The lure will be too powerful for Zalor to resist. He'll rear his ugly head, show his miserable face, unable to pass up a chance to destroy everything I love.

As I'm no longer connected to my Earth body, I assume my quantum-magical connection to Solera has been broken. In death, I've become a natural part of this other, isolated system. I'm no longer the omniscient author who can sculpt fate through the merest magical whim . . . but I *am* a person whose choices and actions can make a difference. And now that I've tapped into Kyla's lightmagic, I have a surefire way to kill Zalor.

With the help of Fyr'thal on one side and Temereth on the other, Cendrion rips through the shadowbeasts. He banks when he reaches the mountains and zooms north, surveying the ground troops. Eldrian corpses litter the limestone, but the mortals are holding their own.

Ahead, I spot a dragon I don't immediately recognize. It's landed on the cliffs to fight a unit of shadowbeast foot soldiers. It's small, and it has odd scales—mottled earthy hues, like those of a python.

"Rexa!" I scream.

The dragon, who's busy dismembering a shadowman, pauses in her gruesome work. Her amber eyes rise and meet mine. A brown-haired head pokes up over her shoulder. *Asher.*

Sorrow swells in my heart, and for the first time since my death, I feel the desire to weep. Never again will I see my Earthling darlings. I'll never again speak to Eric. Never hear Lindsay's laugh. I robbed myself of the chance to reconnect with them. I didn't even think to say goodbye.

I didn't think it was necessary. Didn't believe they'd want to hear it.

In making the assumption that they wouldn't miss me, I robbed them of the chance to tell me otherwise. And though I'll be able to live alongside their simulacra in this world, I've now forced them to live on Earth without *me*.

"Follow us," I scream to Rexa as Cendrion shoots past her. She bunches her hindquarters and springs into the sky. An explosion blooms to the left. Asher's using combustible arrows to thin the enemy crowd, allowing us to move north.

One more piece of the puzzle.

I know where to find him, because this part of the battle is unfolding as it did in my manuscript. Valen is where I left him, leading the main division, booming commands, felling shadowbeasts with bolts of blue-white lightning.

I lean against Cendrion's neck as he angles down, grasping a pearly neck spike to steady myself. With my free hand I wield light-magic, summoning another simple yet deadly beam. Shadowbeasts burst apart around us as Cendrion backwings, stretches his hind legs, and alights on the plateau.

Valen runs to me. It creates a soft and confusing ache in my chest. He wasn't based on any Earthling, but as I stare into the depths of his eyes, I can't help but think of the people he *might* have been.

There were a few, along the way. I ended all my relationships before they had a chance to begin, of course. Not because I'm asexual, not even because I'm an asshole who preferred ghosting to honest communication.

It's because I was afraid.

I was afraid people would scorn my identity. Afraid they'd reject me. Afraid I'd break my own heart if I allowed myself to feel something with someone.

There, too, I robbed those other people of a choice. I decided for them. It was my shadow-voice that told me I was unlovable, not theirs. I never gave them the opportunity to say it because I was too afraid of hearing it.

Perhaps I *would* have heard it and been worse off for it. But perhaps

I wouldn't have heard it. What might have happened then?

I'll never know.

"What's wrong?" Valen asks, reaching for me as I slide from Cendrion's shoulder and dismount. "Are you hurt?"

"No, but buckle in. It's about to become a wild ride," I tell him, clasping his hand.

"As opposed to what?" Rexa's voice reaches us over the screams and clamor. She's landed behind Cendrion and resumed her humanoid form.

I turn my face to the blackening sky. The air above me is mercifully free of shadowbeasts. Dragons circle overhead, guarding us. More of the majestic creatures teleport in from further afield. They're following my earlier directive. Following *me*.

Between my darlings and the dragons, I've created the perfect target.

I turn east, facing the never-ending waves of shadowbeasts crashing against our front lines. I raise my fist in the air and wield light around it. An orb of flawless brilliance glows, turning me into a shining beacon.

"Stay with me," I whisper to my friends.

"Until the end," Cendrion replies.

"Zalor!" My voice rises above the thunder of artillery, the screams of mortals dying. "Here we are—come and get us!"

Without hesitation, a space widens in the shadowbeasts. Half a mile from the plateau, shadows solidify into a recognizable shape.

The Shadow Lord reappears on his cloud of darkmagic. His legions part before him as he glides closer.

"Inviting tragedy?" he snarls. "If you want your loved ones to suffer because of your selfishness, far be it from me to deny your dying wish."

Guilt whispers through me, and regret pulls my heartstrings. I condemned my Earthling loved ones to suffering. Of course they'll miss me—they're good people. They'll wonder why I did it. I didn't leave an explanation. A writer who couldn't even write her own suicide note.

"On my command, focus on Zalor and attack," I instruct my friends in an undertone, ignoring the Shadow Lord's taunts. Temereth hovers nearby. I don't have to issue further instruction to the dragons. They're smart enough to understand my plan now that Zalor is in their sights.

"Remember, you can't destroy me without destroying yourself," Zalor continues. He swirls a hand, gathering a maelstrom of shadow to him, preparing a deadly strike.

He doesn't know I've already destroyed myself. From that destruction I have been reborn in the world I cherish above all else.

Now I see the end.

It's a good ending to my story. Bittersweet. Realistic.

It's not a happily-ever-after, because there are no such things. I ended my story prematurely . . . but here, in this final moment of consciousness between life and nothing, I have one tiny chance at redemption.

"NOW!" I scream.

A bolt of lightning, thunderous and searing, explodes from Valen. Combustible arrows whiz through the air, one after the other in blurred succession, heading for the Shadow Lord. A stream of fire joins them, as well as a nebulous jet of darkmagic from Cendrion. Overhead, the dragons aim beams of light at Zalor.

Zalor expertly redirects his maelstrom, converting his prepared spell into a shield of defense. Our spells turn black and wither into nothingness as they collide with his power, even the rays of pure light.

The volley ends. Our spells dissipate, but so does Zalor's shield. We've matched his god-tier energy output, all of us together. Even from this distance, I can tell that's rattled him.

He takes a breath before wielding again. In that breath, I strike.

"Goodbye, my darlings."

Light engulfs me, and I disappear from the plateau. For a moment, I'm weightlessly expanding to blanket the cosmos. Then I'm small and compact, shoved into a broken, aching mortal body. I've teleported, appearing in front of Zalor.

I no longer have my sword, but that doesn't matter. While the sword weakened him, it wouldn't have killed him. Only my magic can do that.

He doesn't have time to react before I throw my arms around him. I draw energy and light and power and life into my body and then—I release it.

CRACK!

The two of us explode as I become a sun, a *universe*. I expand into a supernova, destroying both Zalor and my simulacrum-self, exorcising my soul from my beloved world.

Yes, I think as agony sears me, as every fiber of my being ignites and burns away. *It's a good ending.*

Solera will go on without me. As for my Earthling darlings . . . that's a mistake I'll have to live with. Or rather, die with. For now, as far as I can tell, I'll be well and truly dead. There is no *after*-after. There is only nothing.

And for one terrible, unending moment, I *am* nothing—

Nothing at all—

Unconsciousness, oblivion, no feeling, no thought—

Then thunder bursts through my chest and I gasp. Everything—sensation, thought, memory—comes roaring back.

CRACK!

My torso feels compressed, like something heavy is sitting on it. But the fact that I can feel *anything* is suspiciously not like death.

"Clear!"

CRACK!

Energy slams into me. My muscles contract and my heart stutters, lurching into a normal rhythm.

My eyes open a sliver. Two angels hover above me. I'm in a shiny white room. Not my bathroom. My bathroom is smaller (and far dirtier) than this place.

Ambulance.

"She's stable," says one angel to the other—or rather, one human. An EMT, based on the uniform.

Their words blur in my ringing ears. I hear something about "hypovolemic shock." One of them talks on a radio. In contrast to my dream, reality feels hyper-real, *too* real. Too bright, too loud, too immense for me, swaddled on a stretcher—but the realness tells me I'm alive.

I'm alive.

"It's a miracle," I hear one of the EMTs mutter. "How she survived that much blood loss is beyond me."

I send a silent prayer to Ohra and to all the gods of Earth, present and past, thanking anyone and everyone who might be listening.

I want to thank the EMTs, too. I want to ask what time it is. How much blood *did* I lose? How long did I wait, curled naked on the floor, for my salvation to arrive? Mount Sinai is half a mile from my apartment complex, but Astoria traffic is brutal.

The EMTs are bustling like bees, doing EMT-things, chattering above me. One of them thumbs my eyelid fully open and shines a blinding light into my retina. My pupil shrinks away from the painful beam.

They keep up their constant stream of jargon-chatter. I vaguely hear their voices, but I can't find mine to speak to them. It seems I'm not awake, not really. Darkness is once again claiming me, though it's not the darkness of death. It's more like the feel of Cendrion's dark-magic, warm and safe.

As I drift into an aching, exhausted sleep, a tiny smile plays across my lips.

It *is* a miracle that I survived.

Maybe Earth has a spark of magic, after all.

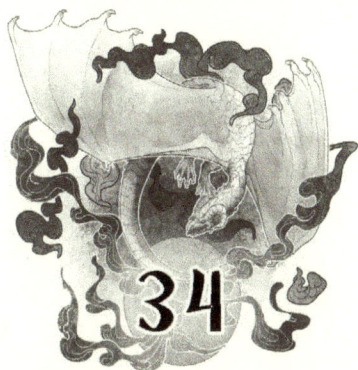

34

THIS IS A DREAM, and I know it by heart.

I awake in a different world. I know the pulse of every tree, the lore of every stone, the deepest desires of every creature. This universe lives and breathes alongside me.

I'm lucid, and I *know* I'm dreaming. Because I know I'm alive.

Solera is pristine and beautiful again. Soft summer grass tickles my bare arms as I lie on a Lenkhari hilltop. Sunlight filters through the emerald boughs of a dwarf-lily tree. The honey-sweet scent of the pink flowers drifts toward me on a gentle breeze.

The fact that I've lived another day to feel these things, to see and smell and taste and touch, is still overwhelming. And I know there are many more overwhelming things awaiting me when I return to Earth. Hospital bills. Explanations and an apology tour. Psych eval? Most likely. Having never attempted suicide before, I don't know how this will play out. Will they force me into counseling?

At this point, I'm willing to try anything. There's no shame in needing help. If I'm going to be open, honest, and vulnerable—if I'm going to make *changes*—step one is acknowledging that.

Instead of pushing help away, I'm going to thank people for offering it.

But this is not reality. I don't have to worry about reality until I return to it, and that might be hours. I'm hopped up on morphine, which is why this dream is beautiful yet hazy. Or maybe that's the natural haze of late summer, the thick tinge of magic that pervades the Soleran atmosphere.

One arm strays from my side, snaking through the grass until I find what I'm searching for. I close my fingers around a warm hand, running my thumb over the calloused palm.

"You're awake," says Valen.

"Mhmm."

He sits up, leaning into my field of view. He doesn't bend down, and I don't think he will. He knows who I am and what I want—or rather, what I don't want. My subconscious has finally taken the hint.

Maybe we can be at peace with ourselves.

A slight frown creases his smooth brow. His eyes widen. "It's you," he breathes. "You're here."

"Where else would I be?"

He stares at me, speechless, emotion dancing in his stormy gaze. I sit up and stare back at him, nonplused. Is this lucidity, or something else?

Valen reaches for my hand and clasps it. "You survived."

I nod, playing along, following the flow of the dream. He pulls me close and wraps his arms around me. I nuzzle against his chest, breathing in his fresh, clean scent.

"Thank you," he whispers, his lips brushing my ear. "You saved us."

Smiling, I draw away from him. "Let's go home."

He nods, and I close my eyes. I extend a tendril of thought toward the place behind my sternum where I imagine my soul lurks, testing to see if I can wield magic.

It doesn't feel like anything's happened, but when I open my eyes once more, the dream has changed. No longer are Valen and I lying side by side on the country hill. Now we're standing on the gleaming cliffs of Midgard, gazing at a golden sunset. We're not alone—all my darlings are there.

This is a real dream I'm having in the hospital. That means Valen and Cendrion, Asher and Rexa, the demons and dragons—they're part of my world. The real world. This is canon. All in-universe. I'll see them again, when I sleep and when I write.

And oh, will I have something to write about now.

"We've reached the end of the journey," I tell them.

"I don't think so," Asher says, surprising me (and everyone else, judging by their expressions). "It's the end of a *chapter*, not the book. You're not even halfway through your story."

My eyes water, and I don't bother hiding it. I'm grateful to have this mouthpiece, this little part of me that never loses hope, no matter how dark the shadows grow. There are no happily-ever-afters, of course—but there can be a happily-for-*now*.

"You're right. I have a lot of work to do when I wake up." My mouth twists. "Like, a *lot* of work. More than I care to think about. But one thing I'm looking forward to is rewriting that manuscript of mine."

"Good," says Rexa, smirking. "I want to know how *our* story ends."

We share a chuckle before settling into peaceful silence. I watch the sun sink toward the peaks of the Midgardian Mountains. They've been restored to perfection and glory. No trace of the Shadow War remains. At least, not in this world.

I glance at my bare arms, which are silky smooth in the dream.

On Earth, they bear long and wicked scars.

I'll carry those scars with me forever. They'll serve as a reminder of everything I'm fighting for and what I almost lost. They'll be proof of my strength.

Proof I survived.

A host of dragons wings past, drawing my eye. I wave to Temereth and her fellows, happy that I can see such magnificent creatures in my dreams. I was given a gift—I was given *many* gifts, and I very nearly squandered them. To have destroyed a mind that can dream up such visions would have been a terrible tragedy.

I don't know how much time has passed, but my dream begins to fuzz at the edges. The sunset grows less vibrant. The soft warmth of summer gives way to a scratchy, less pleasant warmth: my somewhat sub-par hospital bed.

I exhale softly. In my semiconscious state, I feel my physical body emulating the gesture.

"What happens now?" asks Asher, perceiving my shift in mood.

I gaze into the distance, considering his question. What happens in the afterdeath? The life-after-life?

What do you do with a second chance?

"Now I'm going to try to save the world."

My writing never made a difference before, but perhaps that's because I was writing the wrong words. Maybe I'll tell *this* story. Maybe someone, somewhere, will read it—and maybe it will mean something to them.

I know my story is powerful, because it already saved one life. How many more lives might I save if I shed my fears, walk in the light, and own my scars?

"I'm going to talk to my parents. Guess I'll probably have to get a therapist. There's gotta be a decent local one who takes Medicaid, right?"

Asher nods encouragingly. Rexa wiggles a hand side to side, expressing doubt.

"I'll call Lindsay. And when I'm well enough, I'll see Eric. I'll tell them ... well, not everything, because I'm not sure they'd believe what happened to me in this world. But I'll at least tell them I'm sorry."

"You don't have to apologize," Asher assures me.

"I feel like I should." I can't help but worry about what everyone will say to me. What they'll think of me. How they'll judge me.

As if he's guessed my thoughts, Asher says, "The people who love you won't need to hear it. You're apologizing to them because you're angry at yourself."

The shameful truth burns my throat, and I grimace.

"Forgive yourself," he continues. "Don't waste your second chance being angry about a mistake."

"Live to fight another day," says Rexa, slugging me on the shoulder. I crack a reluctant smile, rubbing the spot she punched. If my arm's sore, that probably means I've been sleeping on it funny. So much to look forward to when I return to Earth.

But it'll be worth it. I believe that.

"We never did catch your name," Cendrion muses, rustling his wings.

I think for a moment, wondering if I should tell them. My smile turns secretive.

"Next time," I promise.

Cendrion vanishes like a heat mirage, as things sometimes do in dreams. One moment he's there, and the next, it's like he never was.

Asher and Rexa are gone, too—but it feels like I'll see them sooner than the others. On Earth, Eric and Lindsay are waiting. That makes me want to wake up. The Eldrian horizon fades to the dark of dreamless sleep.

Only Valen remains, as crisp and clear as anything I've ever seen.

He raises a hand and wipes a stray tear from my cheek. His touch is tender and heartbreaking. It's him I'll miss the most. He's the only one I'm truly leaving. There's no equivalent on Earth. No one comes close.

"Why are you crying?" he whispers.

"I'm scared," I say, since I'm now in the unfortunate habit of being honest.

"Why?"

"Same old reasons. I can't magically change overnight."

He takes my hands in his. "Why did you believe there couldn't be a happy ending?"

"Dunno. That's sort of the way it works on Earth. I guess that's why people like stories so much."

He hasn't moved, at least not that I've perceived, but somehow he's closer to me. My chest, my heart, is inches from his.

"I'm scared of living a dark life." A sluggish, familiar fear sloshes in my stomach. "I'm scared of suffering. What if it gets really bad again?"

Valen tilts his head as he looks at me. I fidget under the scrutiny. Yet now he, too, is growing faint. His face, his voice, they're dimming.

"A wise author once told me," he says at last, "that though the darkness may be infinite, it is weak, because even the smallest light has the power to shine through it."

"So you *were* listening to my lectures," I say, trying to inject some levity into our final moments.

"Every word," he assures me. "They mattered to me. And you—you're the one who wrote them. That means you must believe them."

I don't have time to say farewell, or even *see you later*. The clatter of hospital equipment and breakfast trays sounds from universes away, pulling me out of the dream and into my body. My eyes are closed, but I sense the brightness of dawn filtering through my lids.

I steel myself.

I take a deep breath.

And I awake.

ABOUT THE AUTHOR

L.E. Harper is a dragon-obsessed recluse who prefers living in the world of her novels to living in reality. This book was pretty much just her autobiography, so that probably tells you everything you need to know about her.

www.allentria.com

If you liked *Kill Your Darlings*, please consider leaving a review on Goodreads, Barnes & Noble, or Amazon!

And if you want to read the books that started it all...

THE SHADOW WAR SAGA

Enter the universe of Kill Your Darlings . . . kinda.
See your favorite characters again . . . sorta.
Everything is the same, yet vastly different!
Mind = blown.

I began this five-book series (lol) half a lifetime ago.
It helped me grow as a writer.
It helped me grow as a human.
And it kept me alive.

Ingram Content Group UK Ltd.
Milton Keynes UK
UKHW010640250523
422339UK00001B/52

9 781792 366628